THE CONNECTION

Boris Borodov was the most beloved figure in Soviet Russia, for decades the legendary star clown of the Moscow circus.

Jil was the name that his grandson had taken to become the most famous mime in the West, wildly applauded in every country of the free world.

But the relationship between this old man and the young heir to his genius went beyond their shared blood and artistry.

Together they held the fate of world leaders in their hands . . . in a gigantic drama of deception and danger that moved from Moscow to Washington . . . from the Island of Cyprus to a lavish Spanish villa . . . from Palestinian camps in Lebanon to a Holocaust survivors' synagogue in Brooklyn . . . from irresistible sexual seduction to unspeakable savagery . . . as victim by victim the pieces of a master plan of murder dropped into bloody place. . . .

HOUR OF THE CLOWN

Great Reading from SIGNET

HOUR OF THE CLOWN

AMOS ARICHA

A SIGNET BOOK

NEW AMERICAN LIBRARY

TIMES MIRROR

Copyright © 1981 by Amos Aricha

SIGNET, SIGNET CLASSICS, MENTOR, PLUME, MERIDIAN AND NAL
BOOKS are published by The New American Library, Inc.,
1633 Broadway, New York, New York 10019

First Printing, April, 1981

1   2   3   4   5   6   7   8   9

PRINTED IN THE UNITED STATES OF AMERICA

For Gail

PUBLISHER'S NOTE

HOUR OF THE
CLOWN

PART ONE

1

I N THE DIZZYING heights above the arena of the great Moscow Circus, the acrobat Katya Morozov soared through the air, gliding to her brother Aleksei, who leaped toward her from the opposite direction. As the audience gazed in horror, they passed one another, bodies almost touching, nearly colliding.

Boris Borodov watched them as they executed the mid-air bypass with precision and professional skill, a thin, almost paternal smile half-hidden beneath the curve of his great Cossack moustache. He knew Katya's and Aleksei's artistry, had indeed worked with three generations of Morozovs, all of them outstanding acrobats. The old people had died some years before, though they had been younger than he, but not before passing on the secrets of their extraordinary control in the towering heights of the circus to their children, born during the circus's travels from one city to another, in the days when he himself was one of its stars—Borodov the Clown.

A thunder of applause signaled the end of the Morozovs' performance. The old man inhaled deeply, then withdrew into the shadows. Spots threw shafts of colored light over the circus's three interlocking arenas as acrobats, horse trainers, dogs and bears, crowding into the three rings, put on a brief show as a prelude to the next feature: the clowns—all members of a new generation that had vied to capture the old clown's glory when he abandoned the circus so many years before. Had his grandson Yan remained in the circus, he would have taken his place, but instead Yan had become an agent for the KGB and was now traveling somewhere in Europe under the identity of Jil, the mime.

Borodov noted the glances the circus people cast at him as they rushed past to perform their various jobs. No matter how great their haste, each one stopped to exchange a few words with him, a mark of their respect and affection. The old clown's visits were infrequent; he always arrived suddenly, unannounced. He would come when his longing for Yan so overwhelmed him that his heart could no longer contain it. Leaving his small apartment in the building on Kalinin Boulevard, he would walk to the circus. It was a long walk, but he made it regardless of the weather, for an hour in this singular world, intoxicated by its special atmosphere, brought him relief from the pain of his longings.

Now it was time to leave. He turned toward the back gate used by members of the circus during their performances. The guard bowed his head as he passed.

"Good to see you again, Comrade Borodov."

Boris Borodov smiled and continued on his way. Outside, November's bitter frost engulfed him. The contrast between the heated building and the raw cold of Moscow's early winter was especially sharp, but he was used to it and merely turned up the fur collar of his overcoat. As he did so, he saw Sergei Padayev leaning against the door of his battered old Volga.

Borodov stopped short; Sergei Padayev's appearance at the circus was most unusual. He never waited for him there, or at least had not since Boris had retired. Colonel Sergei Padayev was in charge of the Liquidation Section of the KGB's Department V. Pavel Ramizor, the head of Department V, a division empowered to sabotage various regimes around the world by stirring dissension, aiding terrorism, and carrying out assassinations, considered Padayev one of his most dependable men.

Borodov strode purposefully toward the waiting car. Something must have happened for Sergei to act so impetuously.

"What is it, Sergei?" Then, noting that his friend's complexion was the color of old parchment, the old man observed quietly, "You don't look well. The heart acting up?"

"No," the KGB officer answered curtly.

"Shall we go?"

"Yes, let's," replied Sergei Padayev. "It's a long drive, and I have a lot to say, brother Borodov."

The two men exchanged glances. Long years of shared experiences had enabled them to express themselves through their eyes so that at times they had no need for words. Sergei Padayev opened the door for the old man, and Borodov lowered his head and got into the car.

They drove in silence for a few minutes, then Padayev began to speak in a low voice.

"I have the information for you," he said slowly, as if choosing each word with utmost care. "But I want to ask something before I deliver it." Inside the automobile, well insulated against the bitter cold, his voice had a metallic ring.

"Ask."

"I ask because I am afraid, Boris," said Sergei Padayev. "We must know exactly what is happening and who is backing this insane act. Do you understand?" The old man remained silent. "Boris . . . the source of the information that reached you, that prompted you to request I begin an investigation—was it a senior source?"

"A senior source, Sergei."

"From the leadership?"

"Yes."

"Close to the Politburo?"

"Close to the Politburo," he replied without hesitation.

For a moment there was no sound but Sergei Padayev's labored breathing. Boris Borodov waited for him to go on, although he already knew what Padayev's next question would be. He was not mistaken.

"Is he one of ours?"

"Of course he is one of ours," the old man said quietly.

This was the one point Sergei Padayev had wanted to be sure of before reporting the results of his investigation: that the informant was totally trustworthy. That he was in addition a high-ranking official, perhaps even a member of the Politburo, was irrefutable proof that Pavel Ramizor had not acted on his own, that the operation had the backing of the head of the KGB himself, Yuri Andropov, with the approval of the political leadership. Once again Sergei Padayev was reminded that among the hundreds who clandestinely served the clown some of the old man's agents had reached the highest echelons of nearly every institution of the Soviet government.

"Now, what did you discover, Sergei?"

Padayev rubbed his high forehead absentmindedly, as if trying to expel troublesome thoughts. "Confirmation of what you told me. The KGB is instigating a massive terrorist campaign against the Jewish lobby in Washington. They intend to launch the operation in a few months, in the United States.

"It's the first time Pavel Ramizor has personally planned an operation of this size. None of the other section heads participated in the planning, not even myself. And it's quite evident that they intend to prevent the slightest possibility of connecting the Soviet Union with the operation."

"They mean to crush the Jewish lobby?"

"That's the intention."

"By what means?"

"Kidnappings, murders, bombings, other reprisals. And there's no greater expert than Pavel Ramizor. He's drawn up a list of the most influential members of the lobby in Washington, both Jews and non-Jews."

"Do you have any specifics?"

"I know there is a final list, one that includes the names of fifteen men. Believe me, Boris, every detail will be planned very thoroughly. The aim is to shock. To deter. To prove to both the Jewish and non-Jewish leadership that support of Israel can be very costly."

"This is insanity . . ."

"Aren't we used to that, you and I, brother Boris? Haven't we both seen madness run amok? And this operation will serve many purposes: retribution for the anti-Soviet activities of influential Americans who have been working on behalf of human rights, as well as the settling of accounts with the lobby itself for its activities in support of Israel and of Jewish emigration. Moreover, an operation like this can greatly strengthen ties with various terrorist movements, particularly the Palestinians. We both know, Boris, how much the KGB needs the Palestinians. Without them, it would be difficult to keep the Middle East in a constant state of agitation."

The car was not far from Red Square and they could see the Kremlin's soaring towers illuminated by floodlights.

"Up to this point, everything is clear," the old man said softly. "The general implementation of the plan will be in Pavel Ramizor's hands. But who will be in direct command of the operation? And who will carry it out?"

"I don't have those answers," Sergei Padayev replied. "I only have conjectures. It's my guess that direct command will be conferred on the intelligence services of one of the satellites, perhaps the East Germans, the Poles, the Czechs, or the Bulgarians. Any one of those countries has a number of men who could organize an operation of this magnitude very efficiently. As to who will actually implement it in the field, this group will undoubtedly be composed of international terrorists, with the Palestinians playing the major role, so that it will seem to be just another insane terrorist plot."

The car now approached the intersection leading to Kalinin Boulevard, a broad expanse of concrete lined on either side by tall apartment buildings. Sergei turned his head for an instant to look at Boris Borodov, but in the flickering light he found it difficult to make out his expression.

"Anything is possible, Boris. Believe me—anything. Pavel Ramizor has his reputation on the line on this operation. It would be very difficult for him to survive a failure. You know that Pavel has been considered as a candidate to head the First Chief Directorate, a position second only to that of Chairman Andropov . . ."

"Yes, but there are rumors that he has fallen into disfavor."

"Quite true. The collapse of his scheme to plant agents among Jewish emigrants leaving the Soviet Union was a severe blow to his prestige. And his subsequent inability to uncover the identity of the KGB men collaborating with U.S. intelligence hasn't improved his standing either. Right now, he needs a breakthrough, Boris. A conspicuous, unequivocal success."

"What else did you find out?"

"A few names. I noticed that Ramizor's secretary had signed out some personal files from the American archives, using her own name. A routine error on her part."

"We owe our existence to routine errors like that."

"True."

7

"How many names did you get?"

"Five." And he gave them, pausing a few seconds between each one. They were names that had been appearing daily in the American press, often in banner headlines.

"Can you get the other ten names?" Borodov asked.

"Yes," he replied, "and probably in just the same way."

"Then stay with it, Sergei. In the meantime we must contact the Israelis. They'll be able to persuade the Americans of the authenticity of this information. This time we have to act quickly and spare no effort, even if it means endangering ourselves."

Sergei Padayev turned to look at Borodov. Never before had the old man suggested the need to endanger himself or others.

"I'll act immediately, Boris. The information will be on its way to Paris shortly, and from there to the proper hands."

Sergei Padayev parked the Volga in front of a large apartment house on Kalinin Boulevard, one of several new buildings. He got out quickly and hurried around to open the door for the old man. Despite their long intimacy, he treated him with marked respect.

Boris Borodov slid nimbly out of the car. Although many years had passed since he had last appeared in the circus, his movements still had the same characteristic spring, for his lithe, erect body had lost none of its suppleness. He placed a hand on Sergei Padayev's shoulder, his face serene, only his eyes revealing his tension.

"This time we shall have need of all our powers of prayer, Sergei," he said faintly, almost in a whisper.

2

JOHN SALZBURG, SPECIAL counsel to the President, studied the list of names in the report Earl Dickson, a senior official of the CIA, had just handed him, following a meeting the CIA man had set up with General Dan Negbi, the head of the Israeli intelligence services.

Senator Daniel Moynihan; Senator Jacob Javits; Max Fischer, advisor to presidents on Jewish affairs; Morris Amitay, head of the American Israel Policy Affairs Committee; and Rabbi Alexander Schindler, past chairman of the Conference of Presidents of Major American Jewish Organizations in the United States. All five men were known for their unqualified support of the Jewish state—and now all five were marked as targets of a terrorist plot. And there were more to come.

"So you see why I need to see the President right away," Dickson said.

The dreary gray light of a late November morning seeped through the tall windows of the spacious office in the West Wing of the White House where the two men were conferring.

"You say there are other targets as well?" Salzburg asked.

"Altogether there are fifteen names," Dickson replied. "General Negbi will have the remaining ten sometime today."

"Where is he now?"

"In New York. But he plans to fly to Washington."

"And you trust his source of information—without any reservations?"

"Absolutely."

During his first year of service in the White House, John Salzburg had heard a great deal about Earl Dickson's intelligence background. Early in the 1960s, Dickson had been appointed head of the Israel Section, a department that handled the CIA's special ties with the Mossad, the Israeli Secret Service.

"In the report you indicate that Negbi's source is in the Soviet Union."

"That's correct. No intelligence service has finer sources of information within the borders of the Soviet Union than the Mossad." Earl Dickson lit a cigarette. "The Mossad has a Hasidic underground connection, a Jewish network that it cooperates with on a regular basis."

"What do you mean?"

"It seems there's a network of religious Jews affiliated with a worldwide movement that started in Eastern Europe in the eighteenth century. This movement of Hasidim, as its members are called, is devoted to the preservation of a common set of religious beliefs. It's also set up a variety of mutual aid organizations that provide for the welfare of its members, with particular emphasis on education. During periods of religious persecution, the movement was forced to go underground in order to preserve its beliefs and way of life."

"But how did they get involved in intelligence?"

"I gather that it grew out of the events of the Second World War: basically as a means of easing the plight of the Jews. The Hasidim apparently managed to plant individuals in various government positions. Once installed, they were able to be of assistance by providing false identity papers, passing along information, and warning Jews of danger. Evidently some of these people found their way into the KGB, where they now have access to all kinds of important intelligence data."

"So the Hasidic network functions within the KGB as a subversive intelligence operation."

"Not exactly, John. The network was established solely to protect the lives and spiritual values of the Hasidim. All the network's efforts are directed to that end. However they do maintain ties with the Mossad and are willing, through them, to pass on information about Russia's activities behind the Iron Curtain and in the free world. For example, it was Israeli intelligence that tipped us off that a large ring of Soviet agents were operating in the West, disguised as Jewish immigrants, but the original source of that information was the Jewish network."

"Amazing!" John Salzburg paused for a moment. "I've heard of the Hasidim, but I don't really know anything about them."

"When I first heard of the Jewish network and the Hasidic movement, I asked General Negbi a whole slew of questions. According to him, the name comes from the Hebrew word for 'pious one.' Negbi told me that there are many Hasidic sects, that each one is headed by a Rebbe, or Tzadik as he's sometimes called. Among the numerous Hasidic groups, the most well known is right here in the States—in Crown Heights in Brooklyn. The Rebbe is a spiritual leader whose power can be likened to that of the Pope, and his influence on his followers is literally without limits—as is the veneration with which they regard him, and the degree to which they comply with his dictums.

"In all Hasidic groups other members may call themselves 'Reb' or 'Rabbi,' but there is only one Rebbe, and he is believed to embody the highest ideals of Judaism; his life is expected to serve as an expression of all Jewish values. No follower will take a step of major importance—like marrying off a daughter or starting a new business—without first consulting with the Rebbe and receiving his blessing."

"The Rebbe is an authority figure, then?"

"Exactly. I'll give you an example: let's say the wife of a Hasid needs an operation. Without the Rebbe's okay, the husband will not sign a release permitting the operation, even if the woman's life is in danger—"

"Why is that?"

"Because the Rebbe must first be told of the illness so that he can approve the operation."

"And if he doesn't?"

"Then it won't be performed—which leaves two possibilities: the woman will either recover on her own or she will die."

"So the Rebbe takes on himself the role of God?" John Salzburg said in amazement.

"Almost," responded Earl Dickson slowly, "but not quite. To the Hasidim, the Rebbe is a mediator between man and God. He is the final authority and one does not question his judgment—even if the woman in our hypothetical example should die, ostensibly because she didn't have the operation her doctor recommended. You see, John, the Hasidim would say the woman was marked for death, and the fact that the Rebbe didn't agree to the operation merely attested to his knowledge of this fact. An operation would only have added to her suffering and to the suffering of her family during her final days . . ."

"So they follow the Rebbe's commandments unquestioningly?"

"They aren't commandments, John. The Rebbe doesn't order; he advises. However, his followers have complete faith in his wisdom. They trust him implicitly. After all, as I said, they regard him as an emissary of God."

Earl Dickson got up from his chair and crossed to the tall, narrow window overlooking the rose garden; for a moment he stood in silence watching as wild gusts of wind bent the bare branches of the trees.

John Salzburg waited, then asked, "Just how large a group is this?"

Dickson turned from the window and walked back. "It's hard to know. Many of the followers, perhaps tens of thousands, are very easy to spot. Bearded—always dressed in black hats and black frock coats. But then there are the disciples whom you wouldn't be able to identify: the secret followers of the Rebbe. They look like you or me. The engineer who lives in the apartment across the hall from you could be one. So could your accountant. Anybody could be a secret follower."

"Even you, Earl?"

"Even me, John. Even men like me in the KGB."

"So then they *do* form a network of spies in the KGB?"

"No, not really. You see, these men see themselves as embarked on holy missions. Their Rebbe is the emissary of God, they are the emissaries of the Rebbe, and everything they do is done in the name of the Almighty. The Hasidic network in Russia is run by a very small cadre of dedicated men. I really don't know many details, but I do know that their leader is a man they call the Grand Emissary. He serves as the Rebbe's personal emissary to the Soviet Union."

"The Grand Emissary . . ." Salzburg murmured. "And you don't know who he is?"

"Neither I nor anyone else in intelligence does." Earl Dickson grinned. "That is perhaps one of the best-kept secrets. The man has succeeded in concealing his identity. He may not even be known as a Jew. In any case, the network's effectiveness lies in its ability to keep his identity secret—to remain silent generally."

"And it was the Grand Emissary who was the source of the hit list?"

"Right, John."

"Okay, Earl," Salzburg said, reaching for his direct line to the President's office. "You've convinced me."

New York was so flooded with sunlight that it would have seemed like autumn were it not for the occasional blasts of raw winter wind. As the new Dodge glided along First Avenue, Yudke Kantor sat beside his son, his eyes closed. Although he had lived for more than thirty years in the United States, Yudke had never driven a car. In that little corner that he had found for himself in Crown Heights, he had recreated a private world that, in its customs and mores, was like prewar Poland, where he had been known as Yudke, the master carpenter of Warsaw. Fortunately, his eldest son, Reb Shlomeh-Yitzak Kantor, was always willing to leave his work at the computer company when his father needed to go on an errand or make a visit to the city.

A stranger looking at the two men would have thought they were brothers, so similar were they in appearance, with wide noses and high foreheads. Yudke's face, however, bore the stamp of sadness. His three sons had a certain lightness, a zest for life, perhaps because they had reached the shores of the United States in their youth and had absorbed some of the joy of life that characterized the Hasidim of Crown Heights.

As Yudke Kantor sat with his eyes closed, he returned again to the terrible war years. He once told his sons that his life appeared to him like a panoramic film, from which he could at will isolate a single frame—beginning with those fearful days in September of 1939, when the tanks of the Third Reich rolled across Poland and the Luftwaffe dropped a rain of death. It was as if the constant replay of this film had served to isolate him, keeping him shut up for hours on end in his ground-floor carpentry shop. It was there that he devoted himself to the study of the Torah, when he was not engaged in the other task he had undertaken—to help assure the personal security of the Rebbe. Yudke modestly described himself as only a minor emissary. It was his brother, Volodia Kantor, the Parisian restaurateur, who was carrying out the real mission for the Rebbe. Volodia was an authentic emissary. All his waking hours, his entire being was consecrated to the Rebbe's *mitzvot*, to the religious commandments assigned him.

The *mitzvah* that consumed Yudke, when he was not concentrated on the Rebbe's safety, was the completion of the holy chair, the chair of the Rebbes from time immemorial. Of its ten components, nine were already in his possession. Only the tenth and final part of the ancient chair was missing, somewhere out in the Russian steppes, perhaps, or still in transit from parts unknown. Wherever it was, Yudke was convinced that the last part of the holy chair was intact. It had not yet appeared simply because the propitious hour had not arrived. He had to wait for the miracle, for the appearance of the last wooden leg. When the Creator of the Universe willed it, then and only then could he begin to restore the chair to its former glory—as it was in the days when the sainted Rebbes had sat in it before their congregations.

Yudke gave a little sigh and opened his eyes.

"You are thinking of the chair again, Father."

Yudke gazed at the troubled countenance of his fifty-one-year-old son and nodded slowly.

"Everything will fall into place as it should be, Father. Didn't the Rebbe himself take the trouble to say that it would be so? The chair will be reassembled, and it will be just like it was in 1939. We don't question the Rebbe, Father."

"I am not questioning the Rebbe. Heaven forbid." It would never have occurred to Yudke, the humblest of Hasidim, to do that. "But I cannot get the chair out of my mind. If I fail to complete it, I'll leave this world as one who hasn't fulfilled his obligations to his Creator—"

"But the Rebbe, Father!"

"True, true. As the Rebbe ordains, so it will come about, so it will be . . ." Yudke closed his eyes again and thought about the meeting to which his son was driving him. It was actually a mission he had undertaken for his brother: to serve as liaison in New York between Volodia Kantor and the head of the Mossad.

"Father, we're here."

Yudke opened his eyes and saw the tall buildings of the UN before him. As he got out of the car across from the spacious gardens that surrounded the complex, he brushed his dark coat, straightened the brim of his hat, and smoothed his thick beard into shape, unconsciously tidying up his appearance. His body showed few traces of age. Neither his hair nor his beard had grayed visibly. Were it not for the deep wrinkles in his broad face, it would have been difficult to even approximate his years. His enormous shoulders, as powerful as those of a young man, were slightly rounded, and he walked with his head pitched forward, like someone searching for a lost object.

He was to meet the Israeli in the rose garden. An open space was far better from every standpoint. Yudke found a bench and sat down. The afternoon sun was pleasant and he tilted his head back and lifted his face toward its warmth.

The war years and his long, hazardous flight had made him alert to even the faintest sounds, so he was quick to hear the Israeli's approaching steps. Had Yudke not known that the smiling Israeli standing over him was an ex-military man, a veteran of the Israel Defense Forces, he would have assumed he was a bank clerk or a merchant. The thin gold frames of General Dan Negbi's thick glasses accentuated his high forehead. Yet, despite his poor eyesight, his glance was penetrating. Although his features were fine, almost delicate, and his face had a sensitive expression, the broad, cleft chin gave him an overall look of stubbornness and determination. Past meetings with the General had taught Yudke to respect the keenness of his insight and the agility with which he made decisions. Ordinarily Yudke waited until the General came to the carpentry shop in Crown Heights, but this time he had received urgent information from his brother Volodia.

"Reb Yudke Kantor." General Negbi extended his hand and regretted it a moment later. The carpenter had the hands of a giant and a viselike grip, and it always took several minutes after the man's handshakes for the pain to subside.

"*Shalom*, Mr. Negbi." Military terminology was alien to Yudke's nature and he never used the title "General" when he addressed the Israeli directly. "I hope all is well with you."

" 'Well,' Reb Yudke, is a relative term." Dan Negbi tucked his large coat carefully under his body and sat down on the bench. He handled Yudke with patience, aware that he didn't like to be pressed. After a convivial conversation about various things, he would ease him gently on to the subject of their meeting. They had spoken briefly on the telephone only an hour and a half before. The list of names was complete. Yudke had received the information from Paris.

"But you are waiting for the list," Yudke finally said, taking an envelope from his coat pocket and presenting it to the General. Negbi opened the seal, removed the piece of paper, and studied it, then looked up, puzzled.

"Something is wrong here. There are only nine names. Together with the previous five, that makes fourteen. Yet Volodia spoke about a list of fifteen names."

Yudke answered without hesitation. "Volodia said to tell you that there was a numerical error. All the names we obtained have been passed on to you now. At this point we step out of the picture . . ."

"How can we possibly do that?"

"Very easily." Yudke drew a small silver snuff box from his inside coat pocket. "Because we have no further information." He opened the box, took a pinch of snuff between his fingers, and breathed it first into his left and then into his right nostril. He inhaled deeply, filling his lungs with air and swelling out his broad chest. "Do you understand?"

"But we have to have facts—information we can sink our teeth into."

"Understood. I was asked to tell you that if we get any additional facts, we'll pass them on to you."

"Are you telling me that you have nothing more concrete than the names?"

"Correct."

Negbi was distressed. It was the end of the line. The man sitting next to him offered the only avenue to the information he so urgently needed. But Yudke had proved to be a dead end, at least at this stage. It was incomprehensible. The Grand Emissary's men did not make mistakes like this. Something was confused; he needed the missing pieces that could shed light on just how far the preparations for this act of terrorism had advanced.

"Reb Yudke," General Negbi said slowly, choosing his words carefully, "I understand that too much digging on our part could disrupt certain things for you."

"It could endanger lives, Mr. Negbi. Precious lives."

"Then I will call a halt to all activity behind the Iron Curtain connected with this."

"I understand that's precisely what's wanted. You are not authorized to function behind the Iron Curtain, except as directed." Yudke Kantor met the Israeli's intense gaze. "In time, so it was hinted, our paths will cross again . . . God willing."

The message was clear. Intelligence gathering within the borders of the communist block was expressly forbidden. Poking around for information would produce nothing beyond what had already been obtained and would only hamper whoever was working to get more information.

"I'll do as you've requested, Reb Yudke," the head of the Mossad promised. "We'll restrict our activities to the areas outside the Red block."

The two men got up from the bench and turned toward the gate leading out to First Avenue. Nothing remained to be discussed.

During the trip back to Crown Heights, Yudke remained silent. His son drove slowly, as usual, to please his father who hated high speeds. Man—Yudke often said—must go slowly so as not to hasten his last hour.

If his brother had not requested him to, he would not have left Crown Heights for even an hour, for that was his world, both physically and spiritually, and when he left its narrow confines, he felt uprooted. Still, he told himself, carrying out my brother's wishes is only fair since Volodia has put himself out for me many times.

Long ago, Yudke had poured his heart out to his brother, telling him that he could depart this world and be on his way to the next in peace, only after he had finished restoring the chair of the Rebbe. But, since the outbreak of the war, the tenth part had been missing. It had been entrusted to the great Talmudic scholar Rabbi Shmuel ben Menachem Gillerman, of whom all trace had been lost. In Paris Volodia promised to question every Hasid who managed to escape the Soviet Union about him, but for the last thirty years no one appeared to have come across Shmuel ben Menachem Gillerman. Without him, Yudke would not realize his dream.

The carpenter sighed at the thought. He stirred himself and opened his eyes as the car turned into Kingston Avenue where his carpentry shop was located.

"We're home, Father," Shlomeh-Yitzhak said, and quickly stepped out to open the door for his father.

Yudke got out of the car slowly and turned to his son. "When you get home, call Uncle Volodia in Paris and tell him I carried out his request. Tell him that the Israeli noticed that something was wrong in the totals, asked about the disparity between fourteen and fifteen names."

"Father . . ."

"Yes?"

"Do you know what this is all about?"

"No." He shrugged almost nonchalantly. "But whatever I am obliged to do, I do. So my father conducted himself before me, and so you and your brothers will conduct yourselves."

"Yes, Father," Shlomeh-Yitzhak agreed, getting back into the car. "God bless you, Father."

Yudke lingered in the entrance of the building until his son's car had passed out of sight. Then he turned and began walking toward the corner where a small synagogue was located on the first floor of a two-story building.

When Yudke entered the synagogue, he found it already occupied by three old Jews, each one deep in prayer. He sat on the wooden bench and slowly undid the buttons of his heavy winter coat. He removed his hat and placed a knitted skullcap on his head, all the while gazing at the Holy Ark. Its curtain was ancient and frayed by countless years of handling. Still, it was the cover that protected the doors of the Holy Ark, and thus, holiness clung to it. Gazing at the curtain he attained complete concentration. Even with his eyes open he found himself in another world, a world in which man can converse with his Creator with nothing intervening between them. The Rebbe called these conversations "identification with the Creator."

Yudke's lips began to move. "Act, God, so that my dream may be realized, for your glory and for the glory of the Rebbe. Please, God, you who are omnipotent . . ."

The American Airlines flight from New York landed in Washington at 3:10 P.M. Earl Dickson was waiting on the tarmac to greet General Dan Negbi as he disembarked.

"I'm happy to see you, Dan."

"The feeling is mutual," Negbi replied as he handed the envelope with the additional nine names to the CIA man and got into Dickson's waiting car.

Dickson slid behind the wheel, pausing to open the envelope and glance at the list before starting the car. He threaded his way through the maze of access roads, pulling onto the George Washington Parkway.

The drive from National Airport to Dickson's home in Chevy Chase took almost twenty-five minutes, during which time the two men discussed the background of the new security development.

Dickson's home was nestled into the slope of a hill on West Beach Drive: a two-story house faced with light gray bricks and white siding. Dan Negbi recognized it from previous visits, although it seemed much larger now than he remembered it. It was the first time he had seen it in winter and the frost had bleached and withered the surrounding rich vegetation. A long row of cars was parked in front of the house.

"You've moved quickly this time," Negbi commented.

Earl Dickson nodded. "Every hour is important. I've only invited the special task force. You know all of them. They're people you've had contact with in the past."

They entered the house and descended a narrow flight of stairs into the basement where a steel door opened onto a large meeting room. Inside the room seven men awaited them: three were from the CIA, two from the FBI, one from the Secret Service, and the seventh was the President's special counsel, John Salzburg, who had been appointed by the Chief Executive to serve as his representative and furnish him with up-to-date reports on the task force meetings. It was unusual for a personal representative of the President to participate in a meeting of this kind and his presence had produced a certain amount of tension among the others.

After a few brief exchanges and handshakes, the men sat down and Dickson began to talk.

"Well, gentlemen, we've all of us had experience in 'assassination prevention.' We all know exactly how tough this work can be. Some of you undoubtedly would be happier not to be sitting here, because this is going to occupy us for some time. Unfortunately, this isn't just a single assassination attempt. According to the meager information in our hands at this stage, we seem to be faced with a Soviet-inspired international terrorist plot to crush what's known as the 'Jewish lobby.' And contrary to previous intelligence reports, the targets are not only Jews, they include other individuals known for their support of Israel or their sympathy toward the aims of the Jewish lobby."

His glance moved slowly from face to face. Then he drew a list from his breast pocket and read off the names in the order they had been passed on to him by General Negbi: Daniel Moynihan, Jacob Javits, Max Fisher, Morris Amitay, Alexander Schindler, Henry Jackson, Henry Kissinger, Hyman Bookbinder, Arthur Ochs Sultzberger, Arthur Goldberg, Frank Church, Daniel Mann, Marvin Kalb, Richard Stone. The names fell like the blows of a hammer.

Earl Dickson looked up and, with a slow movement of his hand, wiped the perspiration from his face before going on.

"At this stage we have no idea who will actually carry out this operation. Nor do we have any idea whether they will move simultaneously against all fourteen men or whether they will pick them off one at a time in order to escalate and prolong the terror. We do know now the names of their targets, and also we know that the entire operation is the brainchild of the KGB—more precisely of Department V, which is headed by Pavel Ramizor. Ramizor is considered an expert in political intrigue and sabotage. And one other important fact: we know that the operation is only in its initial stages.

"Given these facts, there are several courses of action open to us. First of all, within the next few days, we need to set up a special security force to protect the targets. And we plan to monitor all terrorist activity in Europe and the countries of the Middle East very closely. We'll carry this out cooperatively, using a staff composed of our people and agents of the Mossad. By channeling all information into a single intelligence pool, we can immediately pinpoint the locations of those men known to be key figures in European terrorism.

"A possibility also exists—slight perhaps, but it shouldn't be disregarded—that we can halt this entire campaign before it reaches the operational stage. If we can obtain irrefutable proof of Soviet complicity in this plot fast enough, it can be presented to the proper Soviet authorities and they'll have to halt it in Moscow, before it gets off the ground."

When Dickson finished speaking, the men of the task force had a clear picture of the vast scope of their mission and the extreme gravity of the situation.

"Our next meeting will take place tomorrow at eleven o'clock," Dickson said as he showed them out. "I want each of you to give me your ideas in writing then. We want to establish a brain trust."

A few minutes later, he returned with a bottle of Scotch and some ice, which he placed in front of his guest from Israel.

"We have time before dinner to belt down a few glasses of this."

"Good idea," General Negbi responded, and taking his straight, lifted a small shot glass and said, "Cheers!"

They sipped their drinks in silence for several minutes and began to analyse the operation again from various angles.

"Past experience has proved that if you succeed in cornering the Russian bear, though he may twist and dodge desperately, in the end he always surrenders," the Israeli observed.

"At the moment, Dan, I have a very reliable man operating in Europe trying to pinpoint the extent of Soviet involvement in this operation. An old friend. Our association goes back to the Korean War. We did our combat stints together and then some intelligence work. His name's Paul Mansfield." Dickson laughed suddenly. "The bastard has a filthy mouth, but he's tops in the field. I'd like one of your best men to team up with him. What do you say?"

"Of course. We've got an expert on both terrorist organizations and the inner workings of the KGB operating in Europe right now. You'll recognize his name: Evyatar Miller. We just have to set up a meeting between the two of them."

"Mansfield is in Germany at the moment," Dickson said, pouring another round of drinks. "He's working with the anti-terror unit and the counterintelligence branch of the West German government. And from the phone conversation I had with him this morning, he seemed quite pleased with the results so far."

"You activated him quickly, Earl."

"Yes. Actually, I began to plan the entire operation on the day you informed me of the list of targets . . . When was that exactly?"

"Eleven days ago."

"Eleven days! God! It seems like years . . . Only eleven days ago when you told me about the list of fifteen . . ."

He poured a little whiskey into his glass and leaned back, his gaze on Negbi's face.

"I'm waiting for an answer, Dan," Dickson said slowly. "At the beginning, the list was supposed to include fifteen names. Suddenly, this afternoon, someone vanished. The fifteen-man list became a list of fourteen names. What's happened?"

"I don't know," Negbi admitted. "My reaction was the same as yours. The disparity hit me right away. The source maintains that it was just a faulty computation, a numerical error."

"Do you believe that?"

"It strikes me as strange, but at this stage we have no way of investigating the error."

"If it was misinformation . . ."

"Or intentional," the Israeli said soberly.

3

THE BEGINNING OF December in Europe was marked by a cold wave that rolled across the continent and by an unusual upsurge in the movement of terrorists from one country to another. Although the various intelligence agencies were well aware of this activity, they found themselves utterly helpless to prevent it. The terrorists were spirited from one country to another by a loose network of sympathizers who had elevated the smuggling of people across European borders to a fine art. The very adroitness and the audacity with which these magicians breached the frontiers was a constant source of vexation to the intelligence community.

The Palestinians in particular had made their presence known through public assemblies, mass meetings, and rallies at the universities, where student sympathizers could be found in abundance. At the University of Bologna, leftist students turned out to demonstrate on "Palestine Day," which had been scheduled for Saturday, the first of December, 1979.

By Friday, fighting had broken out between the Israeli and Arab students, and it seemed likely that the administration of the university would have to intervene, particularly since several students had been injured in the course of these altercations.

The day was to be devoted to study groups on the various aspects of the Middle East conflict. In the evening, the long day of study was to culminate in an entertainment program by a number of well-known artists, among them the English actress Claire Lockridge, Pierre Murad, an internationally famous French guitarist, and, perhaps the biggest draw of them all—Jil, the mime.

News that Jil was to make one of his rare appearances had fired their enthusiasm, for he was regarded as the creator of a new tradition in pantomime, far different from the classic school of Étienne Décroux. The new mime had come from nowhere, it seemed, and his origins were shrouded in mystery. Since he gave no interviews he neither confirmed nor denied any rumors. Many of those who regarded him as the Charlie Chaplin of their generation were eager to see the man beneath the clown makeup, but it was one of his ironclad rules never to expose his face. And when the performance was done, he would slip into a secluded corner, remove his makeup, and vanish as anonymously as he had come.

In truth, Jil's reputation as an artist, which he acquired almost at once, and which drew a steadily increasing following, had its roots in the Moscow Circus, but no viewer, seeing his legendary "gallery of clowns" routine, would know that his performance was based on Boris Borodov's famous clown act of many years before.

Jil's circus skill provided the cover for his KGB activities and because it allowed him to travel, gave him entry to the centers of European terrorism. Unlike his earlier mission as an assassinator for the Liquidation Section of the KGB, his present job was limited to intelligence gathering. He was one of a number of KGB agents assigned to report on the activities of various terrorist organizations and their supporters, information that enabled the Soviets to use international terrorism as a means to further their own ends.

Among the European leftist-socialist elite, sympathetic to a variety of terrorists' causes, were many artists and intellectuals, and Jil joined their ranks.

As rapidly as his artistic renown spread, so did his reputation as an expert in smuggling terrorists across borders. He seemed to be able to pluck them from under the very noses of the security services and police departments of Western Europe, and he quickly gained the respect and trust of various terrorist groups. Of those who sought his services, none was aware that, under his dual guise of artist and smuggler, Jil was in reality an agent of the KGB.

Yet, as time went on, he was forced to minimize his conspicuousness. He had become far too famous, achieving a notoriety that could jeopardize his needs in carrying out intelligence assignments. But when he reduced the number of his appearances as a pantomime artist, the public's craving for his performances simply intensified, and the demand for this extraordinarily gifted performer, who had given the art of mime a new dimension, soared. Recently, concerned that the fame he had so quickly achieved might endanger his cover, he had reported the situation to Department V and asked to be repatriated and transferred to a new assignment.

The scores of fans who had lined up to await his arrival on the wide staircase of the old auditorium of the University of Bologna carried hand-lettered signs saying, "Jil—We love you." He heard their shouts as he sat in the dressing room that had been placed at his disposal on the third floor of the university auditorium. His long fingers moved nimbly over his face, as he pressed the white paint into his skin with his fingertips. He was creating a hybrid, a cross between the classical clown and the sad white mask of the pantomime artist. He painted a red dot at the tip of his nose, reminiscent of the big red apple that clowns traditionally fastened onto their noses. Afterwards, he outlined his lips with a black pencil, leaving the mouth unpainted. Over his immense eyes, he drew brows short and thick as fingers. With a single movement he could immediately alter the expression on his face—from serious to mocking, from ironic to pained, from sad to joyous, from scornful to scorned.

Outside, the crowd became more restless. Those waiting now gave voice to the silent entreaties scrawled on their placards.

"Jil . . . Jil. . . ."

It was apparent that the hundreds of students who thronged the foot of the staircase and spilled out into the square could prevent the evening from beginning as planned. The dressing room door opened and the medical student who

25

had organized the evening program stepped inside. Although it was a bitterly cold night, he was sweating.

"Jil!" He seemed out of breath as he wiped beads of perspiration from his face. "They don't know that you're here . . . Please . . . show yourself . . . otherwise the whole affair will be spoiled—completely . . . please!"

Jil looked at him, raising his eyebrows in astonishment. Then, his face fell, his mouth gaped open, and its derisive expression brought an explosion of laughter from the student.

"Fine . . . Suppose I go to the window."

"Thanks, Jil." The student sprang to the high window, opened it wide, letting in, as he did so, the roar of the crowd; cupping his hands over his mouth, he yelled down to them: "He's here!"

He was forced to shout it several more times before he finally succeeded in catching their attention. When they understood what he was saying, the clamor started up again.

"Jil . . . Jil . . . we want Jil! . . ."

As Jil rose from the makeup table and turned toward the window he picked up his flat, wide-brimmed hat and placed it on his head, concealing an abundance of chestnut curls. He was a man of average height and slender build, although his body was supple and powerful. He wore a white blouse whose tails fell over black trousers that clung tightly to his long legs.

He skipped over to the wide marble windowsill and leaned out over the square, his arms spread before him, like wings, ready to soar from the room and float out over the velvet night. With a light, graceful movement he leaped onto the windowsill, and his sudden appearance caused a total silence to fall over the crowd, a lull nearly as unanticipated as his appearance in the third-floor window. He scrambled down from the sill, waved his hands in benediction, and gave a courtly bow. The voices seemed to follow him.

"Jil! . . . we love you, Jil! . . ."

He waved his arms, fashioning them into a pair of mighty wings, and backed into the room. He seemed to disassociate himself from the window frame, giving the impression of soaring aloft.

As Jil did so, the student quickly shut the window and the voices faded. He gazed down for a moment, a faint smile on his lips.

"They're going inside . . . we'll be able to begin. Thank you, Jil."

Alone again, Jil felt overwhelmed by fatigue. The past year had left its marks on his mind and body. A weariness born of frustrated hope engulfed him. The years had gone by, one after the other, and he was still far from fulfilling the mission about which the old man had spoken so often: that mission, carried out in the name of the Rebbe, on behalf of a people dispersed to the very ends of the earth, the mission that awaits every true Hasid at maturity. It was as if destiny had forgotten him, and as time passed, the contradiction between his inner world and his external life, performing brutal missions for the KGB, became increasingly harder to bear.

He closed his eyes for a few seconds, trying to alleviate the mounting tension, then gazed for reassurance at the familiar clown's visage. The large eyes were as he had painted them—staring in wonder, asking the endless questions of childhood. In the circus they had called him "Putchimu"—"Why"—the child forever asking questions. For the man, a central question still remained unanswered.

Although he couldn't see the audience that packed the auditorium, Jil could sense the atmosphere. The students were passionate sympathizers of the Palestinian cause. Jil himself had wondered more than once what his feelings really were toward the struggle raging in the Middle East. As a Jew he knew how he was supposed to feel, but his attitude toward Judaism was intellectual rather than emotional. Everything he knew had been acquired secondhand, and while he had occasionally come across Israelis, he had not felt any kinship toward them whatsoever. They too were alien to him. Perhaps because he was alien to himself—a man still in search of his true identity.

As he moved into the wings, Jil watched Claire Lockridge as she read a short story written by his friend, the English writer, Margaret Aston, about the life and death of a young Palestinian. Jil had first heard it read by Margaret at one of the parties the French lawyer François Ripoll had given at his villa in St. Tropez.

Claire Lockridge was followed by guitarist Pierre Murad who played and sang the songs of George Brassens, Jacques Brel, and Yves Montand. And then it was Jil's turn to go on stage.

He waited until the applause for Murad had subsided. Then, as his name was announced, he heard the stamping of feet, the shrill whistles, and the tumultuous cries of "Jil, we love you."

The spotlights were extinguished and the hall was enveloped in darkness. Suddenly two beams of light crossed at center stage, catching in their brightness the upper half of Jil's body encased in an iridescent white blouse, on his face the look of the eternal lost child. Because he was submerged in darkness from the waist down, the audience saw what appeared to be a large head atop a small body, the hands serving as a pair of nimble little feet.

With the upper half of his body, Jil performed a succession of spectacular and breathtaking acrobatic feats, inducing laughter that verged on tears by showing how a large head, despite its disproportionately small and ludicrous body, could lead an active and independent life as a gay, frolicsome juggler and acrobat. The very absurdity and perfection of this portrayal produced a tidal wave of convulsive laughter that swept over the audience.

The second sketch brought even more peals of laughter as Jil depicted a slightly tipsy clown who passes a hat shop, breaks in, and, out of curiosity, begins to try on hats. Standing before an imaginary mirror, he acted out the person appropriate for each type of hat. Every movement was suggestive and precise, down to the last detail of walk, gesture, and facial expression. One characterization was quickly replaced by the next, to bursts of delighted applause as the audience roared its enjoyment.

The final sketch had been prepared as a tribute to the Palestinians. Jil presented their conflict with Israel as the battle between David and Goliath, with David as the humble Palestinian, and the giant commander of the Philistine army as Israel. His perfect portrayal of the two contenders and the adroitness with which he shifted from one to the other completely captivated the audience. The spotlight faded as the young David stood over the huge body of the dead Goliath, brandishing the Philistine's sword.

In the darkness, Jil fled the stage to a pandemonium of applause. The crowd was not ready to let him go, but he was already on his way to his dressing room on the third floor. He had to hurry. He must reach Paris. François Ripoll had sent a message that he needed him urgently. Undoubtedly, some terrorist on the run had to be spirited from one country to another before the police closed in. Although Jil still didn't know who controlled the French lawyer, he was convinced that Ripoll maintained close ties with the Baader-Meinhof gang in West Germany. To date, most of the terrorists whose transport François Ripoll had arranged were Germans.

Jil made his way quickly to the rented Ferrari parked a few hundred yards from the auditorium. Inside the building, thousands of students still waited in the hope that he would return for an encore. By the time they realized that Jil would not reappear, he was already speeding toward the border.

Margaret Aston leaned into the cold December wind that buffeted her body and whipped the ends of her long blond hair against her face as she strolled with François Ripoll through the court of the Tate Gallery. She stopped before a large bronze statue by Henry Moore. "The Family of Man" she called the conglomerate of hollows and cavities that represented the figures of a man, woman, and child.

"Photographed from the proper angle," she said to the French lawyer, "this statue would make an excellent closing shot."

"The film will be good no matter how it ends," Ripoll replied firmly.

"Do you really think so?"

"Yes," he said, passing a hand protectively over his bald spot where the icy winter gusts blowing in from the Thames stabbed at his skin. "It will surely give a good picture of the lives of the refugees."

"A lot of people are waiting to see it."

"Quite true," he agreed. "How much money do you need to finish?"

She circled the statue once more before answering. "About ten thousand dollars."

François Ripoll blew into his palms. "All right. I'll send you the check right away. In return, I'd like to be the patron of the first showing."

He broke off as a group of men and women passed by; they had recognized Margaret Aston and were obviously talking about her.

"They know who you are," the lawyer commented.

"More because of my political views than because of my books," she answered dryly. She felt slightly uncomfortable. Ever since her appearance on television and radio, defending the rights of the Palestinians, she had become the object of fierce criticism.

As they headed toward the street, Margaret suggested they walk along the bank of the Thames. Traffic was heavy and they had to dash across the wide avenue. By the time they reached the other side the Frenchman was breathing heavily. Margaret laughed.

"You're not very fit, François."

"No," he admitted, somewhat embarrassed. "Not like I used to be!"

Ripoll, who had come to London that morning, was scheduled to return to Paris the following day. He had come expressly to see Margaret Aston and settle two important issues. The first had to do with the money needed to complete the film; the second involved Horst Welsh.

"You must help us with Welsh." Ripoll paused in the shelter of a high stone wall to light a cigarette. "The Palestinians need him."

"What for?"

"I don't know; I didn't ask. I don't want to know any more than I have to. Excessive interest might turn out to be dangerous. I'm only the connecting link—no more than that, Margaret."

She studied his face for a moment. Ripoll had never impressed her as being particularly courageous, but she was beginning to understand his reputation for extreme caution.

"Why me, François?" She didn't want that kind of involvement either. She was a writer, not a freedom fighter. The Frenchman's appeal bothered her. He was asking her to broaden her commitment, to assume a much more active role than any she had previously been willing to undertake.

Edging a little closer, Ripoll again cupped his hands and blew on his chilled palms. He smiled.

"Occasionally we all contribute more than we've bargained for," he said.

"This isn't a contribution," she protested in anger. "You're asking me to help transport a terrorist fugitive when all the police departments and security agencies in Europe are trying to track him down."

"You must understand, Margaret. Horst is now hiding out in Vienna. The Palestinians need him. He has to be taken out of Vienna and brought to Spain."

"And then what?"

"From Spain you can easily get him to Morocco, and from there it should be no problem to bring him to the Middle East. You have to go there anyway, to finish your film. And you know your way around Spain. You can meet Horst there. Da'ud el-Za'id will help you with the arrangements."

"Where is Da'ud?"

"He'll meet you in Spain. You have an excellent base there after all—your father's villa near Toledo."

"Leave my father out of this!" Margaret objected sharply.

"We have no other way," Ripoll continued, unmoved. "As you know, Horst is 'hot.' They're closing in on him. It may be only a matter of days before they find his hideout in Vienna." He inhaled deeply, coughing slightly. "I was simply asked to arrange for you to receive him in Spain. From there, you and Da'ud will move him on."

Margaret hesitated. During the past year she had found herself engaging more and more in real terrorist activity. Until then her involvement had been peripheral, primarily in the sphere of information and propaganda. The burden and complications of practical action were proving onerous, as were the constantly increasing demands that she identify with the Palestinians in deed as well as word.

"Who can possibly get Horst out of Vienna and into Spain?" she asked.

"There is one person." Ripoll tossed his cigarette butt over the low stone wall that lay between them and the riverbank. "Someone you know."

"Jil?"

"Yes."

She had not seen Jil for a long time, not since the party at Ripoll's villa in St. Tropez when the lawyer had informed her that the money for her film had been raised. Since then she had covered the long route between London and Lebanon innumerable times. For many weeks she had lived in the refugee camps near Beirut. Then she had locked herself in a room in one of the few still-undamaged hotels on Pigeon Beach—once considered the Riviera of the Middle East—to write the film script. *Sacred Homeland* was a propaganda film with which the Palestinians planned to open their public relations campaign at the beginning of 1980.

"Now, what about Horst, Margaret?" The lawyer was determined to bring her around. "Your father's home would be an excellent waystation."

"I don't know," she murmured.

She thought of her father, the artist Miguel. There were moments when she felt an almost painful longing to see him. In her childhood he had been only a vague presence. Occasionally she received a postcard from him with one of his red and black paintings on the back. When she was seven years old she had seen him once: all that remained from that encounter was the memory of a tall, slender man with a strong, rather sad face, the mouth a bit askew, as if caught in the grip of a dying smile. He had vanished the next day without a trace, as if he had never existed. Her grandmother, the rigid, correct Lady Annabel Aston, made every effort to erase his memory, maintaining that the single disastrous error of her daughter's life needn't mar her granddaughter's as well.

But Miguel surfaced again after the publication of the short story which had made her reputation. The note he had sent her was engraved on her memory: *I read "Death of a Little Man of the Underground." A powerful story showing great talent. I am proud of you. Miguel.*

François Ripoll touched her arm, rousing her from her thoughts. "Margaret, I'm still waiting for an answer."

She gazed at him for several seconds.

"All right, François. Find Jil. Make whatever arrangements are necessary."

François Ripoll was a remarkably adaptable man, and one who asked few questions. That most of the pieces of his mosaic were unknown to him did not disturb him or prevent him from carrying out his role. He had received his orders from the German nightclub owner Klaus Schmidt to arrange for Horst Welsh's swift transfer out of Vienna. Welsh, who was known as "the Fox," was an expert in complicated terrorist actions. Always the first man to appear in an area targeted for a terrorist operation, he would case it thoroughly, analyze the problems, and then plan the action, from beginning to end. But the German police dragnet had begun to close on him. It would be only a matter of days before agents of the anti-terror unit of the West German security police would find him.

Ripoll was one of Klaus Schmidt's functionaries. The Frenchman knew that Schmidt had considerable influence on the leaders of the Baader-Meinhof gang. A major part of the gang's most daring operations were undertaken only after Schmidt had given his approval and after a preliminary plan had been prepared by Horst Welsh. Beyond this point, François Ripoll's information ran out, nor had he tried to probe further. He had learned not to be too curious. Some time ago, in fact, he had begun to fear for his skin.

As soon as François Ripoll returned to Paris from London, he met with Jil to enlist his help in smuggling Welsh from Vienna into Spain. Once Jil had accepted the mission, Klaus Schmidt sent a cable to Cyprus, to Mussa el-Dalil, commander of a suicide squad of the People's Popular Front, telling him that the German would be brought to Spain within a few days, and that he should dispatch one of his men to help Margaret Aston transfer Welsh from Spain to Larnaca in Cyprus.

The next morning, Klaus Schmidt received a brief reply from el-Dalil. Da'ud el-Za'id would be sent to Spain. Horst Welsh was scheduled to arrive there on the ninth of the month, the day Jil was to appear in Madrid at a convention of pantomime artists. Jil would have Welsh with him and would deliver him to Margaret Aston.

4

"**Y**OU ARE SIMPLY prone to tension," said Dr. Rostovitch gravely as he examined the pale face of Sergei Padayev, head of the Liquidation Section. "I saw that even before I gave you the EKG."

Sergei Padayev smiled faintly. He felt so weak it was difficult to move, but he didn't take his gaze from the doctor's eyes, trying to communicate without words what he wanted. Dr. Rostovitch cast a cautious glance at the concerned face of Pavel Ramizor, the department head, who stood a few feet away with his secretary.

"It will be all right, Comrade Ramizor," Dr. Rostovitch said dryly. "I wouldn't be at all surprised if Sergei Padayev admitted that he hasn't eaten anything today."

Sergei Padayev nodded his head, confirming the doctor's diagnosis. He felt a wave of gratitude: Dr. Rostovitch had correctly interpreted his plaintive look.

They were sitting in Ramizor's spacious office where Padayev had been called to consult with the head of the department about the merits of a group of agents from the Liquidation Section, candidates for a special mission in the United States. Only one man was to be selected. No sooner had they exchanged a few sentences than Sergei Padayev suddenly felt ill. Sweat flowed from every pore in his body, his breath quickened, pressure built in his chest, and a hard lump formed in his throat. Dr. Rostovitch, one of the heads of the medical staff of the special clinic at the KGB headquarters, had been summoned at once. Although the experienced physician had immediately known what was wrong, he was unable to do what he thought advisable, constrained as he was by Sergei Padayev's order that the gravity of his condition be concealed.

Sergei Padayev's vision still had not cleared. The solid, compact figures of Pavel Ramizor and his secretary appeared slightly blurred. Nonetheless Padayev began to behave as if the sudden weakness had passed. He lifted his head and inhaled deeply. Actually the presence of the doctor inspired a feeling of confidence in him.

"I'm fine," he said slowly. "The truth is that Dr. Rostovitch is right. Preoccupation with work robs a man of his health ... it prevents him from eating properly ..."

Dr. Rostovitch regarded him casually as he gathered up his instruments and closed the valise containing the portable EKG apparatus. Then, placing a hand on Padayev's shoulder, he said, "Brother Padayev, when you finish your business here, step into the clinic. I'll give you a new medicine ..."

"For the sake of variety!" joked Sergei Padayev. His face seemed less pallid. There was even a touch of color in his sunken cheeks.

"For the sake of variety," Dr. Rostovitch mocked, and turned to leave.

As the secretary escorted the doctor out, Pavel Ramizor sat down again behind his heavy wooden desk. He drew out a handkerchief and wiped his perspiring face and glistening bald head.

"You alarmed me, Sergei," he said softly.

"I didn't intend to," Padayev rejoined feebly.

"I know."

Ramizor gazed with warmth at his ailing colleague. He knew that Sergi Padayev's health had declined in the last year, and that heart trouble was part of it, but he didn't know just how acute the ailment was. This was the first time he had actually witnessed Sergei Padayev's debility, but he had faith in Dr. Rostovitch, and he hadn't appeared overly concerned by what had happened.

Ramizor and Padayev had been discussing a subject that had preoccupied them of late. It appeared there was a traitor in the ranks of KGB agents operating on the American continent. The turncoat had begun to sing to CIA agents and his songs had had dangerous repercussions for the KGB, among them the recent exposure of a number of important KGB agents.

It was essential to find the traitor quickly and liquidate him on American soil. Sergei Padayev had several candidates for this mission, but information he had uncovered in the last few days had compelled him to reject their candidacy. He was now proposing a new candidate, a man who for some years had not been part of the section's permanent staff: Yan Borodov.

Pavel Ramizor, still concerned about Padayev, suggested postponing the preliminary discussion of candidates to another time, but Sergei Padayev was insistent. Given what he now knew, it was imperative he fight for Yan Borodov's candidacy, that he secure his appointment at any cost.

"Please, brother," he said in a low voice. "I feel fine now. If we postpone the discussion, I'll get the impression that I'm sicker than I think I am." He chuckled softly. "Please."

"Very well," Pavel Ramizor responded impatiently. "Go on then."

Sergei Padayev inhaled deeply, drawing air into his aching lungs. He was aware of his heartbeat as he discussed the candidates for the mission to the United States, a mission that might take several months. He himself had trained these men, and he had closely followed their progress. But, in his analysis, Yan Borodov was a better choice, despite his not having participated for three years in the activities of the section. During these years he had been operating in Europe, providing up-to-date intelligence on various terrorist organizations.

"When Yan was in the field, he was good," Pavel Ramizor acknowledged. "Very good. But three years out of the section is quite a long stretch . . . it can dull the abilities." He hesitated. "There is no doubt, Sergei, that if Yan Borodov were active in the field today, I would agree with you."

"He is still the best," Sergei Padayev said decisively. "Believe me, Pavel."

"I believe you." Ramizor fell silent. He had no trouble remembering Borodov. The man had moved like a shadow, carrying out assignments in various parts of the world. He had always completed his mission with great effectiveness and he covered his trail, so that the KGB was never linked with any act of murder. Yan did not blunder. He understood only too well the meaning of error—the hastening of one's own doom; it had prevented him from making mistakes.

"I don't recall a single instance where we mobilized a man who had been deactivated for an operation of this kind," Ramizor said slowly.

"The fact that there aren't precedents shouldn't prevent us from establishing them."

"True . . ."

"We've absorbed too many shocks in the last few years, Pavel." The observation, though sharp-edged, was made with tact.

"True." Pavel Ramizor knitted his brows together and his eyes narrowed.

"We've known very few agents as reliable as Yan Borodov," Padayev went on.

"Yes, yes." Ramizor suddenly laughed. "I'm reminded of his grandfather, Boris Borodov. The Emperor of the Clowns! And what's the name the young man goes by?"

"Jil."

"Ah, yes. Jil the mime." The smile faded slowly from Ramizor's round face. "He's done some very creditable intelligence work."

"Well, he's reached the point now where you'd have to think of repatriating him in any case." Padayev began to relax; he knew the crisis had passed. "He had to follow a path that entailed a good deal of personal publicity. From our point of view, his lingering on too long in Europe might actually endanger him. He's already done what he could there; neither you nor I would want to lose Borodov . . ."

Sergei Padayev's voice trailed off. It was apparent from the expression on his face that Ramizor was thinking it over.

The department head studied Padayev's calm, inscrutable countenance. He knew that Padayev's recommendation of young Borodov had been prompted by several things. Perhaps Yan was the best candidate for the assignment in the United

States, but, beyond that, he was also the grandson of Sergei's closest friend, the old clown Borodov.

The two men were, he knew, bound together in a friendship that went back to the war with the Nazis. Theirs was the brotherhood common among soldiers who managed to survive the changing fortunes of war. For men like himself and Sergei, one's friends could be counted on the fingers of a hand. Life had taught them to be wary, to count only on those who were willing to put their lives on the line for their friends. The true test of comradeship would always be found on the battlefield. And so it had been with Sergei and the old man, Borodov, who had fought together with the partisans. It was only natural for Sergei to see himself as Yan Borodov's patron and to push for his advancement within the ranks of the KGB. It might very well be that childless Sergei took a paternal interest in Yan, that he regarded him as the son he never had.

"Let me give the matter some thought," Pavel Ramizor said finally. "The idea appeals to me more and more. As you said, we are free to create precedents. I'd like to look over Borodov's personal file."

Sergei Padayev felt relieved. A weight had been lifted from him and even his breath came easier. He had blazed a modest trail—a narrow path he would have to widen, slowly, cautiously, one step at a time. Now, at least, Ramizor was weighing the advantages of recalling Yan Borodov to active duty in the Liquidation Section. Padayev rose slowly from the chair, steeled against another attack of dizziness, but this time he felt no lightheadedness.

"Borodov's file is ready any time you want it," he said with a smile.

"Sergei . . ."

Padayev stopped before the wide oak door separating the department head's office from the outer chamber and turned around slowly.

"Sergei." Pavel Ramizor looked at him tenderly. "Please take care of yourself. I haven't many friends left of our generation."

Sergei Padayev was surprised. Ramizor was more inclined to manifestations of vulgarity than delicate expressions of affection.

"I'll take care of myself," he said in a suddenly husky

voice. He was touched by Ramizor's concern, by his expression of friendship. "Everything will be all right, Pavel."

"If you'd like to take a vacation," the department head said, "my dacha is at your disposal."

"I won't be able to. Not now anyway."

"Why not?"

"Because you need me, Pavel. You know that. And I can't go off when you or the department need me. Later perhaps. In the spring."

Pavel Ramizor smiled. As usual, Sergei was right. They had worked together for many years now, and in a few more their tour of duty in the KGB would be over. Over the years, Ramizor had always been amazed at the calming effect Sergei Padayev had on him, as if he knew just how to diffuse the wrath that was Pavel's almost constant companion.

"Very well, Sergei. In the spring."

When Sergei Padayev returned to his own office, not far from Ramizor's, his secretary informed him that Dr. Rostovitch had already called several times, asking to be notified when Padayev returned.

"Can I tell him you're back?"

Padayev nodded his head as he shut the door separating his office from that of the secretaries. Both his office in the old KGB headquarters in the heart of Moscow and this one in the new building were almost spartan in appearance: plain cabinets for the various files and documents relating to current projects, a comfortable but simple desk, a few wooden chairs. He walked slowly over to his desk and sat down, then took a bottle of vodka from the desk drawer. He poured a drink into a small glass and tossed it down. The heat that spread through his body made him feel instantly better.

When the door opened, he knew without looking that it was Rostovitch.

"You'll have a drink?" he asked, picking up the bottle and filling a second glass. Rostovitch sat down and, lifting the small glass, said, *"Nazdrovya."* He drained the glass and rapidly flicked his tongue over his lower lip to catch a drop of vodka that lingered there. The doctor tugged nervously at his little beard for a moment before speaking. "Sergei, you know you can't continue like this."

"I hear you."

"Your condition is very grave. You know it and I know it. But Pavel Ramizor doesn't."

"He doesn't have to know, Grisha."

"I can't keep it from him indefinitely. Your condition has deteriorated in the last few months. It's a wonder that you can still function."

"There is a God in heaven," Sergei Padayev whispered.

"You believe in miracles."

"Yes, Grisha, I believe in miracles. I am obliged to believe in one miracle, and you will help that miracle to happen. Not one word to Pavel Ramizor about my condition!"

"In the end he'll discover the truth."

"Perhaps. But by then it will be of no concern to me."

"He will know that I had a hand in the cover-up. I'll have to pay the price."

"If you must, Grisha, you'll pay it . . . like the rest of us."

It was clear now to the doctor that the situation had passed out of his control, perhaps even out of Padayev's. He hesitated before asking his next question.

"What is happening, Sergei?"

"I can't tell you—what I need now is time. Perhaps several months. Pavel Ramizor must not know my real condition." He fixed the doctor with a piercing look. "You must do everything you can to give me this time. Is that clear, Grisha?"

The commanding tone was not characteristic of Padayev. Hearing it, Rostovitch began to understand.

His lips moved slowly. "The Grand Emissary?" Rostovitch didn't utter a sound but Sergei Padayev read the question from his lips.

"Yes," he responded. "For the Rebbe . . ."

Grisha Rostovitch fell silent. The discussion was closed. He had received an order in the name of the Rebbe, from the Grand Emissary. The Grand Emissary was the Rebbe's alter ego in the Soviet Union, the ultimate authority. It was forbidden to question him. Rostovitch did not know the identity of the Grand Emissary; he only knew that within the KGB, Sergei Padayev was the highest authority who functioned in his name. Grisha Rostovitch was obliged to obey that authority as if the Rebbe himself had issued the order to him personally.

"I must submit a medical report on you to Pavel within the week," the doctor said. "He wants to know precisely what your condition is."

"You know what you have to report."

"I know." He rose and turned to leave, then paused. "Sergei . . ." He wanted to say something more, but reconsidering, decided to remain silent. Padayev's condition was clear to both of them. Perhaps in other circumstances he could expect a few more years of life, but under the present tensions . . .

For a moment after Rostovitch left, Padayev leaned back in his chair and closed his eyes. He needed to rest before he roused himself to relocate Yan Borodov's personal file.

The challenge that lay before him exceeded his wildest dreams. From the moment he had discovered the fifteenth name on the list of those targeted for assassination, Sergei Padayev knew that this was a momentous mission, for Pavel Ramizor had selected as his prize target their Rebbe, Shalom Baruch Abrahamson.

Once the initial shock subsided, it seemed a natural enough choice. Yuri Andropov, the chairman of the KGB, had made constant references to the "Jewish network," and in the past, Sergei Padayev himself had heard Pavel Ramizor refer to the Rebbe as the man who headed this network. Ramizor spoke of the Rebbe with a bitter, almost fanatic hatred; he was convinced that several plans, which were to have crowned his long career, had been smashed by the Rebbe's secret network.

When the list of names had been forwarded to the Mossad, Boris Borodov had expressly forbidden the inclusion of the Rebbe's name. The old man believed that the Rebbe's fate was in the hands of God, that neither friend nor foe could do anything to shape or alter his destiny. Moreover he knew that the Rebbe's health had recently deteriorated; doctors had ordered complete rest and any unnecessary tension would only further enfeeble him. Borodov was convinced that the network in Russia could be entrusted with the preservation of the Rebbe's welfare, without disturbing the life of the Hasidic community in Crown Heights.

Boris Borodov had been prepared to sacrifice himself, but in the end, his advanced age presented an insurmountable obstacle. In his mind only one man was fit to act in his place, a man whose entire life up to now had been no more than a divinely orchestrated prelude to a great mission. His grandson had to return immediately, for only with Yan's assistance could they halt the diabolical operation that had already been set in motion by the KGB.

Sergei rose from his chair and walked over to the cabinet that held the personal files of everyone who had worked in his section. He knew exactly where he had placed Yan's file a few years before. Without hesitating, he reached for the top drawer and, beneath a pile of folders, found the file he wanted. Back at his desk, he opened the file and glanced at the photograph of the handsome young man. The details describing Yan's appearance held true, but others in the file had been fabricated.

Padayev vividly remembered the first time he had seen Yan, toward the end of the Second World War. The boy was only two years old then; he had been brought to Boris by the old clown's sister, Zina. The child was the only young survivor of what had been a very large family before the fires of war and the Nazi gas ovens had consumed them.

Sergei pressed the button on his intercom. His next step was to check out Yan's updated file, which was in the archives of the division that dealt with "liberation movements"—the KGB euphemism for terrorist organizations.

5

LE CHATEAU, ON Rue Pierre Charron in the heart of Paris, was a modest and unassuming hotel that provided excellent service. It was, moreover, very conveniently located just off the Champs Elysées.

The Israeli Evyatar Miller had checked in there the day before. He was to meet American agent Paul Mansfield, who was coming in from Germany at nine o'clock. Miller glanced at his watch; the American was late.

He stretched out on the double bed. Under other circumstances, he might have enjoyed this spacious, airy room, but at present it was small compensation for the gray routine that characterized his days in the espionage service.

General Negbi's order to meet Paul Mansfield, Earl Dickson's man, had reached Miller while he was in Rome; it had been followed by a written briefing on the mission. Miller had come to Rome after a short stopover in Vienna, a city he visited regularly. Since both Vienna and Rome were transit centers for Jews emigrating from the Soviet Union to various countries in the West, agents of the Hasidic network were active in both cities, helping the Israeli Security Service expose agents planted among the immigrants by Department

V of the KGB. Miller acted as liaison between the Mossad and the Hasidic agents. The order to proceed to Paris was not unwelcome. He needed a change of scene.

At the sound of steps approaching his door, Evyatar Miller got up slowly, listening attentively. He heard the double knock, the same signal Paul Mansfield had used to announce his arrival the year before when the two men had met to exchange information.

"It isn't locked," the Israeli said.

The door opened and Paul Mansfield stood in the threshold, a tall, solidly built man with massive shoulders. He hadn't changed since their last meeting, Miller noted. The Israeli, who was only thirty, estimated that Mansfield must be close to fifty. His face was deeply lined and he had the ruddy complexion typical of men who have been exposed to the out-of-doors.

"May I?" Mansfield asked, as he draped his heavy topcoat over a chair.

"Make yourself at home. If you can call these lousy hotels home."

"It's not a bad room." Mansfield smiled. "Le Chateau is tailor-made for high-class characters like you and me." He sat down on a chair near the bed on which Miller had stretched out again. "I apologize for the delay, buddy. The meeting with the DST ran a little longer than I anticipated. I try to keep a rein on them but it's pretty hard."

"Something come out of the trip to Germany?"

"Yes. I wasn't loafing. It seems you and I have another mission," Paul Mansfield said, stretching out his long legs. "It's funny," he went on. "You know, Earl Dickson and I started out together. I envied him when he moved to the administrative end, but sometimes, like in this case, I consider myself the fortunate one. Think what it must be like from an organizational standpoint to be responsible for the security of fourteen men! You have to be damn unlucky to get involved in a rotten business like that."

Paul Mansfield took a leather case from his jacket pocket. He opened the case and took out a short thick cigar and lit it. He blew out a few puffs of heavy, pungent smoke as he returned the case to his coat pocket. "You know, Miller, I don't like to lose. I'm considered a good fighter—maybe too old for some people's taste—but tough and competent. I know that

44

you're considered a good man too, despite your age." He looked at Miller penetratingly.

"You're sensitive about your age," Evyatar Miller remarked quietly.

"True. It's not an easy adjustment." Paul Mansfield squared his wide shoulders. He seemed defensive.

"What did you find out in Germany?"

"First of all, the Germans are very ready to cooperate. Not just lip service like the French give you." He drew in a quantity of smoke, rolled it around his tongue, and let it out slowly. "I got some interesting information. I'll tell you about it because I have the impression that it's important. You have something to drink here?"

"I think so." Evyatar rolled off the wide bed and went over to the cabinet the hotel stocked. "What will you have? There's whiskey . . . brandy . . ."

"Let's start with whiskey."

"Okay. Fine with me."

He took out glasses and got some ice from the small refrigerator. He brought out the whiskey and poured two drinks. He held out a glass to Paul and took the other back to the bed, where he stretched out.

"The Germans believe that a number of men who have been working for some time with the Baader-Meinhof gang are Soviet operatives. They seem to be chiefly involved in smuggling terrorists from one country to another."

"They must be experts."

"They are that. Definitely," Paul agreed. His cigar had gone out. He relit it and dragged on it a few times until it had rekindled and was burning brightly. "The Germans know of at least three men who are smuggling the terrorists. One they call the Miracle Worker. The second is called the Clown. The third goes by the name the Trainer. Odd, isn't it?" Paul gave a weary smile.

Evyatar felt a strange sensation when he heard the code names. It was the first time someone had uncovered information consistent with the data he had forwarded several weeks before to Mossad headquarters in Tel-Aviv. His report, however, had mentioned only two code names, and they were different from the ones that Mansfield had just given.

"I know of two more," the Israeli said slowly.

Paul Mansfield's excitement was evident immediately. "What are they?"

"Acrobat and Fortune Teller."

"Acrobat and Fortune Teller," Mansfield muttered in a low voice. "They fit together! . . . There must be a connection . . . it can't be a coincidence." He searched Evyatar Miller's face. "Have you ever heard of the Soviet Circus?"

"No."

"A German police official, a sovietologist, told me about it."

"What does it have to do with us?"

"I think it has some significance. You're close to intelligence sources operating in the Soviet Union." He raised his hand when he saw that the Israeli was about to protest. "Don't tell me it isn't true."

Evyatar chose to remain silent.

"Fine. A clever response." Paul chuckled. "Now, as I was saying. You have sources. I'm not trying to expose them. But we need you to make use of them on our project."

"What do you want to know?"

"The significance of the term Soviet Circus."

"Why?"

"Because if that West German sovietologist was correct," explained Mansfield, "then we'll find that we have a real clue to the operation. One that will help us find direct proof of Soviet involvement, which is what Earl Dickson and General Negbi are both looking for."

"I'll try to check . . ."

"Every hour counts." Paul Mansfield rose from his chair and pulled on his topcoat with one quick motion. "If you need me, you can find me, even in the wee hours of the morning, at our embassy. The duty officer will know which room I'm in," he said as he left.

Evyatar Miller remained stretched out on the bed, immobile, his eyes closed.

"Soviet Circus." He said the words slowly. He had to follow up on that.

One of his best sources was only a short distance from the hotel: the man who had helped expose Soviet agents planted in the West—Volodia Kantor, the restaurateur. Miller glanced at his watch. It was ten-thirty. The restaurant closed at nine-thirty but Volodia would still be there. The Israeli slid agilely from the bed, grabbed his overcoat, and headed for the door.

Volodia Kantor finished mopping the restaurant's tile floor, and took the chairs down from the round tables and stood them in their proper places. Now he could devote his attention to the letter he had been meaning to write to his brother Yudke. He sat down at the table next to the kitchen entrance and, in pencil, wrote at the top of a sheet of paper the Hebrew letters "Beth" and "Hay," the initial letters of the words meaning "with the help of God."

He began the letter to his brother with news of his life in Paris, which he disliked intensely. The longing to again be among the great congregation of Hasidim in Crown Heights was ever present. Volodia thanked his brother for meeting General Negbi in his behalf:

> Believe me, my brother, we all do these missions with a full heart and soul. The more so if it is a mission in the name of the Grand Emissary—may he be granted a long life. I don't know what it concerns this time. I don't ask, and therefore I am not able to cast any additional light on the mission you performed. I was requested to tell you that if you are needed again, I shall notify you at the proper time.
>
> I know, dear brother, that you are waiting primarily to hear good tidings. But, to my sorrow, I am not able to add anything new. I have yet to come across a man who has recently seen Rabbi Shmuel ben Menachem Gillerman, whose appearance you have awaited these many years. Yet I am convinced and have complete faith that you will one day hear from him. And on that day the nine holy parts already in your hands will be joined by the tenth—and the chair of the Rebbe will be completed. Until then, please send my kind regards to your blessed wife, your sons, daughters-in-law, and grandchildren—may they be granted long lives. I remain, as always, your devoted brother. With love and respect, from all my heart,
>
> *Volodia ben Mayer Kantor*

Volodia heaved a deep sigh and poured himself another

cup of tea. He was sipping it slowly when the door opened and the handsome Israeli entered.

He greeted the young man enthusiastically. Despite the difference in their ages, and the very different worlds in which they lived—Evyatar was a totally nonreligious Jew—they truly liked and respected one another. The Hasid took the Israeli's hand in his powerful grip and shook it vigorously. Volodia was a stocky, broad-shouldered man with the ascetic face and thick beard of a student of the Law. His sage eyes seemed to take in everything around him with understanding and humor.

"Well, well," he said, chuckling, "a good deal of time has passed, eh, Reb Yid?"

The two men generally conversed in Yiddish—Volodia's a rich, Lithuanian Yiddish, Evyatar's a castrated German. But they understood each other well, and that was the important thing. Volodia always joked about the Israeli's efforts to butcher his German in the hope that it would at least sound like Yiddish.

"Fool," he would say with a laugh, "what do you gain? Your German is not German and your Yiddish is not Yiddish. You end up with a dead loss."

He never tired of telling Evyatar the history of the language that had been created by the Jews to serve a people dispersed throughout the world; Hebrew, on the other hand, was a sacred tongue, he maintained, to be used only in prayer. Evyatar listened, always with patience.

This time, after he saw to it that the Israeli was comfortably seated, Volodia busied himself bringing food. There were blintzes and Volodia's famous Russian borscht—a delicious sweet-and-sour beet soup with a pungent flavor that delighted the palate.

"Volodia," said Evyatar, as he pushed his empty soup bowl aside, "I must talk to you about something."

"Have you ever come only to eat?" the Hasid mocked.

"Something very serious."

"Such as?"

"Tell me what these words suggest to you: Miracle Worker, Clown, Acrobat, Trainer, Fortune Teller." He said the five names in a single burst.

"Soviet Circus," Volodia replied at once.

There was a short silence. "Why Soviet?" asked the Israeli.

Volodia paused before answering, his brow furrowed. The question clearly disturbed him. His response had been perfectly natural to him. But Evyatar was right.

Volodia's sharp, intelligent eyes gleamed provocatively. He lifted his cup of tea and took a long sip.

"To answer you," the old man said quietly, "I must pose a similar question. Now, you tell me: what do flutist, violinist, drummer, and trumpeter remind you of?"

"An orchestra."

"Exactly." Volodia grinned. He ran his hand over his forehead. The long day in the restaurant had taken its toll. "But, for me, the image is slightly different."

"Meaning?"

"I would have said: Red Orchestra."

The answer took him by surprise, but the concept of the Red Orchestra was not unfamiliar to Evyatar. During the Second World War, the Red Orchestra was the name of a renowned espionage ring the Soviets established in Nazi-dominated Western Europe. The ring, which was headed by the Jew Leopold Trepper, gathered intelligence of crucial importance to the Soviet Union. When Leopold Trepper left the Soviet Union for Israel many years later, he published a book telling the story of the group. "Does the term Soviet Circus have similar connotations?"

Volodia's gaze softened. "Yes," he murmured. "There was another network, much much smaller than the Red Orchestra. But what it did was no less remarkable, no less daring. Perhaps more . . ."

"It was called the Soviet Circus?"

Volodia nodded.

"Do experts on Soviet affairs know about it?" Miller was thinking of Paul Mansfield and the German sovietologist.

"Professionals in the field may know," Volodia said. "They may have heard of it. It was a small espionage ring on the Stalingrad front; its members moved around disguised as a band of circus performers, gathering information behind the Nazi lines. They were only a few men, but they plagued the Nazis in every way conceivable. They were associated with the partisans; they actually were the first to report that the Soviet winter would vanquish the Nazis, just as it had vanquished Napoleon's army. And that is what happened." Volodia chuckled. "History does repeat itself."

It was after midnight when the taxi pulled up at the entrance of the hotel. Evyatar Miller leaped from it and walked with long strides to the elevator. He had to get in touch with Paul Mansfield immediately. A few minutes later, he had located him at the United States Embassy.

"You are very diligent, Mr. Miller," said the American in a sleepy voice.

"Your assumptions were correct," Evyatar said. "Someone among the KGB agents apparently knows about the activities of a World War Two group called the Soviet Circus and is using the code names of that group for a similar network of agents. If this information is accurate, we might have the key to it all."

Paul Mansfield was suddenly totally awake. "If that's the case, I'm going to enlist the cooperation of the DST. It means we'll probably have to use steam-roller tactics on a certain French lawyer who's known to be deeply involved with the Baader-Meinhof gang and Terror International. I'll have to go to Germany again, Evyatar, to get more information on this man. Do you want to join me?"

"No," said Evyatar. "I'd rather get more background on the Soviet Circus. I'll hop over to Tel-Aviv and burrow into our archives, see if I can find something concrete. We'll be in touch. I'll contact you shortly."

"Fine . . . Well, good night, Miller. This may be the last night that you sleep well."

6

THE FIAT MINIBUS made its way quickly from the airport outside Madrid to the Hotel Royal on Avenida de Jose Antonio. It turned into the hotel's underground parking lot. The driver pulled the minibus up to an elevator entrance on the first level and leaped out to help a passenger who was carefully extricating an elderly woman in a wheelchair from the vehicle.

Jil turned to the driver with a somewhat embarrassed smile. "Thank you," he said, offering the driver a substantial tip.

The elevator stopped in the lobby and Jil carefully pushed the elderly invalid's wheelchair toward the reception desk to register. Their reservations had been made several days before by François Ripoll.

The frail old woman sat immobile, her eyes closed, completely dissociated from the world around her. While the young bellhop carried their suitcases, Jil wheeled her back to the elevator and they ascended to their rooms on the third floor.

Jil waited until the bellhop had left and then closed the door.

"Okay, Horst," he said. "You can slip out of your fancy carriage."

Horst Welsh opened his eyes. They were a blend of gray and light watery blue that gave the impression of being on the verge of tears. With his lithe body encased in a long dark dress and his face made up to give the appearance of old age, he looked both pitiful and ridiculous.

"It's all over, eh?" he asked as he got out of the wheelchair.

"You can leave the hotel and begin to move about like a free man."

"I . . . don't know." Horst moved with difficulty; the long dress impeded his progress and he lifted the hem to facilitate walking, looking as he did so like a venerable matron trying to step over a puddle of water without getting her dress wet. He moved to the window and gazed at the breathtaking sunset which cast a red hue over the entire city.

"I'll be busy this evening," said Jil. He was to appear that evening at a congress of dancers and mimes.

"I know. I don't intend to leave the hotel. How long will we be here?"

"Till we hear from Margaret."

A muscle spasm ran the length of Horst's sunken cheek. His hand went swiftly to his jaw, and with the pressure of his fingers he attempted to bring the rebellious muscle under control, but to no avail.

"I'll be in my room for now," said Jil. He was tired, and the German's nervousness irritated him. He glanced at his watch. Six o'clock. In another three hours the performances would begin. The annual congress in Madrid, which was opening that evening, was an important one and Jil wanted to prepare himself physically for the effort that would be required of him during the few minutes of his act.

"Jil . . ."

He stopped by the door.

"You won't be gone long, will you?"

"I don't know, Horst," Jil answered quietly. He abhorred the role of nursemaid. "You're perfectly safe here. This country isn't willing to cooperate with German security services."

He closed the door behind him and went to his room where he shaved, washed, and set out the things he would need. Then he stretched out on the bed and closed his eyes, still aware of the anxious man in the next room. The German was frightened, like all the terrorists that Jil had been called on to rescue from the manhunts of various security forces.

Not that he was so safe himself. Jil was well aware that the security forces could discover his own involvement and ultimately his true identity. As a smokescreen, he had created the impression that he did not act alone in smuggling fugitives, that he was only one of a unit of professionals dealing in human contraband.

To create this illusion, he operated under a number of circus code names, gleaned from the stories he had heard in early childhood about the exploits of the Soviet Circus, a tiny partisan espionage unit that had wreaked havoc on the German army during World War Two.

The stories of his grandfather, Daidushka, who was the leader of this group, had excited his imagination for years. Now Jil brought new life to the little circus, using its characters in such a way that it appeared as if a column of men were vexing the security services of the countries in which he operated solo.

The terrorists he had transported intrigued him. Usually when he found them they were as frightened as any confused, vagrant youths cut off from their pack. He was curious to learn their motives. At first he thought that some kind of bond must exist between him and them. They killed men. He too had killed. But they seemed without remorse, whereas he, on the other hand, was so conscious of his transgressions that he experienced deep spiritual pain.

True, in his days as an assassinator for the KGB he had for a long time functioned as a machine of death. He had always performed meticulously, in accordance with the rules and guidelines of the KGB, which prohibited him from thinking about those he had eliminated in the performance of his duty. Daidushka, however, had raised him to honor the commandment that explicitly stated "Thou shalt not kill." It was clear that a conflict was bound to arise within him. And it did, very suddenly. Up until then, he had been given a mission, learned it thoroughly, located the target of the reprisal, and committed the murder. But things had become utterly and irrevocably confused four years ago. The victims refused burial in his subconscious. They lived there, waiting for retribution. Then he began to relive the assassinations.

The first time that this happened, he awakened suddenly from his sleep after a series of terrifying dreams—dreams so painful that they caused him to cry out. He was in a hotel in Rome, in bed with a movie starlet, a one-night stand: he had always been wary of extended relationships, preferring chance encounters. He opened his eyes in terror, bathed in perspiration. The young woman lying naked beside him continued to sleep, unaware of what was happening, lost in the pleasure and utter tranquility that had followed their love-making. In his dream, he had seen the face of a man he had killed not long before. Then the face shifted suddenly to that of a curly-headed man with a flushed countenance and large, gloomy eyes. It was his own face that he confronted!

Fatigue was the word he seized on as a last resort in his attempt to be transferred out of the Liquidation Section. Sergei Padayev had interceded for him, and he was transferred from the Liquidation Section and given a new assignment, the infiltration of European terrorist groups. He refused to kill anymore. He wanted peace of mind. Perhaps the ultimate mission that awaited him, the one promised by the old man, would give him that longed-for peace. Perhaps he would then gain the tranquility that comes from the knowledge of having embarked on a true life mission. Perhaps in serving the Hasidic community he would finally attain a completeness of spirit.

There were moments even now when he had glimpses of this completeness—moments in his performances when his body expressed his inner world. He had been forced to create a cover for himself and he seized the rare opportunity that befell him to transform his art into his cover. In so doing, he discovered anew the world that had been lost to him, the world of the circus.

Jil opened his eyes. He could hear Horst Welsh pacing in his room. Up and down, up and down. He had been in hiding for many weeks, fleeing for his life, before Jil was called to transport him to Spain. From Spain he would be taken somewhere else; Horst couldn't tell Jil where that would be—he didn't know himself.

The German had been a bundle of nerves when Jil found him in the small apartment on the second floor of the building in Vienna. His only contact with the outside world had been an eighteen-year-old university student. It was he who had brought Jil to the apartment.

They had set out that night in Jil's Ferrari. They sped along winding roads toward the Austrian border, roads that would bypass the border checkpoints; roads that were relatively untraveled. They crossed the border and drove into Italy; they reached Milan in the early hours of the morning and stopped to rest until evening. At nightfall, they continued to drive toward the French Riviera until they reached the airport in Monaco where they boarded a direct flight to Madrid. That part of the trip had been easier. Horst Welsh had been so successful in the role of the sick, paralyzed old woman traveling with her very concerned companion that he gained the sympathy of everyone on the flight.

In the next room, Horst continued his pacing. Jil glanced at his watch. It was seven-thirty—time to go.

Nearly one hundred and fifty artists had gathered in "the Club," as the assembly hall on Calle Morenas was known. Twenty-two artists were to perform during the course of the evening. Some were choreographers, others dancers and pantomimists.

His appearance before these artists inspired a special feeling in Jil. He had prepared a short sketch of powerful dramatic impact which would give them a deeper understanding of his craft. He had devoted many years to the study of movement and he had finally mastered his grandfather's art. He knew how each movement must give rise to another. This was the secret of his unique perceptiveness. Many artists of mime failed to choose from the possibilities before them the precisely correct movement which followed inevitably from the one preceding. The old man had understood this. And he himself knew now—but only after long, uninterrupted years of study with the old clown.

It was after midnight when Jil appeared at the center of the stage. The upper part of his torso was bare, and his legs, widespread, were sheathed in black tights that revealed his supple muscles. His feet were bare. Someone held up a small sign with the name of the scene to be portrayed: "The Dying Eagle."

A spotlight threw a beam of light over Jil's erect, immobile body. His head rose slowly, the mane of chestnut hair throwing into bold relief the white skin stretched over his long face, the high cheekbones and the arch of his straight nose with its narrow, pinched nostrils. His expression, his entire bearing, was that of a proud eagle perched in a mountain-top eyrie.

Then Jil's head described an arc in short, spastic jerks, like a bird studying its surroundings. The muscles rippled from his powerful neck down to his massive shoulders in long, graceful undulations. The forearms rose slowly like the wings of a huge eagle. They fell and rose again until they seemed to form a perfect extension. His feet remained planted in one place, his body slightly at an angle. With his right leg stretched backward, rising off the floor of the stage, he seemed to be flying through space, parallel with the platform, his body actually supported by his left leg. Suddenly all motion ceased. The head bent downward as if he were watching the land far below, alert to danger. The outstretched leg began to rise as he lowered the upper part of his body until he appeared to be hovering just above the planks of the stage. He slapped the leg he had been standing on sharply, and the report resounded like a rifle shot. From somewhere on the winding trails below, a hunter had been stalking the eagle. Excruciating pain was etched into the pantomimist's face. A tremor passed through his body as the fatal bullet began to sap the great bird's life.

His back was now toward the audience. The muscles of his shoulders and arms created a starkly powerful illusion of wing feathers as they twitched and fluttered while he struggled to rise to his eyrie to find refuge. Then the leg supporting him crumpled, and he crouched on the stage. The mortally wounded eagle had escaped the hunter, but not death. The neck arched and he buried his head beneath a protective wing. The bird's dying tremors passed along Jil's shoulders to his arms, which drooped lifeless on either side of his body. The spotlight flickered spasmodically to express the transition from life to death, as the fingers of Jil's outstretched hands fluttered once and ceased.

The light died out and the hall was plunged into darkness.

Before the lights came up on a standing ovation, Jil was on his way.

The Spanish winter was pleasing to him, compared to the

fierce Russian winters. He found himself walking up a hill overlooking the Prado Museum. He had a profound fondness for this ancient quarter of Madrid. It had a special grace that was reflected in every element of the landscape, from the Plaza del Prado, the wide road leading to the museum, to the dwellings along the modest lanes that criss-crossed the top of the hill.

A gentle wind caressed the trees, shaking the branches and producing a muted rushing sound. Jil stood before the great entrance doors of the museum. He closed his eyes, envisioning what he knew lay beyond the doors. He had spent many hours in the museum, especially in the large room containing the paintings of Hieronymus Bosch. The fifteenth-century Flemish painter was his spiritual guide. Jil had studied his canvasses, focusing his attention on the scores of tiny figures, seeing in them ideas that inspired the figures of pantomime that he fashioned with his body.

As he slowly turned away and walked in the direction of the hotel, he knew that, despite his triumph tonight, he had still to realize his full potential as an artist.

7

THE MEDITERRANEAN WAS unfriendly to the small boats
that brought refugees from Lebanon to the ports of Cyprus,
but the boats continued to come, nevertheless, most of them
making their way to the port of Larnaca. The promise of
money kept these boats churning through the rough waters.
Refugees from war-torn Lebanon were willing to pay vast
sums to any seamen ready to challenge the waves and bring
them to a safe haven. Some of these small craft were lost at
sea, but even this danger didn't prevent others from undertaking the journey; the Lebanese Christians, skeptical that their
militia could protect them, seized any opportunity they could
to escape the fate that awaited them at the hands of the
Moslem forces, who were now reinforced by Syrian artillery
and Palestinian fighting units.

Cyprus was a base for the Arab terrorist organizations as
well. For some time their headquarters had been entrenched
in the main cities of the island. Cyprus was convenient since
it was easily accessible from all parts of the Middle East and
Europe. Larnaca, on its eastern coast, had become a center of
operations for Arab terrorist movements, and as a consequence was flourishing.

On this stormy Monday morning, Mussa el-Dalil sat in the restaurant of a hotel that overlooked the Larnaca harbor, his view of the port slightly blocked by a row of tall palms that stretched almost a mile from north to south. El-Dalil, the son of a Sudanese father and an Egyptian mother, had been born fifty-seven years earlier in Palestine, where his parents had come during the great famine, seeking relief in an area bordering on several Jewish settlements. El-Dalil had a military background, beginning with a four-year stint in the British Army during World War Two. Years later he became one of the founders of the Palestinian Liberation Organization, and during the past few years he had commanded the "Suicide Squad" of the People's Popular Front, a dangerous radical faction of the PLO.

Next to Mussa el-Dalil sat Vladimir Zoska, a Czech who had arrived in Larnaca just a few days before. Zoska, who spoke fluent Arabic, had been sent to assess the military abilities of Mussa el-Dalil's men. He had been invited, at this early hour, to watch the mouth of the port for the ship of the Greek captain Dario Papadopolus, which was due in shortly. The Greek had no inkling that his fate had been decided several days before. The Palestinians had discovered he was an informer as well as a sailor, and unfortunately he had shared his knowledge with the wrong people.

"Do you know how your man intends to get rid of the Greek?" asked Vladimir Zoska, scrutinizing the Palestinian fighter's profile.

"No." Mussa el-Dalil held up binoculars and looked out over the sea. "That's his problem. The order he received was to liquidate the Greek when he reached the harbor. How he does it is his affair."

The force of the wind blowing in from the sea intensified, its gusts swirling around and through the patio, which was open on three sides. During this time no boats made any attempt to leave the calm water of the harbor for the rough, open sea, although from time to time ships arriving from Lebanon approached the entrance of the port.

The *Larissa*, the Greek's ship, hove into sight. Mussa el-Dalil studied the small boat through his powerful binoculars, identifying it immediately by its wide stern. Broad-beamed, it followed its course slowly but surely, as the waves crashed over it and battered it from right to left. They crashed against the hull and the murky foam rose up and scattered in the air before falling back and being enveloped again in the raging sea. On deck one could make out a multitude of passengers: men and women of all ages, children, even a few tiny infants. Mussa el-Dalil felt the touch of Vladimir Zoska's hand on his arm. He lowered the binoculars.

"Can you see the Greek yet?" Zoska asked. His tension was evident in the frown that furrowed his face. He wondered how Da'ud el-Za'id, the Palestinian fighter assigned to execute the Greek, would carry out his mission. He assumed the Greek captain would be killed after the *Larissa* had tied up at the pier.

"The distance is still too great," responded Mussa el-Dalil. He tried to make out the features of the passengers, but decided he would have to wait until the ship came closer.

A great broad-crested wave slipped under the *Larissa*'s hull. The skilled captain took advantage of the opportunity to steer the boat toward the calmer waters of the port. The wave rolled out like a wide carpet, padding and cushioning the *Larissa*'s course. The Greek grabbed the wheel firmly, steadied the ship, and steered it along the center of the wave, which gathered power as it approached the harbor entrance. At this point the ship sprang free of the churning waters. An instant later the *Larissa*'s solid keel was visible as the wave broke and mixed with the placid waters of the harbor. The green ship again steadied itself and gradually lost momentum, coming closer to shore.

"Are you sure of Da'ud el-Za'id?"

Mussa el-Dalil smiled contemptuously. He glanced briefly at the Czech.

"He's my best man. He is wild, but I restrain him." El-Dalil clenched his fist and held up his arm. "I am making him into a man . . . he needs to be restrained and he needs training. But he is courageous. He is a good example for the others."

"I wonder how he will get rid of the Greek."

"We'll have to wait and see."

They did not have long to wait. Within seconds there was a thunderous explosion. A giant tongue of flame rose twenty yards in the air. The boat appeared to rise slowly above the water of the harbor and suddenly shattered into pieces. Reverberations from the explosion were heard in remote neighborhoods to the west of Larnaca.

The Palestinian was thrown backward out of his chair by the force of the blast. The binoculars shot from his hand as he tried to break his fall with his open palm. As he got up, he realized that the same thing had happened to Zoska. The Czech sat on the ground in shocked disbelief, staring at the black cloud mushrooming over the spot where the Greek's ship had been only seconds before. Nothing remained. At first the victims caught in the sudden inferno were thrown up in the air; afterward, their bodies fell and were submerged in the water, then bobbed to the surface. Debris was scattered far and wide over the churning waters, and splinters of broken boards, blown into the air, landed on the broad stone steps of the dining room patio, the front windows of which had been shattered by the blast. Small burning fragments of the ship lay on the harbor's main dock. Shredded bodies, disgorged from the depths of the sea, floated on the surface of the water, which was beginning to calm down after the shock of the explosion.

For a moment, nothing stirred, nothing moved. It seemed that even the wind was paralyzed. Then pandemonium broke loose as several of the dock workers, who had been thrown into the water by the force of the explosion, swam ashore and, leaping into small boats, sped through the waters of the harbor in an attempt to retrieve bodies.

Mussa el-Dalil and Vladimir Zoska bolted from the patio of the restaurant and ran toward the harbor. They cut quickly across the palm-lined avenue and, sweating and panting, reached the concrete dock. Scores of dazed and confused men ran to and fro, shouting. Two small boats, loaded with the victims' bodies, approached the dock, and one of the port workers called to the sailors aboard, "Is anyone alive?"

"No" came the brief response.

Ropes were thrown ashore, and experienced hands quickly tied them to heavy iron rings. The bloody remains were transferred from the deck of the ship and placed one on top of the other on the cold, damp concrete of the dock. It was a gruesome sight, especially the mutilated bodies of children and infants. Sickened, Vladimir Zoska sank to his knees at the edge of the harbor and vomited, his face green. Mussa el-Dalil gazed at him in wonder. He tried to help him by supporting his head, but Zoska pushed his hand away.

"Leave me," he said, gasping for breath. "It will pass."

The wind continued to lash the harbor. Zoska turned his gaze from the confusion around him to the Palestinian. He could read nothing: the face of the dark-skinned man with the sparkling eyes was a frozen mask.

"Let's go," Mussa el-Dalil said, turning back to the main avenue. A low, murmured prayer seemed to rise from the wind-filled palm fronds. Vladimir Zoska wiped the perspiration from his face as he rose and began to follow el-Dalil. They walked from the harbor area in complete silence back to the large Mercedes, in the front seat of which sat two of el-Dalil's bodyguards. They headed back to the villa which served as their headquarters in Larnaca. It was here they would meet Da'ud el-Za'id, the man who had detonated the explosive charge from somewhere near the harbor.

"So, he achieved his aim," remarked el-Dalil. When the Czech didn't respond, Mussa el-Dalil turned to stare at him.

"You wanted to see action," he said. "You saw it."

"He was to kill only the Greek," replied Zoska. "What we witnessed was a slaughter . . ."

Mussa el-Dalil grasped Zoska's shoulder angrily, then inhaling slowly, he regained his self-control, his hand falling from the Czech's shoulder.

"I raise fighters, not little chicks." His voice was hoarse with emotion. "You came to see if my men were capable of undertaking the actions that will be required of them. And they are. What do you think? That picking off targets like Kissinger or Jackson is a job for weak stomachs?"

"I hadn't thought that—" Zoska broke off. There was no point in going on with the conversation. He had been sent by his commander to learn something of the capabilities of the men in Mussa el-Dalil's fighting unit. He had discovered that they were courageous, decisive men, but he had also discovered they had no regard for human life, and he found this extremely discomforting.

Mussa el-Dalil glanced at the European beside him: a man of forty, with a broad face reflecting his Slavic origin, sharp features, and an open, friendly expression. But his gray eyes gave evidence of a certain reserve, as if he kept his distance.

They were the eyes of one who did not miss the tiniest detail, the faintest nuance.

"I expect to hear something more definite from you," el-Dalil said.

"Within a short time we'll know the answers to most of your questions."

"Have you decided yet on the first target?"

"Not yet. But you know all the names. The order will be determined within a few days."

"My men are thirsty for action." Mussa el-Dalil drew a cigarette from a silver case and lit it. "I have held them on a short leash for a long time."

The Mercedes stopped at the foot of a wide staircase leading up to an isolated villa. They got out and went into the house. Da'ud el-Za'id, a tall, handsome youth of twenty-five, was waiting for them in the hall.

He smiled as they entered. "I brought it off as promised!" he said excitedly.

"You did indeed," Mussa el-Dalil agreed. "Now, tell me how you detonated the bomb."

"Very simply." El-Za'id laughed. Outside they could hear the wail of sirens as ambulances rushed by on their way to the port. "I played on the Greek's avarice. I paid him fifty dollars in advance on the condition that he bring a suitcase from the port of Junea, with the promise of another hundred on delivery. He brought it. And you saw the results. I had only to be near the pier and press a little button—and whoosh!" His burning eyes glittered. "One day we shall surpass even the Israelis. You know," he said, turning to Vladimir Zoska, "it was from the Israelis that we learned to detonate explosives from a distance. They struck at us many times using this method. Today we are just as skilled as they, and in the end we shall be better. It's just a matter of time." He clenched his fists, his body taut, as if he were about to explode in anger.

Mussa el-Dalil's glance moved from the face of the youth to that of the European, but Vladimir Zoska's expression told him nothing.

"You carried out the mission you were given," declared Mussa el-Dalil. "You are a good example to your comrades."

"I never make mistakes!" el-Za'id announced proudly.

"Should you make a mistake, you'll pay for it," rejoined el-Dalil. "I'll see to that. As you well know."

Da'ud el-Za'id did not reply. Mussa el-Dalil was known as a man who did not forget a grievance, who stubbornly held on to a grudge; a tough commander from whom it was wise to keep a cautious distance.

"You have to be at the airport within an hour," el-Dalil said. "A friend of ours awaits you in Spain. You and Miss Aston are to bring Horst Welsh to Larnaca."

Da'ud el-Za'id's dark cheeks suddenly reddened.

"Your assignment is to bring *him*, Da'ud, and that is all," said el-Dalil, lowering his voice. "I know that you are fond of Miss Aston. See that her honor is preserved. She is important to us. Keep your personal feelings out of it."

"Our relationship is purely professional," the youth protested. "I served as an advisor for her film. You yourself recommended me."

"Therefore I am sending you to her now. She knows only you and me from our unit." Mussa el-Dalil lit a cigarette. He drew the smoke deep into his lungs. "I am sending you because she knows you and trusts you. Don't annoy her."

"I—"

"There is nothing for you to add!" Mussa el-Dalil raised his hand to stop the youth from going on. His voice was sharp. "Behave as I tell you to behave. Go now, and return with your things. I'll take you to the airport."

Da'ud el-Za'id rose quickly and left. Throughout the entire exchange, Vladimir Zoska had remained silent.

"We seem strange to you," remarked Mussa el-Dalil. "There's no need to respond. It is the truth. We are alien to you. As you are alien to us. We come from different cultures. But we too have one thing in common—our goal. We would do well to focus on that. Now, I want to know where we stand. When do we move? What is our target?"

"We'll have all the missing details in a few more days," Zoska explained. "Don't forget that this is a complex operation. You and your men will spearhead it, but many others are also involved in it."

The Palestinian rose from his chair and went to the large window where he stood and watched the ambulances which still shuttled back and forth from the harbor.

"I have prayed for an operation like this for years. Something that would shock the world . . ." He turned back to the Czech. "I'm tired of taking little bites. This operation . . . striking down men like these . . . carrying out reprisals in the heart of America . . . This is something that will justify the long road . . .

"I don't know if, in my lifetime, I'll see the establishment of my own state." Mussa el-Dalil's voice was steady, but Zoska picked up a nearly inaudible tremor. He had heard these sentiments in the past, from other nationalists. A freedom fighter in one part of the world expressed himself exactly like his counterpart in another. "My mother and father didn't dream. They had no time for dreams. They were always hungry, always scrounging for food. I was fortunate. My parents concentrated their energy on feeding me. Thus, I could begin to dream. Now I dream and I work to realize my dreams. The land of Israel belongs to us. Perhaps I will not live to see a Palestinian State there. But these young men like Da'ud el-Za'id will see it."

"You are fond of him."

"Yes. As I told you, he is a wild man but a superb fighter."

"Because of his extremism?"

"Perhaps." Mussa el-Dalil chuckled. "To be a good fighter one must be an extremist. Even a little obsessed. But there must always be someone at your side who can direct you."

"And you can give direction?"

"I have participated in many operations—I believe a commander must be in the field with his men—to serve as an example. This time will be no different. You will be here for some time," the Palestinian went on serenely. "It will become clear to you that we have our own means and our own approach. Quite different from yours, but no less effective—"

He broke off as Da'ud el-Za'id appeared carrying a small suitcase. The young fighter had changed into an impeccably tailored suit. He was a remarkably handsome man. Vladimir Zoska knew that he came from a cultivated and wealthy Jordanian family that had contributed generously to Mussa el-Dalil's special fighting unit.

Zoska accompanied Mussa el-Dalil and Da'ud el-Za'id to the door of the villa. At the foot of the stairs a group of bodyguards waited beside two parked Mercedes. The unit's commander and the young fighter got into one car, the bodyguards took the second, and both automobiles sped off on their way to the Larnaca airport.

The Czech sat on the marble wall in front of the villa for a long time, trying to assemble his initial impressions. Mussa el-Dalil had been right when he described them as belonging to different worlds. Zoska was a functionary who was obliged to do the bidding of his master in Moscow. He had never met Pavel Ramizor, but he knew of him and was aware of his power over Anton Karlov, his commander. Now he was in Larnaca, a small link in Pavel Ramizor's extensive network. Oh hell, thought Zoska, cursing himself and his luck. Once again the images of the mangled bodies of today's victims rose before him. Although he did not have an especially sensitive stomach, he felt a wave of nausea. Pale and shaken, he rose and strode toward the villa. He needed a drink desperately.

8

It was the third day of the snowstorm. Moscow lay under a heavy white quilt as snowflakes, falling from the leaden skies to the frozen ground below, fluttered wildly in the wind, bringing a grayish white curtain down around the entire city. From the large window it was nearly impossible to see the high wall of the Kremlin. The glittering white carpet that covered Red Square reflected the dazzling rays of the dying sun. Soon winter's early darkness would fall, swallowing the square, the walls, and the archaic crenelated towers.

Sergei Padayev turned back from the window as a senior assistant in Department V droned on, reporting in a slow, monotonous voice the details of the defection of the second secretary of the Soviet embassy in Canada. The man had disappeared a week before, after declaring he was going on a hunting expedition in the Canadian Rockies. That evening the Canadian government had announced that the diplomat had requested political asylum.

The past year had been a difficult one for Department V and, consequently, Pavel Ramizor's standing in the KGB had declined. He had sustained blows to his prestige from two directions. Someone at a senior level had been cooperating with the Western security services, revealing the identity of KGB operatives in key positions in the West. The second blow had undermined Operation "Red Immigrants," Ramizor's plan for creating the largest espionage network ever conceived by the KGB. Hundreds of agents, men and women of different nationalities—Russians, Czechs, Bulgarians, and East Germans—had been planted in the West as Jewish emigrants. The massive program had been implemented within a few months in an exceptionally smooth manner, with only a few mishaps.

The program—a remarkable one for its innovativeness and daring, for its meticulous and farsighted planning—had demanded and received the very best of Pavel Ramizor, and it was to crown his long career in Soviet espionage, thrusting him into a position of power at the very top of the intelligence pyramid, close to Yuri Andropov, the chairman of the KGB.

From the very beginning, Ramizor had included Sergei Padayev in each phase of the planning, for he trusted his judgment implicitly.

"I've always remained a strict believer in man," the department head had said during one of their many conversations. "Certainly, technology has offered new approaches to the problems of espionage. But, believe me, brother Sergei, there is no substitute for, nor will there *ever* be a substitute for, man himself. Before us we have a rare opportunity to flood the centers of Western power with hundreds of our agents, hundreds of sensitive, well-trained antennae to gather information of the greatest importance from our point of view."

Then, inexplicably, after so promising a beginning, Operation "Red Immigrants" fell apart. Its failure became apparent to the KGB when the CIA began flushing out the plants and exposing them as Soviet agents. No one knew better than Sergei Padayev the significance of the failure of Operation "Red Immigrants."

For Pavel Ramizor, the operation's miscarriage provided additional evidence to bolster his claim that a Jewish espionage network, operating against the interests of the Soviet Union, was at work within the KGB. In the wake of the operation's failure, Chairman Andropov gave Ramizor a free hand to investigate his charge.

Dozens of officials were questioned, including the section heads of Department V, but not a single suspect had been uncovered. Ramizor then concluded that the informer was to be found within the ranks of those agents who had been dispatched to the West as Jewish emigrants. He assumed that several of these operatives were, in fact, Hasidim masquerading as Russians and functioning as double agents, who, as soon as they reached the West, had revealed their true identity to the Rebbe and exposed the KGB operation.

In point of fact, when he was made aware of the plot, the Rebbe had been deeply shocked, for, had it been successful, Operation "Red Immigrants" would have made Jews throughout the world suspect. Once informed, he instructed his far-flung Hasidic congregations in the West to cooperate with the Israeli security services in exposing anyone suspected of being an agent planted by Department V. Had it not been for the work of the Hasidim in uncovering these agents, the Soviet Union, in the course of the 1980s, would have established an enormous communist espionage network in the West.

Now that his master plan was in shambles, Pavel Ramizor feared for his position. His reputation, the product of hard work and diligent planning over a long period of time, was being undermined, like an impressive facade that is decayed and crumbling underneath. At times, Ramizor would curse the Jews with great bitterness as if they had conspired to bring about his downfall.

Sergei Padayev studied Pavel Ramizor's face as the assistant went on with his report on the defection of the second secretary in Canada. Ramizor was known as the "Tatar," a nickname inspired by the glittering bald pate that complemented his round, fleshy face. His small eyes were nearly engulfed in swollen, fatty pouches of flesh. His neck was broad and his shoulders solid, like those of a wrestler.

The nasal voice finally droned to a halt and the assistant began to fold the papers before him. Pavel Ramizor ignored the report, returning to more pressing problems.

"So," he declared, his glance passing over the faces of the section heads, "you know what to do. I want this bastard who is collaborating with the Americans rooted out from our ranks." His glance came to rest on the man in charge of the Liquidations Section. "Sergei Padayev will remain with me to conclude a small matter. The rest of you can go."

The section heads rose as one and gathered their files together. Each one knew what this "small matter" was. Pavel Ramizor and Sergei Padayev were to decide on just who would be sent to the United States to find and liquidate the traitor.

When the four men had left, the department head took a bottle of whiskey from one of his desk drawers. He poured out two shot glasses and handed one to his colleague.

"Whiskey is the best medicine for a weak heart, Sergei." Pavel Ramizor smiled. His little eyes became two tiny slits. *"Nazdrovya!"* The section head raised his glass in a toast to his colleague's health.

"This younger generation! Technocrats all!" Pavel Ramizor went on derisively, referring to the four men who had left the office a minute before. "They believe that our power has been sapped. That our time has passed. Eh, brother Sergei?"

"So it seems."

"This business of a deserter in Canada is secondary, almost without significance compared to the Jewish network. Just wait and see, Sergei, how these youngsters react when I uncover the impostors who have been betraying us."

"Those youngsters apparently feel that the exposure of the department plants is a personal failure for you," Sergei Padayev remarked cautiously. Despite the frozen expression on the department head's face, he decided to proceed further with this dangerous line of talk. "One must admit that the religious Jews seem to have a special sense . . ."

"Sense?" Ramizor pounded the desk with his fist. He was enraged. "Sense . . . You know as well as I, Sergei, that this 'special sense' is nothing more than a detestable termite boring from within. It's true that I have absorbed some heavy blows. Let me crush this termite!"

"Termite? Only one?"

"Maybe more."

"Do you really believe that it is someone from our headquarters?"

"Yes, I'm convinced of this, Sergei. It is someone, or several individuals in one of the departments. Maybe in several departments." He tossed down another shot of whiskey. "Sometimes I think I have been trapped in an intricate net . . . there's no other explanation for the failures. No explanation whatsoever . . . the damn Jews . . ."

Ramizor had no doubt that the Hasidim were in touch with one of the senior KGB officials. He studied Sergei Padayev pensively. If his old friend were not in poor health, he would assign him to locate the source of the leak. But Padayev, in his debilitated condition, would not be able to help. It even pained Ramizor to have to ask him for advice. It was a shame to put unnecessary pressure on the man. Dr. Grisha Rostovitch had made it clear that if the pressure could be minimized, Padayev might very well reach retirement age without any trouble.

"I have a blood account to settle with those kikes," the department head cursed. His face was gloomy. "But we're not dealing with them now." He drew Yan Borodov's personal file from a corner of his desk and opened it. "You and I have a special matter to attend to—the elimination of the double agent who is collaborating with the Americans. The erosion must be stopped there too. If these young men of ours," he said, referring to the other section heads, "succeed in discovering this fellow's identity during the coming weeks, then I will want his head immediately. I don't want to kidnap him. I don't want him brought back. I want him liquidated."

"Yan Borodov is the man for the mission," Sergei Padayev remarked quietly.

"I looked over the file you sent to me, Sergei. I am in total agreement with you that he should be returned and prepared for the mission in the United States. You were right about his being the best man for the operation. He's familiar with the American continent, and at the same time, he hasn't been there for several years—two important factors to take into account."

"And therefore?"

"He is our man." Pavel Ramizor closed the file and passed it over to Sergei Padayev. "Don't worry, Sergei, we haven't lost our fight yet. We'll show those youngsters that they still have a lot to learn from us."

For a moment it again seemed to Padayev that his heart was unable to withstand the pressure. He felt the blood course wildly through his veins, until they seemed to expand almost to the point of exploding. "God," the words of the prayer passed through his mind, "do not forsake me. Not now." He smiled and breathed deeply in an effort to slow his heartbeat.

Pavel Ramizor looked at him with concern. "Something isn't as it should be?"

"Oh, no." Sergei Padayev laughed, and the laughter seemed to rend the blood vessels pulsating in his temples. The pain was sharp, almost cruel. "Everything is fine, Pavel. I'll take care of all the arrangements on Yan Borodov's mission." As he pulled himself up and turned to leave, his footsteps were measured and confident.

Sergei had slowed down considerably by the time he reached his office. He needed a brief rest after the emotional ordeal he had undergone. Boris Borodov, anxiously awaiting Pavel's decision on the matter, would be pleased to learn that the department head had approved of sending Yan to the United States. Sergei Padayev had known all along how terribly important it was to return Yan to Moscow so that he might be briefed for his real mission, the mission ordained by the Grand Emissary, and he was relieved that the department head had, once again, ultimately heeded his recommendation. But the whole process had left him completely drained.

He sank into his chair. The pressure in his chest had abated and no longer annoyed him, but his temples throbbed painfully. The blood pulsing through his veins like a long chain of dull pinpricks left him feeling weak. In a few moments, when his discomfort eased, he would be on his way to Boris's apartment. He took a deep breath and closed his eyes, and his thoughts turned to the curious way that Heaven had linked his destiny to that of Boris Borodov, the Grand Emissary.

He had first met Borodov, who was many years his senior, in his youth in Warsaw, when he was not Sergei Padayev but Shmuel Gillerman, a young Hasid. At that time, Boris Borodov was known as Reb Mendel Gruner, the Rebbe's emissary throughout Europe. Sergei never dreamed, before the war, that they would one day meet again among the partisans in Russia and wander about the countryside together disguised as vagabonds of pure Russian stock.

They were both in flight at the time and had found themselves trapped in the Stalingrad district, which was then surrounded by the Army of the Third Reich. No one could break out of the German encirclement. The Grand Emissary had been on a journey to the far reaches of the Soviet Union, a trip he had undertaken in order to prepare sanctuaries for the Hasidim who had escaped Occupied Poland. Sergei, too, had been fulfilling a holy mission. He had been instructed to proceed first to the northern countries and then to make his way to the Hasidic community in America. But it was the will of the Almighty that both their paths were blocked.

For months Sergei Padayev had roamed the frozen Volga River, occasionally earning a bit of food by working at farmhouses in forsaken villages. In the course of these wanderings, he chanced upon a small band of partisans entrenched in one of the forests along the way. A tiny unit of men, drawn from this partisan group and led by a man named Boris Borodov, was carrying out the most daring actions in the guise of a band of circus performers. At first, Padayev hadn't known why the Cossack with the great moustache had recruited him for the unit. Only later did he discover that Boris Borodov was, in fact, Reb Mendel Gruner, the Rebbe's emissary. Borodov had recognized him as the young Hasid from Poland, despite the fact that he was calling himself Sergei Padayev and passing as a Russian. The two were the only Jews in the small band of partisans, and they both guarded this secret carefully.

During his first few months with the unit of circus performers, Sergei had feared Boris Borodov. When the older man was involved in a sabotage operation or an armed skirmish with the Germans, he became a bloodthirsty, vengeful warrior. Sergei knew that Borodov's wife and four of his five children had been murdered by the Nazis, but the clown kept his anguish and his sorrow to himself, never demonstrating his inner feelings. Then one day a message reached him from his sister Zina: the husband of his surviving daughter, Rachel, had been killed in battle, and Rachel herself had died shortly after giving birth to a son. Zina was now caring for his grandson. It was the only time Sergei saw Boris weep.

After the war the Rebbe sent them instructions to remain in the Soviet Union and rebuild the devastated Jewish communities. The Rebbe had determined that Jewish life must be sustained both physically and spiritually, even in Joseph Stalin's godless, repressive republic.

As the Rebbe's emissary, Boris's specific mission was the resurrection of the Hasidic communities from the ashes of the Holocaust. He was to gather up those who had escaped annihilation at the hands of the Nazis and build new Hasidic communities for these survivors. Traveling all during Stalin's reign with the Moscow circus to the far reaches of the Soviet Union and its satellite countries, the famous clown was able to organize a network of centers—wherever Hasidim were to be found—helping them to propagate traditional Jewish education and worship. Sometimes the establishment of these tiny islands of Judaism required the smuggling of books of learning or prayer; at other times, Torah scrolls had to be obtained and then secreted in the clandestine Hasidic synagogues. Boris functioned as their link to the Rebbe—and to life beyond the Iron Curtain. In return, he depended totally on the representatives in these communities to safeguard the secret of his true identity.

As a further safeguard both Boris Borodov and Sergei Padayev acquired documents that certified to the purity of their Russian origins so that they could safely fulfill their mission, and thus they had operated for thirty-four years. But now the end was in sight. Many of the Hasidim had emigrated to the West. Those who remained would surely find a way out of the Soviet Union within the next decade. Yan was to have taken his and Boris's place, to have acted in their stead until the last Hasid had left the Soviet Union. However another mission awaited him.

Sergei heaved a sigh. It was time to leave for his meeting with the old clown. He rose, took down his heavy fur coat from a hook, and put it on slowly. Then, placing his fur hat on his head, he closed his office door behind him. A few minutes later he strode out of the large gray building. Darkness closed in around him as he walked slowly to his old Volga.

Padayev noted, to his satisfaction, that the snowstorm had almost entirely abated during the past hour. Only a few flakes drifted down, not enough to interfere with visibility. Regardless of the weather, he had decided to drive to the large apartment building on Kalinin Boulevard, only a five-minute ride from the old KGB headquarters.

Although the car had been fitted with snow tires, Padayev drove carefully. His vision wasn't as sharp as it once had been, and after dark he always proceeded with great caution, his head bent forward, his face nearly touching the windshield.

Visibility was better along Kalinin Boulevard. Light flooded from the office buildings and shops that lined the avenue and continued all the way to the circle in the heart of Moscow. As the car approached the large block of apartment buildings allocated primarily to middle-level functionaries and a few retired VIP's he slowed down, turning into the entrance of the underground parking lot.

Boris Borodov's modest apartment was on the second floor. Sergei Padayev decided to use the stairs since physical activity in moderation was good for his circulation. Standing before the door of the apartment, he rang the bell, then pulled off his hat and opened the collar of his coat. Boris Borodov's sister, Zina, a frail old woman, opened the door and greeted him with a radiant smile.

"Brother Sergei!" she exclaimed, spreading her arms wide to welcome him. He bent down and embraced her gently.

"Babushka Zina." He uttered the Russian word for grandmother with affection. She released him and moved back to study his face. He smiled and straightened up.

"How is Daidushka?"

"As usual, Sergei," she answered. "Nostalgic."

He followed her into the small kitchen and placed his briefcase and hat on the table, then proceeded to remove his overcoat.

"Keeps thinking about Yan, eh?"

"At his age, Sergei, there is a fear, here"—she placed a hand over her heart—"that every day you do not see the young one is a loss that can never be recovered. My brother misses him." Sergei Padayev expected a sign, perhaps even tears, but cruel as fate had been to her, Zina, like her brother Boris, had learned self-restraint.

"All will be well, Babushka," he promised, smiling. "I have a special New Year's gift for you."

Her eyes widened and a fragile hand rose to her lips to suppress a cry of joy. He saw a tremor pass through her body.

"Yes, Babushka," he said gently, "but I want to tell Boris this news myself."

She embraced him excitedly and he patted her thin shoulder gently.

"Enough!" he scolded. "Come, take me to Daidushka."

Her tiny, trembling hand resting in his, she led him to a

small room at the far end of the apartment: the old man's room and a museum-in-miniature. Zina opened the door slowly. A lamp was burning on the table and behind it the old man sat reading. Assuming she was alone, he objected to the intrusion and, without looking up, said, "What do you want now?"

She said nothing. In the ensuing pause, Sergei Padayev studied the thin, sharply chiseled features of the eighty-five-year-old man. It was the face of a man who had led a stormy life, but despite the lines of old age, his features had retained their power. The shock of hair that had turned silver many years before was still thick. It curled above the high forehead, accentuating the arch of the nose and the sensitive nostrils. The thick moustache, its ends proudly twirled, had gone from silver to glistening white, yet it was still as dashing as that of a young Cossack.

Finally, noticing that no answer was forthcoming from his sister, Boris Borodov raised his head and saw Padayev.

"Dear Sergei," he cried out. He smiled and the ends of his moustache spread even farther apart.

The two men were openly demonstrative in their affection, although they had seen each other only a few days before. A week's separation seemed long for men who, for several years, had lived side by side, day and night, their lives hanging in the balance every moment. That that common past had been so very unusual, and could not be shared with anyone else, tended to draw them even closer together.

Zina retreated from the room, quietly closing the door behind her. As he seated himself, Sergei Padayev glanced up at the wall behind the old man. Dozens of photographs and newspaper clippings hung there, all recording events and performances in the life of the greatest clown of the Moscow Circus, Boris Borodov. Among the many pictures showing the clown in his ridiculous costume, surrounded by a flock of admirers—which often included many of the country's most prominent men—one photograph caught the eye. It showed two clowns of the same height in identical costumes, their faces made up identically as well to show the same expression: a mixture of surprise, gaiety, and a strange touch of sadness.

The picture of the great clown had been taken following

his final performance with the Moscow Circus. He was seventy years old at the time. That was in the spring of 1964, one of the most beautiful Moscow had seen in many a year. The twin clown at his side was the young circus performer Yan Borodov, the old man's only grandchild.

On that intoxicating evening at the end of May, with the fragrances of distant fields permeating the air over Moscow, the renowned circus gave one of its most exciting performances. It was bidding farewell to the seventy-year-old man who, years before, had been crowned by the Russian press as the "clown whose weepy eyes make you laugh till you cry." In the presence of Moscow's most important officials, artists, and writers, the entire circus participated in a grand salute to the aging clown.

Boris Borodov caught his friend's glance and smiled, his face radiating vitality, as if illuminated by an inner light.

"That was indeed a special night, brother," he murmured softly. "You remember, I see."

"It was unforgettable, Daidushka." Sergei Padayev moistened his thin, dry lips with his tongue. "I also remember that it will be thirty-seven years this month since first we met in the forests. Do you remember that?"

"I forget nothing, Sergei!" They both laughed. "I have never forgotten that day I added you to my little circus . . . or the night we scrambled the orders of the German tank brigade . . . or the many nights we demolished railroad tracks. Not as long as I live will I forget."

Sergei Padayev remembered too. The little group of seven men had provided intelligence to the Red Army High Command that had helped break the German siege of Stalingrad in the winter of 1943 and pave the way for an assault along the entire front, a counterattack that ended that summer in a death blow for the Nazis near Korsk.

Their partisan brigade had operated from a forest behind the front lines. Boris was forty-nine years old at the time; the other six men ranged in age from twenty to thirty. He never spoke of his past; they knew only that he loved clowning and acrobatics. It was he who trained them, turning one into a juggler, another into the trainer of two hungry dogs they found in an abandoned village. He taught one of them to read fortunes from cards and from the dregs of coffee. He trained another as an acrobat and still another as a miracle worker who performed magic. The sixth man he showed how to play both heartrending and irresistibly joyous tunes on a paper-covered comb—that sixth man was Sergei Padayev. Boris was the clown.

These men who had lost their families to the Nazi murderers took revenge on the Germans whenever they found them. In tattered rags they wandered from village to village, masquerading as hungry peasants whose village had been devastated by the war. This was how they presented themselves to the weary German troops as well. In the field, they amused the tired, embittered soldiers with fascinating circus acts. It was a humble performance, but one that nonetheless met with great success among the war-weary soldiers of the Third Reich. The war came to an end for the members of the circus in May of 1945, when the Red Army planted its flag in the ruins of Berlin. In the years that followed, only two of the circus members remained in close contact: a retired clown and a high-ranking KGB officer with a weak heart.

Sergei Padayev heaved a sigh and turned his gaze again to the large picture of grandfather and grandson.

"That last night," the old man said, "was a farewell for me, and for Yan, too. That was when you took him. And now, just see," he went on, with a gesture that encompassed the room, "thanks to his position as a Resident, we old folks were given a good apartment, and Mother Russia takes care of all our needs." The old man, conversant with KGB terminology, knew that only those agents who were sent to live abroad, completely cut off from the homeland for extended periods of time, were accorded the title of Resident.

Padayev nodded. "Yes, he is one of our best."

A light knock on the door interrupted their conversation, and Zina appeared, bearing a tray. On it was the vodka Sergei had brought and two small plates of black bread and salt herring in cream sauce, which she had prepared herself.

"You have to warm your insides, too," she said, carefully setting the tray on a table before them. "Enjoy yourselves."

Sergei Padayev laughed. "Thank you, Babushka." As the door closed after her, he opened the bottle and poured the clear, sparkling liquid into two large glasses, which they lifted high in a gesture of friendship.

"To your very good health, Daidushka!" said Sergei. "*Nazdrovya.*"

"*Spassiba*, brother," the old man responded, raising the glass to his lips.

"Some news has arrived from across the ocean," said Sergei Padayev. He speared a piece of herring and took a helping of black bread. "Our information has been received most gratefully. Volodia Kantor, with his brother Yudke's assistance ..."

"The carpenter from Crown Heights?"

"That's right, Boris. It was the carpenter who transmitted the information to Volodia in Paris. The fourteen men are now under protective guard day and night in the United States."

"So, the Israeli general succeeded in convincing them." The old man became pensive. He was satisfied that the Americans had moved at once to protect the targeted individuals. He began to question Sergei Padayev on what steps Pavel Ramizor had taken.

"I didn't succeed in obtaining additional information," Padayev admitted, disappointment obvious in his voice. "The operation is being conducted as if it were completely dissociated from the KGB. As I said, Boris, he's consumed with suspicion. He thinks that someone in one of the departments is connected with what he calls the 'Jewish network.' "

"That's what he said?"

"In those words."

"He's never spoken to you about this explicitly?"

"No."

"He never couched his suspicions in such clear terms."

"Not until our conversation this evening."

"We'll have to be careful, Sergei," said Boris Borodov, softly. "Pavel Ramizor is far more dangerous than the others. What seems a coarse and unsophisticated manner is simply an excellent cover for a brilliant mind. He's trying to find concrete evidence. If he succeeds, that discovery will surpass all his past accomplishments. He might even win the directorship. Nobody is better suited for that position than he is."

"In his opinion."

"In his opinion." Boris Borodov tugged at the ends of his moustache. "He thinks that if he succeeds in proving that the Jewish network penetrated KGB headquarters, he can repair his damaged image. He is behaving now like a wounded elephant. He's dangerous, Sergei. You must be careful."

"What should I do?"

"Memorize every conversation you have with him on this subject. I have to know every detail in order to turn the tables on him at the proper time. He is laying a trap for us."

"You think you'll come up against Pavel Ramizor one day?" Padayev asked.

"I came up against him a long time ago," was the old man's rejoinder. "Here." He pointed a finger at his forehead. "Ah, you're laughing, Sergei. Yes, one day I'll confront him face to face. Then I'll have to be prepared for the last phase of the action. At the moment you are my antennae." He smiled faintly.

"Yes, Daidushka."

"But you haven't come just to report on your conversation with Pavel Ramizor."

Sergei Padayev grinned as he refilled the two glasses with vodka.

"I did indeed come to report on other things."

"You maneuvered Ramizor into agreeing?"

"I did. Today Pavel Ramizor approved the repatriation of Yan. In a short time he will be here, with us . . ."

"And he will be sent from here to America?" The old man's voice was choked with emotion.

"As you planned it, brother Boris."

"Praise God!" The old man's voice trembled. A deep blush came to his pallid sunken cheeks and his eyes glittered with tears. Their glances met for a long moment. "You worked cleverly, Sergei."

"Yan will be with us for a while before being sent on from here," he explained. "I'll see that he is free for several days so that he can be with you and Babushka."

"God points the way," the old man responded.

Their spirits soared. By revealing this plot to them, God had placed the fate of the Rebbe in their hands. Yan's return merely served to reinforce their conviction. Both men were seized with a profound sense of having entered God's mystical realm, of having divined His commandments. It was God's will that Yan be entrusted with this mission which, they were convinced, constituted the final link in a chain of events initiated in Heaven.

Outside, the snowstorm had begun again, this time in earnest. Sergei rose to leave.

"Be careful," was Boris Borodov's parting entreaty, as it had been years before in the frozen forests.

"I will," Padayev promised.

As Boris Borodov closed the door behind him, Zina appeared in the doorway of the kitchen.

"Lord of the Universe," she said, "how long?"

"Until the last day," responded the old man. He knew exactly what she meant. His sister had often expressed her desire to live openly among Jews, to live a complete Jewish life, something she had been prevented from doing since the outbreak of the war in 1939. "Until the final day, Zina." Only his lips moved. They had become adept at reading each other's lips. In this manner they could carry on long conversations without fear of someone overhearing them.

She studied her brother; her tall, wise, older brother, who by virtue of his great learning in the Torah had the honor of fulfilling missions for the Rebbe.

"May we reach that day in peace."

"Zina," the old man said in a low voice, "you must prepare your best dishes for Yan."

"When will he come?"

"I don't know exactly, but perhaps within days, weeks at most." He suddenly contorted his features to portray a clowning simpleton, trying to conceal his feelings behind a comic mask. He looked so ludicrous that the old woman laughed.

"Boris, I'm so happy."

"Yes, yes. So am I," he said, and strode toward his room.

Once there, he stood staring at the large photograph of himself with his arm around his grandson Yan, the last descendant of a long line of clowns which began with the first Yan Lakosta who had fled to Russia from Portugal in 1716 after the proclamation of the anti-Jewish edicts. Soon after he arrived in Moscow, he achieved fame as jester in the court of the Tzar Peter the Great. The Lakosta descendants spread through Russia and Poland. At the outbreak of the war in 1939, the family numbered over a hundred men, women, and children. When the Holocaust had ended, only Boris, his sister, and young Yan, the last Lakosta, remained.

Now the tears flowed unabated, salty drops scorching the

old man's cheeks. The world would have been startled to witness Boris Borodov weeping in earnest—the clown whose tears had brought peals of laughter from crowds of jubilant spectators.

9

LATE MONDAY NIGHT, the hotel bellhop brought Jil a telegram from Margaret Aston. It informed him that she was leaving for Spain the following day, arriving at her father's villa in the evening. She suggested that Jil arrange to meet her father, Miguel de Salit, in Toledo and go with him to the villa.

At Margaret's suggestion Jil telephoned de Salit. Miguel was expecting the call and the two men arranged to connect in Toledo the following morning at eleven o'clock. Since they had never met before, and so would not recognize one another, they agreed to meet at the entrance of the El Greco museum.

At nine o'clock the next morning Jil and Horst Welsh took the elevator down to the underground parking lot where they got into a small car which Jil had rented for the fifty-mile drive from Madrid to Toledo.

A few minutes after they had left the parking lot, they were caught in heavy traffic. It took almost a half hour to extricate the car from the throngs of automobiles choking the streets of the city and turn onto the winding highway on the outskirts of Madrid.

Jil had been in Spain a number of times before. On his first visit he had felt a pang of nostalgia, as if he were returning to a familiar childhood scene. His ancestors, the Lakostas, had lived in Spain and Portugal for hundreds of years. Only after they had been forced to flee for their lives from the Inquisition did they emigrate from the Iberian Peninsula to Russia.

Horst Welsh, sitting at his side, talked incessantly, mainly about his yacht in Hamburg, which he had purchased with the proceeds of a bank robbery he and the Baader-Meinhof gang had carried out. He also talked about his girl friend, Anna-Maria, an Argentine guerrilla fighter whom Jil had smuggled out of South America to West Germany.

He was eternally grateful to Jil for having saved her life, and he was planning a wonderful future with her. In a few years they would leave the world of international terrorism behind and sail the yacht to the Middle East, to the sunshine and warm blue waters of the Mediterranean.

"Horst."

The German looked at him questioningly. "Yes, Jil."

"Have you ever been in Spain before?"

"No. Why?"

"If you love nature," Jil said quietly, "take a look at the scenery. You'll see how beautiful it is right here. Look around you; you won't be disappointed."

As they climbed higher in the mountains, the landscape gradually unfolding before them revealed a majestic country. The road was typical of Spanish roads, narrow and winding in spots, badly in need of repair in others. Some sections had been widened to two lanes, and along these the car moved ahead swiftly. Then the two lanes would suddenly reconverge into one, requiring enormous attention and skill to avoid an accident. The road ascended and meandered in sweeping ellipses around the foothills. Then, fifteen miles outside Madrid, the climb grew steeper, each hairpin turn revealing marvelous vistas—ravines and valleys covered with lush green carpets of grass and vegetation.

It was Jil's first visit to Toledo, the once proud and beautiful capital city. During his previous trips to Spain, he had avoided the city with which the fortunes of the Lakosta family had been so closely intertwined, avoided it deliberately although Daidushka had begged him to go and visit the

Jewish synagogue there, now a depressing museum housing the relics of the once proud and flourishing Jewish community.

He remembered the stories the old man had told him and remembered too his wonder at his grandfather's knowledge about the history of the Jews: how the Roman Empire had trampled tiny Judea underfoot when the Jews tried to fight for independence, and how the victors had brought his ancestors to Imperial Rome as slaves. His grandfather had described how many Jews had liberated themselves from bondage by embracing the teachings of Jesus, while others remained faithful to the Law of the Patriarchs, settling, after endless wanderings and vicissitudes, in affluent Spain.

"When you are in Toledo, go to the synagogue," the old man had pleaded. "There you will find proof that the Lakosta family was among the founders of the Jewish community ... Go, Yan, and see for yourself ..."

The old man angered him with his entreaties, but Jil had merely bit his lip and remained silent in order not to hurt his grandfather's feelings. How could he shout to the aged clown what was in his heart: that he had no desire to seek his roots, that he felt no need for affinity with those who had been persecuted, even killed because they chose not to be like other peoples?

Jil rolled down the window and inhaled deeply as if to air his tangled thoughts.

The sun was climbing high in the blue transparent sky, its soft light caressing the mountainous landscape. Ahead, walls, castles, and towers came into view as the city of Toledo gradually materialized before them like an artist's illustration of an old Spanish legend. The ancient capital seemed to have come into the twentieth century directly from the pages of Cervantes.

The small car climbed quickly and effortlessly and, passing through the ancient wall, entered the city. Jil found a parking space at the end of a narrow road. Small signs directed tourists to the path that wound up to El Greco's house. As he turned off the motor and pulled out the key, Jil glanced at his watch. It was a few minutes after ten.

"I'm going to meet Senor de Salit. I should be back within an hour."

"An hour," Horst repeated, looking troubled.

"Sooner, perhaps," said Jil as he left the car.

He started up the path, turning up the collar of his short coat against the cold mountain winds. As he crossed the square he could not ignore the small sign pointing to the Jewish synagogue. The doors were open and he could make out officials in gray uniforms just inside. Anyone interested in visiting this house of prayer, whose worshippers had been expelled centuries before, could purchase a ticket from them for thirty pesetas. Jil was about to continue on his way, but suddenly stopped, and looked inside, and on an impulse paid the ticket seller and entered the El Transito Synagogue.

Daidushka had told him about the synagogues—some poor, some sumptuous—in the towns of Russia, Poland, and Lithuania. Jil had never been inside a house of prayer, Jewry's symbol of the Temple of Jerusalem that had been destroyed centuries ago. Now he was entering a hall which he had been told his ancestors had once prayed in.

The hall was large enough to accommodate hundreds of worshippers, but he was surprised to find it completely stripped of furnishings. Everything had been removed. The vast hall was still and lifeless as a tomb. Only the high walls remained, testimony to the building's former splendor. The walls and ceiling were engraved with beautiful Hebrew calligraphy, the intricate adornments reflecting the Arabic style prevalent during the rule of the Caliphs in Spain. With great effort he was able to decipher some of the words.

Jil turned toward the eastern wall, aware that in the past the Ark containing his people's holy books and scrolls had stood there. There had also been a wooden dais from which the priests, descendants of the tribe of Aaron, had blessed the congregants; here too the rabbi and leader of the congregation had prayed for his flock. Before the anti-Jewish persecutions there had been eight synagogues in Toledo. Now only two remained, remnants of departed glory.

To his left was a passage from the hall to a small museum. In that room the memorabilia of the dead community—of the learned men of law, science, medicine, and literature—were displayed. There were a few tombstones engraved with the names of the dead and glass cases containing 800-year-old phylacteries, prayer shawls, and ancient bibles. Jil paused over these exhibits, vaguely aware that something was, indeed, happening within him.

In the third and last room of the somber museum he found an ancient register listing the names of members of the old community. He scanned the lists. Familiar names appeared—Maimon, Levy, Shlomo—as well as many others, long forgotten. Some had converted to Christianity under duress and never returned to Judaism. Others, whose progeny still adhered to Jewish tradition, had held fast. Suddenly, Jil was seized by an emotion so powerful it welled up inside him and nearly choked off his breath. A veil of moisture descended over his eyes, blurring his vision. He stared through a curtain of mist until the letters before him steadied and clearly formed the two words of a familiar name: Isaac Lakosta.

For the first time in his life Jil knew the meaning of divine awe. The intense feelings surging through him were new to him. It had been a long time since he had prayed. He had abandoned his efforts to reach spiritual communion when he began to doubt the existence of a just and merciful God. Yet, here, in the museum that had once served his ancestors as a temple of prayer, it dawned on him that he was rooted to something that transcended himself. Here before him lay irrefutable proof that, far from being mythical tales, his grandfather's stories were drawn from a long and distinguished genealogy, from the annals of a glorious past he could no longer deny.

Shortly after Jil had met Miguel at the El Greco house, they went back to get Jil's car and then set out. The artist's villa stood on a peak, some ten minutes' drive from Toledo on the mountain road leading to Córdoba.

Miguel received the visitors foisted on him by his daughter politely, but with a certain air of reserve. He hoped that these two strangers, apparently part of his daughter's rather odd circle of friends and aquaintances, would not keep him from his work. For several months he had been preparing a series of prints on the bullfight. He had built a bull ring on his spacious grounds and had acquired four very fine bulls. His friend Pepe Manuelete, a matador who had been famous in the fifties and sixties, visited him regularly, entering the small arena and pitting himself against the bulls while Miguel made rough preparatory sketches. Although Miguel was not happy about the interruption these visitors would cause, he was pleased that Margaret would be with him that evening. He had not seen her for a long time, and he had missed her.

As they parked the car next to an elegant yellow Mercedes, Miguel explained that it belonged to his friend the matador, whom they would meet when they reached the house.

"You will find him an interesting man," he said. Then, glancing at the winding footpath, he added: "It's a bit of a climb to the house."

"We'll manage," said Jil.

Miguel went first, followed by Jil and Horst Welsh. The path twisted some twenty yards up to a flat crest and from there, a paved walk led to a wooden gate in the white fence that encircled the grounds.

As Jil paused to take in the view, the artist stopped beside him. Jil studied his strong, sharp features with interest. He had known of him by reputation and had seen some of Miguel's large oils in various museums in Europe. Despite his sixty-five years, the man's step was light and springy; he was not even breathing hard after the strenuous climb. He led his guests through the gate, and up a flagstone walk that led to the wide veranda along the front of the house. This was Miguel's home, studio, and workshop.

The artist looked back at the two young men. "Congratulations! You climb like true mountaineers."

Without waiting for an answer, he led them on. He had built his home so that it afforded a breathtaking view of Toledo. From the top of the cliff the city appeared to be within arm's length, although it was actually quite far away. Opposite the house rose sharp crags and peaks, offset by deep crevices and ravines covered by thick, verdant vegetation.

A corpulent, middle-aged servant opened the door for them, greeting the master of the house and then bowing to the two guests. Inside they found themselves in a large, high-ceilinged hall. At the southern end, a wooden staircase led to the second story, where, fifteen feet overhead, an enclosed balcony overlooked the area they were standing in.

"Carlos will show you to your rooms," Miguel said, removing his black cape and tossing it over the back of a chair. "He will see that you lack nothing." He bowed in parting and walked to the stained-glass door at the end of the hall. As he opened it, Jil saw that it was the entrance to his studio.

Jil went up the stairs slowly, pausing to examine the pictures hanging on the white walls. They had been painted by Miguel de Salit at various periods. The rooms prepared for Jil and Horst Welsh were in the east wing, overlooking a large courtyard that contained the bullpen and arena.

Once alone, Jil removed his coat and lay down. He concentrated on regulating his breathing, using a method he had learned long ago from an old man, a member of an ancient tribe of Siberian sheep herders and tradesmen, who had been an expert fortune-teller and mind-reader. He had joined the circus as a horse trainer, a job at which he excelled, having grown up with the wild animals of the frozen Siberian steppes. But his specialty was the remarkable world of the spirit, the future, the unknown, and he had taught Jil many of his secrets.

Now, in this great white house in Spain, Jil floated off to distant realms. His fatigue vanished. He recalled the day when, as a little boy, the elderly woman had brought him to his grandfather, and a charmed world had opened up to him: a dazzling world of wonders, of variegated colors and unusual people, of marvelous animals—from tiny dogs to superbly disciplined Indian elephants. Even then Jil knew that Daidushka had joined the circus by order of the Rebbe, the leader of the Hasidic sect to which his grandfather belonged.

Jil breathed deeply. The visions of the past faded. He rose from the bed and went to the window. Across the mountain range, he could see Toledo, the city of his ancestors. He tried to define what he felt at that moment. Although he had always known intellectually about the tribulations his ancestors experienced, he now felt as if he had traveled the long road with them.

He stepped out onto the balcony and leaned against the high wooden railing. From here he could see the arena and the bullpen, which was enclosed by a solid fence of huge logs, strong enough to withstand the tremendous impact of the charging animals. In the center of the arena stood a thin man of average height. He swung a yellow matador's cape in rippling waves with grace and remarkable agility, creating the illusion as he did of a massive bull hurtling forward with menacingly lowered horns. Pepe Manuelete arched his body backward as if leaving room for the bull to storm past, following the tantalizing wave of the cape. Then he walked toward Miguel, who sat atop the wooden fence, and appeared to be explaining the movement to the artist. Jil's curiosity was aroused, and he decided to go down to watch the retired matador more closely.

The sun had sunk low in the west as he walked outside and into the garden. Long shadows fell over the grounds, and from the height of the cliffs the wind could be heard sweeping through the valleys below. He passed beds of red and yellow roses. Petals plucked from the full-blown blossoms by the wind drifted in the air. As he rounded the house, Jil found himself some twenty yards from the arena. At his approach the matador and the artist fell silent.

"I hope I'm not disturbing you," Jil said, smiling apologetically.

Something in his expression diffused the artist's irritation. "Of course not."

"Thank you, Senor Miguel," Jil said, looking into the other man's eyes. "I simply want to learn."

Until then Miguel de Salit had not noticed the young man's extraordinarily large eyes. Even now he could not determine their color—they were dark, yet glowed as if illuminated from within. A strange man, he thought.

He introduced Jil to Pepe Manuelete, and the matador resumed his explanation of why he had arched his back and moved his left hand—the hand that held the red swath of cloth, called the muleta, and the slim sharp sword beneath it.

"Watch, Miguel," he explained. "I'll repeat the same movement with the cape. But take note: because the muleta is smaller, I have to get closer to the bull's horns."

Pepe Manuelete tensed for the demonstration. In the silence, only the matador's quiet breathing was audible. He stood straight, his left leg slightly crooked. His right arm was bent at the elbow and extended before him; his eyes followed the sword as it shot forward to pierce the nape of the imaginary bull. At this stage, the matador held his pose and, without turning his head, explained the stance to Miguel.

"This is the moment that counts. Our chances are even. The bull or the matador . . . I must not miss! . . ."

The artist's hand moved quickly over his drawing paper as he sketched the matador's figure in the light cast by the rapidly setting sun. As he approached Miguel, Pepe Manuelete's walk was that of a victorious matador leaving the arena to the accolades of the crowd.

"You have captured the movement and atmosphere; the feeling is just right," he said as he studied the sketch.

Miguel looked up at him gratefully.

"Thanks to you, Pepe." He laughed with pleasure. "It is you who give the drawing vitality."

It was almost dark when they returned to the house. The sun had vanished behind the mountain range, leaving only a trace of crimson in the darkening sky.

Jil went up to his room to shave and take a long, refreshing shower. After dressing, he put out the overhead light and lit the lamp on the night table, then sat by the window, trying to visualize in his mind's eye the landscape that had been swallowed up by darkness. He lost all sense of time until a soft knock on the door roused him from his meditation. He rose and opened the carved wooden door to find Margaret Aston. She opened her arms to him.

"Jil!"

With a mischievous smile, he hugged her to him.

"Hello, Maggie!"

He studied her for a moment. She was a woman of many facets. Though she was his age, thirty-six, she could sometimes behave like a mocking, teasing schoolgirl; at others like a mature woman, whose personality combined a gravity of demeanor with a startling intelligence.

Margaret remained in his arms for somewhat longer than was necessary for a friendly hug. Her fingers slid along his shoulders, then to his waist. She was lovelier than ever. Her face glowed with a special radiance that never failed to amaze him. She drew back for a moment and looked at him intently.

"I've missed you, Jil. I've missed you very much," she whispered. "You left so suddenly."

She was right. He *had* fled from her, perhaps out of cowardice—like a thief fleeing by cover of darkness. After the night he had spent with her, he knew he had to get away from her. She was his first encounter with a woman whom he respected intellectually as much as he desired her physically. The strength of his longing to be with her had frightened him. He feared the strong tie, the deep relationship that might have grown between them. As a Resident, he had received clear directions from his instructors at the intelligence academy: he was to guard himself against any emotional ties, for they could bring disaster. That directive had become a warning system within him which enabled him to protect himself against emotional involvements. But the system could be breached. He discovered this after their first encounter: a few hours of passionate lovemaking which he tried to forget, and which she tried constantly to resurrect subsequently at every chance encounter between them.

He studied her face. It was difficult to disengage his glance from her gray eyes. The skin of her face, stretched tightly over the bones of her finely sculpted features, was almost transparent.

She was one jump ahead of him. "You are running away again," she teased.

"Maybe." He was embarrassed. He felt the blood rushing to his cheeks. Margaret laughed. She had succeeded in confounding him. He saw the familiar sparkle in her eyes, the desire. She wanted him.

"Close the door, Jil," she said mockingly, as she passed by him and entered the room.

He didn't move.

"This is my father's house."

His gaze did not waver.

"Not this time, Margaret."

Her laughter died and was replaced by a nervous smile.

"I've heard that before, Jil."

"I said what I did just to make it clear where we stand." He spoke with deliberate restraint. Then, he shut the door and remained standing there, leaning against the jamb.

"I need you . . ." she said slowly.

She always succeeded in disconcerting him. He envied her rebellious, mocking candor. Sometimes he wanted to express himself as she did, openly and freely, but it seemed he was incapable of such liberated self-expression.

"I'm sure that even this time you are not alone."

"Jil!" She pointed at him mock-accusingly. "That is jealousy speaking!" She chuckled.

"Who is it this time?"

"Da'ud."

Jil had heard that Da'ud el-Za'id, a handsome young Palestinian terrorist, was one of Margaret's more enthusiastic suitors.

"El-Za'id," he said quietly.

"There is nothing between us, Jil. Believe me." Her manner became serious. "What he may feel is his problem—not mine."

She didn't want to waste time speaking about Da'ud, or anyone else. She only wanted Jil, craved him passionately. His long face with its strange eyes fascinated her. She had first met him at François Ripoll's villa. Until then she had only heard of him, the pantomime artist who was the darling of students all across the European continent. After she saw him she understood his reputation at once. To her surprise, she discovered he was greedy for knowledge, eager to extend the borders of his intellectual experience, and she had opened the doors for him. She had never known anyone so starved for intellectual enrichment as he was and, in his presence, she felt his hunger. And then she found herself stretched out naked next to him. He had made love to her as no man had before. And after that, he fled from her, as if something happened to spoil the relationship before it had even begun.

Her hands tingled; she longed to bury them in his thick auburn curls. She looked deep into his eyes—those large, sage eyes that sparkled with perceptiveness, with humor, with gentle mockery. She raised her arms swiftly and put them around his neck. She pressed her lips to his. He didn't move, and she released him but kept her face close to his, inhaling his scent.

"There is something so special about you," she whispered hoarsely.

He was studying her, but his look was remote.

"The time hasn't come yet, has it, Jil?"

He didn't answer. The faint suggestion of a smile flickered at the corners of his mouth. Margaret felt the heat rise in her cheeks. Jil's arms closed around her. His hand pressed the nape of her neck, and his long, powerful fingers entwined themselves in the flowing mane of hair. He brought his mouth down to hers, and his lips seemed to scorch into Margaret's soul, stirring her desire into lust.

They stripped away their clothes, thirsting for the joys of their passion. He wooed her slowly, tracing the mounds and hollows of her body with his tongue, restraining his mounting desire, prolonging the erotic foreplay as if it were an end in itself.

Quickening to his touch, Margaret longed for him to take her—to enclose her with his arms and legs and bring her to fulfillment. She felt a sharp twinge of pleasure as she watched him arch over her. She responded to his rhythm, felt the rising force of tension, and then the final surge of energy as they came together in an ecstatic moment of release. They lay back, languid and peaceful in each other's arms.

"Jil . . ."

His lips parted slightly, but he remained silent. She bent over him and brushed her lips over his.

"When are you leaving?"

"Tomorrow at three in the afternoon, from Madrid."

"Will I be seeing you again soon?"

"That's impossible to know," he said with a sad smile.

"You know that I'm in love with you."

"Are you?"

Margaret knew that she would never be able to elicit a clear response from him. All his answers were evasive, ambiguous. Both his "yes" and his "no" were double-edged. At times she believed he could read her thoughts. She rose and slipped into her clothes.

"Jil . . ."

He looked at her questioningly.

"Are you a mind reader?"

"Get out of here, Maggie!" he called out in ridicule.

She laughed and turned toward the door. "By the way," she said, halting at the threshold, "Miguel wants to know more about you. You've aroused his interest."

"What does that mean?"

"That he likes you."

Dinner that night, presided over by Miguel de Salit, was an uneasy affair. Pepe Manuelete had stayed on, and now he and Miguel exchanged despairing glances as Horst Welsh and Da'ud el-Za'id, who had evidently met before, proceeded to embark on a conversational marathon, neither one permitting the other diners to speak. Horst's self-confidence had returned and he had become quite cheerful, his mood greatly improved by the appearance of the young Arab, who treated him with open respect and deference.

Desperate to stop the flow of their conversation, Margaret finally turned to her father and asked, "How's your work coming along?"

Miguel brightened. "Thanks to Pepe I have solved some difficult problems. I've already completed a few prints. Some I am satisfied with, others still have to be worked on."

"Perhaps you'll show us the ones that are finished?"

Miguel smiled with pleasure. "Gladly, Margaret."

After dinner, Miguel led his guests into his studio, a large, high-ceilinged room with a northern exposure. Finished and partially finished canvasses filled nearly every corner of the room. A large cabinet standing at the center of the room brimmed with tubes of paint, thinners, and brushes. A few steps from the table, two large basins had been installed in the wall, under metal faucets, for the acids used to develop the copper plates. The large press was in the far corner of the studio, and behind it stood a case containing powders, acids, and other chemicals needed for developing and printing plates.

When they were seated, Miguel began displaying a series of large prints depicting the confrontation between man and bull.

"Your prints remind me of Goya's etchings." Jil approached the easel and pointed to a print that showed a dying bull stretched out in a pool of blood, the matador still standing over him. The agony of the bull and the solemnity of his slayer were graphically depicted. "You've captured the essence of the bull ring. The real loser is the man . . ."

Miguel looked at Jil with renewed interest. "You have paid me a great compliment. You have seen what I wanted to say."

The conversation drifted to bullfighting and its significance in Spanish culture. Da'ud el-Za'id was full of praise for the matador. He spoke with fervor as he justified the killing of the bull, an essential act.

"All killing is justified if it serves a just aim!" he said heatedly.

"I don't consider death in the arena as proof of the matador's courage," Jil said in a quiet voice. "One must always remember in looking at bullfighting that it is not a struggle between equal forces under equal conditions. There is more than one man against a single bull; there is the picador, who severely wounds the animal, and there are the many assistants."

"Perhaps you know better forms of courage?" Da'ud el-Za'id taunted.

"Well, in ancient times there were more interesting contests, more evenly matched struggles between man and bull."

A profound silence followed Jil's words. Miguel felt uncomfortable, fearing that they might have offended his friend Pepe.

"You speak as one who knows the history of the Corrida," said the matador. "Do you also know something of the special training a matador must undergo, the courage demanded of him if he is to really become a matador?"

Jil listened attentively and then the two men began to discuss bullfighting—the great matadors, their abilities and their shortcomings.

"Your knowledge is equal to that of one who has lived the Corrida experience," Pepe Manuelete said admiringly.

Unknowingly he had hit on the truth. Jil had been taught the lore of the Corrida and the secrets and mysteries of the ring by none other than Manuel Jimenez, one of Spain's greatest matadors in the 1920s. During the Spanish Civil War Jiminez had fought with the leftist brigades, taking refuge in the Soviet Union when Generalissimo Franco's forces won. There, he earned his living in a different arena, the Moscow Circus, where he was put in charge of the large Rumanian bulls that lumbered around the ring with mischievous monkeys on their backs. Before performances he would play music on his guitar that sounded like the soul weeping for its beloved homeland. Jil, standing next to him, would listen to the Andalusian songs, and between these songs the great matador, now an aging man, would regall his little friend with fascinating stories of the ring.

Through these stories Jil learned the secrets of bullfighting. How, by gazing into the eyes of the bull, the matador could foresee the animal's next move. How the stamping of its foot indicated a decision to change suddenly, to crush the man standing before him.

"Have you ever considered measuring yourself against the bull in the ring?" the matador asked.

Jil shrugged evasively. Da'ud was pleased at his discomfort.

"Aha!" the Palestinian exclaimed gaily. "Anyone who talks

about other people's courage should look for a bit of courage in himself."

Jil ignored the comment. He looked at Pepe Manuelete's openly inquisitive face.

"Yes," he said. "I can go into the arena with a bull."

"Don't boast!" Da'ud scoffed. "There is an arena right here. Are you prepared to enter it?"

The tension heightened as all eyes were riveted on Jil.

"Nonsense," said Margaret, pressing her fingers into Da'ud's arm to restrain him. "Jil, he didn't mean it seriously—"

"Why not, Margaret," interrupted Da'ud. He turned to Jil. "Let's see you go into the arena with a bull for two minutes. No more. What do you say?"

"All right," Jil answered calmly. He saw that Margaret was about to intervene again, and he stopped her with a glance. "Tomorrow I'll show you how a man can pit himself against a bull, with both coming out of the ring unscathed. This is not a test of courage," he stressed with irony. "I am doing this for Pepe Manuelete and Miguel de Salit."

The next day he would demonstrate something he had learned from Manuel Jimenez and then perfected into an act under the guidance of an acrobat and trapeze artist in the circus.

It was after one and the big house was silent. Jil lay in bed, his eyes closed, listening to the wind. It reminded him of the Russian winter winds as they howled outside the train carrying the Moscow Circus from city to city: Riga, Minsk, Baku, Leningrad, Samarkand, Yakutsk, Tashkent. Fascinating large cities; drab small ones; little towns; miserable villages and settlements. The train with its endless string of cars rolling along, and outside the wind constantly howling and moaning against the windows of the cars as if begging for admittance. When someone did open a window, the air would enter, whirling through the train with the frightening power of a storm.

Suddenly the memory triggered another, and the remarkable face of the Rebbe loomed up before him. "Almighty God," Daidushka had murmured in his ear, as he showed him again the tiny picture of the Rebbe concealed under the lid of his pocket watch, "may this youngster, the last of our line, be worthy of inclusion among the Rebbe's Hasidim . . ."

Then, the old man had sighed, stooping over the boy and tucking the blankets around his body. Gently kissing his grandson's forehead, he had whispered: *"Mein einikel*, my grandson . . ."

A hybrid tongue—a mixture of ancient Hebrew and Russified Yiddish—was the language in which he and his grandfather had secretly communicated. For brief, stolen hours, they would sit clandestinely studying the Bible, the Law of Moses, the story of Abraham. Passage after passage he learned by heart, for Daidushka had no books. It was all stored in his remarkable memory—one who studies law in his youth, repeating it and practicing it, does not forget. Thus Jil learned about the holidays of Israel: the New Year, the Day of Atonement, Succoth, Hanukah, Passover. Some days joyous, some sad, some set aside for the soul's petitions for mercy.

And Daidushka would tell him about the Rebbe, who worked for the spiritual perfection of his Hasidim and whose main concern was the development of an educational network through which every one of them could study the law of his ancestors.

Jil tried to blot out the Rebbe's face, tried to free himself from those searching eyes. which seemed to penetrate and expose the secrets of the heart. Dear God, he murmured. He needed help in seeking his true identity, in trying to find his true self.

10

T HE NEXT DAY was clear and bright. A few minutes before ten, the first bull was let out of the pen. He was a nervous, rambunctious animal, easily the most dangerous of the four. As he stormed into the arena, a servant quickly closed the gate behind him.

The bull lifted his massive head, the ivory horns in sharp contrast to his sleek black hide. His stance was belligerent and his left hoof pawed at the ground in anticipation. On the other side of the fence a small group had congregated.

"This is a dangerous bull," Pepe Manuelete stated flatly. "Even an experienced matador would think twice before entering the ring with him."

Jil nodded his agreement. Margaret came toward him and seemed about to say something, then changed her mind and turned away. It was Miguel who expressed the group's trepidation.

"I have no idea what you want to show us," he said, "but nothing obligates you to go in there. Your very willingness to try is testimony to your courage."

"It's not my intention to enter the arena to demonstrate courage. That would be foolish," said Jil.

"I don't understand . . ." Miguel began, perplexed.

"I intend to demonstrate the art of an ancient culture," Jil explained, removing his jacket and tossing it over the top of the fence. "Five thousand years ago the Minoans played these games in the bull ring."

As he removed his shirt, Jil felt the chill of the December morning on his back. It was a pleasant sensation. He bent down to take off his shoes and socks. Then he straightened up, naked to the waist and barefoot, and turned to the matador.

"Senor Manuelete," he said, "no matter what seems to be happening, even if I appear to be in danger, do not enter the ring. Leave me alone with the bull. He will not be hurt and I too will come out of the ring unharmed."

The matador nodded. "As you wish." Inadvertently, in a gesture repeated from earliest childhood, Pepe's hand rose to his chest and made the sign of the cross, as if he himself were about to enter the arena to confront the bull.

Jil bent down and passed into the arena through a gap between the two lowest logs in the fence. Once inside he straightened up and began to walk toward the animal. He was now completely alone with the bull. He stopped when he was four yards from the animal.

The bull, trained to attack, did not need the enticement of a cape waved before him: he needed only a moving target. The instant Jil began walking again, the bull was off; head lowered, piercing horns directed at the moving figure, he charged. With a dazzling flash of hooves, the bull quickly covered the short distance between them and shot past Jil, who had lightly leaped aside just at the moment of collision.

Margaret held her breath, certain that Jil had exaggerated his ability. This was not a stage for pantomimists and dancers. Beside her, Pepe Manuelete stood silently; despite the coolness of the morning, small beads of sweat were evident on his forehead.

A few paces from him, Da'ud el-Za'id watched with an odd smile on his face: a smile of bloodthirsty anticipation. Horst Welsh leaned with his arms against the topmost beam of the fence, his head bent forward in concentration.

The bull, taken by surprise, had been unable to brake the momentum of his charge and now found himself thirty feet from his adversary, just as Jil had planned. He was now in control of the animal. He stood motionless, ready for the furious animal's next assault.

Jil felt a stab of fear. The black bull was quite different from the ones in his circus act. He was far faster than they had been, and he was wild and savage. The slightest error in timing or judgment could be fatal. Jil felt lead forming in his legs, impeding the swift, precise movement of his body. Ever since he could remember, he had had to overcome fear and terror. He had learned to live with both, to cope with them, to vanquish them. He knew that fear was the parent of courage, which was nothing more than the ability of the intellect to overcome paralyzing terror.

It had been many years since he had appeared with the Rumanian bull. He had to recall every detail of those performances and be doubly cautious because of the astonishing speed of the black bull before him. He concentrated, trying to recall Manuel Jimenez's exact instructions: first of all, determine, according to the inclination of the bull's head or the angry movement of his leg, how he intends to proceed; then maneuver him so he is standing opposite the sun in such a way that its light will blind him.

This time Jil would not retreat before the animal. He stood his ground and waited as the bull approached. There was frightening power in the animal. He weighed over half a ton, and the earth trembled under his hooves as he gathered speed. The pounding of the hooves grew louder and faster. Jil could hear the animal's snorting breath. In a moment the large horns would tear open his stomach. In that split second he vaulted high in the air and the bull passed under him. Jil seemed to overcome gravity as he hovered in the air for what appeared to be several seconds. Then, he fell to the ground and pirouetted immediately so that he again faced the bull.

The rays of the sun caressed his naked back. The bull turned, his tail lashing from side to side. The second miss had only increased his rage. His head swung heavily from side to side. With slow, cautious steps, he lumbered toward the powerful figure silhouetted against the blinding rays of the sun. Like an experienced matador, Jil had used the sun's angle correctly to blind the animal. The bull froze in place, and the two adversaries stood studying one another. Jil had waited for this moment. He flung out his arms and grasped the bull by the horns. Before the beast could comprehend what was happening, Jil's feet had left the ground. He executed a handstand on the dazed animal's horns, his body arched like a tight bow. As he felt the shudder of rage and rebellion pass through the bull's thick neck, he let go of the horns in a single moment and performed a backward somersault. The soles of his feet were now planted on the animal's back. He straightened, spread his arms, and leaped to the ground, like some agile, fleetfooted dancer using the bull as a springboard in the performance of magnificent acrobatic feats.

He zigzagged now before the bull, teasing and goading the confused animal, increasing his wrath and his speed. And the angrier the animal became, the more remarkable were the acrobatic feats that Jil executed. The spectators held their breath as he performed a variety of graceful and light-footed somersaults, dashes, and leaps, all the while vaguely aware that they were witnesses to a strange and magnificent ancient rite.

As Jil completed the final somersault and began to make his way to the fence, the bull seemed to regain his senses, and in a murderous rage came thundering after his opponent. At the sound of the bull's mighty hooves, Jil grasped the top beam of the fence and vaulted over it. As his feet touched the ground, the bull's heavy body struck the fence resoundingly. The bull pounded his horns against the wood, then backed up, stretched out his neck, and let out a long, thunderous bellow of protest.

The onlookers surrounded Jil, voicing their admiration. Pepe Manuelete's reaction was the most eloquent and the most significant. Ordinarily a nondemonstrative man, on this occasion he made no effort to restrain himself. He embraced Jil, released him, regarded him with a moving smile, and then embraced him again.

"That was beautifully done," Da'ud el-Za'id said grudgingly, "but it was only an exercise in body control, in agility—nothing more."

Jil doused himself with cold water from a nearby trough and began to put on his shirt. As he bent over to lace his shoes, Miguel approached him.

"That was a rare exhibition of courage," the artist said.

Jil straightened up, smoothing his hair with his hand. The chestnut curls caught a glint of the golden sunshine, and the expression on his face seemed to soften.

"I think it would be more proper to speak of fear," he said.

"What kind of fear are you talking about?" interrupted Da'ud.

"The kind that must be suppressed." Jil smiled. "Perhaps it would be more accurate to say that the courage you witnessed was nothing more than my ability to overcome fear . . ."

"Why, Jil," said Margaret, "it was more than that." She slid her arm through his. He glanced at her, knowing that she had understood him.

They walked toward the veranda, where fruit, cake, tea, and coffee had been set out. There was an oppressive tension in the air fostered by Da'ud's open resentment and animosity toward Jil.

"You know," he said, as Jil rose to leave, "someday I'll show you what I call courage. An act so bold that it will surprise even someone like you."

Jil nodded politely as he picked up his small bag. "Perhaps you will indeed have the opportunity to do just that."

He turned to say good-bye to Miguel and Pepe. They shook hands in silence. Words were superfluous. Margaret rose and followed him as he started down the steps toward his car.

"Will you be in London soon?" she asked.

"Possibly."

"You won't forget me?"

He turned to her, an affectionate gleam in his eye.

"I have a comfortable house there, Jil, as you know. It's at your disposal at all times. You owe me nothing, but I would like to see you again."

He opened the door of the car and tossed his suitcase into the back. Then he turned to her and brushed her cheek with his lips. The touch of his mouth scorched her skin. Before she could react, he was in the driver's seat. He started the motor and the small car began its descent down the steep slope. Margaret stood and watched his departure under the glaring sun, shading her eyes with her hand. She followed the car until it had left the private road to the villa and turned onto the Madrid-Córdoba highway.

Only then did she become aware of the labored breathing behind her. She turned around to confront Da'ud el-Za'id, his features contorted. His expression frightened her. His eyes were riveted on Jil's small car with a strange, savage glint. She suddenly realized the reason for his resentment of Jil.

"You will not go to bed with him," he whispered hoarsely.

Margaret laughed. "That's my business, Da'ud."

"It is my business, too." His face was twisted in anguish. She understood in a flash of insight that he was motivated not by jealousy of her, but from an explosive mixture of emotions that had nothing to do with her at all. The revelation left her dumbfounded: Da'ud el-Za'id wanted Jil.

"I didn't know . . ." She immediately regretted her words, but it was too late now to retract them.

His lips tightened. Two deep furrows extended from the corners of his mouth to his square chin, twisting his face into an expression of stark cruelty.

She stepped back, intending to go around him and start back to the house, but his hand shot out and clamped her shoulder. She groaned in pain as his fingers dug in.

"I mean what I say, Margaret." His face was pale. "If you go to bed with him . . . I'll kill you . . ."

She knew she must conceal her terror at all costs. She managed to smile almost seductively, despite the flashes of pain shooting through her shoulder.

"Don't do anything foolish," she said soothingly. "Solve your personal problems in your own way. But in the meantime we have a problem to solve together; we have to get Horst Welsh out of here. Don't forget that someone is waiting for him and for us, someone who will not be pleased with unnecessary delays."

Reason and common sense prevailed. Da'ud released his grip and his hand fell to his side. Then he turned and started quickly up the path, leaving her behind, her heart pounding.

Now, more than ever, she wanted to complete *Sacred Homeland*. She had believed that in giving the Palestinians moral support she had done the proper thing, but she had been assailed by doubts of late. She was beginning to find herself an accomplice to actions she wanted no part of. She needed time to re-evaluate what she was doing. Fortunately, she would finish the movie within a few days. The premiere was scheduled to take place at François Ripoll's villa in St. Tropez.

She didn't know what would happen after that, but the

more closely she examined her situation, the more gloomy the outlook became. She glanced up at the top of the cliff and saw Da'ud standing there. She waited until he turned toward the house and disappeared before she began to climb slowly. She stopped from time to time and looked toward the main highway. Jil's car was out of sight.

When Margaret reached the gate, she found Miguel waiting for her. His glance was fixed on the distant highway, and like her, he seemed to be looking at the turnoff where Jil's small car had disappeared only minutes before.

"Margaret," he said, hugging her, "what do you know about him?"

"Very little, Miguel. Almost nothing at all."

"I would like to see him perform," said Miguel, smiling. "Perhaps even sketch him."

They turned and walked toward the arena where the black bull moved about restlessly, still searching for the antagonist who had mocked him and vanished.

11

B Y THE BEGINNING of December almost 130 agents were directly involved in assuring the security of the fourteen men on the hit list. And this was only the beginning. Additional measures would shortly be taken and additional personnel assigned. Earl Dickson, having succeeded in putting together an exceptional network of men, now worked twenty-four hours a day, round-the-clock, leaving his post only for short rest periods. He was to meet personally with each of the fourteen men in order to discuss security measures and to obtain their cooperation. It was essential that they accept his decisions with regard to the arrangements of their personal schedules, including daily meetings, family events, and trips in and out of the United States.

He not only flew across the country, from city to city, pursuing the few men on the list who were in almost continual transit, he also directed the task force headquarters in Chevy Chase through the communications systems placed at his disposal in each airport.

When he returned to Washington, intelligence reports awaited him. He spent several hours one night in his basement room in Chevy Chase reading them and comparing them with the intelligence that had been transmitted by General Negbi's men almost daily, sometimes two or three times a day. The unofficial covenant between the Soviet Union and the terror organizations had been known to both American and Israeli intelligence for several years. In the estimation of Israeli intelligence experts, the Soviet Union had backed the program of reprisals against the Jewish-Zionist lobby in order to harness the Palestinian terror organizations to her own policy of sabotage. These experts determined that the Politburo had formulated a policy designed to strike at United States' spheres of influence in the Middle East and to cause the closing off of America's sources of oil. To attain such leverage, the Soviet Union needed a provocative ally like the Palestinians, an ally able to foment turmoil at every point in the Middle East. In return for their help, the Soviet Union would assist the Palestinians in striking at Israeli and Jewish targets. The Soviet Union was prepared to accept the risk that her involvement entailed, even on American soil, in order to prove to the heads of the Palestinian terror organizations that they could indeed rely on her almost unqualified assistance.

In the detailed report that Earl Dickson prepared for the President, there was a special paragraph that discussed the alternative modes of reprisal against the targets: either as a single action or as a series of actions. He presented three possibilities. First, fourteen assassination squads could be activated against all fourteen targets simultaneously. Second, a lesser number of assassination units could act almost simultaneously. And finally, it was possible that a chain of fourteen separate actions would be attempted one at a time. This would serve to maximize the shock felt in America. In the conclusions that Earl Dickson appended to this section, he expressed his opinion that the third possibility was the most likely.

General Negbi of the Mossad was inclined to agree. Furthermore, Negbi believed that either Senator Henry Jackson or former Secretary of State Henry Kissinger was the prime target. The Palestinians had long regarded the former Secretary of State as the man directly responsible for the sharp turn of events in the Middle East; the initial contacts between Israel and Egypt had awakened a sense of dread in them. The Soviets, on the other hand, had good reason to place Senator Jackson at the head of the list. They had an old account to settle with Jackson, who was known as one of the sharper critics of political interchanges between the United States and the Soviet Union, and was generally considered by them to be one of the more vigorous anti-communists in the Senate. He was, moreover, an enthusiastic supporter of the Jewish state.

Now a long series of meeting with his European operatives and with senior officials of the European security services awaited Earl Dickson. On Thursday, December sixth, he flew to London, and from there went to Rome and Munich. The results of the meetings were meager and quite disappointing. The intelligence agencies could not confirm the information that had been passed on to the head of Mossad, nor had Dickson's own men found anything much, beyond the fact that there was an obvious movement of terrorists from one country to another. Dickson's tension mounted. If something concrete wasn't discovered soon, the tight security network for the fourteen might prove to be absolutely worthless.

On his arrival in Munich, Dickson met with senior officials of the anti-terrorist unit of the federal police. They promised their full cooperation and assistance, but they emphasized that they would have to rethink their position if it were discovered that Palestinian terrorists were involved. In almost every place he stopped, at almost every meeting, Dickson smelled the sickening odor of oil. He saw clearly how in the higher echelons of the security agencies there was a tacit acceptance of the new economic-political situation and the conditions it imposed: cooperation in fighting terror was withheld if the slightest hint of Palestinian involvement arose. The oil-producing countries were, in effect, the third greatest power in the world, after the United States and the Soviet Union, and the Palestinians were in league with this power.

Earl Dickson met with Paul Mansfield in Mansfield's room in a modest hotel not far from Munich's commercial center. Paul had found himself a partner among the Germans: a man by the name of Hermann Kruger, an investigator expert at dealing with terrorism. Kruger was also well versed in Soviet history. It was he who had told Paul Mansfield about the Soviet Circus; he had also brought to the American's attention the French lawyer François Ripoll, whom he suspected of being involved in smuggling members of the Baader-Meinhof gang from one country to another. Kruger thought Ripoll might be a good lead to follow.

Earl Dickson and Paul Mansfield sat in armchairs on either side of a low coffee table. On the table were bottles of beer—a beverage that Paul Mansfield particularly enjoyed.

"What proof does this German have," Dickson asked, "about the Soviet Circus intelligence unit?"

"There's a book that mentions the unit by name."

"Which book?"

"A book of testimony on the Holocaust," Mansfield explained. "The testimony of partisan troops. Someone in the book says that he and three of his comrades were saved by members of an espionage unit called the Soviet Circus. He relates how the members of the unit were welcome guests in the German Army field camps. He mentions some of them by name—the 'Miracle Worker,' the 'Acrobat' . . ."

"Would it be possible to locate that witness, or any of his comrades?"

"I doubt it." Mansfield took another swig of beer. "That's why I asked my Israeli contact to look around in their archives in Tel-Aviv. Maybe he'll find something more solid."

"You know it's quite possible that circus code names were adopted coincidentally, without any connection to the unit that operated during the war."

"No." Paul glanced at Earl Dickson's lean, tired face. "It's not coincidental, Earl. The nicknames used by the group that has been smuggling terrorists are identical to the members of the Soviet Circus. That's why Kruger made the connection."

"The names are *all* he has to go on?"

"It hinges on more than just that. Kruger commented on something unusual about one of the names—the 'Miracle Worker.' A Miracle Worker is really a magician."

"So?"

"For years no one has used the term 'Miracle Worker' in connection with a circus performer. It belongs to bygone days when people believed in rainmakers and medicine men. When Kruger heard the code name, it immediately reminded him of the one other time he had come across that name—in connection with the Soviet Circus. Then, when all the other names fit too . . ."

"I guess when you have nothing else, this is worth a lot."

"We have nothing," Mansfield agreed, "except the code

names and the French lawyer. And what he knows will have to be squeezed out of him."

"How do we go about doing that?"

"Kruger rounded up a great deal of information on this François Ripoll. The man is a piece of trash. But I'm having a hard time getting a hold of him."

"Why?"

"The French. They're a bunch of whores." He got up and turned toward the window. The other side of the street was bathed in the glow of lights from nightclubs, coffee houses, and brothels. "The DST is afraid to move its ass. It's controlled by a little group of functionaries. Oh, there is one fellow who has been sympathetic—a good man. His name's Louis Etienne. He can set up a meeting for me with Ripoll. But Etienne is scared. He's worried about his hide. He has a wife and two daughters."

"I see you're learning about global politics," Earl Dickson said cynically.

"Global politics!" Paul exclaimed. The tone of his somewhat hoarse voice was characteristically contemptuous. He drew a cigar case from his pocket and lopped off the end of a short, thick cigar. "Global politics is a farce. We're in the same situation we were in before World War Two: terror casts a shadow across the world, and nobody does anything to prevent it from spreading." He turned from the window, cupped a match with his large hands and lighted his cigar, expelling a cloud of smoke, and then another. "You see, everyone's afraid. They're shaking in their boots—all the dwarfs and pygmies. You know, if they would all lend a hand, cooperate, there wouldn't be any terror. Not here in Germany. Nor in Italy or Ireland or the Middle East. We could smash terrorism, destroy it completely. Instead, the world is being dragged to the edge of an abyss . . ."

He fell silent and glanced at his watch. It was 7:40 P.M. Earl Dickson's El-Al flight to Tel-Aviv was leaving in another two hours.

"We had better start to move," suggested Dickson. "The Israelis are very meticulous about their security checks." He picked up a small overnight bag and his attaché case as he went on, "I want you to stay with this. You may have a solid lead, and in any event, to date you're the only one who's come up with anything whatsoever."

"I need Louis Etienne's help. I have to put the squeeze on that French lawyer—get him by his skinny neck—or his balls—whichever works to get the information out of him."

"Give me a day or two," Dickson said. "I'll meet with your partner Miller in Tel-Aviv and see what he's got on the Soviet Circus."

"And if he's found something?"

"I'll return to Paris. And get Louis Etienne to cooperate."

Earl Dickson's flight to Tel-Aviv was delayed more than an hour by a bomb threat at the Munich airport. On his arrival he was met at Ben Gurion Airport by an FBI agent stationed at the United States Embassy, who drove him to the Hilton Hotel on Yarkon Street a few yards from the shores of the Mediterranean.

At ten o'clock the next morning he began a series of meetings with General Negbi and other senior officials of the Mossad. The Israelis, who had dispatched teams of agents to Lebanon and Cyprus, were more and more convinced that the Palestinians would spearhead the assassination operation, with the support and protection of European terrorist organizations.

The meagerness of the information that had been gathered by Dickson's men and the Mossad underscored Paul Mansfield's request that they seek the assistance and direct involvement of the DST, a request that was seconded by the Israeli agent Evyatar Miller.

It was the first time that Earl Dickson had met Paul Mansfield's Israeli counterpart in person, and he was impressed with the young man's professionalism and his familiarity with the ins and outs of European and Middle Eastern terrorism. The Israeli had done some thorough research in the archives of the Mossad and had uncovered the names and addresses of five men who, many years before, had given testimony about the Soviet Circus. All five had been assisted in their escape from the Nazis by members of this sabotage and intelligence unit.

"According to them," Miller said, "the Circus was a crack commando unit of seven men who caused great damage to the Germans. They stole ammunition, arms, and explosives from German military camps and used them to attack and liquidate other German encampments. They also blew up German tanks, railroad tracks, trains . . ."

"What do we know about these men individually? What happened to them? Where are they now?"

"At the moment we don't have any other information on them," the young Israeli admitted as he shifted uncomfortably in his chair. "Apparently they just disappeared during the last stages of the war."

"But the stories about them didn't die."

"No," agreed Evyatar. "The stories were hard to forget. Take that German police investigator, Kruger. In his youth he heard stories about the Soviet Circus from his father and he remembers them to this day."

"He's not alone," commented General Negbi.

"Apparently not," Dickson agreed. "From what we know, it seems clear that a Russian agent heard about the Soviet Circus and is putting it to use in his activities in Europe today." As he uttered the words, Dickson suddenly understood Paul's insistence on pursuing his hunch about the Soviet Circus. It seemed less a hunch and more a possibility.

"What do you think?" Dickson asked the young Israeli.

"That Paul has some important information. We just have to put in some hard work to corroborate it, and then we'll get results."

"How do we go about getting those results?"

"Find men who are acquainted with someone in this group that's smuggling terrorists," Miller explained. "Somebody must be able to describe one of them—the color of his eyes, his build. We have to catch one of the smugglers and squeeze him. And when we do, maybe we'll have what we need so badly: proof that the Soviets are part of this operation. It's probable that this group is smuggling several terrorists who are central to the assassination operation."

When Earl Dickson left Tel-Aviv late that night for Paris, he had decided to enlist the help of the United States Ambassador to France. He would ask the ambassador to meet with the French Interior Minister and request that he direct a junior inspector named Louis Etienne to cooperate with Paul Mansfield. Once that was done, Dickson would report the results to Paul and return to Washington immediately.

12

PAUL MANSFIELD WAS tired, and the sweat that soaked his shirt only added to his discomfort and irritability. He found it difficult to follow the argument between the French police inspector and the evasive lawyer, and the effort made him weary. Although Mansfield had a fairly good command of French, François Ripoll and Inspector Etienne of the DST, the French anti-terrorist squad, spoke so rapidly that he kept losing the thread of their conversation.

Earl Dickson's cable had reached him in Munich:

All clear. Etienne expecting you. Lawyer is all yours.
Nibble with caution. Earl Dickson.

Yet, when Paul Mansfield arrived at the headquarters of the anti-terror unit, it turned out that there was a hitch. Louis Etienne, who looked more like an insignificant bank clerk than a police inspector, received him apologetically.

"Something's gone wrong, my friend."

"Don't tell me there won't be a meeting!" Mansfield roared. "I didn't come here just to be told that!"

"No, no. But, to my regret, the meeting will not be held

here." Etienne spoke quickly, attempting to stave off the American's anger.

"Not here?"

"No. We finally received the go-ahead and we can deal with him. But, it seems, on condition . . ."

"Which means?"

"That we must treat him with kid gloves. Interrogate gently . . ."

"Where will we be meeting him?"

"At his office. François Ripoll still has a great deal of influence in high places."

"Gently . . ." Mansfield repeated angrily. "Gently . . . On his home court we will *have* to be gentle with him."

"That is precisely his intention," Etienne agreed. "In his own territory it will be easier for him to play the game, at least at this stage."

"You know as well as I do that he's a despicable son of a bitch," Mansfield growled.

"It is not at all a simple matter—conducting an interrogation of a French citizen in the presence of an agent of a foreign country," Louis Etienne explained, "and even more difficult when the subject is a lawyer. He knows his rights—and maybe a good deal more."

Mansfield smiled wanly. "We both know how easy it is to twist the law—interpret, circumvent, even turn it inside out. So that's what we're up against, eh?"

At three o'clock they drove in Louis Etienne's car to Ripoll's offices on Avenue Victor Hugo. They occupied the entire fifth floor of an impressive six-story building; Ripoll's living quarters were on the floor above, connected to his offices by a private elevator.

The two men entered Ripoll's elegant reception room where they were received by a receptionist who seated them in comfortable chairs and offered them something to drink, which they refused.

As they waited for her to return, they looked around the reception room. It was furnished with expensive antiques and several fine oil paintings, among them a very good Gauguin. From the surroundings it was not hard to conclude that the lawyer was a rich man.

François Ripoll, who took the trouble to come out to the waiting room to greet them, was a well-dressed man of average height. Although he was only in his late thirties, his thinning hair aged him at least ten years. Glasses accentuated his beaked nose, which curved sharply down to his thin lips. His face reminded Louis Etienne of some predatory hawklike bird. His cordial, straightforward manner did not fool either the police inspector or Paul Mansfield.

They shook hands, and there was something in Ripoll's manner that made it clear he was in charge. He intended to let them know their place if they had any doubts to begin with—to impress on them that he was to be treated with respect. The message was not lost on them. Although the lawyer was meeting Louis Etienne and Paul Mansfield for the first time, he obviously knew something about them already.

"It never occurred to me, Monsieur Etienne, that I would have the pleasure of entertaining you here, in the company of your American colleague." His voice, though thin and somewhat high, was carefully modulated so that it was almost pleasant. "But, then, life is full of surprises."

"Indeed it is," the Frenchman agreed, as he and Paul Mansfield sat in two straight-backed chairs near the desk. It was obvious that behind the screen of smiles, each side was carefully measuring the other. The very fact that the lawyer had chosen to seat them opposite his desk rather than in the deep leather armchairs arranged for a comfortable chat was an indication that he was receiving them not by choice but under duress. His attitude implied that they should conclude their business as quickly as possible and leave.

When François Ripoll reached over to a series of buttons at the right of his desk, Louis Etienne startled him, saying: "Please, Monsieur, this is not an official conversation. It is not to be recorded."

The lawyer smiled smugly. "I record every conversation—official or unofficial—that takes place in my office," and he turned on the tape recorder that was installed in one of the drawers of his desk.

Louis Etienne stared helplessly at his American colleague. The Frenchman was toying with them and Mansfield did not enjoy the little game, but despite his annoyance, he maintained a serene look.

"And so, gentlemen, here you are," said the lawyer.

"Yes, here we are," concurred Louis Etienne.

"I should like to know how I have earned this honor," said Ripoll, the mischievous smile never leaving his lips.

"I suggest that we cut through all this clever repartee," Etienne interrupted sharply. "You may find it convenient to look on this meeting as an unexpected honor, but we regard it differently. I want to have your full cooperation, Monsieur Ripoll."

They knew how deeply Ripoll was mired in terrorist activity, but the lawyer was convinced that they had no chance of forcing him to cooperate. If they did, they would be richly rewarded, for the information he possessed easily equaled any contained in the files of the French and American security agencies.

"Always be assured of my complete cooperation," the lawyer rejoined, as calm and relaxed as if he were passing the time of day with a client. "From my standpoint, first, as a law-abiding citizen, and second, as a lawyer, I would always offer my full assistance to representatives of the law and government of France."

Louis Etienne had no doubt that the lawyer was mocking them, and he chafed at the restrictions that had been placed on him by his superiors.

"Let me explain why we are here." Etienne was aware that the American was observing the proceedings with impatience. "We need to have information which we know you possess, concerning the political and criminal activities of certain terrorists."

"Monsieur Inspector." Paul Mansfield caught the disdainful tone in Ripoll's voice. "You've taken up my time to no purpose. You know very well that if I had information of that nature I would not hesitate to put it at the disposal of the authorities."

He was now addressing the tape recorder, his eyes gleaming derisively. Every word could be used to prove his willingness to cooperate with the police. As he listened to the lawyer speak, Paul Mansfield squirmed uncomfortably in his chair and finally got up. He rested his hand on the desk and, leaning his weight on it, turned to Inspector Etienne.

"Etienne," he said in a quiet but resolute voice, "with all due respect, may I have five minutes to speak with Monsieur Ripoll? Let's just pretend you are not here!"

Ignoring the lawyer's look of astonishment, Mansfield sat

down suddenly on the desk, and, before Ripoll could digest the drastic change in the impassive American's demeanor, Mansfield's stubby hand grabbed the lawyer by the knot of his tie and, with a powerful jerk, yanked him out of his chair. He held Ripoll's face close to his own.

"You can kiss my ass!" he growled in a low, husky voice. "It's garbage like you we're fighting against. You can play your games as much as you want, with whomever you want—just don't try them on me, you little bastard."

Stunned by the American's sudden metamorphosis, Ripoll turned beet-red as he struggled to catch his breath. When the American finally released him, he sank back in his chair, gasping for air, his heart beating wildly.

"Get this madman out of here!" he ordered Louis Etienne, but the police inspector seemed not to hear him, choosing instead to walk over to the shelves crammed with law books. He took down a volume and slowly leafed through it. "You're out of your mind!" Ripoll shouted.

"Now, now," said Mansfield as he pressed the "off" button of the tape recorder. Then, ignoring the lawyer's vociferous protests, he opened the drawer containing the recording device, removed the tape, and dropped it into his pocket.

"I tell you . . ." the lawyer sputtered, trying in vain to complete a sentence.

"No. I will tell you. I will tell you exactly what we want."

Filled with murderous rage, the lawyer tried to stand up, but Mansfield's arm shot out and clamped a viselike grip on his thin nose. Groaning in pain, François Ripoll sat back in his chair. Louis Etienne looked on in amazement; it had never occurred to him that Mansfield was capable of such violence.

"We want your full cooperation," said Mansfield, his powerful fingers twisting the lawyer's nose. "And we are going to get it. There are gangs of murderers loose in Europe. Our job is to wipe them out and you are going to help."

The only response he received was a tortured groan.

"Don't play the lawyer with me," said Mansfield unrelentingly, "because with you I won't behave like a representative of the law. Consider me a fighter, fighting for my life, for the life of a society I believe should continue to exist. I don't want terrorists running amok. I want a sane, law-abiding world. And if the law can't protect law-abiding people, then

I'll make rules of my own. And I won't learn law and morality from you, because in your jungle and your friends' jungle, I'll enforce regulations that you haven't even heard of, clever *monsieur avocat!*"

The American was breathing hard as he stared into the angry, frightened eyes of François Ripoll.

"As for you, you suck up to that gang of lunatics. Well, I'll teach you whose ass to lick. You know how? With the stuff I'm collecting on you, I'll prove to your crazy friends that you've been working with us all along—then it will be our asses you'll have to kiss. I'll show them that you're the first to enjoy the money they get robbing banks. I'll let them know where you've made your little investments . . ."

It was difficult to ignore the cold terror in the lawyer's face.

"You know, Monsieur Ripoll," declared the American, "the moment I reveal to your partners who you are, there will be only one solution to the problem of François Ripoll: death. I can even tell you how you will die . . . At first they will place you under siege. You will start to sweat . . . sweat will roll down the entire length of your spine. Then you'll begin to live in terror. They will surround you from every side . . . in the daytime . . . at night. Fear will dominate your life. After that, they will catch you. Suddenly. Unexpectedly. They will trap you—not to kill you immediately—oh, no. They have time. Slowly, very slowly . . ."

François Ripoll moaned and broke loose from Mansfield's grip.

"You won't dictate how *I'll* die!" he exclaimed. The pain in his nose was unbearable and the injury to his pride no less so. Moreover, he had experienced fear such as he had never before encountered. For the first time in years he had been caught off balance and the American had terrified him. "I—I'll tell you how *you* will die . . ."

"Shut your beak!" Mansfield boomed, making a derisive gesture. As he watched the lawyer rubbing his injured nose, he thought how much he looked like a bird. "You had better understand that not a soul is to know about our little meeting. You will, for example, make no move that will hurt Louis Etienne. Because if you do, a number of facts I happen to possess in connection with you and your business dealings will be used to make things very unpleasant for you, even at this stage. Don't forget, Monsieur Ripoll, that both my friend here and I are still considered a bit more trustworthy than you."

Paul Mansfield took out a leather case and extracted a half-smoked cigar. He lit the stub, drawing deeply and exhaling a single, thick ring of smoke that billowed and diffused over their heads.

"What do you want to know?" The question seemed to burst from the lawyer's mouth. His voice was dry and hoarse.

"For starters, how a man named Horst managed to disappear. What's his surname? What does he look like?"

"I haven't heard the name."

"I see," said Mansfield, laughing derisively. "Well, it may be necessary to work you over a bit more, just to refresh your memory. Another thing. There is a Soviet Circus at work here. They say it has something to do with the sudden disappearance of Horst—a name, of course, unfamiliar to you. They also say that you have connections with somebody who belongs to that circus."

"I don't know what you're talking about."

"Don't play the innocent. You know exactly what I'm talking about. I want to know about the Miracle Worker, the Trainer, the Clown. There might be a few more members of the Circus, one of whom may be able to help me in certain matters I am working on. Do you understand what I mean now?"

Paul Mansfield stopped talking and studied the lawyer's flushed face. He wondered to what extent he'd really succeeded in shaking him up.

François Ripoll said nothing in the hope that the American would abandon the brutal interrogation. Mansfield seemed to have alarmingly precise information. The American slid from the corner of the desk and stood over the lawyer's chair. Putting his hand under Ripoll's chin, he raised the lawyer's head.

"Think very carefully about what I've been saying, monsieur."

His voice was restrained now. "You'll be hearing from me again. In another week. Perhaps in another month. But you'll hear from me. Until then, you'd best decide on whose side you want to play—on whom it is best to gamble. And one more thing. I repeat: don't be in any rush to enter a complaint against Monsieur Etienne. He and I are one and the same. You get what I mean, don't you?"

Mansfield knew he could squeeze nothing out of the lawyer just yet, but he felt that he had succeeded in establishing the proper atmosphere for a second meeting. He would get cooperation by working slowly and deliberately. Before departing, Louis Etienne turned to glance at the lawyer who sat slumped in his chair. He wondered what Ripoll would do in the next five minutes. If Paul Mansfield had been wide of the mark, the inspector's superior would have his hide the minute he returned to his office on Sousa Street.

13

Fʀᴀɴçoɪs ʀɪᴘoʟʟ ᴡᴀs shaken by his encounter with Paul Mansfield. It was not the American's assault on his person or the open threats that disturbed him, but rather the simple fact that for the first time since he had become involved in giving legal aid to the terrorists, he had been unable to avoid an interrogation by the police. All he had been able to do was change the venue from DST headquarters to his own office, and in the end that change had not helped him very much.

The smallest breach in the wall of his personal security could bring the entire structure crumbling down around him. In the event of such a debacle, those he had swindled would run to save their skins—some might even demand their pound of flesh. At the same time, they would expose his connection with the terrorist organizations, a connection that had demanded far more of him than the normal lawyer-client relationship.

Then they would begin to question how he, the son of poor farmers in Provence, had managed in only a few years to amass such a large fortune. As long as he maintained his ties with men in the highest political and financial circles, many of whom needed his good offices from time to time, he could rely on their support. Analyzing the scene that had just been enacted in his office, he decided that his wisest course was to refrain from any action whatsoever—not because he was a coward, but because he was a very cautious man.

To allay his anxiety he decided to submerge himself in routine legal activities, working long hours for the remainder of the week. By Friday he needed a release from the tension that he had bottled up. Now that his wife Charlotte and little son Marcel were permanently settled in the St. Tropez villa, he had created a separate life for himself in Paris. He occasionally spent weekends with his family, but in general he preferred to remain in the city. He finished the day's work and went up in the elevator to his suite. After a soothing, perfumed bath he lay down to rest for a couple of hours. When he awoke at eight o'clock in the evening, he found himself in good spirits for the first time since his meeting with Etienne and Mansfield.

He was dining with Madeline Torez at an Italian restaurant near his apartment. Madeline, a film actress, doubled as a high-class call girl, but the lawyer sought her company for other qualities as well. She was an intelligent and stimulating conversationalist in addition to being adept at catering to the special tastes—and weaknesses—of her clientele. That night Madeline could see that François Ripoll was in obvious need of a large dose of coquetry and tenderness.

The few hours that Ripoll spent with Madeline assuaged the anxiety that had been brought on by his meeting with the lawmen two days before. His self-assurance had returned, and as the taxi pulled up in front of his home, he surprised the driver by the generosity of his tip.

The private elevator stopped inside his suite, at the entrance to the spacious salon, and even before he opened the door, François knew that Jil was waiting for him. Through a crack in the elevator door, he could see that the large crystal chandelier was lit. It was Jil's way of informing him that he was waiting. Ripoll had never given Jil a key to the building or to the apartment, but he could enter the apartment at will nonetheless. It was pointless to ask how he did it; even a professional housebreaker would have set off one of the many electronic alarm systems Ripoll had installed, but Jil apparently knew how to silence them.

As he opened the elevator door, Ripoll found Jil sitting, as usual, in the wicker chair opposite him, his long legs stretched out before him.

"I'm sorry about having come so late, François." Jil rose and held out his hand in greeting, his manners polished and courteous, as always. He had apparently not been there long, for he still wore his overcoat.

"I hope everything is all right with the German," Ripoll said in a questioning tone.

"Everything is all right. He is with Margaret Aston now, per your instructions."

"Good." François took a deep breath. "I'm pleased you took the trouble to come and tell me."

"That is not the only thing I came for."

"No?"

"I came also to say good-bye."

Ripoll was genuinely surprised. "For how long?"

"I don't know."

"A family matter?"

"Yes," Jil confirmed. "Someone needs me."

François went to the bar and took out a bottle of brandy. He filled two snifters and put one before his guest.

"I gather that it is sudden." The lawyer moistened his lips with the brandy.

"Indeed." Jil smiled, but he was disturbed. Something in the lawyer's eyes, a glint he caught behind the glasses, troubled him. Ripoll seemed unsettled, alarmed, anxious about something he had no desire to discuss. Jil stared at him and François Ripoll found it hard to meet those large eyes. The black pupils flecked with gold drilled into him, their penetrating stare burrowing into his brain. His forehead burned as if touched by a scorching iron.

"Nobody has asked about you," he blurted suddenly. The words seemed to have been torn from his mouth, against his will.

"I didn't ask if anyone had inquired about me," Jil said quietly. "But I think that if anyone has, François, it might be best if I hear about it from you."

It was unusual for François Ripoll not to have a ready response, but now he seemed to be groping for words; his tongue felt thick. He was confused. Damn, he said to himself, there is something in his crazy eyes that prevents me from thinking clearly. His forehead was beaded with drops of sweat.

"I don't know why I said that," he stammered, "but no one has asked about you, nobody at all . . . It's awfully hot in here, isn't it?" He realized suddenly that he had not removed his coat and he pulled it off, laughing. "Look . . . I'm all mixed up . . . I even forgot to take this blanket off . . . no, don't worry, everything is all right."

"Are you certain?"

"Yes," he said with annoyance. "I'm sorry you're leaving, Jil."

The fear he had experienced on Wednesday was returning. But now, perhaps because it had been diluted in alcohol, the terror produced confusion. He shifted in his chair, restless under Jil's questioning gaze.

"Is there anything special you want of me?" he asked.

"We have shared a few experiences, you and I," Jil said, "and I wouldn't want the details of those activities passed on to others. We'll meet again, François."

The final words were said quietly, but they were a clear warning to Ripoll to keep his mouth shut. The lawyer did not stir until Jil was safely inside the elevator, but before the door closed, he caught Jil's eye and that gaze seemed to penetrate into Ripoll's soul.

Within minutes Jil had reconnected the electric circuit of the alarm systems. Despite the biting cold, his dextrous fingers moved rapidly. He exited as usual, pulling himself through the top of the elevator and emerging on the tiled roof of the apartment house. The edge of the roof was joined to that of the building next door. Under the tiles there was a long, narrow chamber, and by crouching low he could move through this space. The security experts had installed the control panel for the elaborate alarm system in this tiny corridor. Immediately after connecting the electric circuit, Jil crossed to the roof of the building next door, crawled through the escape hatch of the elevator, descended to the first floor, and emerged into the bitter predawn chill.

The day before, he had left his room in the small gray hotel in Montmartre and gone to a coffee house for coffee and a croissant, while he read *Le Monde*. He checked the classified section of the newspaper routinely, for it was here that the notices intended for him appeared—advertisements that were in fact precise instructions from Department V in Moscow. For three years the system had worked without a hitch. Although he had no idea who placed the ads in the paper, it was undoubtedly another Resident agent of the KGB operating in Paris and responsible for maintaining communications with agents like himself. He found what he was looking for under the Personal Inquiries section: *Gilbert, the wedding will take place at the established time.*

For almost a year he had waited for this message. Gilbert. The wedding will take place on time. Return home. The date has not been changed. Return. Return. Return.

The special lexicon that had been prepared for him before he left three years before to burrow like a mole into the power centers of the Western terrorist organizations contained fifty words in various combinations that could be used to convey an almost endless number of meanings. But there was no mistaking the meaning of that sentence. It contained the key words he had been waiting for. His European mission had drawn to a close. Moscow had apparently heeded his warnings that he was likely to be exposed.

It was possible that the old man had been working behind the scenes. Perhaps the time had come for him to embark on the mission that Daidushka had spoken of so often and which he had trained his grandson to expect. Jil had begun to worry lest the old man not have sufficient time to prepare him for his mission. And doubts had begun springing up inside him, not only concerning his Hasidic affiliation but also about the very nature of the Judaism he had learned from the old man. He had never lived with other Jews, had had no firsthand experience of Judaism, no sense of the way its vital spirit could permeate the most ordinary aspects of daily life.

Jil was glad that he had gone to see François Ripoll now that he was to return to Moscow. He had been trained to tie up loose ends, just as a surgeon rejoins nerve endings after completing an operation. He had to clear a path behind him before he left.

He hailed a cab for the ride to Montmartre and sank back in the seat, lost in thought.

The streetlights sprayed sparks of color over the windshield, visions interchanging, images being swallowed up, one being enveloped in another. He thought again about the lawyer. Something wasn't right. He had sensed Ripoll's discomfort right away. Someone had indeed questioned the lawyer about him. Who? Why? What about? Had he not been pressed for time, he would have stayed to get to the root of the matter. It was a poor practice to leave behind people who had questions but no answers.

Montmartre was enveloped in a soft gray morning mist as the taxi pulled up in front of Jil's hotel. He decided to walk in the mist-shrouded silence that had not yet given way to the sound and bustle of morning in the quarter. Jil climbed the summit of the hill, toward Sacré Coeur. Below him, he could see Paris, all gray and blue in the dawn of the winter day. As he stood and took in the city stretched out at the foot of the hill, he realized that he had wanted to take a final look at the now familiar view—to say good-bye.

The last three years would soon be a closed book of memories that he would never share with anyone else. He thought suddenly of Margaret and wished that he could talk to her, discuss with her some of the things that perplexed him and weighed on his heart. But such a relationship was forbidden to him. He dared not surrender to it.

If only he could have told Margaret the truth—that he was, in fact, not an entertainer but an espionage agent and a Jew, that he was, in fact, not thirty-six years old but a man of eighty-five: he was the old man. He had been created in the image of the old man. He thought the way the old man wanted him to think. He lived as the old man wished him to live. He had simply restored to Daidushka his lost youth so that he could continue to carry out the Rebbe's mission.

14

FROM LARNACA, VLADIMIR Zoska continued to report to his superior Anton Karlov, the head of the Czech Foreign Operations section. Foreign Operations was in fact merely a Czech branch of Department V; as such, it provided a convenient camouflage for those activities in which the Soviet Union did not wish her involvement to be known. It was for this reason that Pavel Ramizor had assigned the actual implementation of the reprisals against the Americans to Anton Karlov.

Karlov was known for his intelligence, cunning, and wariness, as was his chief assistant, Vladimir Zoska. Their cautiousness had saved the Soviet Union great embarrassment on more than one occasion, since the two Czechs were quick to cut their losses and abandon a project whenever it was apparent that the plan had run aground.

Vladimir Zoska was charged with the responsibility of setting up a base of operations in Larnaca and of serving as an advisor to the Palestinians. The initial American hit list had been transmitted to them from the KGB, and extensive preparations were underway for separate strike forces. Mussa el-Dalil had been put in charge of the Palestinian units.

Since it had been decided that the assassinations would be carried out one after the other, with an interval of several weeks between each attack, el-Dalil chose to lead the first liquidation unit himself, in order to set an example for the groups that would be mobilized later on. The plan was to prolong, for as long as possible, the uncertainty and terror among Jews and non-Jews considered supporters of the Jewish State.

In Europe, the man whose responsibilities paralleled those of Zoska was Klaus Schmidt. Schmidt, a dangerous killer and a superb and wily tactician, had consistently proved his effectiveness. From a little office in the Cassandra nightclub, near the port in Hamburg, he had cast his nets of terror over the entire continent of Europe. At present, he was recruiting European terrorists, who would serve the Palestinian liquidation squad as a backup unit and guarantee their safe withdrawal from the United States. The plan was to arrive from Europe on a commercial flight and, on landing at Kennedy Airport, to seize control of the craft, holding the crew and passengers as hostages. This was intended to insure the Palestinians a safe getaway from the scene of the reprisal to the airfield, where they would board the plane; the two groups would then join forces and demand to be flown with their hostages to an Arab state. The use of these international terrorists was a deliberate red herring to disguise the Soviet involvement in the killings.

While Zoska awaited the arrival of Horst Welsh, he checked out the fifty men assigned to Mussa el-Dalil's team. He felt uncomfortable in the presence of the fanatic Palestinian. It was one of the few times in Zoska's long career that he had been unable to anticipate the reactions of someone with whom he worked. He was no stranger to the Arab mentality but he couldn't get a fix on Mussa el-Dalil. Which made it all the more imperative that he find someone among the men in el-Dalil's unit who might act as his informer.

The wild and coddled youth Da'ud el-Za'id came to his mind immediately. El-Dalil had shown a special fondness for him, had said he thought el-Za'id the most courageous of all his men. Because he wanted, in time, to make him into a commander, he dealt with him far more strictly than he did with the others. It was precisely because of this approach that Vladimir Zoska decided he might find a way to drive a wedge between el-Za'id and his commander, and he awaited his opportunity to do just that.

The tension between Margaret Aston and Da'ud el-Za'id had increased sharply since the day of Jil's departure. The Palestinian had been pursuing the tall Englishwoman for a long time, and while she had treated him with courtesy and even with a certain fondness, she had never been intimate with him. Despite this, Da'ud el-Za'id had told his comrades titillating stories of his stormy sessions in bed with the beautiful Englishwoman. His relations with "boys," as he referred to his male partners, did not prevent him from having sexual relations with women, and he was hungry for the Englishwoman with the white skin and the seductive body. In his imagination, he regarded her as his personal property. When she discovered that, in addition to being hot-tempered, the young Arab could be extremely dangerous, Margaret decided to cool her relationship with him.

They had traveled with Horst Welsh by car to Tarifa on the southern coast of Spain, arriving there after sundown. At midnight they were picked up by a speedboat and taken to the coast of Africa. From the moment they were on Moroccan soil, there was no longer any reason to be concerned about the security of Horst, the Fox. Their passage to Cyprus was assured.

By the time they reached Cyprus, on Saturday morning, the fifteenth of December, Margaret was pleased to note that Da'ud el-Za'id was leaving her alone, perhaps because Horst Welsh had been with them constantly. In truth, he was merely biding his time.

In Larnaca, Da'ud el-Za'id returned to the villa in which Vladimir Zoska was staying. Margaret Aston and Horst Welsh took adjoining rooms on the third floor of the Palace Hotel. From the window of her room, Margaret could look out over a brilliantly colored landscape to the strip of coast and the sea beyond. It would take only three more days of work to complete *Sacred Homeland*. She had to interview Mussa el-Dalil and photograph the refugee ships arriving in Larnaca from Lebanon. She longed to finish the movie. The determination to dissociate herself from any activities connected with the Palestinians had been slowly growing on her, and with it had come an awakened desire to retire to

Miguel's villa and try to write again. She was uncertain about a great deal now, and her inability to analyze what was happening to her weighed on her, but one thing she was sure of: she wanted no more involvement with Palestinians in the future.

On her first night in Larnaca, Da'ud el-Za'id had tried to enter her room. She told him she would meet him later in the lobby of the hotel, and when she did, she had no desire to have any physical contact with him whatsoever.

"I want to know why!" he demanded, his face flushed.

"I'll tell you." She looked directly at him. "You don't interest me as a man . . . Is that what you wanted to hear?"

She wanted to insult him so that he would leave her alone once and for all.

Da'ud el-Za'id rose from his chair, his face contorted with anger. "The cheapest whore on Pigeon Beach is better than you are," he hissed venomously. "We shall meet again . . . and then *I'll* dictate the terms—*Sharmuta!*" Da'ud pronounced the Arabic word for whore slowly, drawing out each syllable.

For the next two days Margaret saw nothing of him. On the evening of the second day, Da'ud and six of his friends went to a Greek nightclub in the harbor area. As they sat over glasses of ouzo, they joked, watched the floor show, and commented on the voluptuous dancers.

The club offered two types of entertainment: the floor show and a series of back rooms where prostitutes worked. The club manager, spotting a table of young men who were out for a good time and had plenty of money to spend, came over to greet them.

He quickly had three tables put together to make room for any women the young men might want to have join them, and sent over bottles and ice and trays of appetizers: black olives, eggs, salty cheeses floating in pure olive oil, thinly sliced tomatoes, halved onions, and cucumbers. The women in the back rooms, notified that heavy spenders had arrived, began to stream out, one at a time. A few of the women had already joined the party of young Palestinians by the time two heavy-breasted dancers appeared on stage in transparent flowered dresses.

The party was in full force when the dancers, panting and

perspiring from their act, joined the group. The young men joked as they teased the women, and soon hands were sliding over ample thighs and cupping partially exposed breasts. The atmosphere became heated and the men more and more ardent in their caresses, until four of them finally rose and retired with their women to the privacy of the back rooms.

The drink, the music, and the women were having a cumulative effect on everyone but Da'ud el-Za'id, who sat apart and sipped his ouzo in silence, lost in thought. Two days had passed since he had last seen Margaret. His appetite for her was seasoned by a lingering bitterness over the abuse he had suffered. He had thought of nothing but taking her in the most violent way possible, of humiliating her as she had humiliated him.

"Leave those painted bitches alone," he exclaimed suddenly to his friends, angrily pushing aside one of the women who had come over to join him. "Come with me," he said imperiously.

His friends, Adel and Sa'id, exchanged glances. In the past it had always been worthwhile following el-Za'id, and they assumed it would be in this instance too. "Where you go, my brother, I am ready to go, too," Adel said.

"No, dear brother," Da'ud laughed. "Where I screw, you will screw, too."

"What are you talking about, Da'ud?"

"I'm talking about the most beautiful whore on this whole rotten island."

Intrigued, they threw a few bills on the table and, weaving slightly, one man leaning on the shoulder of the other, they turned and followed Da'ud.

When they reached the hotel, the desk clerk, recognizing them as members of an important Arab organization, made no attempt to stop them, although the hour was late and he knew they were not staying at the hotel. Once they reached the corridor outside Margaret Aston's room, Da'ud el-Za'id indicated that they should be quiet. He knocked softly, and a moment later the door opened a crack.

He giggled at the sight of Margaret. "Were you expecting me?"

She looked at him dubiously, unaware of Adel's and Sa'id's presence. "You've had a long day, Da'ud," she said quietly, trying to control her anger, "and I've been working hard, too. You had better go to sleep. Good night."

He laughed derisively and, before she realized what was happening, he had pushed open the door so suddenly that she fell backward. In that instant she saw Da'ud's friends and realized that all three were drunk. Sa'id covered her mouth to prevent her from screaming for help and, with his other arm around her waist, dragged her over to the bed and threw her down. Adel pinned down her arms and shoulders, while Da'ud tore off her flowered nightgown. As her lovely body was exposed, her silky white skin glowing through the tatters of the nightgown, an exclamation escaped Adel's lips and Sa'id began to laugh excitedly.

The thought that he would soon enter her in the presence of his friends stirred Da'ud el-Za'id's desire to a frenzy. He would take her in a way that he had never taken a woman before. He would have her first and then he would stand back and relish the sight of her struggling beneath his friends.

As he came closer, Margaret glanced up at his handsome, distorted features. She felt like a detached observer, witnessing some ugly scene in an anonymous hotel room. The amorphous shapes and forms, expanding, contracting, dividing, conjoining surrealistically around her, seemed like the components of some hallucinatory trip. She wanted to scream, but the hand muzzling her mouth weighed so heavily on her that she could not even move her head.

Da'ud fumbled with the buckle of his belt. He unzipped his pants and with a flick of his hand exposed his erect penis. He placed his face close to hers and tried to force her legs apart, conscious as he did of the profound look of disgust in her eyes. He laughed and, passing his hands over her full breasts, pinched the nipples cruelly. She flinched, her face contorted in pain. Then he slid his hands down to her stomach and, thrusting a finger into her vagina, began a breathless exploration. All three men were beside themselves, sweating and panting in unison. Sa'id and Adel were becoming impatient. "Fuck her," Sa'id growled, unable to contain himself.

"Patience. Everybody will have a turn," Da'ud said, enjoying the feel of her long, muscular legs. He was in no hurry. Each additional moment would only add to the ultimate pleasure of penetrating her and finally exploding inside her.

Margaret felt as if she were stretched out on an operating table. From her angle of vision, the three faces looming above her looked like those of ravenous beasts, moving in for the kill. She felt a mounting nausea. If she could only vomit . . . maybe they would—

At that moment the door burst open and Horst Welsh stood on the threshold. Da'ud, who had just thrown his body on hers, jumped back at the sound. "You want a turn, too?" he mumbled.

The German shook his head in refusal. Only a few minutes before he had been awakened from a deep sleep by the young men's laughter. Before deciding to intervene, he had reached the villa by telephone and alerted Mussa el-Dalil.

"Then what to you want?" Da'ud said, as his pants fell in a heap around his ankles and his erection slowly collapsed.

"Get out of here," Horst said quietly.

Sa'id laughed derisively. "Lousy Kraut . . . son of a German whore and an American nigger."

The insult had no effect on Welsh, but their behavior enraged and disgusted him. He watched the three men for several seconds, a scornful expression on his face, and then removed the large bath towel that was draped over his shoulder and arm. They saw the Kalatchnikov in his hands, and were aware from his firm grip on the trigger that he knew how to use it.

"Get out!" he ordered in a quiet but menacing voice.

"You are a fool, Horst," Da'ud said, pulling up his pants and buckling his belt. "Everything has its price . . ."

"You are absolutely right." The voice of Mussa el-Dalil filled the room as he advanced toward Da'ud el-Za'id. "You are absolutely right. Everything has its price."

Sa'id and Adel had released Margaret. She sat up, her arms aching from their powerful grip. She was surprised to find herself neither angry nor vindictive; she was devoid of any feelings at all.

"I am terribly sorry," Mussa el-Dalil mumbled in embarrassment, his eyes averted from her nakedness. He turned and followed his men out of the room. Horst Welsh closed the door behind them and went to the window where he stayed until he saw them get into Mussa el-Dalil's car and drive away. Then he turned to Margaret. She had neither moved nor spoken. Her breathing was returning to normal, but all the color had been drained from her face, and beads of perspiration covered her body. She suddenly fell back on the bed in exhaustion, overcome by a great lassitude.

"I'm sure you want to be alone, Margaret," Horst said in a low, understanding voice. "You have nothing to fear. I'm in the next room."

Too weak to talk, she could only express her gratitude with her eyes as Horst left, closing the door quietly as if exiting from a sick room.

Margaret went into the bathroom and, as she turned on the tap to bathe her face with cold water, she found that her hands were surprisingly steady. She removed the tattered remains of her nightgown and, turning on the shower, soaped her body over and over again, scrubbing the skin ferociously. When she had finished, she was about to dress when she suddenly began to shiver. The uncontrollable tremors started in her fingers and passed through her entire body, as if she were in the throes of a high fever.

Mussa el-Dalil was fanatically scrupulous about the integrity and virtue of his fighting men. An observant Moslem himself, he regarded the war against Israel as a holy war, the Palestinian fighter as a dedicated and highly moral man.

Da'ud el-Za'id had violated one of the sacred commandments of the Moslem religion, the holy obligation to offer hospitality to guests. But it was not solely for this reason that el-Dalil determined to punish him at once; he wanted to make an example of him to show the others that even the commander's deputy could not transgress with impunity. He now had to decide how he would punish this young man of whom he had grown so fond. In his own youth, men guilty of rape were castrated—a harsh punishment that was a deterrent, since the castrate served as a living warning to other men.

Da'ud el-Za'id had been incarcerated in the basement of the villa, awaiting the decision of his commander. On the top floor, the Czech Zoska, who had been watching the bustle of activity, emerged from his room and learned what had happened from Mussa el-Dalil.

"He must be punished severely," the Palestinian stressed. "I am obliged to humble him in order to maintain discipline among the other men. He is a superb combat soldier. He knew that he was also to serve as an example to the others."

"When will he be punished?"

Mussa el-Dalil glanced at his watch. "Very shortly."

When, fifteen minutes later, they descended to the basement to bring up Da'ud el-Za'id, not one of the six men, whom he knew as close friends, told him what lay in store. In total silence, they took him outside the villa where two large Mercedes waited and seated him between two guards in the back seat of the first car. An additional two guards sat up front. Not a word was exchanged. The remaining men got into Mussa el-Dalil's car, and the two automobiles pulled away from the villa and started up the palm-lined boulevard.

Da'ud recalled el-Dalil's words after the incident in Margaret's room.

"How do you explain your action, el-Za'id?"

"It was only a joke." He smiled. "It wasn't serious . . ."

"Not serious?" El-Dalil's eyebrows rose in surprise.

"No," el-Za'id repeated. "The Englishwoman is a whore . . . I've screwed her a few times."

"Is that all you have to say?" Mussa el-Dalil's eyes flashed with anger. "And the others, what were they doing there?"

"The Englishwoman invited them." Da'ud laughed. "She wanted variety . . . you know those European whores . . . they're very liberated. They have sophisticated tastes."

The commander's expression was grim. "You'll remember that laugh," he said coldly. "You'll remember it for a long time."

Now, sitting in the car, Da'ud suddenly began to tremble. His teeth chattered so loudly that he had to clench his jaws to suppress the sound. Overhead, heavy rain clouds moved across the lowering sky and pale moonlight intermittently broke through the shifting cloud banks and was extinguished. Da'ud felt a heavy weight on his chest. It pressed on his rib cage, choking off the air. He gasped for breath. It was the beginning of fear: a creeping, paralyzing dread that fanned out over his body. He stifled the desire to scream, to make them stop the car so he could crouch down at the side of the road and vomit.

Finally the cars pulled up at a deserted beach. He was

shoved out onto the sand; struggling to regain his balance, he was vaguely aware of the quiet ripple of the sea. The night seemed airless and the cloud masses hung suspended in the sky, precursors to a storm.

The heavy wooden poles that in summer supported colorful food and drink stands now stood bare and forlorn in the sand, their counters removed for protection against the severe winter weather. They dragged him toward one of the poles that rose about a yard and a half from its cement base. He thought they were going to tie him to it and lash him, and he looked in panic at the silent men to see which one was carrying a whip, but no one was. They taped his mouth with adhesive, shutting off any plea he might have made for mercy.

His heart pounded wildly. He had the sense of fleeing, of running madly to save his life, but his body had been tied to the post. He was immobilized.

The men from the second car now approached, Mussa el-Dalil in the lead. He stopped a few paces in front of Da'ud.

"You enjoy playing sex games," he said quietly. "Tonight we are going to teach you a new one."

Da'ud wanted to speak, to scream out; he looked at el-Dalil imploringly, but the commander moved aside and the others closed in. They girdled his hips with a leather belt on which a grenade was hung at precisely the height of his genitals. They tied a cord carefully around the pin of the grenade and then began to move toward the sea, lengthening the cord as they went. At that moment, the clouds parted and illuminated the scene on the beach with a faint bluish light. El-Za'id watched in horror as the man unwinding the cord reached a small boat resting half on shore and half in the calm waters of the bay.

"You and I are playing this game," said Mussa el-Dalil. "In another three hours the tide will come in. The boat will then be set afloat and dragged into the water, thus tightening the rope. You will never remember your last sex game."

Mussa el-Dalil turned and left, followed by his men. Da'ud wanted to beg them to stay; he couldn't bear the waiting all alone.

It felt now as if hordes of stinging ants were crawling over his body, their bites small but sharp. Da'ud wanted to scream. He was unable to shake them off. They seemed to multiply as they reconnoitered his body, until they completely covered him. Suddenly, he began to laugh—a low, hollow laugh that rattled and reverberated through his mind—as he realized that there were no ants, that they were the figments of his feverish imagination. He felt himself slipping toward the abyss, losing his grip on reality. Those bastards were going to blow off his balls . . .

The wind rose up and dense clouds danced overhead. He must have lost consciousness, for he had a sense of his mind going dead. When he opened his eyes, he was bathed in perspiration. He felt a pleasant warmth between his legs as his urine trickled uncontrolled.

Allah the all-powerful sits in the heavens and does nothing. By lifting a finger, Allah could halt time and stop the tides. Allah could extend a hand and free him. But Allah did nothing. No miracle occurred. Perhaps later Allah would feel remorse and weep, and his tears would filter through the clouds and flood the earth. Then people would say: Look, the winter rains have come.

His eyes were riveted on the coil of rope: a magnificent serpent was slowly uncoiling from around him. He sensed the tide was coming in. He heard the waves lapping at the sides of the boat, climbing higher, growing louder. As the boat rocked, it tugged lightly at the metal ring attached to the pin of the grenade. He began to shriek but the tape muffled his screams. No one was there to hear him, yet he felt that if he stopped screaming he would die—instantly, inevitably.

It took a long time for the cord to grow taut as the boat listed in the rising waters of the bay. Now Da'ud rejoiced at the darkness; he would not be able to see the boat moving out from the shore, slowly tightening and pulling the cord, finally jerking out the pin and detonating the grenade.

He felt the slight movement of the grenade over his genitals. He did not know whether he was crying or whether the rains had begun and Allah's tears were streaming down his cheeks. Allah is weeping, he thought, because he cannot help me.

When the ring was pulled and the pin released, he thought he heard himself scream again. In the confusion of his mind, a thunderous explosion resounded as he felt a heavy fog envelop his body. All were figments of his deranged imagination; the grenade remained intact.

Early the next morning, before sunrise, Mussa el-Dalil and his men returned in the driving rain to free him. His head lolled, his eyes wide open, the pupils rolling from side to side. His hair had turned white.

As they pulled the tape from his lips he stared vacantly at Mussa el-Dalil and whispered: "Allah—I knew we would meet. Allah the merciful . . ." And Da'ud el-Za'id began to laugh and weep.

Drops of rain as large and heavy as hailstones pounded against the panes of the tall window on the second floor of the villa. Outside, the gray sky hung over the city.

Vladimir Zoska walked from his room to the one next door where Da'ud el-Za'id reclined on a sofa, his face expressionless. The Czech brought a chair over to the bed, sat down, and began gently stroking Da'ud's shoulder. The white-haired youth looked up. His face was a mask of death.

"I know what you've been through," Vladimir Zoska said quietly.

Da'ud did not respond, but his eyes suddenly gleamed with life. He had regained his sanity, although the terrible, crushing fatigue persisted.

"You are a very able man. You made a mistake and paid a heavy price for it." Zoska spoke slowly, weighing each word carefully. "But Mussa el-Dalil made a bigger mistake than you did."

A tremor passed along Da'ud's shoulders. The simmering wrath boiled up from within, melting and reforging the frozen mask of his face with an expression of insane ire. He still said nothing, but now he looked at the Czech and listened.

"We need men like you. You have a future." Zoska spoke softly, choosing his words carefully. "You have only to learn self-restraint. If you learn that, then the future is yours. In every respect. Do you understand me?"

Da'ud el-Za'id wanted to answer but his throat was too dry. He blinked his eyes to indicate that he had grasped the Czech's meaning. Vladimir Zoska again patted his shoulder amicably. He was convinced that he would be able to establish rapport with Da'ud and that the youth could be developed into an important channel of information.

Zoska was close to his goal. Anton Karlov would be pleased to learn that the prospects of having an informant working within Mussa el-Dalil's organization had improved considerably.

15

Early monday morning, December 17, the Air France "Airbus" approached Moscow, bringing Jil, who would soon resume the identity of Yan Borodov, back home.

Homeland. What a strange concept. The old man had raised him to recognize only one homeland, that of the soul of the man of faith. The old man's homeland was the kingdom of heaven, the seat of God.

"Do we love Russia?" the seven-year-old child asked once and his grandfather had laughed, ever tolerant of the child's questions, always good-natured and patient with him.

"No," he had replied, "we do not love Russia."

"Then why are we here?"

Daidushka had sighed and said: "Putchimu, maybe we are here because many years ago our forefathers did things that were not good in the eyes of the Creator of the Universe. And so He became angry and rose up and uprooted our forefathers from their homeland and scattered them over the world, dispersed them among all the nations of the earth. Do you understand?"

During conversations like this, the old man would quote from the Prophets. From Isaiah and Amos. He would review their bitter prophesies and the boy's heart would pound with fear, as if the words predicting a holocaust for his people had been uttered that very day, and not two thousand years before.

"If they let us leave here, would we leave?"

"I don't know," the old man admitted. "If the Rebbe permitted us."

"If so, where would we go?"

"To wherever the Rebbe says."

The old man had often discussed the concept of faith with his grandson. From his point of view, faith was the allegiance of a human being to his God. This was the ultimate level of faithfulness. Just below was the Hasid's unlimited trust in the Rebbe; the Rebbe was the leader. One could take no important step in life without first receiving the Rebbe's blessing. The Rebbe could stand before the Creator; he could plead with the Almighty on behalf of each member of the congregation.

Often when they finished talking, his grandfather would lean over, kiss him on the forehead, and say, "Always remember, silence is the fence guarding wisdom."

They were bound together in a covenant of silence. This world was theirs, and it was a world that other people must not know about. They studied during minutes and hours stolen from the routine of the circus, a strange world indeed in which to nurture and educate a child as a Jew. They studied in secret, away from the prying eyes and inquisitive ears of other members of the circus. Time and again the old man would warn him that their lives depended on keeping silent. Only years later did Jil realize that, even then, his grandfather's hands had been molding him, forming and shaping him into a man and a Jew.

Every lesson was a complete, self-contained experience. The boy grew up with a vivid concept of the covenant between himself and God, well aware that it was a relationship he might not share with any other member of the large circus family. Only Daidushka and Babushka Zina knew about this secret bond between himself and God.

The circus traveled great distances, over the endless expanse of Russia. Jil remembered railroad tracks winding off into infinity, broken only by customs and immigration checkpoints as they crossed the border into Bulgaria, Czechoslovakia, Yugoslavia, Rumania, East Germany.

During these trips he learned not only from his grandfather but from the other circus performers as well. His desire for knowledge was insatiable. He tried everything, sometimes failing, but always striving.

As his thirteenth birthday approached, he prepared to celebrate his bar mitzvah clandestinely.

"From now on," said his grandfather, "you carry responsibility. You are a grown man."

According to the Jewish religion, a boy was considered an adult when he turned thirteen; every morning thereafter he was obliged to fix the phylacteries to his arm and above his forehead for the morning prayer. But even Daidushka did not do this, nor did they own a set of phylacteries. They did, however, cover their heads each morning and silently recite the prayers, facing toward the east.

One day while the circus was in Zagreb, the old man and his grandson went out for a walk so that they could speak freely.

"Daidushka, what is the difference between our Hasidic sect and other Hasidim?"

"The others are a closed circle. They are not accessible to outsiders. We, on the other hand, welcome and accept all who, in their hearts and souls, desire to worship God as we do."

They walked in silence, the old man's arm around his grandson's broad, muscular shoulders. A slight breeze had broken the heat of the day and the sky glowed with banners of yellow and red light from the setting sun.

"Daidushka." The boy had stopped walking. "How is it that we're so isolated?"

"What do you mean?"

"You, Babushka Zina, and me. The three of us are alone in the circus. We are the only Jews," he said sadly. "I have learned what Judaism is and I still don't know what it means to live like a Jew. I don't know what it is to be a Hasid. I only know your stories."

"One day you will be among Jews and among Hasidim," the old man said slowly. "Then you'll see the difference between us and the others."

"What are the differences?"

"Perhaps in the way we try to get close to God. The others worship God in their way, we in ours. We wish our souls to be perfect, to be complete, like the soul God put in the body of Adam."

The boy seemed disturbed. Finally, he asked: "The Rebbe—is he a perfect man?"

"So it is said. He is a Tzadik."

Even then Jil understood the concept of a Tzadik: a man who has been specially favored by the Almighty; a man who knows the secret of maintaining perfect harmony between body and soul.

They fell silent as they approached the circus. It was growing dark and people were streaming in from every direction. A long queue had already formed at the ticket office as they entered their car. The old man removed his jacket and shirt, and setting out his makeup, he signaled to Zina to keep watch outside while he and his grandson engaged in a conversation not meant for the ears of strangers.

"Daidushka . . ." The boy stood watching his grandfather as he spread a few drops of oil on his face.

"I'm listening," said the old man.

"My mother and father—were they good people?"

"They were."

"Yet the Nazis killed them. Why? Where was God then?"

The question was a difficult one for the old man. On very rare occasions, the boy asked about his father and his mother, the old man's daughter, Rachel.

"It is not for us to judge the actions of He who sits in the Heavens," he said in a hoarse whisper.

"You don't judge God because you believe in Him, right?"

The pointed question flustered the old man. He turned around and placed his hand on the youth's shoulder.

"Yes. Because I believe in Him."

"Then I am not sure that I want to believe in Him."

"Why not?"

"Because I want to judge Him."

It was his first act of rebellion against the old man.

"Those are the words of heresy." His grandfather's voice was all but inaudible. "It is forbidden to lose faith in God . . . remember the story of Job . . ."

The boy fell silent, but it was a moody, rebellious silence, and from that moment on, he began to pay more attention to

143

the outer life of the circus than to the inner world that the old man had wanted to share with his daughter's son.

To the outside world, his grandfather was the great clown, the beloved Boris Borodov—so ludicrous, so absurdly human and vulnerable that he drew great thundering bellows of laughter from exalted party officials and lowly peasants alike. But Borodov was more than just a clown. He was a master of mime, and it was from his grandfather that Jil learned the art of pantomime, how the movement of the body could create an entire world.

Jil noticed that during their tours the old man would often absent himself for hours at a time. He found this surprising because he knew that outside the world of the circus, Boris had only one friend—Sergei Padayev—who visited them regularly in Moscow. After these absences, the old man would closet himself with Babushka Zina, and the two would talk privately. He came to realize that there were aspects of the old man's life about which he knew nothing.

One day when the boy was sixteen and practicing on the trapeze, he lost his grip and fell to the ground. Fortunately, he had not been on the high wire, and so was not badly hurt. During the period that he lay in bed recuperating from his fall, he and Boris Borodov had many long conversations, and it was then that his grandfather told him about his part in the Soviet Circus during the Second World War. He told him too about his family, which included several rabbis, all of whom had been destroyed by the Nazis.

"Your father, Shimon-Haim Levinson, was a student of the Torah and the Talmud. He was only nineteen when he married my Rachel. During the early years I supported them so that your father could continue his studies in the Yeshiva. Your mother helped me in my work among the Hasidim; I was an emissary of the Rebbe, carrying out missions for the Tzadik in Russia and Eastern Europe."

"Emissary? What does that mean?"

"The emissary is one who bears the word of the Rebbe," the old man explained patiently. "The Rebbe cannot be everywhere, but since congregations of his Hasidim are spread throughout the world, he needs representatives—emissaries—to carry his word to them, to all Jews, wherever they may be. There were many emissaries in our family. It became a family tradition, serving as the Rebbe's emissary. In Russia the emissaries were particularly important."

"Why?"

"Because in this country it is forbidden to worship God. The Rebbe was forced to flee Russia and go to Warsaw. Before leaving, however, he sent emissaries to the various communities to save lives and souls—to see that every community had an institution of learning and that the Torah was being studied."

"Then you and your family might have escaped if the Rebbe hadn't ordered you to remain as his emissary in Russia?"

"Possibly."

The silence that followed his answer was oppressive.

"If you had not been an emissary," the boy said slowly, "then perhaps my father and mother would still be alive."

"I do not know." The boy's questions were torture for the old man. "Your father was also an emissary of the Rebbe and therefore remained to carry out his own mission."

"You paid a terrible price for your obedience to the Rebbe."

The skepticism that his grandson had voiced had more than once in the past given Boris Borodov pause, and he had had to summon all his faith in God to accept the terrible anguish to which he had been condemned.

"Yes, we paid a heavy price," the old man concurred. "I lost a whole world . . . a large family . . . parents, brothers, sisters . . . my sons and daughters . . . grandchildren." His breathing was labored. The burden of so many haunting memories weighed heavily on his heart. And now his only remaining grandson had placed an additional burden on his weary soul. The boy questioned, doubted. "Don't forget that for each soul I have lost I may have saved two others as the Rebbe's emissary."

The old man fell silent. Outside, they could hear the roar of the lions and tigers being put through their paces in the ring.

"A man must never lose faith in his God or in his Rebbe," he whispered with finality. His hand covered Jil's as if seeking with his touch to transmit to the boy his own abiding faith. "Remember, even when the devil himself overruns the world, a man can overcome him if he carries within himself a faith in God, a belief that, somewhere, the Almighty exists. As long as one man—only one—retains God in his heart, the devil will be unable to extinguish the creative light that comes from God in Heaven."

The old man talked through the long night, telling the boy how Jews, Christians, and Moslems throughout the Soviet Union had been severely persecuted when the communists seized power. Jews continued to worship and teach the Torah. Even during the most repressive years under Joseph Stalin, the Hasidim had maintained a strong, vital educational underground in communities throughout the country. During the great purges in the mid-1930s, when millions of innocent people were sent to concentration camps in Siberia, and so many thousands died, the Hasidim maintained this educational network through the efforts of the Rebbe's devoted emissaries.

The old man stared blankly into the distance as he told of the terrible Holocaust years of the Second World War, when millions were killed in gas chambers and most of the Jews of Occupied Europe were annihilated. During that period the Rebbe was in New York and, through his emissaries, he tried to help those of his congregation who were left. One by one, the survivors began to appear. They came from the victorious armies; from the forests of the partisans; from hidden caves and bunkers under the shattered houses of the ghettos. They searched for those who remained, and they looked for those who had perished, to record the names of the dead—for the sake of the living.

"I could have lifted you and Babushka Zina out of the ashes of Europe, taken you both from this scorched, burnt-out charnel house," the old man said wearily. "But through a messenger, the Rebbe ordered me to stay and continue my mission; to rebuild the Hasidic community for the survivors; to establish institutions so that those who remained could study the Law. I had to build an educational network—underground—in the name of the Rebbe. The authorities could never be allowed to find out about it. Day after day I was in danger of being exposed and imprisoned. It was like living and dying each day of the week, every month of the year. But by the grace of the Rebbe and the mission I am performing, I am alive today."

As the light of the oncoming day scattered the stars, the

old man drew his watch from his pocket. He opened the lid and again showed his grandson the tiny picture of the Rebbe. This sight of the serene, radiant countenance was engraved on Jil's memory: the wise eyes looking out from under the wide-brimmed hat; the expressive eyebrows nearly meeting over the bridge of a small, straight nose; the great moustache flowing into a black beard which even then showed the first traces of gray.

The old man closed the lid and returned the watch to his pocket.

"One day," he said wearily, "you will live among your own people. Only then will you know all the answers to your questions. The day will come when you will be an emissary in your own right. Perhaps then you will understand the concept of the holy mission. We are the creations of God. But we have the power to influence what God's image will be in our generation. God's image radiates from the soul of man. We must take pains to preserve the purity of our soul so that the divine spirit, too, will retain its purity."

The boy who had fallen from the trapeze recovered from his injury and left his sickbed a man, but Jil had never forgotten how the old man's face looked that morning.

A few years later, when Sergei Padayev plucked him from the circus, the young man learned that his grandfather's only friend headed the Liquidations Section of Department V of the KGB.

Sergei Padayev sat in a quiet corner of the airport cafeteria set aside for senior officials of the regime. A few days before, Boris Borodov had instructed him to gather information on Pavel Ramizor. Although he was given no details, Padayev suspected the old man anticipated a showdown with the head of Department V, and intended to be ready when the time came.

Sergei Padayev looked at his watch. With Jil's arrival in Moscow a new phase would begin. In a few minutes the plane would land, and he would again see the man who was his and Boris Borodov's only hope. Yet Sergei could not overlook his reservations about Jil. The man had one very conspicuous weakness: a lack of genuine commitment. Unlike the old man, he did not possess an absolute faith in God nor in the Rebbe and his congregation of Hasidim.

Even as he thought that, he found himself overcome with a longing to see Jil—or Yan as he thought of him—for he was like a son to him too.

As soon as he entered the terminal building, Jil spotted Sergei Padayev standing near the passport control center. He had not seen Padayev since he had left for Europe as a Resident agent and Jil was shocked when he caught sight of him. Sergei's face was thinner and more elongated, and as he approached him, Jil saw that his skin was withered and sallow. A moment later they were hugging one another affectionately.

"It's good to see you," Jil said.

"Yan, I'm so happy to have you back." Sergei Padayev smiled and took Jil's arm. "Your suitcases will be brought to the hotel."

As they started toward the exit, Jil noticed that Sergei walked slowly, his movements no longer swift or confident. Under Jil's scrutiny, Padayev grimaced and pointed to his chest.

"My heart is acting up on me," he explained. "The clock is not ticking properly . . ."

"Since when?"

"For several years, but the past few months have been very difficult."

Sensing he was obviously reluctant to discuss his health, Jil steered the conversation to other areas.

"How are the old folks?"

"Much the same, Yan. Oh, perhaps a little more stooped." He looked at him affectionately. "Now don't look so worried. We're all of us all right."

Jil wondered why Daidushka and Zina weren't there to greet him, and for the first time, it struck him that he had not been brought back to Moscow because he had requested a release from his duties; he had been brought back for a reason that he as yet knew nothing about.

From his room on the fifth floor of the Intourist Hotel, Jil could see the Museum of the Revolution and Pushkin Square. Fresh snow had fallen and hard, bright shafts of light slashed the frozen streets, making the city gleam with a silvery brilliance. Staring down at the streets below, Jil realized how much he had missed the city of his youth. Padayev had insisted that he stay at the city's most comfortable hotel as long as he was in Moscow. It was not far from Zina's and Boris's apartment on Kalinin Boulevard and was also convenient for Sergei, who would be shuttling him between the new and old offices of Department V.

Padayev congratulated Jil on his successful penetration of the European terrorist organizations and stressed the fact that Pavel Ramizor and the KGB's top men were well aware of Jil's accomplishments.

And then, in an abrupt shift, Sergei Palayev asked, "How many times have you been in the United States?"

"Five."

"How much time did you spend there altogether?"

Jil paused a moment. "Altogether, about a year and seven months."

He wondered what the section head was leading up to.

"Come," said Sergei Padayev, "let's have a drink together."

He studied Jil as the young man took a bottle of Scotch from his valise and partially filled two glasses. He had been one of the Liquidation Section's most effective operators. The cumulative pressures of intelligence work could frazzle one's nerves, but Jil showed no signs of tension. The circus world in which he had grown up, and the influence of his grandfather's unique personality, had endowed him with an inner calm. He never came apart under stress.

Sergei recalled the meeting at which he and Boris came to an agreement regarding young Yan's future: he was to be initiated into the KGB a few months after his twentieth birthday—the year his grandfather planned to retire from the circus. And from that moment, his education, his entire upbringing had been directed toward that day. Boris Borodov had explained to his grandson that he would one day have to join the KGB, for only there could he acquire the experience that would prepare him for his real mission.

Although Padayev had promised the old man that his grandson would be put in to espionage, he had been assigned to the Liquidations Section, and there was nothing Padayev could do to alter that assignment. For a long time, Sergei had avoided telling the old man, afraid of his reaction, and it had been a great relief to him when, on learning the truth, Boris had simply sighed and said that fate had decreed it so. Yan's subsequent transfer out of Liquidations had eased Padayev's conscience, but now yet another shift was in store.

"As you may have guessed, your European chapter is closed," he said.

"I thought as much." Jil shrugged. "And what am I to expect in America?"

Sergei smiled at him. Jil had drawn the right conclusion. "A job awaits you there that we believe you are eminently qualified for."

Jil studied him for a moment before he spoke.

"I'm not going back to Liquidations."

"That is exactly the job that is waiting for you."

So that was it. For reasons unknown, he had been returned to his old job. Again he would be sent on missions of murder, and afterward the frightful nightmares would assail him. He would awaken in strange hotel rooms in the shadowy throes of terror, perspiration oozing from every pore. Suddenly he felt the cold sweat overtaking him. He closed his eyes, trying to shut out the ashen faces of his victims.

"There are others who are at least as good as I am. A whole new generation coming up that is even better."

"That may be so, but you are the one to whom this assignment has been given."

His voice was flat, almost metallic. Jil had never known Sergei Padayev to speak with such finality. There was no appeal, would be no reprieve. And yet Jil had no doubt that the section head, whom he had known since childhood, could sense his distress and had compassion for it.

"Now, Comrade Ramizor is waiting to brief you. He will explain just what you can expect."

"And I'll say to him what I said to you," Jil said defiantly.

"Not this time," Padayev declared sharply. "Not this time. You will accept the assignment and you will inform Ramizor that you intend to carry it out to the best of your ability. You will accept—and later Daidushka will explain to you why."

"What does Daidushka have to do with a liquidation operation?"

Padayev's voice softened. "A great deal. Everything perhaps."

Pavel Ramizor had been in his office in the new KGB building on the outskirts of Moscow since seven o'clock. For several days now, he had been preoccupied with the implementation of the plan to rout out the Jewish network. He was still unwilling to abandon his idea of placing the investigation in Padayev's hands—he needed a man with Sergei's experience—but it would mean he would have to transfer him from the Liquidations Section. At first he had thought he could use the excuse of his poor health, but the last two reports he had received from Dr. Rostovitch were too optimistic to justify the move. The day before, Ramizor had consulted Dr. Goridin, a cardiac specialist, to get another opinion but the results of that consultation had only confused matters, for when Goridin had finished scanning the medical reports, he had announced, "There is no doubt that the man is sick. Very sick. It's angina pectoris."

"But the last reports . . ."

"Yes, I know. They are very confusing. It's unlikely someone with such advanced angina would show any improvement. Quite the reverse, in fact. Frankly, if the doctor were anyone other than Grisha Rostovitch, I would be suspicious, but I know him. He's an excellent—and a fine cardiologist."

No sooner had Goridin left than Ramizor buzzed his secretary and asked her to bring him Grisha Rostovitch's personal file from the archives. He had gone through the file twice, but everything seemed to be in order. Every year of the doctor's life was accounted for. Nonetheless there had to be something he had missed. Experience had taught Ramizor that no fabric was absolutely free of defect.

He had stopped to reexamine the memo, dated September, 1967, that listed the names of the men who had recommended Grisha Rostovitch's recruitment by the KGB. Among the names, one immediately caught Pavel Ramizor's eye: Sergei Padayev, the head of the Liquidations Section.

Not that it necessarily had any special significance. His own name also appeared as a reference in at least ten files like this one. But the discovery of even so fragile a connection as this between Sergei and the doctor was food for thought.

The sound of the buzzer on his desk jarred Pavel Ramizor back to the present. He looked at his watch: a quarter past ten. It must be Sergei and Yan Borodov.

Despite his doubts, Ramizor received Sergei Padayev with an open display of affection, then turned to scrutinize the young man whose credentials he had gone over thoroughly. His faith in Padayev's judgment had been corroborated by the material in Yan Borodov's file.

His glance lingered on the agent's face. Several years had passed since their last meeting. Had Ramizor not known that Yan Borodov was thirty-six, he would have guessed him to be much younger. Perhaps it was his finely delineated features which combined the sensitivity of youth with the steely resilience of manhood.

Ramizor extended his broad, square hand to Jil. "So you are with us again, Yan Borodov." Ramizor's lips were compressed into a thin smile. "You belong to an outstanding family. I knew your grandfather, Boris Borodov," he said, rubbing his palms together. "Ah, what a great clown he was." He paused, then shifted to business now that the token amenities had been dispensed with.

"You are here," he explained, "at Sergei Padayev's recommendation. We had other candidates for the job, but Sergei insisted that you were the best. He also said that you were tired of your work in Europe, and he convinced me that the time had come to bring you back to the Liquidations Section."

Jil's expression revealed nothing.

"You know, we are not in the habit of bringing people back to a field they have left. But this time we have a special reason for doing so." Ramizor's face became downcast. "We are out to expose a traitor, a double agent who has caused untold damage. Because of him, the Americans have been phenomenally successful in engineering the defection of many top KGB agents. We need to expose him, and when we do, we want him dead, Comrade Borodov. Dead!

"We want you to leave for the United States very soon. You are to get established there, build an American identity for yourself. This is the most important mission we have sent you on to date."

Behind Ramizor's cool remarks, Jil realized that the department head was desperate; his position in the KGB was on the line. Unless he was successful within the next few months, he would be held accountable for a succession of setbacks.

The long, exhausting meeting ended a few minutes before one o'clock. Sergei and Jil returned to their car in silence. As they approached the main road leading into the center of

Moscow, Jil suddenly asked Sergei to stop for a minute. He slowed down and pulled off to the side of the road, parking the car carefully so as not to get caught in the snowdrifts that lined the roadside. Jil got out and began to walk in the crisp, cold air. The meeting had left him very perturbed. He couldn't understand what had motivated his friend Sergei to misrepresent facts, even lie, to have him assigned to a mission that involved murder, when Padayev knew all along that Jil was psychologically unable to undertake such a task.

The crunch of dry snow underfoot was calming. Jil filled his lungs with the cool, fresh air, and bent to pick up a handful of snow. It had fallen late in the night and so was still quite soft. He rubbed it over his face and licked it with his tongue, as he'd done as a little boy. For a moment he was filled with the same sense of wonder he had experienced as a child rejoicing in the miracle of falling snow.

He returned to the car and got in but did not close the door. He looked at the trees lining the roadside, etched against the sky by the rare winter sunshine.

"You know, Sergei," he said sadly, "I have the feeling that I will never see this country again."

Three years is a long time in the life of an elderly person. The old clown no longer stood as straight as he had when Jil left for Europe, but even though his shoulders were stooped, he still held his head proudly erect. The white moustache was somewhat thinner, the ends did not curve up as before, but his eyes had the same clarity and sharpness and were, Jil thought, as pure a blue as the spring sky.

Jil and the old man embraced, kissing each other on the cheek, while Zina wept.

"Silly old woman," Boris Borodov said, pretending to scold her. He looked at Jil in helpless confusion.

"Babushka, you look wonderful—but why the tears?"

Wiping her eyes, Zina laughed. "Tears of joy, Yan."

Jil took her trembling hand in his. The white skin, almost transparent, looked like parchment. He bent down and gently kissed the back of her hand, then straightened up and kissed her forehead. He had always treated her gently. She had lost her entire family in the war, and had devoted her life to raising little Yan, the last precious remnant of her brother's family, while her brother fought with the partisans. She had cared for him single-handed until just after the war when she learned that by some miracle her brother had survived.

"Silly boy," she scolded jokingly, as Jil presented her with the gifts he had brought. "Is that what I was waiting for?"

"For that and for this," said Jil, hugging her again.

"Now, Boris," she warned her brother as she turned to leave, "don't take all of his time; leave some for me, too."

"Don't worry," said Jil, smiling. "I'll be here for a while, possibly a few weeks. You'll be wanting to get rid of me."

When the two men were alone, Boris put his hands on Jil's shoulders, those remarkably beautiful hands that Jil had inherited, and studied his grandson's face. He noted the tiny wrinkles at the corners of Jil's large eyes, the crease in his high forehead, partially hidden under the thick lock of auburn curls, which reminded Boris of his daughter Rachel's.

"I see signs of wear, of the passage of time. You are a sad man, Yan—a man without joy in his heart. Your sadness is hard for me to bear."

"You know, Daidushka, I am beginning to pile up years, meaningless years. I am not a youngster anymore. In another few months I'll be thirty-seven, an age when other men are watching their children grow up."

"Sit down, Yan," said the old man, taking his place in the armchair behind the desk, silhouetted against the old circus photographs.

For a long time they reminisced, recalling the circus people with whom they had lived and worked, reliving their successes and failures in the years they had spent together, the old man teaching and the child learning.

The old man had always succeeded in avoiding any confrontation, but this time Jil was determined not to let him off. Painful as this moment of truth might be for both of them, it could no longer be deferred.

"Daidushka," Jil said, leaning his elbows on the table, "how much longer?"

"What do you mean?"

Jil smiled gently. "I love you, old man, but let go of me. Let go."

There was a plaintive undertone in Jil's voice that Boris caught at once. His grandson was openly rebelling, was fighting for the right to be himself, to blot out every trace of all that was precious to the old man.

"I don't want to live with your shadow constantly falling over everything I do," Jil whispered.

"Explain yourself . . ."

"Explain?" His voice was bitter. "Where do I begin? I can tell you that I live in a way that is diametrically opposed to anything you've taught me. I can tell you that I don't want to wait anymore for the mission—whatever that may be. I am tainted, Daidushka. You understand? I am tainted."

The old man was silent.

"I eat pork. I sleep with Gentile women. I steal. I murder." He spoke slowly, pausing deliberately. "I don't live like a Jew and I cannot live like a Jew. My way of life, in which you had a hand, has transformed me into a monster. You lived lies in order to protect the essential falseness of my life. You understand?" He paused wearily, and then continued. "Of course you understand. My lie is so great that I can't even express it to you. I love you, Daidushka. But go your way and let me go mine. I'm a man who has lost his way. I want to find a path that's completely mine. Then maybe I'll be able to rebuild myself and my life. But not in the image of Boris Borodov—as someone who is really me."

Jil fell silent. The bright, almost golden flecks glittered in his dark eyes.

"Have I ever hurt you?" Boris Borodov attempted to still the storm.

"You have always done with me what you thought had to be done with me. You molded me into what I am today—a man without a past, without a present, perhaps even without a future. True, I have memories: wonderful, beautiful memories of the world of the circus. But that is all. I am a storehouse of memories."

"Is that really all, Yan?"

"That is all." The words came quickly now, exploding from within. "I lived a double life from the moment I began to understand. You forced me to live that way because you were performing a mission for the Rebbe."

He knew that the old man shared his spiritual torture and sensed his pain, as if he himself were undergoing it, but he could not stop.

"I've waited years for the moment when I could say what I am saying now," Jil continued. "I know that you wanted to make a man of me, according to your beliefs. And that included faith in God. But you see, I don't believe. I have not yet found a way to God. Perhaps if you would leave me alone, I might find it, but you continue to determine every step of my life. You and Sergei engineered my recruitment by the KGB, and now I feel your long arm again, and again Sergei is in on it with you."

This was the moment the old man had feared, for he had always known that a confrontation with his grandson was inevitable. He began to speak, haltingly at first, but without apology.

"You were educated as your father would have wished, in accordance with the terms of his unwritten will. He might have paid with his life for remaining the Rebbe's emissary, but still, that was his world—the world of the Hasidim—and he would have wanted his son to know that world."

"You did what you wanted with me."

"True," admitted the old man in a voice choked with emotion. "But not in the way that you think. I was carrying out a last will and testament. I acted with the conviction that I was doing the right thing."

"I did not mean to accuse. I wanted to ask . . ."

"No!" The old man shook his head. "You are not asking questions. You are presenting me with charges and I must defend myself. There are many things you may not yet understand. There is always more hidden than revealed. It is true that I molded you—your convictions, your inner life. But I also schemed, together with Sergei, to give you experience, position, status . . ."

"For what purpose?"

"So that you could complete your mission."

Jil laughed bitterly. "The one entrusted to me by the bloodthirsty Pavel Ramizor? Sergei hinted that you were in some way involved with this liquidation assignment."

"Yes, that's true." Boris raised his steely blue eyes to meet Jil's gaze.

He knew the old man so well and yet he never failed to be astonished by him anew. "What's your connection?"

"A very intimate one," Boris responded with a slight smile. "Of course, Pavel doesn't know this . . ."

"He expects me to liquidate the traitor."

"True. But first he must be exposed. You know as well as I that the number of KGB operatives in the United States and

Canada is in the hundreds; any one of them might be a double agent. It's a very difficult enterprise, locating a traitor when there are so many possibilities. And a time-consuming one. It sometimes takes months to smoke out a double agent. Occasionally the search turns up nothing. Do you understand?"

"I'm afraid I don't follow you."

"Take heart, Yan. You must be a little patient with an old man," said Boris, dropping his voice to a faint whisper. "You know almost everything there is to know about me and Sergei. You also know that one day you were to take my place. But things have changed.

"You understand, Yan, in this game of espionage, there is always a traitor someplace, always some kind of leak. With a little daring, a little stirring of the pot, it was possible to leak information to the West through a double agent that we created and fostered in the minds of the KGB directors."

"Sergei assisted you in this?"

"Precisely." The old man tugged at the ends of his snowy white moustache. "We created a figure whose identity could never be uncovered since he didn't exist. We then convinced the leaders of the KGB that the information transmitted by us had apparently been leaked by him."

"And no one here in Moscow could prove otherwise," said Jil, his eyes riveted on Boris Borodov's face.

"No. No one could prove otherwise. We've created dummy agents many times over the years. They served us well."

"So I won't have to carry out Ramizor's orders!"

"You can't kill a man who doesn't exist."

"How well do you know Ramizor?"

"I know his strengths, but I also know his weaknesses, know how to use them to my advantage. He is adamant that this traitor must be found and liquidated. We simply persuaded him that you were the most suitable candidate for the job. But, in fact, *we* are the ones who need you in the United States, for that is where you will carry out your true mission."

He then told Jil all that he knew about the Jewish hit-list operation that Pavel Ramizor had planned. He enumerated the fifteen names, ending with that of Shalom Baruch Abrahamson, their Rebbe.

When Jil heard that name, the pieces finally fell into place.

The KGB had found a way to hurt them. If the old man had been able to ensure the Rebbe's security, he would have done so. But his age had placed limitations on him, and he was therefore sending Jil in his stead.

"Daidushka, I understand everything now . . ." He rose, walked around the desk, and knelt beside the old man's chair.

Boris Borodov placed his hand on Jil's head. "I shall never ask anything else of you. Go on this final mission, and then you are free to find yourself. Go and become a whole man. Do not come back here and do not worry about us."

"You are asking me to abandon you?"

Their glances met. Boris Borodov's clear blue eyes were filled with sorrow and his lips quivered: "I swear to you that we will not be harmed, that we will all be left in peace. I have survived thus far. Trust me to find a way to prevent reprisals against us."

Jil rose and touched the old man's hand. "I'll do what has to be done."

Sergei Padayev had a twofold task: to prepare the way for Jil's exit from the Soviet Union and to smooth his path to the heart of the Hasidic community in Crown Heights. The latter would be difficult; since the older Hasidim treated strangers with suspicion, it ordinarily took a long time before they accepted a newcomer to their community. From Jil's point of view, this could be disastrous. He had to be received immediately and gain all the assistance possible. Sergei now had to get word to the Kantor brothers, Volodia in Paris, and Yudke, the cabinetmaker, in Crown Heights, and enlist their aid. He spent the better part of the afternoon arranging for this, and by the time he returned to KGB headquarters at five o'clock in the evening, it was pitch dark.

He found Pavel Ramizor waiting for him. The department head greeted him with an amiable smile and began to ask questions about Yan Borodov's reacclimatization to his homeland.

"Patience," Sergei chuckled. "He has been here less than twenty-four hours."

"One can often tell right away. What is your impression?"

"He's somewhat confused."

"That's natural. How was the reunion between him and Boris Borodov?"

"I don't know." Sergei shrugged. "I just dropped him off. I didn't stay."

"Very wise," commented Pavel Ramizor. "I know how close they are. When does Yan begin his training?"

"In the morning. It's the usual training program. Drills and examinations for ten days. A test of fitness. A test of emotional stability. The standard medical exam."

"You've spoken with Dr. Rostovitch?"

"Yes. He'll start the medical tests tomorrow."

"An excellent doctor." Pavel Ramizor's eyes were fixed on Padayev's face. "He has treated you for a long time. Isn't that so?"

"For many years."

"How many?"

"Let's see." To an observer, Sergei Padayev was merely calculating the number of years he had known Grisha Rostovitch, but in actuality, his mind was racing to determine the significance of Ramizor's question, for the conversation had turned from a trivial discussion into an inquiry. Sergei Padayev read Pavel Ramizor well enough to know that he had to be careful. The man sitting opposite him was exceptionally sharp. His small, beady eyes sparkled almost mockingly, and Sergei knew the meaning of that gleam. Pavel Ramizor was zeroing in on something.

"I believe about fifteen, perhaps sixteen years," Sergei responded. "I met him when he was a young doctor . . ."

"I am certain that Yan Borodov does not have any medical problems." Pavel Ramizor changed the subject in a totally natural way, as if the present thought had simply sprung from the previous one. He smiled pleasantly.

"I have no doubt that his health is excellent. He is still a young man."

"Who will his dispatcher be this time?" Ramizor referred to the man in KGB headquarters who maintained contact with a Resident for the duration of his mission. The dispatcher was the agency's liaison, the man who transmitted orders and provided whatever assistance the Resident required.

"I haven't decided yet," Sergei said. "I thought you would want me to take charge of this personally, since this is such an important assignment."

"Thank you, Sergei." Pavel Ramizor regarded him with

satisfaction. "I didn't want to suggest it, but that is indeed what I'd like."

A few minutes later, Sergei entered the archives of the Department of Manpower. He looked for and found the veteran employee who was permanently in charge of the night shift. She was an old acquaintance of his and permitted him to look through the sign-out index.

As he had suspected, Grisha Rostovitch's personal file had been taken from the archives; it had been signed out to Pavel Ramizor. Perhaps it was of no significance, but Sergei decided to report this incident to Boris at once. Until now, the old man had always managed to keep a few steps ahead of Ramizor.

17

ON FRIDAY, DECEMBER 28, four days before the advent of the year 1980, the door of Yudke Kantor's carpentry shop in Crown Heights swung open and the Rebbe's secretary entered, his face beaming.

"Yudke," he announced as he opened his attaché case and drew out a large envelope, "I have a letter for you from your brother Volodia."

Although he recognized Volodia's elegant script, Yudke hesitated.

"Is there good news in this letter?" he asked slowly.

"Wonderful news, Reb Yudke. News that you have awaited for years."

"Open the letter, please." Yudke's hands began to shake and to hide this, he thrust them quickly into his pockets. "Please . . . read it to me . . ."

Glancing affectionately at the carpenter, the secretary opened the envelope and began to read the short letter.

My dear brother Yudke:
May this letter find you and your family in good health. In the name of the Grand Emissary, I inform you that

161

the tenth part of the holy chair will reach you very soon. And, as a sign that the message is authentic, I was told it is the right front leg. I have been instructed to ask that you receive the messenger with the greatest warmth, for he is truly a brother to us all. May you prosper in all your undertakings, and some day, when the chair of the Tzadikim is standing in its proper place, with God's help I shall come and be among the celebrants.

Your brother, Volodia Ben Meir Kantor

When Yudke made no move to take the letter, the secretary laid it down on the carpenter's bench.

"You have brought me wonderful news," said Yudke, his voice sounding strange to his ears, "news I had despaired of ever receiving."

Later, as he gave thanks to God, Yudke recalled that day in 1939 when he had been called upon to break the chair into ten separate parts. It was the first of September, the day the German Air Force had launched its attack on Warsaw. The Rebbe, persecuted in the Soviet Union for promulgating Jewish law and religion, had fled to Poland, and shortly before the outbreak of the war he had left Poland for the United States. He had been forced to leave behind the holy chair, which had been passed down through generations of the Hasidic dynasty.

Foreseeing the Holocaust, the Rebbe had ordered nine disciples to remain behind in Warsaw with instructions to try to save the members of the Hasidic congregations. But the German forces swept through Poland so swiftly that the disciples had been forced to separate, each departing for a different country. Since they were unwilling to abandon the holy chair, they suggested that it be split into nine parts so that each man could take one part with him. They would meet when the war was over in Crown Heights and reassemble the chair. They called in Yudke the cabinetmaker to dismantle it. He agreed, but only on condition that the chair be divided into ten parts so that he himself could partake in the mitzvah—the sacred deed—and take one part with him.

He worked slowly, painstakingly, and finally the four legs, two arms, the red-velvet cushion, the upholstered cushion's wooden frame, and the two halves of the back lay next to Yudke's toolbox. Each part was then wrapped in a piece of soft velvet and placed in a coarse brown sack so that it would attract no attention. The ten Hasidim then dispersed, each going his separate way, bearing a part of the chair.

Hordes of people, Poles as well as Jews, were fleeing the country. Yudke Kantor took to the road with his wife and three sons. In an effort to keep his family alive, he cut off his earlocks and shaved his beard, for all along the way peasants lay in ambush, waiting to attack Jews and rob them. Most of their meager possessions were lost in the course of their travels, but he guarded the arm of the Rebbe's chair with his life.

Yudke reached Finland with his family, and at the end of the war they were transferred to a Jewish refugee camp in Occupied Germany and, in the spring of the following year, were permitted to join the Hasidic congregation in Crown Heights. The small sack came with him and, on his arrival in Brooklyn, he found three of the disciples already there with three other parts of the chair. Yudke had kept the two arms, a leg, and one half of the backrest in his shop, and over the years other parts had arrived, until he had gathered nine parts in all. Only the last part—a leg—was missing, and now that too was on its way to him.

He drew his hands from his pockets and studied the calloused fingers, as if trying to decide whether they would be capable of this ultimate act of restoration.

That Sabbath eve, in the synagogue, Yudke recited his prayers with great fervor, and later, at the dinner table, with his large family seated around him listening in wonderment, he chanted the Sabbath songs with unusual joy.

At night, as he lay in bed, Yudke wondered if the man who would deliver the long-awaited part would be the missing disciple, Rabbi Shmuel ben Menachen Gillerman. And for the first time in many years, the carpenter fell into a deep sleep that brought peace and refreshment to his soul as well as his body.

18

NEW YEAR'S EVE at François Ripoll's villa in St. Tropez was to be celebrated with the premiere of Margaret Aston's film *Sacred Homeland*. Very few of the invitees, even those who were not Palestinian sympathizers, had declined Ripoll's invitation since the lawyer had a reputation as a lavish host.

On his way to the Riviera from Paris, Ripoll stopped off in Monaco where he kept one of his many bank accounts. There were others in Zurich, Paris, London, Cologne, and New York. By four that afternoon, he was being driven along the Riviera by his chauffeur Claude. A farmer's son, Claude had been Ripoll's childhood friend. On those rare occasions when the inequities of their situations touched him, the lawyer would quickly assuage his conscience by saying, *"C'est la vie. Some people are meant to rise to the top and others to stay at the bottom."*

They reached the St. Tropez villa as darkness fell. Clusters of clouds moved across the sky like billowing sails, and Claude remarked that he thought the good weather would hold for the next few days, so that they might go fishing the next morning.

Ripoll's four-year-old son Marcel was waiting impatiently,

although it was not evident in his manner as he walked toward his father with short, measured footsteps, his small, delicate hand extended before him.

"Good evening, Papa." The child seemed like an adult in miniature, and as François kissed him on both cheeks he saw in the child's features the face of the slim, attractive woman he had married. The boy's manners were a product of his mother's petit-bourgeois notions. At times François felt an urge to shout "*Merde!*" but the impulse to confront his wife on anything was always short-lived.

"How are you, Marcel?"

"Fine, Papa, thank you." The boy regarded the suitcase avidly, obviously eager to s e what gifts Papa had brought him from the city.

François laughed. In spite of everything, Marcel was a normal child. As he was unpacking the gifts, Ripoll heard Charlotte's labored breathing.

"*Mon Dieu*," he thought gloomily as he watched her emerge from the library. There seemed to be no limit to her obesity. Fortunately, she at least had the good sense to attempt to conceal her girth under a white caftan. The expensive diamond pendant François had brought her from Brussels three years before hung around her neck. Her smile, which she now flashed at François, was all that remained of her former beauty.

"I'm glad to see you, darling."

She approached him with the small, mincing steps of the very fat, her feet barely able to carry her immense weight. He gave her a perfunctory kiss on the cheek, the minimal show of affection for the benefit of the watching servants and their son.

They sat down to dinner at a beautifully carved eighteenth-century table under a magnificent crystal chandelier that had been purchased at auction by Charlotte from the estate of a prominent aristocratic family. Had their title been up for sale, Charlotte would gladly had bought that too.

But no sooner had they settled down than Ripoll was called to the phone. It was Kurt Sherman, his broker in Cologne.

"Excuse me, *chérie*," he said to Charlotte as he pushed back his chair and rose.

She smiled pleasantly but said nothing until she saw he was

gone. Then, with a contented sigh, she pulled the large silver tray of hors d'oeuvres toward her and began to heap her plate.

Picking up the phone in the library, Ripoll sank slowly down into a chair as he listened to Sherman's news.

"Monsieur Ripoll, there were some investigators here yesterday, inquiring about the source of certain investments," he began.

"Income tax?"

"No . . . police."

"Go on." Ripoll's mouth went dry.

"Two of them just appeared in the morning. One was an American. They had information—so they said—that monies obtained in armed robberies had been invested through my company in legitimate businesses."

"What did you say to them?"

"Of course I denied it! I told Herr Kruger and Mansfield—"

"What was the man's name?"

"Kruger."

"The other one!"

"The American? Mansfield . . . Why do you ask?"

"Doesn't it seem strange to you that an American is involved in an investigation like this?"

"Well, yes, I did ask Herr Kruger about that. He said they suspected a portion of the money had been transferred to the United States."

"What happened then?"

"That's all, Monsieur Ripoll." There was a brief pause. "As a friend, I just thought you should know about the visit."

"I appreciate your concern." Ripoll had regained control of his voice, but the blood that had rushed to his head had left his cheeks aflame. "I'm sure it's a misunderstanding, but it was good of you to call."

Ripoll dropped the receiver as if it were a hot coal. Only then did he realize he was bathed in perspiration. He pulled out a handkerchief and dried his face. His heart was pounding, and he found it difficult to breathe.

"That son of a bitch Mansfield!" he growled.

Although Mansfield had made no bones about the fact that he would continue to pursue him, Ripoll had not anticipated that the American would so quickly have uncovered the money he had invested with Kurt Sherman—money transmitted to him by Klaus Schmidt in Hamburg from the Baader-Meinhof gang's holdups and robberies. Ripoll's cut of their take was fifteen percent.

Now Ripoll had to deal with the German, Klaus Schmidt. He knew he should notify him of his conversation with Kurt Sherman, but he was afraid of how the meticulous, secretive, and vengeful Schmidt would react. He would, of course, do some checking, in the course of which he would discover that some of the money he had transferred to Ripoll had never reached its proper destination; Ripoll had siphoned off a bit more than his share. Schmidt was a dangerous man. He could react savagely. On second thought, Ripoll decided not to report his conversation with Kurt Sherman just yet.

Margaret Aston's arrival late Monday afternoon marked the beginning of the festivities at the St. Tropez villa. François Ripoll studied her face discreetly as they sat, drinks in hand, on the terrace of the house, watching the sunset. She was as beautiful as ever, but he detected a restlessness he had never noticed before.

"You are satisfied with the film?" he asked.

"I believe it says what I wanted to say."

Averting her face from him, she ran her long, slender fingers along the edge of her glass. Margaret did not want the lawyer to get wind of her growing doubts, her general confusion. He knew nothing of the incident in Cyprus nor the extent to which it had caused her to reexamine her support of the Palestinian cause, although periodically she took herself to task for allowing a bitter personal experience to so affect her up-to-now unshakable intellectual convictions.

"I'm very tired, François," she said suddenly. The sky was now turning dark; only a narrow ribbon of scarlet hung over the farthest mountain peaks.

Ripoll led her to her room, then walked to the wing he shared with Charlotte. He was relieved to find that his wife was still in the playroom with their son. It meant he could shave, shower, and relax without being stifled by her oppressive presence. As he pulled up the trousers of his well-tailored suit, he noted with satisfaction that he was as trim as he had been as a youth. He studied his image in the mirror and laughed to himself. His social and financial position might have changed, but his face had not: it was still the plain peasant face of the Ripoll tribe.

His guests began to arrive at seven. Arc-lamps illuminated the garden paths that wound through flowerbeds filled with plants chosen for their ability to withstand the briny air that blew in continuously from the sea. Tonight there was a gentle breeze and not the slightest hint of rain. It promised to be an exceptionally lovely winter evening.

Charlotte and François Ripoll greeted their guests at the entrance to the main hall where cocktails were to be served. The hall, which opened on to the formal gardens, was on the upper level of the house. The powerful lights fixed to the building's stone façade illuminated the lawn all the way down to the procession of palm trees on the cliff above the private jetty. Charlotte had managed to wedge her immense body into the semblance of a compact mold by means of a powerful corset. The constriction hampered her respiration but was a small price to pay for the gala. The villa was the scene of such festivities only two or three times a year, and she made the most of her few fleeting moments in the limelight.

By eight-thirty the house was crowded and the champagne flowing. Just as Ripoll, in high spirits from the wine and the company, was launching into a story, Claude caught his eye and he broke off.

"You have visitors."

The lawyer laughed. "Quite right, Claude"—he squeezed the chauffeur's arm affectionately—"the house is full of visitors."

"These are different," said Claude quietly, his face as expressionless as his voice.

Ripoll sobered at once.

"Where are they?"

"In the library . . . I hope I did the right thing."

"That's fine," the lawyer murmured and, excusing himself, he quickly left the room.

The heavy carved oak doors of the library had been locked from the outside; Claude dealt instinctively with unusual situations, and his instincts, François thought, as he opened the door, had been quite sound. These guests *were* different, and most unwelcome: Inspector Louis Etienne, the police detective from Paris, and the American Paul Mansfield were waiting for him in the company of a third man, younger than they, tall and quite handsome.

They had made themselves at home. Louis Etienne sat in the center of the leather couch, his legs stretched out before him and an expression of unconcealed derision on his thin, narrow face. Mansfield was ensconced in Ripoll's armchair behind the desk. The stranger stood at the window overlooking the sea.

Ripoll was suddenly seized with anger over this intrusion on his privacy. "Up to now I have had to deal with only two uncouth individuals," he declared bitterly, closing the doors. "Now it seems another has sprung up. Good evening, gentlemen," he added ironically.

Louis Etienne smiled apologetically. "I'm sorry, Monsieur Ripoll, but we have been waiting for your answer . . ."

"I was under no obligation to reply, and certainly I am not obliged to receive you here," he retorted sharply. "You may have noticed that I am engaged this evening. May I request that you defer your questions until the holiday is over? I suggest we meet in Paris next year, gentlemen," he added contemptuously.

Inspector Etienne's smile faded and he sighed.

"There is no need for belligerence, Monsieur Ripoll. We have come all the way to St. Tropez simply because Mr. Mansfield has a few things to tell you that may make it easier for you to reach a decision."

Ripoll turned from them and strode toward the door.

"Unless you show me a legally signed warrant," he said, his hand resting on the doorknob, "I shall call the head of the St. Tropez police department."

Louis Etienne nodded sadly, then drew a long envelope from his coat pocket and placed it on the desk.

"I'm sorry you have forced me to do this," he said. "As you can see, the warrant is duly signed. I realize, of course, that there's nothing to prevent you from manipulating some influential people in order to clip my wings one day, but nonetheless here it is."

The lawyer's hand slid from the doorknob and he gazed at Louis Etienne with undisguised hostility. The situation was worse than he had thought. Only the highest authority would have approved an order giving the police legal entry into his home, forcing him to submit to an interrogation and perhaps even a search. As he picked up the envelope and read its contents, he began to sweat.

"Yes." His voice was inflectionless. "Now I understand."

"I am not so sure," commented Paul Mansfield truculently.

Ripoll gazed at the American's grim face. Apparently they were not going to let him off easily this time either, but in less than a half hour he was to host the premiere of Margaret Aston's film, not that these rude, mulish men could be prodded into concluding their business quickly.

"Let me clarify a few things for you," the American went on. "First of all, I am certain that the telephone call from the investment company in Cologne will not be the last of its kind—"

"Don't threaten me!" François Ripoll interjected.

Paul Mansfield took a deep breath. His quarry was obviously frightened.

"And don't you interrupt me," he advised. "I know exactly who you are behind that honest, upstanding lawyer front. You are just a blood-sucking parasite who is turning a profit from terrorist insanity." His gesture silenced any protests the lawyer might have made. "We have no time for formalities. Now, if you want us to leave you alone for a while, you are going to have to cooperate."

"Look." Ripoll's voice was cool but his mouth was dry and his chest felt constricted. He was desperate to get rid of his visitors. "I repeat, my involvement with those circles is purely as a representative. I resent the implication that I am involved in any other way . . ."

Mansfield grinned sardonically. "Cut the bullshit, Ripoll. I'm not some judge you can con." He jabbed his finger against the Frenchman's chest. "What interests us is the Trainer. The Clown. The Miracle Worker. The Acrobat. The Fortune Teller." Paul Mansfield drew out each word, his piercing gaze never leaving the lawyer's flushed face. "You promised us an answer and we're still waiting. Talk."

François Ripoll stalled for time to organize his thoughts. It occurred to him that since Jil in all probability would not be returning to Europe, he might be able to tell them just a little about him without placing him in any jeopardy. And the information would keep them occupied and out of his hair.

"We are ready to listen to whatever you have to tell us, Monsieur Ripoll." Etienne was playing the good guy.

"Well," he began, pausing to convey the impression that the information he was about to transmit had been acquired with considerable difficulty, "I made use of a variety of connections." A wave of relief suddenly swept over François Ripoll. He had taken the inevitable step and crossed over an invisible boundary of silence and discretion in order to save his own skin.

"And the result?" Paul Mansfield's tone was harsh.

"I'm afraid that what I learned after our meeting in Paris was not all that much," Ripoll said apologetically. "But it does appear that your conclusions about the espionage ring are well founded. Those circus names are the cover for a group of people who assist terrorists in various spheres—training, occasionally smuggling men from one country to another . . ."

"This is all very general information," Mansfield commented. "You know very well you are not telling us anything new."

"What do you mean?"

"Give me something I can dig my teeth into. Do I make myself clear?"

"I have no details about the group. Nothing precise, at any rate. On the other hand, I do know of one man who is supposedly connected with the group."

"Who is he?"

"A Canadian, apparently of French extraction."

"Are you certain of that?" Mansfield was incredulous.

"Yes, quite sure. I have spoken with him once or twice." The lawyer's tone of sincerity dispelled their doubts and mistrust.

"How do you know he is part of the group?"

"My informants." François Ripoll was careful to speak in generalities in order to make it clear that his own connection was very limited. "They said that he deals mainly in smuggling terrorists from place to place."

"Does he have a name?"

"I know him as Jil."

"Jil what?"

"Just Jil. Apparently short for Gilbert, as we pronounce the name in French. Jil. The clown."

Ripoll's use of the code name had an electrifying effect.

"The Clown," muttered Paul Mansfield.

"Yes," confirmed Ripoll. "He is called that because he is a pantomimist and many of his acts include portrayals of clowns."

"How do you get in touch with him if you need him?"

"I never said that I am in contact with him." The lawyer was quick to protest. "I said I have met him . . . no more than that."

"Sorry," Mansfield said. "Suppose I rephrase the question. How can we reach him? Does he have an address? Is there any way he can be contacted?"

"Not that I know of. He makes the contact—whenever and with whomever he chooses."

"Can you describe him?"

Ripoll poured a glass of cognac. "He's a young man, although it is difficult to determine his actual age. Maybe twenty-five or thirty. Average height. He is extremely handsome, a fact that's difficult to forget."

"What's special about him?"

The lawyer seemed perplexed. "I don't know," he admitted, "but there is something very unusual about him, something strange and unforgettable, but hard to describe."

"Give it a try," said Mansfield, who turned to the silent third man and said, "Take down the details, Miller."

As Ripoll tried to describe Jil's features in detail, Evyatar Miller wrote the description in a notebook so that experts could later reconstruct the face of the mysterious clown.

The interrogation ended shortly thereafter; as Ripoll prepared to return to his guests, Mansfield gave a parting shot.

"Ripoll?"

"Yes?"

You may run into the Clown, right?"

"It is possible."

"We will want to know when that happens."

"I'll try."

"Do more than try," Mansfield declared. "And thanks for your cooperation."

The lawyer pressed a button on his desk and Claude appeared to escort the visitors to their car. François Ripoll watched from the window as the three men descended the broad steps to the brightly lit parking area.

On one hand he felt a sense of relief: in deciding to cooperate with the authorities, even in a limited way, he had acquired insurance against future uncertainties. On the other hand, however, he knew that if Klaus Schmidt got wind of his collaboration with the police, he would be in grave danger. Unless he moved with utmost caution, it could cost him his life.

Voices, rising in a dissonant swell of praise, buzzed unintelligibly in Margaret's ears as people crowded around her. It appeared that the film was a success, although Margaret had watched without seeing, and the moment the fund-raising began for the Palestinian refugees, she slipped away. She was drained.

She went up to her room, put on a warm coat, and then went down to the bar on the first floor. Taking a glass of whiskey with her, she stepped out onto the wide patio overlooking the sea. She stood for a moment, inhaling the fresh, salty air. It was good to have a breather, to stop and think. She had returned from Larnaca a week before in order to complete the film, and for four days had worked on the last phases of editing. Three of these days were spent in solitude, and now she knew she had to return to her desk, to write in earnest. And to do that, she had to shake off every other obligation, above all to terminate her political activities.

Miguel had asked her to translate a book on his work from the Spanish for a British publisher. She was captivated by the idea of spending a few months in the large white house on the rocky cliffs overlooking Toledo. Perhaps this would provide the isolation, the refuge that she needed, and work on the translation would draw her gradually back to her own writing, hopefully to a renaissance of creative energy and a harvest of new stories.

The sudden hush in the large hall behind her was broken an instant later by cries of jubilation. Midnight. The new year. Margaret did not even register the transition from one year to the next, swept up as she was by memories of other times and other places.

On the first day of the new year the intensive manhunt began for the shadowy figure on the fringes of European terrorism code-named the Clown.

At eight o'clock in the morning, Paris was still celebrating the new year when Louis Etienne, Paul Mansfield, and Evyatar Miller arrived at DST headquarters on Sousa Street. They stayed only long enough to dictate the description of the anonymous Clown which they had obtained from François Ripoll. Paul Mansfield then went to the American Embassy, Evyatar Miller to the Israeli Embassy, where each transmitted brief coded accounts of the events of the previous evening and a description of their first concrete achievement.

Five hours later, at two o'clock in the afternoon, Mansfield and Miller were sitting in Louis Etienne's office, their faces still lined with fatigue. The reconstruction experts arrived at the office a few minutes later with their likenesses of the Clown, based on the details Ripoll had supplied. In this technique, developed in the 1950s in the United States, one portrait was prepared using slides of features while the other was sketched by an artist. When the two were compared, there was a very marked similarity.

Louis Etienne thanked the experts and apologized for having to call them in on their day off. Paul Mansfield studied the reconstructions. "Interesting how Ripoll will react to the results," he commented. "Louis, please see to it that he gets a look at both of these soon and approves them."

Evyatar Miller examined the haunting, enigmatic face depicted in both—the high cheekbones, the vaulted brow that accentuated the large eyes—an expression of sadness and irony, and great sensitivity. He found it hard to tear his eyes from this face, as if he had been transfixed by the penetrating gaze of those enormous eyes. An hour later, as he lay stretched out on his bed in the hotel, he found the image of the Clown's face still fixed in his mind.

He got up quickly at the sound of footsteps approaching his door. He waited for the double knock.

"Come in, Paul."

The door swung open and Paul Mansfield barreled in. Draping his coat over the bed, he headed to the small refrigerator and took out a can of beer.

"What happened?" asked Evyatar.

"I heard from Earl Dickson." Paul stretched wearily. "He's arriving in Paris tonight."

"What?"

"Yep! And not only him. Your boss, too. General Negbi."

He drew out his cigar case, opened it, and let out a curse. In his fatigue and preoccupation, he had forgotten to refill it.

"Don't tell me that they're coming because of the sketch of the Clown?"

"Right. And that isn't good."

"I don't understand you! For weeks we chase around, we can't turn up even a crumb of information, and when something finally falls into our hands, you act like the sky has fallen in. You know, sometimes it's hard to understand your moods."

"It's not my moods you don't get, young man." Paul took another sip of beer. "It's the significance of both our bosses coming to Paris with instructions to have hundreds of copies of the Clown's portrait prepared."

"I'd say that showed they're treating what we've uncovered seriously."

"Too seriously."

"You mean to say . . ."

"I mean to say that from our point of view the fun is just beginning." Paul Mansfield contemplated his empty case; he really needed a cigar. "On the basis of their reaction I'd say they apparently have obtained nothing further, which means we are the only ones who have even caught a scent of anything concrete."

If he were right, Evyatar Miller realized, then the other units in Washington and Tel-Aviv had drawn blanks, as had the teams of agents operating throughout Europe and the Middle East, to say nothing of the Mossad's sources in the Soviet Union. It appeared that Department V had managed to create a remarkably thick smokescreen around the preparations for the reprisal operation.

Paul drained his beer, then rose and picked up his coat.

"Well, one thing is certain—I have to grab a little sleep."

He stopped at the door and turned around, the glimmer of a smile on his lips.

"Come what may, Evyatar, let's enjoy the chase. In the end, you and I will capture the Clown."

PART TWO

19

ON THURSDAY, THE third of January, 1980, the training period of KGB operative Yan Borodov was scheduled to conclude. It was to end in the evening, in a sub-basement of the agency's headquarters.

Sergei Padayev had three hours to wait before he could pick Jil up. He had been prevented from seeing him for the last ten days, during which time he had occupied himself with the details of Jil's dispatch to the United States. Although he had no doubts that Jil would pass the tests, his anxiety about Dr. Grisha Rostovitch, whose file had still not been returned to the archives, had increased. Had this merely been a regular review, Pavel Ramizor would have returned the file within a day, but it had been in his office for many days now. Ramizor's interest in Rostovitch was a matter of some concern to both Sergei Padayev and Boris Borodov. It had been a topic of conversation for over a week, until one day the old man had announced, "I think I understand what has aroused Pavel Ramizor's interest. It was a mistake of yours, Sergei."

"Of mine?"

"Yes, I'm afraid so." And then the old man explained that

in going along with Padayev's request for a good medical report, the doctor had left himself open.

"Ramizor is no fool. He knows the nature of your illness—and the severity. Faced with that optimistic report, he can either assume that Grisha Rostovitch is a poor doctor, or, more likely, that for some reason he was doing you a favor."

Padayev said nothing.

"I have no doubt," the old man went on, "that Ramizor made some inquiries about Grisha Rostovitch's medical competence. And, afterwards, he undoubtedly checked to see if there was some connection between you and the doctor."

This had been the second mistake, Padayev thought with a sinking heart.

"I was one of Grisha's references," he admitted.

"So Pavel knows that the association between the two of you goes back many years."

Padayev nodded.

"We must think about what else Ramizor sees when he looks at that file." The old man sat in silence, studying his interlaced fingers. Despite his age, his hands were surprisingly delicate and graceful.

"Undoubtedly he is struck by the record of a man who graduated from medical school with high honors. One could have foreseen a brilliant future for Grisha Rostovitch. And yet he settled for a very unchallenging career. Why?" The old man paused to take a sip of tea. "I think Pavel Ramizor will begin to make inquiries about Grisha. He will want to find the reason that a doctor with Grisha's prospects so suddenly and unexpectedly agreed to such a boringly bureaucratic job. And then he will interrogate Grisha personally."

"Using every means at his disposal."

"Every means, Sergei. You know that."

Sergei Padayev already knew to what extremes Pavel Ramizor would go, particularly when the investigation concerned something that he cared about personally.

"And when he is through with Grisha, he will get to you, Sergei."

Padayev was frightened, for though he was confident his spirit could not be broken, he knew that his weakened body could not withstand one of Pavel Ramizor's "interrogations."

"He will do all this, Sergei," Borodov went on, "in order to get to me through you. But have no fear; you won't have to undergo torture." The old man's voice imparted his deep affection for Padayev. "When he gets to you, you will bring him to me."

"But . . ."

"I shall be ready, believe me. I will be prepared for Pavel Ramizor. Trust me, Sergei."

"I have always trusted you."

"Bring Yan to me," the old man said. "We have some decisions to make."

"I hope he will have the strength to stand." Sergei's tone was doubtful. "Right now he's undergoing the most difficult examination in the whole training program."

"What is that?"

"It's a new apparatus, Boris," explained the section head. "The technical name won't tell you anything, but the men who operate it call it by a nickname: the Centrifugal Force Machine. It tests a person's capacity to withstand stress. It's used to determine an operative's ability to take interrogation by enemy agents. You're completely drained at the end of it, sometimes to the point of unconsciousness."

The expression on Boris Borodov's face did not change.

"He will pass this test, too, Sergei. Bring him to me when he is through."

The KGB had only been using the Centrifugal Force test for about two and a half years. Its inventors were two scientists who had been engaged in space research, assembling apparatuses used in training astronauts. One day, by chance, they had observed that an astronaut who had been in a large, hermetically sealed capsule for some time, spinning on an axis at tremendous velocity, lost consciousness when his direction was changed at the same time that the capsule's speed was altered. But, more important, they found that when the man came to, he had experienced moments of absolute terror before blacking out. The first man on whom the test was tried said he would have done anything they wanted him to if doing so would have brought an immediate halt to the effects of the centrifugal force.

When it became clear that the Centrifugal Force device could be used to overcome a man's willpower without in any way damaging his mind or body, an examination employing this machine was incorporated into the series of tests that every agent had to undergo.

Jil's past ten days had been crammed with various examinations: a test of fitness; a check of his reflexes, of his ability to defend himself and to attack; of his knowledge of and facility with an assortment of weapons, from handguns to small arms to explosives of various types. During this period Jil managed on only four hours of sleep a night. The training regimen demanded tremendous exertion on his part, and at times he felt weak and exhausted. In the past, he had coped better with these training periods, but three years had taken a toll. Nonetheless, Jil had passed each of the tests and examinations.

On the last night he was unable to fall asleep. That night he saw his body as the instrument by which he would break away from the old man, once and for all. He had always longed to create a world different from that of Boris Borodov's clowns, and now he had to break out of the orbit of Judaism and the world of the Hasidim, as well.

Three rings, three orbits, three ways of life from which he would have to exit in order to equip himself to return. Only then would he know precisely who he was. He must acquire this self-knowledge on his own. Only then would he comprehend his worth as a man and as a Jew.

At five o'clock in the evening of the following day, Jil found himself in a circular chamber in the large sub-basement where the machine that was to test his ability to withstand interrogation and torture was housed. The technician in charge explained that the test was more effective and precise than any administered in the past using the classical method of cross-examination. The interrogation no longer ran through an entire day and into the night. Now, results were obtained in a short time. This was the great achievement of centrifugal force.

Jil was stretched out, immobile, on an iron table and his body and head were fastened with special belts. The table was attached to an axle by means of which it was hoisted into the air. The technician sat behind a small control box with one red button. Jil was to be asked questions. If he responded falsely to his interrogator's question, the button was pressed, activating the machine so that the iron table was spun on its axis at a dizzying speed, and at the same time, and almost the same velocity, it was raised to the ceiling and lowered, generating feelings of fear and helplessness. In short order, most examinees would begin to respond to each question with complete candor—a victory of machine over man.

"Your name is Yan Borodov?"

The voice, which was deep and mellow and abounding with amicability, emanated from every corner of the room by means of amplifiers. Jil answered, "No," curious to experience the effect of centrifugal force. He discovered it precisely ten seconds after he had given his answer to the question. The spinning produced instant vertigo. It seemed to him that his internal organs had shifted positions, his stomach in the place formerly occupied by his heart, his heart was where his stomach had been; his legs where his arms had been. And then, suddenly, his breathing was cut off. There was no air. There was only fright—the maddening terror of being alone, of utter isolation. He was hovering in space. The lights went out, plunging him into total darkness, and mercifully the table returned to its place. He had returned from a long journey to hell.

"You are an agent of the KGB?"

"You are from Department V?"

"You are with the Liquidations Section?"

"You are an orphan?"

He longed to reply truthfully—*Yes . . . I am an orphan . . . an orphan!* but he said "No!" and by his response brought on the whirling, unearthly horror once again. He cried out but did not even hear the shout torn from his insides.

Fatherless, motherless. Only an old man and an old woman. All his life he had responded falsely; had prevaricated. The warp of truth, the woof of falsehood. The order of veracity and the order of mendacity arrayed one against the other. The lie for the sake of truth.

"You are an orphan?"

Yes! he thought, but still he responded "No," and again the awesome roll of the machine, the terrifying dizziness. He lived a lie. He had denied the truth, fled from it. Daidushka was his father, was everything. His mother was the old woman. He wanted no connection with the dead. A bond only with the living.

"You are Russian?"

"You are a Party member?"

"You liquidate enemies of the state?"

"No . . . No . . . No . . ."

And again the mind-deranging gyrations. The awful revolutions. Perhaps it was a product of the imagination, not a condition of reality. It was not possible that this reeling dizziness was real. It had no significance. No purpose. But now he had a purpose. To carry out Daidushka's mission. To protect the Rebbe. This was his mission. To liquidate those men who would kill the Rebbe. To murder. One more time and not again . . . once more . . . the last time . . .

Afterwards, he would again flutter his wings and lift off the ground, an eagle soaring through the sky, hovering free over the earth. In the vortex of the universe. In the realm of the Almighty . . .

When Jil opened his eyes, he found Sergei Padayev on one side of him and Dr. Rostovitch on the other. He had to blink several times in order to adjust to the light that flowed from a lamp near the couch.

He knew he had completed the Centrifugal Force test, even knew without being told, that he had passed. He had coped successfully with the abominable machine. He was swept by a strange gaiety, a joyous lightness. He wanted to rise from the couch, but felt too weak.

"What time is it?"

"Ten to six."

"In the morning," he muttered. The night had passed quickly.

"No," said Sergei, looking at Jil curiously. "In the evening. Ten to six in the evening."

Jil felt a dull pain in his head. It was not possible. It seemed to him as if hours had passed. Had it only been fifty minutes?

"It's one of the characteristics of the apparatus," explained Dr. Rostovitch. "It makes you lose all sense of time. There are no seconds, no minutes, and no hours. Just an undefined mass of time stretching out before you."

"How long was I unconscious?"

"Twenty minutes."

So he had been strapped to the machine for only thirty minutes. He knew he would remember that half hour for a very long time, for in that frightening interim they had dislodged his mind and torn his body and his soul to pieces, scattering the remnants to the winds. He had had to chase after them, to take to the air to recapture the pieces, for they ranged farther and farther away from him. He had to gather them together so that he would again have a soul, for the absence of the soul was death.

They were driving now from KGB headquarters on the outskirts of the city to Kalinin Boulevard, the Centrifugal Force test receding in Jil's mind like some dreadful surrealistic hallucination that would never be totally forgotten. The flakes of snow were blown wildly, descending in increasing volume and velocity, then borne suddenly aloft on a gust of wind and whirled in a dizzying spiral skyward, making driving difficult.

"You completed the training," said Sergei. "Pavel Ramizor has already received a detailed report. You were given an exceptional evaluation."

Jil remained silent. That night he would work with Sergei and the old man on the real mission before him. He knew that for the entire training period Sergei had been busy on behalf of Pavel Ramizor, arranging a new identity for Yan Borodov. Unofficially, he was at the same time securing still another identity for the mission Jil was to carry out for Daidushka. They discussed these two identities when they had gathered in the back room of Boris Borodov's apartment, and Boris and Sergei agreed that the moment Jil was beyond the borders of the Soviet Union, he should get rid of his departmental identity. He would enter the United States bearing his name from birth, which would facilitate his absorption into the Hasidic community in Crown Heights.

"I have been assigned the role of your dispatcher," explained Sergei. "So in the future every contact with the department will be made through me. All you'll have to do is contact Gregory Galenkin, the press attaché at our United Nations mission. Give him an address at which you can be reached so that he can contact you when the time comes to act in behalf of Ramizor. Of course, we know that that time will never come, that they won't be needing you. Realistically you can forget Galenkin and treat that mission as if it never existed. The problem is to make sure you are accepted by our people."

This was the one dangerous loophole. Since Jil was a Russian emigrant who was unknown to the Hasidic community, it was essential that they eliminate any suspicion that he might have been planted by the Soviets. Jil had only to be suspected of contact with the KGB for the entire operation to collapse.

Jil had to become an integral part of the Crown Heights community, for only then would he be in a position to frustrate any attempt on the Rebbe's life. They had to find a way to convince those close to the Rebbe that Jil was indeed the grandson of the Rebbe's emissary, Reb Mendel Gruner. This point had disturbed Boris Borodov, and it was Sergei Padayev who finally offered the solution. He would provide Jil with the one token that would remove all doubt as to his authenticity. And in a voice choked with emotion, Sergei told the story of the Rebbe's nine disciples and the carpenter, Yudke Kantor. He told of the pious young men who had dispersed, each bearing one of the parts of the chair of the Tzadikim. They had not only vowed to meet again in Crown Heights after the war, where Yudke would reassemble the holy chair; they had also vowed not to entrust this sacred obligation to anyone else, unless they felt their end drawing near. In such a case, a trustworthy man might be selected to fulfill the mission in place of the original disciple.

"I don't know what happened to the other pieces of the chair," said Sergei. "But I know where one piece is—the right front leg. And you, Jil, will take it with you. There can be no better testimony of your true identity."

Neither Boris nor Jil uttered a word. Their eyes were fixed on Sergei's pale countenance.

"Yudke the carpenter is awaiting you in Crown Heights— you and the last part of the chair. I notified him through his brother Volodia, the Rebbe's emissary in Paris."

"That was the sack you never let out of your sight," the old man declared in a tremulous voice.

"Yes," Sergei confirmed.

"You were nearly killed because of it," said Boris Borodov, his voice lowered to a whisper. "You went back for it that time the Germans pursued us into the forest . . ."

Sergei said nothing.

Jil watched them with open envy. He possessed no such faith. His Jewishness was an abstraction, the product of study and learning, not a way of life. He wondered if he would ever be able to fully understand these two men, to identify completely with their outlook or share their unshakable faith. They acted and never looked back, never questioned their actions. Although their self-assurance angered him, Jil knew that each of them—the one awaiting death at the end of a long life, the other facing it imminently from an illness that already ravaged him—looked upon him as their only hope. He alone could prevent harm from befalling their beloved Rebbe.

He heaved a deep sigh. With each passing hour, his time in this city, in this country was running out. For the first time in his life he would be himself. His documents would bear the name he had been given at birth, Yacov-Moshe Levinson. He was to receive them in Paris—Volodia's people were taking care of that; he would enter the United States with bona fide papers and an authentic immigration visa in his own name.

"You're on your own," remarked Sergei. "We have no target date and we don't know the name of a single person who is directly involved. The only thing we do know is that it's a complex scheme, which means you may have the advantage of time."

"But you think the Rebbe will be the first target?"

"It seems likely. We're fairly sure the radical Palestinians will form the backbone of the assassination plot," Boris Borodov said. "And since the Rebbe is recognized as one of the keenest opponents of a Palestinian state, he would be an obvious first target."

"Do you have any idea who is the contact between the Palestinians and the KGB?"

"According to Sergei," explained the old man, "during the past few months experts in terrorist operations have come to Moscow from East Germany, Czechoslovakia, and several other satellite countries for a round of secret talks with Pavel Ramizor. Sergei checked and found that all of them have had dealings in the past with various Palestinian terrorists."

"I probably know some of them."

"I have no doubt that you do," said Sergei.

"It seems you have a forest of conjecture and zero information."

"That's your job, Yan," the old man cut in. His voice was hoarse with fatigue. "To determine which of these suppositions are correct and to uncover all the details of the plan."

"I'll have to get help from the Mossad and the CIA."

"Yes, but only after you have the most clear-cut evidence in your hands. At this point, they must not know that one of our people is operating concurrently with them in the field. Don't forget, they aren't the only ones who employ double agents. If they have men in the KGB, you can be sure that there are CIA and even Mossad operatives on the payroll of the Soviet Union. A leak can develop anywhere. And, from our point of view, a leak means exposure for all of us—as well as disaster for the Rebbe."

"As their first move," Sergei Padayev interjected, "I think they will send a man into Crown Heights, a fox whose job it will be to become thoroughly acquainted with the neighborhood in which the Hasidim live so that he can plan the final stage of the actual strike."

Jil nodded.

"You will have to keep your eyes open. If you manage to single out the fox—and that may not be too difficult in a section as homogenous as Crown Heights—then you will have the first lead. Don't lose it. It will provide the key. You will be able to get to the others through the fox."

"As one man working alone, I'll be able to do little more than expose. What then?"

"Consult with Volodia, or his brother, Yudke. They are our liaisons with Israeli intelligence," Sergei explained. "If it becomes necessary to mobilize greater power, like the CIA, do it only through them."

"Then I am not as alone as I thought." Jil smiled.

"You have never been alone," Boris Borodov commented quietly. "This time, too, our Father in Heaven will watch over you."

Jil looked at the two men sitting before him and saw neither an old clown nor a shrewd intelligence agent but two wise men of the Law—Hasidim whose sole purpose in life was to honor their God. They had been compelled by circumstances to lead double lives, but circumstance had not forced them to eschew their faith or abandon their sacred mission for the Rebbe.

"Daidushka," said Jil in a low voice, "you made me a vow."

"I know." Boris's eyes radiated warmth and affection. "I made you a vow: no one will harm us. News of our safety and well-being will reach you. We shall both carry out our vows."

On Monday, January seventh, Pavel Ramizor concluded his meeting with Anton Karlov with a word of warning. "It is essential that we do not fail. The slightest slip-up and we will be exposed."

"I am personally supervising every stage," said Karlov quietly.

The Russian smiled and nodded his appreciation. "You have my approval. Go ahead." He extended his hand and once again Anton Karlov was surprised by the powerful grip of the department head's deceptively delicate-looking hand.

During their previous meeting, Ramizor had reminded him that if they valued their necks, it was essential to guard their tongues, and at all costs prevent the discovery of any connection between the assassination plot and the KGB. At the first sign of trouble, they agreed that the entire operation was to be halted.

On his flight back to Prague, Anton Karlov reviewed his meeting with the head of Department V. Karlov was a man without illusions. He knew he was just one block in the pyramid of Russian intrigue, and at the top of the pyramid there was room only for the KGB.

In this instance, the Soviet intent had been clear from the outset. Control over Palestinian terrorist organizations would enable the Soviet Union to continue fomenting upheaval in the Middle East and would permit them to carry out the subversion of non-communist regimes. The Russians had to eliminate American influence in an area they considered geographically to be their own backyard, so that they could assume control of the oil sheikdoms of the Persian Gulf.

Anton Karlov respected Pavel Ramizor's ability to translate Politburo policy into practical programs of action, but he loathed him nevertheless. In fact, he hated all Russians, knowing, as did every Czech, Pole, Bulgarian, and Romanian, that the Soviets were daily plundering his country's resources and exploiting its population, who were only puppets animated by strings pulled by the lumbering Russian bear. He too was so manipulated, he thought; little more than a damned KGB puppet himself.

20

At FIVE O'CLOCK the first shadows of dusk began to touch the sides of the deep ravines beyond Miguel de Salit's villa, and in a slow, inexorable ascent, they finally enveloped the foothills in complete darkness. From the window of the large second-floor room, Margaret could see the last rosy blush of sun on the ancient walls of Toledo.

Below her stood the stone bull pen and arena, and she remembered that magnificent morning when Jil, leaping and gamboling, had led the bull through the breathtaking pagan rite. That morning seemed to belong to another world, to a child's world of dream and fantasy, too vivid and enchanting for adults.

Miguel was waiting for her in his studio, where he was to show her the book he wanted her to translate as well as the most recent prints in his "Matador and Bull" series. He had chosen to have dinner in the studio rather than the dining room since the atmosphere was warmer and more intimate. Food and a bottle of chilled Malaga had been set out on a low square table before the fireplace where logs burned and crackled.

Though they had never discussed her private life, Miguel

had noticed a change in Margaret, sensed that something was amiss.

"Have you seen Jil?" he asked abruptly.

"No. Why?" She looked at him incredulously: how had he succeeded in reading her thoughts?

"No reason. I suddenly thought of him . . ." Of all Margaret's acquaintances who had appeared at the house, only Jil had captured Miguel's imagination.

When they had finished their modest meal, Miguel stood up and pulled the cork from another bottle of wine.

"I like this Malaga," he said, smiling. "And I see you do too." He filled her glass and his, then sat down on a small stool near the fireplace and watched his daughter as he sipped his wine. The fire threw flickering shadows across her face, and her long, soft hair shone with brilliant tints of gold.

Margaret raised her head from the book he had given her and looked at him.

"I'd like to translate it."

"I'm glad, very glad. Shall I send word, then, to the publisher in England?"

"Certainly," she said. She put the book down and picked up her wineglass. "Miguel . . ."

"I know," he said as she paused. An encouraging smile spread over his face. "You want to talk. Go ahead."

"I want to tell you about myself . . . I think you should know something about me that you aren't aware of. Please, just listen. Don't say anything . . . at least not tonight."

And she told him of her involvement with the Palestinians and various other terrorist groups. His face became grave. As she went on to describe the doubts that had assailed her in recent months, he relaxed somewhat. She realized that this was the first confession she had ever made to him.

He moved beside her on the couch and embraced her. She no longer seemed a strong, independent mature woman but rather the little child he had lost so many years before. She clung to him and he tightened his arms around her.

21

At NOON ON Tuesday, January eighth, Jil said good-bye to Boris and Zina. The old clown knew that this was the last time he would ever see his grandson, ever hold him in his arms, yet he had been strangely silent. Only the deathly pallor of his face indicated his agitation. Babushka Zina appeared terribly old and frail; each passing day seemed to diminish her height. Jil embraced her carefully as if her frailty would not withstand a hug.

Sergei took him to the airport. They drove partway in silence, and then Sergei spoke. "I have a request to make of you."

Jil waited for him to continue.

"I am ill. I have no one. My wife was killed in the bombing as we were fleeing Warsaw . . . we were very young and had no children . . ." He paused. "I know you promised Boris you would say kaddish for him after his death."

Jil held his breath, and a tremor passed through his body. Kaddish: the prayer one recites daily for eleven months after the death of a loved one.

"Yes, I did promise that."

"I want you to promise me, too. There is no one to pray

193

for me." Sergei's voice was thick with emotion. He cleared his throat and continued: "I want you, who have been like a son to me, to pray for my soul when I am gone."

Jil put his hand on the older man's arm.

"Of course I will say kaddish for you too."

"You must know my Jewish name for the prayer."

"Tell me. I'll remember."

Sergei Padayev spoke in a whisper: "Shmuel-Menachem Gillerman. Will you remember? Shmuel-Menachem Gillerman . . ."

And for the first time, Jil heard Sergei's Jewish name. Ironically, it was the last time that they would ever see one another, for both Boris and Sergei had made him a promise that, no matter what happened, he would never again set foot on Soviet soil.

Two days later, in Paris, Volodia Kantor produced official Soviet immigration papers for Jil in the name of Yacov-Moshe Levinson—it was the name his father had given him, a name he had never before used. Shortly thereafter, an immigration visa to the United States was issued to Yacov-Moshe Levinson, who had been granted the right to enter the United States as an immigrant. On Wednesday, January sixteenth, Jil left Paris.

Now, as the plane circled over New York, his primary concern was to pass the immigration desk. He had no way of knowing that at that moment the largest security and espionage agencies in the world were mounting an intensive manhunt for a French-Canadian pantomimist known as Jil, the clown.

Jil's previous arrivals at Kennedy airport had been either as a tourist or a businessman. Now, as an immigrant, he walked with the other passengers down the wide corridors of the terminal toward the cubicles manned by immigration officials. He carried two pieces of luggage: one, a small case, contained all his documents, and the second, somewhat larger, held the leg of the holy chair. He was attired in the dark, ill-fitting garb of a religious Jew. He had not shaved for six days and a reddish fuzz covered his cheeks and chin. His worn gray suit was conspicuously "foreign," as was his long, oversized topcoat. He had crowned this outfit with a worn fedora.

The check made by the immigration officials was more

rapid and cursory than he had expected. He was released in short order and permitted to go to customs to pick up his old leather suitcases.

He emerged from the terminal into the cold, winter twilight.

It was a quarter to six when his taxi pulled up in front of a small hotel on Forty-fourth Street between Second and Third Avenues.

Jil decided that first thing the next morning, he would get in touch with the liaison, Gregory Galenkin, and give him the name and address of the hotel. Then, before leaving for Crown Heights, he would arrange with the desk clerk to hold any mail or phone messages that might arrive for him in the coming weeks. Once this had been accomplished, he would be free to concentrate on his real mission.

Jil began to explore Crown Heights. He left his hotel early each morning and did not return until after dark. At first he studied the perimeter of the neighborhood, where the population was mixed—a majority of blacks with a light sprinkling of Jews. After he had become completely familiar with these areas—every street and alleyway, every rundown building and shabby storefront—he penetrated to the heart of Crown Heights, to the center of the large Hasid community that clustered around the Rebbe.

He had to be even more cautious here, for the Hasidim were intensely suspicious of any strangers lurking in their neighborhood. By now, his beard had thickened, and he had exchanged his gray fedora for a wide-brimmed black hat like those worn by members of the Hasidic community. He discovered that the spiritual center was on Eastern Parkway while the business and shopping centers were on Kingston Avenue. He even found the Rebbe's house, though he did not see the Rebbe himself. Jil learned later that, because of his weak heart, the Rebbe had been confined to his house for the duration of the winter.

It was during his first visit to the area that Jil came to understand the meaning of the term ghetto. Though the section was not fenced in—was in no way physically separated from the surrounding neighborhoods—he felt its isolation; the will of its residents had sealed it off from the secular world outside.

The ghetto was approximately a mile square and entirely self-contained: the children attended school within its boundaries; the women shopped there; it provided for all its residents' spiritual needs. There were numerous houses of prayer and Yeshivot, in which scholars of Jewish Law instructed the young men who were embarking on lives devoted to the study of the Torah, the Talmud, and the Kabala.

There were many Hasidic communities throughout the United States, but Crown Heights contained the Rebbe's own congregation; about a thousand of his disciples and their families lived here—some six thousand souls in all. The international headquarters of the Rebbe was housed on Eastern Parkway. Jil had passed the building several times; nothing in its external appearance gave any indication of its importance as a worldwide spiritual center, yet it was to this building that heads of state, diplomats, renowned scientists, and distinguished figures in the arts were drawn to consult with the Rebbe—the man under whose direct inspiration the Hasidic religious network functioned, an individual who was considered one of the towering Jewish personalities of the age.

Jil had no trouble locating Yudke Kantor's shop. One evening he saw the elderly artisan leave his shop and he followed him, wondering at his youthful stride and his broad, powerful physique. Jil trailed him for two days, until he had his daily schedule down pat.

Then, deciding it was time to begin living among the Hasidim of Crown Heights as Yacov-Moshe Levinson, the grandson of Reb Mendel Gruner, Jil left his hotel on Friday, January twenty-fifth. By the time he reached Crown Heights, snow was falling. Lowering his head against the blasts of wind, Jil pressed on to Yudke's shop. The door was slightly ajar; he pushed it open and found himself staring squarely at Yudke's broad back. The carpenter was finishing the door of a holy ark that would shelter the sacred scrolls.

"*Shalom Aleichem*," said Jil.

"*Aleichem Shalom*," responded Yudke, returning the stranger's greeting.

"I have special greetings from your brother Volodia," Jil said, meeting the carpenter's inquiring glance. He placed the two cases he was carrying on the floor and rubbed his hands together briskly to warm them. "Greetings, Yudke," he said, holding out a hand.

Yudke hesitated; could this be the messenger for whom he had waited impatiently ever since his brother's letter had arrived? With an apparent effort, he extended his hand and shook Jil's. "Welcome," he said finally. "And whom do I have the honor of addressing?"

"Yacov-Moshe Levinson."

"Levinson," the old man repeated. "Where from?"

"From Moscow."

An inner light was suddenly kindled and shone luminously from Yudke's eyes. This stranger could indeed be the man whose arrival Volodia's letter had announced.

"I have brought something for you; I was told to give it only to you."

"Who is the sender?" Yudke's voice was unsteady.

"Shmuel, the son of Menachem Gillerman."

"The disciple . . . the tenth man. Is he alive?"

"He is alive," Jil confirmed, explaining that Sergei was in poor health and, since he had no hope of getting out of the Soviet Union, had asked Jil to fulfill his mission.

"Reb Shmuel Gillerman said before I left: 'May Yudke's sacred deed be executed and his rewards abundant,' " Jil concluded. He placed the larger case on a wooden bench, opened it, and drew the leg of the holy chair out of its leather sheath.

"There it is," he said to Yudke, moving aside.

The carpenter, his eyes moist, came forward slowly. He looked at the wooden leg for a long time before he finally stretched out his arm and tenderly passed the palm of his hand over it.

"Forty-one years," he whispered, then went to lock the door of the shop; he wanted no intrusions. He opened the lock of the cabinet in which the other nine parts were safely stored.

"See, Reb Levinson," he whispered, "there are the parts. You have been privileged to perform a great mitzvah . . . that is why I wanted you to see them . . ."

Jil regarded the craftsman with interest. He would have thought that after his association with Daidushka and Sergei, this kind of intense, almost fanatic devotion would not surprise him. Nevertheless, observing this man whose entire adult life had revolved around a single burning ambition—to restore the chair of the Tzadikim—filled him with profound wonder.

Yudke went back to the bench and Jil watched as he picked up the leg with the gentleness of a father lifting his infant child. Slowly, carefully, he walked back to the cabinet, raised the right front leg, and placed it lovingly on the single empty shelf at the top of the cabinet. Throwing back his shoulders, he seemed to cast off a burden he had carried daily for many years.

"Come and look, they are perfect twins!" His eyes moved back and forth between the two shelves, his face beaming.

"Now," he said, addressing himself, "tomorrow is the Sabbath, but on Sunday I shall begin to work on the chair, slowly, piece by piece."

Closing the door of the cabinet and locking it, he turned his attention to his guest. "First, Reb Levinson," he said, "we must find you living quarters, which will be no problem at all. But Friday night and Shabbat you will spend in my home. My wife Haya Rivka, may she live a long and joyful life, will be delighted to have you. You'll be like a fourth son."

The apartment Yudke produced for Jil was in a block of apartments occupied by impecunious Hasidic families. The two sparsely furnished rooms on the fourth floor overlooked the street.

"This is your home," announced Yudke. He seemed reluctant to leave Jil, though it was Friday and the hour was late. "Which Levinson family are you from?"

Jil told Yudke his father's name.

"Ah, yes!" The old man's face lit up. "The son-in-law of Reb Mendel Gruner." The carpenter looked inquiringly at Jil. "Do you mean to say, young man, that you are Reb Mendel Gruner's grandson?"

"Yes, I am."

"I was not privileged to know him personally, but I heard a great deal about him in my youth. He was not only secretary to our sage and teacher, the Rebbe, but one of his trusted advisors as well." He sighed deeply. "Well . . . was Reb Mendel Gruner privileged to raise a grandson worthy of himself?"

"You don't expect me to testify on my own behalf," Jil replied with a faint smile. The whole tenor of the conversation was strange to him: cordial, fraternal, couched in terms of endearment and respect. Yet, as he would learn, it was characteristic of exchanges among Hasidim, even those who had just met. "Zaide educated me in the spirit of our Jewish heritage." He did not say Daidushka, but used instead the Yiddish word for grandfather.

"Indeed the response of one learned in the Torah," nodded Yudke, smiling. "And, permit me to ask, has Reb Gruner also been granted the privilege of coming here to the United States?"

"No, not yet." Yudke obviously had no idea of Reb Gruner's real role as Grand Emissary.

"Well, his time will also come." Yudke placed a hand on Jil's shoulder and gazed warmly into his eyes. "I'll be waiting for you at my house, just a short distance from here. You will be most welcome."

The meeting—the first real test of his authenticity, under the penetrating gaze of the amiable old carpenter—had left Jil exhausted. But he felt that he had succeeded in persuading Yudke Kantor that he was a bona fide Hasid.

It seemed to Jil that somewhere in the past he had already lived a Hasidic life. Its details were familiar to him, and his initial apprehensions had been replaced by a curious feeling of comfort, as if he had broken out of a dream and plunged headlong into solid reality. His grandfather had opened the way for his exodus. Now the decision whether or not to remain a Jew and a Hasid rested in Jil's own hands, and he would make it once he had fulfilled his vow. Then the chains would fall from him. Perhaps America, this vast and beautiful land, would be his final refuge.

Jil roused himself from his reverie and went into the bathroom to shower. Half an hour later, he stood in his black hat and large overcoat looking at himself in the long mirror of the clothes closet. He smiled wanly at the unfamiliar reflection of the red-bearded Hasid.

He locked the door to the apartment and remembered to go around to the staircase: an observant Jew was prohibited from using the elevator on the Sabbath. A thin layer of snow covered the sidewalk, but fortunately he did not have far to go to the pleasant house on Union Street, which Yudke had pointed out to him earlier.

Many months later he would recall that night, and the Saturday following it, as the most remarkable days in his life. The prayers that were recited in the small synagogue near

Yudke's house and the sumptuous meal with all the members of the carpenter's large family as well as a few guests that evening were etched on his memory. But it was the Saturday service in the central synagogue that was the highlight, for it was here that Jil saw the Rebbe for the first time.

Word had spread on Saturday that the Rebbe would come to the synagogue following the evening prayers, and that he might even address the congregation. He had not appeared there for several weeks and large numbers of Hasidim eagerly assembled to see and hear him.

At the center of the synagogue sat the elders of the congregation, sages venerated both for their age and wisdom. Surrounding them were the heads of the Hasidic families. On tiers of long benches, lining the western wall, were the younger members of the congregation. As a distinguished elder, Yudke was accorded a seat among the sages, almost at the foot of the Rebbe's table. Jil, sitting next to him, would have an excellent view of the Tzadik.

Suddenly a hush fell over the group, which until then had been conversing loudly in a mixture of Yiddish, Hebrew, and English. By the time the Rebbe, surrounded by his senior advisors, entered the room and mounted the platform, an absolute stillness prevailed.

Jil remembered the old photograph in Daidushka's watch. The Rebbe's beard was no longer black, as it had been in the picture, but for a man of his age, the Rebbe's step was remarkably spry. He moved quickly through the crowd, his head bowed in thought. He took his place on the platform and began to address the congregation in Yiddish in a clear and resonant voice.

So fascinated was Jil by the Tzadik's physical appearance that at first he did not really hear what he was saying. The wide-brimmed hat accentuated the Rebbe's fine, sharp features, which were set off by a silvery beard that flowed majestically over his chest. Never before had Jil seen such a radiant face. It was as if the Rebbe had somehow escaped the ravages of time: his forehead was high and unlined, his skin smooth and clear. Under the glare of the lights, the color of his eyes shifted from gray to blue to emerald green. He drew the undivided attention of the assemblage almost effortlessly. As he rose to speak, all eyes were riveted on him.

After a few minutes, Jil began to concentrate on the Rebbe's words. He spoke first about Israel, saying that no Jew had the right to relinquish any part of the ancestral homeland that had been bestowed by God: a clear warning to the leaders of Israel that as long as peace negotiations in the Middle East were conducted on the basis of Israeli withdrawal, they were doomed to failure. Then he spoke on the elevation of the spirit, of a faith, born of love of God and one's fellow man, and so complete that it is unmarred by even a ray of doubt. He spoke of the many forms of prayer, observing that a man might pour out his soul to God in song or music, in many ways, all acceptable to the Almighty. After he had spoken for almost an hour, he paused to rest.

Throughout the Rebbe's talk many of his Hasidim were on their feet, swaying back and forth with their eyes closed, listening raptly to his every word as if the exalted thoughts to which he had given utterance had been expressed for their sole benefit. During the brief interval before the Rebbe resumed his talk, their bodies swayed more energetically as they chanted prayers and sang the traditional valedictory songs of Saturday evening in praise of the departed Sabbath Queen.

When the Rebbe lifted his head to resume speaking, the singing ceased and the congregation fell silent. He now discussed the true meaning of Jewish education, presenting and examining problems connected with religious education and explaining how solutions reached and applied in the proper spirit could draw the believer closer to the Creator. Afterward he spoke of the necessity of mutual aid for both the individual and the congregation. He stressed the special responsibility that each member of the House of Israel had for his brother—an obligation prescribed in the Torah and particularly important in this dawn of the Age of the Messiah; the more mitzvoth or sacred deeds that Jews performed, the more worthy they would be of the coming of the Messiah. It was the special task of the Hasidim to see to it that Jews outside the Hasidic fellowship also performed mitzvoth, so that the era of total redemption could be hastened.

The Rebbe's talk went on for almost three hours. It was past midnight when he rose, thus signaling a conclusion. The Hasidim also stood, but they waited until the Tzadik and his entourage had gone into an inner office before dispersing. A throng of Hasidim had already congregated on the front steps to catch another fleeting glimpse of the Rebbe.

Yudke took Jil by the arm and led him to a spot near the entrance. "Stand here and do not move," he ordered. "I must go to the Rebbe's office. The Tzadik must be told that you have come as the emissary of Shmuel Gillerman."

A few minutes later, Yudke emerged from the building, smiling joyously.

"Reb Levinson," he said in excitement, "the Rebbe sent you a special blessing: he will receive you in *y'chidut*—alone—this week." Yudke used the Hebrew word which describes a private meeting between the Rebbe and a disciple.

Such an invitation had great significance. Ordinarily the Rebbe received a Hasid privately only at the latter's request—to discuss a pressing personal problem. But when the Tzadik initiated such a meeting, it meant that he attributed special importance to the individual to be received. Word quickly spread among those standing nearby that the Rebbe had invited the new immigrant from Russia to meet him in *y'chidut*.

The Tzadik emerged from the building and, as he passed Jil, he stopped and, with a smile, placed a gentle hand on his arm. In the ensuing moment, as they stood with glances interlocked, they almost seemed to be engaging in a silent conversation. Then the Rebbe turned and made his way briskly through the crowd of Hasidim to his car.

As Jil and Yudke walked home, they discussed what Jil would do for a living.

"Do you have something in mind?" Yudke asked. "Is there something you would like to do?"

Jil hesitated. He had to find a way to be near the Rebbe, some function that would enable him to move freely around Crown Heights.

"I would like to serve the Rebbe," he said slowly.

Yudke looked at him thoughtfully.

"You know," he said finally, "a few days ago I learned that they are looking for a messenger . . . an emissary."

"An emissary?" Jil gave a little start of surprise at the sound of the word, which conjured up images of Daidushka and Sergei Padayev.

"Yes," said Yudke, stroking his beard. "The Rebbe has

had to stay at home recently on his doctor's orders. He isn't permitted to go to his office daily, so a messenger is needed, a reliable man who will maintain contact between the Rebbe's home and his office."

"What kind of contact?"

"Bringing the mail, for example, and books and documents that require the Rebbe's attention; taking things back to the office . . ."

It was the opportunity Jil had been waiting for. "I see. I would be happy to serve as the Rebbe's messenger, at least until I know what it is I want to do in this country."

Yudke smiled. "The apple doesn't fall far from the tree," he said. "To be an emissary is a tradition in your family. In the beginning you will perform small missions, later more important ones. Who knows, Reb Levinson, perhaps the time will come when you will actually carry out a mission ordained by the Rebbe, as did your grandfather. Who knows?"

They might have talked longer, but it was late and very cold. Yudke pressed Jil's hand affectionately and hurried up the steps to his house, while Jil set out for his apartment.

The long arms of Boris Borodov and Sergei Padayev had reached out to pave Jil's way in Crown Heights, yet, from this point on, they were without influence. Now he must enter the struggle himself and engage the enemy without any further help from them.

Sometime soon—in the next week or the next month—the terrorist fox would have to make an appearance to study Crown Heights and prepare a blueprint for the operation. As Sergei had pointed out, Jil would have to find the fox in order to unravel the plot. He hoped Yudke would succeed in arranging the job with the Rebbe. It would justify his spending twenty-four hours a day in the vicinity of the Rebbe's home and at the administrative headquarters.

He thought of the Tzadik and of the odd sense of warmth, the faint excitement he had experienced when the Rebbe had gazed into his eyes and touched his arm. He felt as if he had known the Tzadik all his life.

When the Rebbe had spoken that night about modes of prayer that did not require words, Jil felt certain that he was directing his remarks to him. The thought surprised him. He found it difficult to believe that the Rebbe had been able at a glance to plumb the depths of his being, but in some way he had. The Rebbe knew that all his life Jil had prayed with his body, through movement. His art was his prayer.

Suddenly embarrassed by the effect the encounter had had on him, Jil sought to play down its significance with self-mockery: "Why, I am nothing but a Hasid," he said to himself, "a little son of a Hasid."

22

IN EUROPE A massive manhunt for Jil the Clown was underway. Copies of the composite sketch had been distributed to American and Israeli intelligence agents and to representatives of the police and security agencies throughout Western Europe. Only after the dragnet had been drawn tightly over Europe did Earl Dickson return to Washington and General Negbi to Israel, leaving the operation in the hands of Paul Mansfield and Evyatar Miller.

Although there were many people who were familiar with the pantomimist, having seen him perform, very few had actually seen his face. Among the first people Evyatar Miller went to see was Volodia Kantor, who had told him about the Soviet Circus in the first place, but Volodia was unable to add anything to what he had previously related.

"Believe me, Evyatar," said the restaurant owner, when they had seated themselves at one of the small tables, "I've told you everything I know. But you," he added, casting a sly glance at the Israeli, "you don't tell me anything. Maybe you have a little something to share with me?"

"Not at this stage," Evyatar responded with a smile. "The only thing I can say is that we suspect the Soviet Union is involved in a major terrorist action. It's my assignment to find proof."

Volodia regarded him dubiously. "To prove Russian involvement you'll need a certain amount of luck."

"Luck and hard work," rejoined Evyatar, taking the composite drawing from his pocket. "Take a look at this, Volodia. You see lots of faces. Maybe you've seen this one?"

Volodia glanced at the drawing. The man in the picture seemed to project an air of youthful innocence; he looked almost adolescent. For a moment the restaurateur thought there was something familiar about the face but he dismissed the idea. "Who is he?"

"Someone who goes by the code name of the Clown."

"This is why you're looking into circuses!" exclaimed Volodia with a chuckle. "Sorry I can't help you this time. You know, my customers aren't such youngsters. Most of them are in their fifties or sixties."

Although he hadn't really expected anything from the meeting, Evyatar nevertheless felt disappointed.

"Look, Volodia." There was a tone of supplication in Evyatar's voice. "Try to get more information on the Soviet Circus. Anything you can."

"I'll try. But it isn't always possible to shake a mountain of dust off a chapter of history."

"Maybe history is repeating itself again," remarked Evyatar as he turned to leave. "Who knows?"

Paul and Evyatar kept on the move across the continent, completely concentrated on the chase and their prey. But their quarry seemed to have vanished, swallowed up by the harsh European winter. They met with intelligence operatives who had managed to uncover information on the Clown— vague, meager scraps of intelligence, but not one agent had been able to dredge up anything that pointed to the Clown's present whereabouts.

They did, however, find reports of the Miracle Worker, the Fortune Teller, the Acrobat, and the Trainer. They began gathering details as to their physical appearances.

"If we don't succeed in capturing the Clown," Paul remarked one day, "then we'll take one of the other bastards."

Although they drew a blank on the Clown, both Miller and Mansfield at least came to have a more clear-cut understanding of the interrelationship of various terrorist groups—the Red Brigades in Italy and the Tupamaros in South America, among others. They found that the IRA had been obtaining assistance from the Palestinians, and they learned how the Baader-Meinhof gang succeeded in attracting sympathizers among the students at various universities. They also gained some information on the way high-ranking officials in different European governments cooperated with the terrorists.

Despite these sideline discoveries, they were not diverted from the hunt. They pursued the Clown and his associates in the Soviet Circus relentlessly, untiringly. Others grew weary of the chase and dropped out to be replaced by new agents. But not Miller and Mansfield.

By the beginning of February, they had only a few more details on Jil the mime. The final bit of intelligence had been obtained from a French ballet dancer who claimed that she had seen Jil in December when he appeared at a congress of artists in Madrid. Paul and Evyatar flew there at once and confirmed the dancer's testimony. But the trail was cold. The Clown had vanished. They flew on to Rome and from there to Bologna. There had been a Palestine Day rally in Bologna and Jil the pantomimist had been the star performer. But where he had gone after that no one knew. They continued to investigate doggedly, in transit from one airport to the next, sleeping at odd hours in gray rooms in gray hotels in the midst of gray, desolate cities. When, on February eighth, Dickson informed them that the men he had assigned them for the manhunt in Europe were needed back in the United States, they understood the significance of this order. Dickson and Negbi, too, were losing faith. They had grown weary. But Paul and Evyatar persisted, for they believed they would ultimately succeed in tracking down the elusive Clown.

23

EVERY WEEK SERGEI reported to the old man on Yan's progress in the United States. Information was transmitted from Crown Heights to Paris, from Paris to Moscow, and once Sergei had received it, he immediately passed it on to the old man. Up to now nothing had really happened. They prayed that they had been mistaken, that their assessment had been incorrect and that the Rebbe was not to be the first target.

Sergei Padayev had been keeping watch on Pavel Ramizor's activities and what he saw was disquieting. The department head had embarked on an intensive investigation of Grisha Rostovitch.

The doctor's personal file had been returned to the archives, but the file had been copied in triplicate, which meant Ramizor had assigned the task of digging into Grisha Rostovitch's past to other men in the department.

"He is closing in on us," said the old man.

"I'm afraid so, Boris."

"He discovered our mistakes."

"He took an additional step yesterday."

"Yes, Sergei, I know. He went to Riga. Word reached me

from there. Everything begins in Riga. There, Grisha Rostovitch was born. There the affair begins, and there it will be concluded."

Puzzled, Sergei Padayev looked up at the old man.

"What will happen when he returns from Riga?"

"Another inquiry. He'll continue to investigate in Moscow until he has the answers to his questions."

"And then he will come to me," whispered Sergei.

"You must prepare Grisha," said Boris. "You'll have to alert him to the possibility of detention for the duration of the KGB's inquiry. He may very well have to undergo a very bad interrogation."

"I have faith in Grisha," said Sergei. "He'll be able to cope with it."

"He is a man of extraordinary faith," said the old man quietly. "I consider him no less a Hasid than you or I. He is among the Righteous of the Nations." In saying that, Boris Borodov had bestowed upon the doctor the most exalted title that Jews may confer on a Gentile, a designation reserved for those Christians who endangered their own lives to save the lives of Jews.

"We will have to follow the situation closely," the old man said. "If it will help matters, you must tell Grisha to bring Ramizor to you. You know what to do from there?"

"I do."

"And one other thing, Sergei. On the day that Ramizor returns from Riga, I'll have to go there. Arrange my trip. I will be gone for several days at least."

The request took Sergei by surprise. The old man hadn't left Moscow since his retirement from the circus. There had been no need to drag himself from place to place, since he could supervise the activities of his men from his small apartment. But now it appeared that something exceptional had happened to make him travel again.

"You must understand," Borodov explained, "it is not only we who have made mistakes. Pavel Ramizor is committing his most serious blunder at this very moment. And I intend to trap him."

24

IN A DETAILED communiqué from Larnaca, Vladimir Zoska notified Anton Karlov that Horst Welsh had left for New York. He also gave his evaluation of the combat readiness of Mussa el-Dalil's troops and noted that he had succeeded in finding a rat among el-Dalil's men who would funnel information to him that the Palestinian commander chose not to disclose. That man was Da'ud el-Za'id.

Although the brash and reckless el-Za'id had been reined in, he seethed inwardly with bitter hatred and a burning desire for revenge. During the difficult hours after el-Za'id's return from the beach, and in the days that followed, Vladimir Zoska had carefully and deliberately gained his confidence.

Not long after his insulting, degrading punishment, el-Za'id had stood docilely in front of Mussa el-Dalil. Heeding the Czech's instructions to win forgiveness and regain his standing, he had demonstrated his respect by kissing his commander's hand several times with an unmistakable air of contrition.

The candidates for el-Dalil's group had been transferred to a special training base located near the village of Bint in southern Lebanon. There, a series of brutal exercises was conducted, accompanied by bloody clashes with troops from the Lebanese Christian militia, a group the Palestinians had come to hate because they interfered with their sabotage actions against Israel. In the course of these exercises, Da'ud recaptured his old position in the unit.

On the night between the second and third of March, a group of Palestinian fighters under the command of el-Za'id went out to lay an ambush for the militia troops. The darkness permeating the wadi at the bottom of the rocky foothills was so thick it was difficult to make out el-Za'id's shock of silvery hair. From all sides of the ravine, the five men under his command dragged heavy rocks and piled them one on top of the other, working in silence, until the road had been completely barricaded. Then, concealed by the bushes, they lay in wait for the Lebanese patrol at the side of the road.

In the meantime, el-Za'id finished laying the charge, which consisted of a small quantity of plastic explosives. He drew the thin cord that would detonate the explosives across the path of the patrol, and then rejoined his comrades.

The armored car of the Lebanese Christian militia reached the barricade shortly thereafter. Its powerful floodlight swept over the mound of heavy stones, and the car stopped. Two soldiers armed with Uzi submachine guns emerged from the vehicle, regarded their surroundings suspiciously, and then began to remove the stones, calling to their comrades for assistance. They were joined by two more soldiers; the fifth and last man stood guard near the armored vehicle.

When Da'ud el-Za'id pulled the string and a powerful explosion ensued, the soldiers reacted precisely as he had anticipated. The four militiamen immediately dropped the stones in their hands and aimed a volley of automatic rifle fire at the site of the explosion, turning their backs to the ambush party, as did the fifth man. At that instant Da'ud el-Za'id leaped to his feet and, together with his men, fired a shower of bullets at the Christian soldiers. Clear targets, caught unaware, they were dead before their bodies hit the ground.

Mussa el-Dalil stood on the summit of a steep rise not far from the Israeli border, a good vantage point from which to check the action that was taking place between the Christian troops and his unit. He heard the sudden explosion and watched the tongue of flame rise against the darkened sky. The explosion was followed by a brief volley of automatic gunfire, and then silence. The battle was over.

El-Dalil glanced at the phosphorescent dial of his watch. It was four o'clock in the morning. Very soon the dim glow of dawn would scatter the darkness. He was impatient to learn whether his men would return safely from their mission. The groups he had sent out at the end of February had suffered heavy casualties. Of the forty-seven candidates who had begun the training program, only thirty-six remained after clashes with the militia. Each man who had gone out that night under el-Za'id's command was undergoing his final test. The best of these men would form the hit team for the Crown Heights operation.

Mussa el-Dalil lit a cigarette and spit out the loose shreds of tobacco that had stuck to his tongue. The sky in the east was turning gray. The officer standing next to him was the first to catch sight of el-Za'id's group as it appeared at the foot of the hill. The ambush had been successful: all six men were making their way up the narrow path.

The eastern sky was tinged with the first blushes of sunlight as Da'ud el-Za'id, in a camouflage uniform with a ring of grenades at his hips and an ammunition belt slung over his shoulder, approached his commanding officer, the Kalatchnikov he had used for the brief skirmish still smoldering in his hands. The other five mounted the summit, their legs heavy, breath steaming in the air. One of them had been injured but the wound was slight and had already been bandaged.

"How many did you kill?" asked el-Dalil.

"There were five," el-Za'id responded quietly. "We also destroyed their vehicle."

"What did you do with the bodies?" he asked.

"I put them in the car," el-Za'id explained, his face expressionless. "Then I blew the whole thing up. I don't think anything but a few charred bones are left. Their own mothers wouldn't recognize them."

Mussa el-Dalil studied Da'ud's handsome face for several moments. He had performed the mission efficiently and with thoroughness. He had learned his painful lesson well. He placed his hand on el-Za'id's shoulder.

"I have been watching you for some time," he began slowly. "I think you are a real fighter."

He fell silent, waiting for Da'ud's reaction. The young man knew that some response was expected of him. This was the first time since the incident with Margaret Aston that his commander had singled him out for praise. He knew that the compliment was meant to indicate that the unfortunate incident had been forgotten, that el-Za'id's subsequent behavior had completely blotted it out.

"I had always hoped you would recognize my ability," he said in a low voice. "I am happy that the moment has finally arrived."

Mussa el-Dalil nodded. "For some time you've known that you would participate in the mission. But now you will participate in it as my second in command. You may have to give your life, as may I."

"You and I are true Palestinians," Da'ud responded, his eyes moist with emotion. He took Mussa el-Dalil's swarthy hand and kissed it. "I am at your command," he said in a quavering voice. "You have done me a great honor."

Back at the base, Mussa el-Dalil took el-Za'id aside. It was time to reveal the whole picture. The commander began speaking in a slow voice. He told el-Za'id that the first target from the list had been selected: a well-known rabbi was to be assassinated according to the plan presented to them by the Czech, Vladimir Zoska, a plan approved in Moscow. But Mussa el-Dalil had a scheme of his own, which, until that moment, he had discussed with no one.

"What do you mean?" el-Za'id asked.

"I am no longer a young man, Da'ud. I have been fighting for years, and killing is not something new for me. People are more shocked over ten dead than one, and a hundred deaths shock them more than ten. The bite of a flea does not disturb the lion, but when the lion's foot is crushed, he becomes a cripple. Do you follow me?

"I want a slaughter," he went on in a clear, calm voice. "A slaughter that will shock the Jews, Israel—the world! I want to cause an upheaval. I want to kill the rabbi and another thousand, maybe two thousand men, women, and children with him. They are our enemies! We must destroy the rabbi and his people."

"How?" el-Za'id gaped in astonishment.

"How?" repeated Mussa el-Dalil, folding his arms over his chest. "You know that in order to deal the enemy a blow that will send him reeling, you have to study him first. I *have* studied the enemy. I know the Jews. You and the others do not. I had Jewish friends; I grew up among the Jews in Haifa."

He fell silent, his look abstracted, as he gazed up at the mountains and recalled climbing the steep ridges of Mount Carmel as a child.

"A Jewish friend once told me a story about how the Cossacks in Russia got rid of the Jews. When the Jews would go into the synagogue to pray to their God, the Cossacks would come and lock the doors and windows of the synagogue from the outside. Then they would set fire to the building." He gave a short, mirthless laugh. "You understand, Da'ud? That is what we will do. There is a synagogue in the target area. We'll use the Cossack strategy. Have you any idea what that will do? What its effect will be on American Jews?

"This is not a terrorist action," continued the commander. "This is a holy war. Our enemy is not only the soldier fighting against us on the battlefield. Every Jew who supports Israel is the enemy, and that enemy must be destroyed. You are a brave and daring warrior. That is why I need you. You are as courageous as I am. You are not afraid to kill. And that is important."

Da'ud envisioned large buildings going up in flames, heavy smoke and fire bursting through upper-story windows. He could hear the screams of people trapped inside the structure; he could almost smell the odor of burning flesh. "From this moment on, you are sworn to silence," el-Dalil continued. "Not even the slightest hint of this plan must reach other ears. It will appear that we are simply preparing to follow the instructions of Vladimir Zoska and Horst Welsh. Is that clear?"

Da'ud el-Za'id nodded, unable to speak. He was afraid that if he made a sound his voice would betray his emotions. The moment of revenge, about which he had dreamed so long, was at hand.

Only one aspect of the mission shocked him: that a man

like Mussa el-Dalil, who could put a soldier to death for not obeying an order to the letter, was now plotting a flagrant departure from the basic plan approved by their organization's high command.

25

JIL QUICKLY ADAPTED to his new life. His private audience with the Rebbe, which lasted almost three hours, had been an extraordinary turning point. Jil was astonished to learn that the Rebbe knew every detail of the lives of his emissaries in the Soviet Union. The Tzadik wanted to hear firsthand just how Daidushka had succeeded in raising and educating him as a Jew and a Hasid.

In the course of the meeting, Jil was struck by the remarkable spiritual power that emanated from the Tzadik, by an awareness of the incisiveness that enabled him in a flash to penetrate to the recesses of a soul, comprehending its mysteries immediately and completely. It therefore came as no surprise when the Rebbe suddenly asked the very question with which he had been so long preoccupied.

"You are searching for your identity?"

"Yes, Rebbe."

"And you have reservations about your Jewishness, don't you."

"Yes, Rebbe," Jil replied, "though I don't question the validity of Judaism. I am just not convinced that the way in which it is practiced is the way for me."

The Rebbe nodded his head slowly.

"You need some time by yourself."

"I tried to explain this to my grandfather."

"And he understood . . ."

"Yes."

"Your Zaide is a wise man and a true Hasid," said the Rebbe. "He has made a great sacrifice, he and Rabbi Shmuel Gillerman. Your presence here represents a part of their sacrifice. But have no fear. Almighty God will let no harm come to them. You may be assured of their well-being."

Jil's pulse quickened. He had an uncanny feeling that the Tzadik might know of the danger threatening him and the nature of Jil's real mission.

"Rebbe . . ."

He was about to ask if the Rebbe knew why he had come to Crown Heights, but the latter raised his hand to stop him.

"My son," he said, "some questions must not be asked, not even of me. God guides our destiny and, in ordaining the future, moves in mysterious ways. Our understanding is often too limited to comprehend His intentions."

As Jil rose to leave, the Rebbe smiled at him.

"Bless you for coming," he said quietly. "One day you will know whether you want to remain with us."

As time went by, Jil began to question his hypothesis that as the first stage of the reprisal against the Rebbe the Crown Heights area would be reconnoitered by an advance agent, a fox.

At night, stretched out in bed, his eyes fixed on a spot in the middle of the ceiling, he visualized the territory he covered each day, reviewing in his mind the faces he had seen. He assumed that the fox would operate in broad daylight, when the streets were teeming with cars and people. These were the hours in which, under his cover as the Rebbe's emissary, Jil could move about safely, checking and rechecking details and gathering the information he might need later.

Confident that he would be able to spot any stranger who was checking out the neighborhood, Jil reassured himself that he would find the fox within a day or two of his arrival. What he needed now was patience. It was important that he stay calm. The long period of waiting created its own tensions, which could ultimately only be relieved by action. Jil felt terribly alone. He remembered that Sergei had told him he could turn to Volodia for help, but the time hadn't yet come for that.

On Monday, March third, Jil noticed a group of workers repairing ruts in the street near the Rebbe's home. They had not been there before, and he carefully absorbed every detail. A small vehicle used by the workers was parked on the right side of the road. Behind the wheel sat the driver, and next to him was a worker, his helmet pulled down over his eyes so that he could sleep undisturbed. Three men worked in the street, two preparing the hole and the third pouring asphalt. A small roller towed by the vehicle pressed the asphalt once the holes had been filled. Something about the operation was wrong. Jil crossed the street and looked at the vehicle again, examining it carefully. Everything appeared to be in order. Perhaps his mind was playing tricks on him.

The Rebbe, who had been sitting near the window reading a book, looked up as he heard Jil enter the house. He studied him for a moment, then asked: "Did you learn Hebrew in Russia?"

"A little, Rebbe."

"Then you know that the letters of the Hebrew alphabet have various meanings?"

"How is that possible?"

"Well, for example, take the word that is spelled Beth, Kuf, Resh. What do the letters mean?"

Jil thought for a moment. "*Boker*—morning," he said.

"Correct," the Rebbe said with a slight smile. "But they can also mean 'cowboy,' or 'criticized,' or 'he visited,' and so on . . ."

"But, Rebbe, they can be differentiated by filling in the vowel signs to indicate the exact meaning you want from the word."

The Rebbe smiled again.

"So," he said, "what you have seen, you have not really seen if you haven't learned the signs."

Jil left the house deep in thought. On its face, the conversation was about the vowel signs of their ancestral tongue. But Jil knew the Rebbe did not speak unless he wished to convey a message. He walked a few paces and stopped. He realized that he had overlooked a minute detail in the street tableau, what the Rebbe would have called a sign in the picture. Now he remembered what he had seen on his way to the house and what he had missed. Two people had been sitting in the cabin of the small truck used by the repair crew, but only one, the driver, was necessary. It might well be that the man sitting next to him was not a part of the crew at all. During winter, repair crews went from street to street filling in the potholes created by the rock salt put on the snow. Being part of a crew afforded an excellent cover for reconnoitering a given area. The vowel signs were in place now, the meaning of the word was clear.

What he had been waiting for had happened, was happening then and there. Whoever the fox might be, Jil had to admire his ingenuity: he had found a way to move about freely in an area in which strangers were noticed immediately.

Walking back the way he had come, Jil turned so that he had to pass close by the truck. He drew a newspaper from his pocket, opened it, and edged slowly toward the vehicle. He stopped every few paces, as if an item in the newspaper had drawn his attention, until he came to rest only a few feet from the truck. He raised his eyes over the edge of the newspaper just as the man sitting next to the driver lit a cigarette. As he lifted his head, Jil recognized the face.

The fox was Horst Welsh.

Jil felt a stab of fear: the German had spearheaded the more savage actions of various terrorist gangs, and his specialty was laying the groundwork for liquidations. His appearance meant that the Rebbe was slated for death.

Then the professional in him took hold. Horst Welsh was the first link in the chain: he must keep a tight grip and under no circumstances release his hold on Horst. Through him, he would reach the others—those who would actually carry out the operation. Jil was certain that Welsh did not know their identity. He was familiar with the KGB system; they always split off the links of the chain so that each knew only the identity of the individual to whom he was directly responsible. Even if one link were disconnected, the chain remained intact. It was essential he find the connecting links. Jil knew the rules of the game only too well, and the penalty for failure was death. To carry out his mission he would have to operate as his opponents did, only with greater savagery.

Jil passed in front of the truck. He had no fear that Horst

Welsh could identify him. He was a Hasid now; the figure he cut bore no resemblance to Jil, the pantomimist.

After his initial reaction, Jil was transformed into a hunter. He moved quickly, going first to the Rebbe's house for the second time that day, then to Yudke's shop, where he found the carpenter waiting for him. Word of his impending departure on a mission had spread with astonishing swiftness.

Yudke's manner toward him was deferential. "Word has come down that you are to be given assistance—whatever help you might possibly need. God is with you and the Rebbe's blessing accompanies you." Curiosity was clearly gnawing at him, but he carefully avoided asking about the nature of the mission. Here this poor humble immigrant had arrived only a short time ago from the Soviet Union, and already the word had gone out that he was to be treated as an important emissary of the Rebbe with a mission that obligated every Hasid in the congregation to regard him as the Tzadik's envoy, a man who spoke for and indeed stood in the Rebbe's stead.

"We have people in every part of the United States and Europe," Yudke explained to Jil. "Both open Hasidim and secret Hasidim."

"Secret Hasidim?"

"Secret only in that, while they are Hasidim like you and me, their manner is different."

"I don't understand," Jil said.

"There are Hasidim who have attained important positions in banking, in education, in government, and elsewhere, but our style of dress and life would make it difficult for them to move in these spheres. So they have been granted special dispensation by the Rebbe to dress without any external indication that they are Hasidim."

"But spiritually they are Hasidim?"

"Even as we are. And they will do anything that is asked of them to help you. No matter where you are, if you need something, one of our people will be there to provide it for you. Someone will always be ready to assist you."

"How can I reach them?"

"Contact me," said Yudke. "I will give you a telephone number. Let an hour pass and then call the individual."

Yudke drew a sealed envelope from a drawer in his carpentry bench. "In this envelope you will find everything you need for your travels in the course of the mission."

He took it from Yudke and opened it. The envelope contained five thousand dollars in cash, and a checkbook on an account in a Manhattan bank.

"These things are arranged quickly," said Yudke, smiling at the look of surprise on Jil's face. "You can use as much money as you need, as you see fit. You must understand that one who goes out to perform a mission must not be troubled by worldly concerns. We shall take care of all your requirements. All you need supply is patience and faith in the righteousness of your cause."

Jil had difficulty lowering his gaze from the old carpenter's.

"You said that help would be forthcoming in the United States. But what about other places?"

"In Europe, you may turn to my brother Volodia. You can always find him in his restaurant in Saint Germain des Près. You have been there. Are you familiar with the area?"

"Yes, I'm familiar with it."

"And if you need assistance in other parts of the world, my brother Volodia will tell you where and how you can obtain help. It will be as effective as what you receive here."

"I'll remember that."

"Good. From now on, you are a real emissary."

Yudke replaced the money and documents in the envelope and handed it to Jil.

"We will be waiting for your return. God will be with you."

They shook hands and Jil left the carpentry shop.

It was time to go back and relocate the truck used by the street repairmen. But first Jil stopped at his apartment where he removed the shabby, oversized clothing he had been wearing and changed into a faded pair of jeans and a leather coat lined with sheepskin. With his curly chestnut hair and beard, Jil looked like an ordinary young man. The Hasid was gone, but there was still no danger that Horst Welsh could identify him.

Outside, the weather was almost pleasant, and the air carried the first hint of spring. Jil moved quickly through the streets, trying to locate the truck. He found it by mid-afternoon on Eastern Parkway.

221

The men worked slowly now; their day was drawing to a close and they were tired. The driver sat in the cab of the truck and next to him the wily fox—Horst Welsh. Now, however, it wasn't Horst Jil sought, but the German's bodyguards. He knew that Welsh needed to feel protected from sudden physical attack in order to function. And knowing his weakness Jil knew that the bodyguards had to be close at hand.

After a brief search, he found them—two young men in a green 1977 Ford parked around the corner. The car had diplomatic plates. Jil memorized the number and headed toward a nearby restaurant. Ducking into a pay phone, he quickly dialed the number of the carpentry shop. Yudke's deep, resonant voice answered.

"I need help," Jil said.

"I thought it was you." Yudke chuckled. "What can I do for you?"

"I need a car."

"Urgent?"

"Very."

"Where?"

"Next to the headquarters on Eastern Parkway." Jil described the location of the automobile with the diplomatic plates. "I want it parked behind the green Ford."

"It will be taken care of."

"Oh, and one other thing."

"I am listening."

"I don't know how far your long arm extends. But I need to check who the green Ford belongs to. Apparently it's the property of a diplomatic mission." Jil gave him the letters and numbers on the plate.

"Call a little later. I'll try to have the information for you."

As Jil hung up he realized that in order to obtain the information Yudke would have to have a direct connection with the upper echelons of the FBI.

Jil walked slowly back to Eastern Parkway, stopping about fifty yards from the repair truck. At that moment he noticed the door of the Hasidic headquarters swing open; a young Hasid emerged and hurried off. A few minutes later he returned driving a gray Buick which he parked behind the green Ford. Yudke's forces wasted no time.

The German fox was busy staking out the quarry, photographing the headquarters building from various angles. Overhead, clouds gathered, and the narrow beam of sunshine was engulfed by gray as the sky became overcast. Jil circled back to where the Ford was parked. He was waiting for Horst's arrival. Another hour passed. The workers seemed unusually industrious. Undoubtedly Horst kept their pockets well lined with terrorist money. At four-fifteen the truck finally pulled up next to the Ford and stopped. Horst scrambled out and opened the back door of the car. Before he had a chance to close the door, the driver had already released the handbrake, stepped on the accelerator, and pulled away from the curb.

Jil got into the gray Buick. The keys had been placed in the glove compartment as he had instructed. He started after Horst, forced by the heavy rush-hour traffic to keep a close tail on the Ford.

At five-twenty the green car pulled up in front of the Elliot, an old and rather rundown hotel near Madison Square Garden. Horst and a husky fellow who had been sitting next to the driver got out of the car and went in.

Jil slid the Buick into an empty parking space in front of the hotel. He managed to reach the reception desk just as the elevator doors closed on the two men. He watched the gilded pointer above the elevator as it swept past the Roman numerals indicating the floor numbers. The hand stopped at five—the top floor.

The clerk at the reception desk was young and friendly. He flashed Jil a pleasant smile. "What can I do for you?"

"I'd like a room—on the top floor if possible." Jil contorted his face into an absurd expression and held it until the youth burst into laughter.

"Hey, that was good! How did you do that?"

Jil twisted up his face again, shifting instantaneously from one expression to another: an entire gallery of characterizations. The clerk doubled up with laughter: this fellow in the red beard was a real comedian.

"You must be a nightclub performer, eh?"

"Something like that," admitted Jil. "What's your name?"

"George."

"Mine's Mack."

They shook hands and the clerk handed Jil the key to a room on the fifth floor.

"Listen," said Jil. "I'm alone in the city. What's to do here a little later on?"

"That depends," said George, shrugging his shoulders. "It's a big city. There are a million possibilities. Depends on what you want." He paused. "Listen . . . things begin to slow down here at about ten. A couple of friends and I were thinking about a little card game, in the room behind the information desk. You interested in being the fourth hand?"

"I'm interested, old buddy." He contorted his face again and George laughed.

"Say, you're good, you know? Believe me, the comedians on television have got nothing on you!"

Jil waved good-bye and, room key in hand, turned toward the elevator. A minute later he emerged on the fifth floor and stepped into a narrow, high-ceilinged hall whose red carpet had long ago been worn smooth by use. The square hallway extended to an emergency staircase that lead to a back courtyard. Hotels like this were very familiar to Jil from his previous stays in the United States. Room 517 was like scores of others in which he had lived in the course of the last few years: a bed, a chest of drawers, an armchair, a straightbacked wooden chair near a desk, a floor lamp, a table lamp, even a color television set.

Jil placed his bag on the table and took off his leather coat with the sheepskin lining. Then he went to the telephone and, receiving an outside line from the switchboard, dialed Yudke's home.

"Good evening," he said when he heard Yudke's voice. "Do you have an answer for me?"

"Yes, I do. The vehicle belongs to a man named Simon Alexander; he's a member of the Bulgarian delegation to the United Nations."

"There's no mistake about that?"

"No. Not considering the contact who gave me the information."

So Yudke did have a high-placed source in the FBI, just as Jil had suspected.

The fact that they were using a Bulgarian meant Jil could now begin to shorten the list. The Bulgarians could be eliminated; from the moment they had been chosen to escort Horst Welsh in New York, they became just another isolated link that would be detached from the chain as soon as their task was completed. Jil recognized Pavel Ramizor's salami system: hack off pieces of the communist intelligence community and use each unit separately, individually, discarding it, making it impossible to connect one link to the next.

At ten-thirty Jil found George and his two friends in the little room behind the reception desk. Four glasses and a bottle of Scotch stood on the table. The young clerk greeted him with a broad smile.

"Mack," he said, "I want you to meet Frank and Barry." Like George, they were in their late twenties and part of the hotel staff. "I've been telling these two they wouldn't be able to see what a serious and important guy you are under that red beard of yours."

Jil laughed as he drew his chair up to the square table. George was anxious to show off his new discovery to his friends, who seemed pleasant young men. Jil was in high spirits, his mood enhanced by the fact that George was an unexpected find, someone who would be able to perform small but essential services for him.

In the course of the poker game Jil dropped almost ninety dollars, the lion's share going to George.

"Listen, buddy," George said when the game was over and the other two had left, "I feel bad about your losing so heavily tonight."

"Forget that." Jil grinned. "But there is something you might be able to help me with."

"Name it, Mack."

"Look," he said hesitantly, feigning a reluctance to continue, "you're an intelligent fellow, George. You could see through any bullshit story I might try to tell you, right?"

"Right." George laughed.

"There are two guests staying here, also on the fifth floor. I don't know what names they're registered under. Probably not their own."

"What do they look like?"

Jil described them verbally and then impersonated Horst, mimicking his quick, nervous gait. George burst out laughing.

"Oh, yeah. I know who you mean. And the other guy looks like a professional prizefighter."

"That's them. When did they come here?"

"Wait—let me get the hotel register. We'll see exactly." George left the room and returned a minute later with a thick notebook in hand. "They checked in on Saturday. Room 524. The skinny one is named Korchain. The other one is Mishkin." He closed the notebook. "So, what can I do for you?"

"Listen, George, I want to know whenever they leave the hotel. Okay?"

"That's all?"

"Yes." Jil pulled out his wallet and started to take out a bill, but George grabbed his forearm.

"No need for money."

Jil was surprised. "Payment for service," he insisted.

"I don't perform services like that, buddy." George released Jil's arm. "I'm doing this for a friend."

At six-fifteen Jil was awakened by the telephone. George was as good as his word.

"Morning, Mack." He chuckled. "Sorry to wake you, but you asked for it."

"They left?"

"Five minutes ago."

Jil leaped from the bed and was standing in the hall in front of Horst's door a few minutes later. He easily jimmied the lock and slipped quickly into Room 524. The two suitcases were brimming with personal effects but nothing significant beyond a Swiss passport to which a photograph of Horst Welsh was affixed, bearing the name of Willie Korchain. There was nothing that shed light on Horst's plans.

Jil spent the day in the hotel. It was pointless to travel to Crown Heights. He knew exactly what the German and his two Bulgarian companions were doing there. That night he again sought the company of George and his friends, entertaining them with imitations until they were weak with laughter. Jil spent Wednesday and Thursday at the hotel in the same fashion while Horst continued his reconnaissance of Crown Heights.

Early Friday morning the telephone rang in Jil's room. He knew George was on the other end of the line.

"The chickens are about to fly the coop."

"When?"

"Within a half hour. They asked me to prepare the bill."

"Do mine first. I'm on my way down."

So Horst Welsh had completed his business in Crown

Heights and was about to take off. In a short time the Bulgarian contingent would be replaced by a new group—another link in the chain.

The bill was ready when Jil arrived at the reception desk. As he paid, he glanced up at the clerk.

"Like we agreed," George protested. "No personal extras. Friends don't keep accounts."

"I'll remember this, George."

"Come back again sometime."

After a brief handshake, Jil stepped out of the hotel into the cool, morning air. The Buick was parked twenty yards from the entrance. He put the bag on the seat next to him and started the motor to warm it. After five minutes he turned it off and waited. In a short while the green Ford pulled up in front of the hotel and Horst Welsh and his bodyguard emerged. They got into the car and it took off quickly.

At that early hour the roads weren't crowded and it was easy to tail another vehicle without arousing any suspicion. From the moment the Bulgarians' car entered the Brooklyn Battery Tunnel, Jil relaxed behind the wheel. It was clear their destination was Kennedy International Airport.

The Ford stopped before the American Airline terminal and Horst Welsh got out with his companion. He carried one suitcase and the Bulgarian the other. Jil slowed down and drove the Buick into a large parking lot. He placed the keys in the glove compartment, got out, and closed the door without locking it.

Entering the terminal, Jil peered through the crowd and in a few moments picked out Horst. He was standing at the counter with his bodyguard right behind him. They were waiting for their seat assignments.

Opposite there was a large board that flashed the departing flights: at seven-thirty there was a flight to Los Angeles, at eight o'clock one to Miami, and at eight-ten, a flight to Chicago. The remainder of the flights were scheduled to take off much later in the morning, at times that would not justify Horst's arrival at the airport at this hour. Jil tailed the German and his companion. They walked to gate thirty-four—their destination was Miami.

Jil returned to the ticket counter.

"I'd like a ticket to Miami on the flight that's leaving now."

"I'm sorry, sir. That flight is all booked up. But if you'd like to wait, I'll put you on standby."

The clerk punched the computer and added Jil's name to the list of standby passengers. There were five others on the list; a few minutes before flight time, the clerk announced the names of three of them.

"I'm sorry," she said, turning to Jil.

"That's all right." He smiled. "When's the next flight?"

"At ten in the morning."

He paid for the ticket with cash, thanked the young woman, and walked to the row of public telephones, and placed his call.

The carpenter's voice was thick with sleep. "Yes? Hello?"

"Good morning, Yudke. I need help again."

"What kind of help?" Yudke had immediately come awake.

"I need a tail on two men when they arrive at the airport in Miami."

"I don't have a contact at the moment," said Yudke hesitantly. "Call me again in an hour."

It was a nerve-wracking hour for Jil. Horst Welsh was on his way to Miami. There had to be someone there to tail him. From time to time Jil glanced at his watch: half an hour, an hour; he gave Yudke another five minutes, then went back to the telephone and dialed the number of the house in Crown Heights.

"You'll need a pen—or can you remember?" Yudke asked.

"I'll remember."

Yudke repeated the Miami telephone number twice.

"This man is already waiting for your call. He will help you. He is a well-known criminal lawyer. Anything else?"

"That's all."

Jil hung up and made a collect call to the lawyer in Miami. They conferred briefly and the lawyer agreed.

"Okay, I'll put a tail on them. And I'll be waiting for you at the airport. What do you look like?"

"Thirty-seven years old. Curly red hair, a red beard; I'll be wearing blue jeans."

"Are you also one of the secret followers?"

"I don't know." Jil laughed. "Believe me, I don't know."

The lawyer was waiting for him at the Miami airport, a

man of about thirty, tastefully dressed, his grave expression enhanced by the thick dark frames of his glasses. He led Jil to a chauffeur-driven Lincoln and ushered him into the roomy back seat. Raising the window that separated the front and back seats of the car, he pressed the intercom button and told his chauffeur to take them to the Hotel Belvedere.

"You have a room there for as long as you need it," he explained to Jil. "Everything is paid for. If you need anything else, let me know."

"What did you find out?"

"My men waited at the airport. Your description was very accurate; they picked out the German and his bodyguard immediately. There were two other men waiting for them; Latins, according to my men. They drove to the harbor, to a seafood restaurant called the Santiago. Your men entered the restaurant with their companions. An hour ago the German and his friend left with two other Spanish types who took them to a private yacht basin where they boarded a boat called the *Sierra Madre*. It departed immediately. That's all."

"I assume that isn't quite all," Jil said, glancing at his host.

"You're right."

"Did you try to find out who the *Sierra Madre* belongs to?"

"Yes. There is no boat by that name. It simply doesn't exist."

"What does that mean?" Jil asked in consternation.

"It's a boat used for smuggling," the lawyer explained. "The name is changed every few days. The real name appears only on the documents its captain holds."

"How can I locate the owner?"

"I'll find you a go-between, someone to sniff around and dig up information. You ask him a question, pay, and get your answer. I suggest that you don't leave your room. You'll hear from me within a few hours."

Jil had barely settled in to the comfortable and spacious suite on the eleventh floor of the Hotel Belvedere, overlooking the glittering blue expanse of the ocean, when the phone rang. It was the lawyer.

"I've found your man. His name is Manuel Plati."

"Does he know how to get in touch with me?"

"You should hear from him in a little while. He's willing to sell you the information."

The call from Manuel Plati came half an hour later. Jil explained that he wanted to know who owned the *Sierra Madre*.

"That's a complicated business," Plati replied.

"How complicated?"

"At least a day's work. Maybe more."

"How much?"

"A hundred dollars."

"Okay."

There was a brief silence during which Manuel Plati regretted having quoted his price so hastily. The man had agreed too fast—he should have asked for more.

"There might be some additional expenses," Plati added.

"Forget them. One hundred."

Plati sighed. "Come by my house tomorrow; it's near the harbor. If I'm not there, you don't have to wait outside. Go in. I'll turn up. Okay?"

"Fine."

Manuel Plati described the location of his apartment and set the meeting for the next day at six o'clock in the evening.

When Jil arrived at the apartment shortly before six, Manuel Plati was not at home, but, as he had said, the door was unlocked. Jil entered the apartment. The squalor of the place was appalling. On one side of the room was a wide bed with an old worn mattress partially covered by a soiled sheet. A wooden chair stood next to a small table near the bed. A battered floor lamp stood in one corner of the room beside a large, dilapidated armchair.

Ten minutes later Jil heard the sound of footsteps rapidly approaching the entrance. Then the door flew open as if blown by a strong gust of wind and Plati, perspiring and out of breath, stood beaming in the threshold. His lips parted, framing yellow, nicotine-stained teeth as he flashed Jil a broad, amicable smile.

"Hi!"

He came into the room and kicked the door shut. He seemed in a festive mood. He opened the refrigerator, took out a bottle of cheap wine, and, pulling the cork out with his teeth, raised the bottle to his lips and swilled down a long draft. He then offered the bottle to Jil, who gestured his refusal.

"Have you got what I asked for?"

Manuel Plati smiled. He took another drink from the bottle and waited. Jil took out his wallet, withdrew a hundred-dollar bill, and handed it to him. With a short, vigorous laugh, the man smelled the bill and thrust it into his pocket.

"The boat belongs to Antonio Larado," he said.

"Who is he?"

"Ah!" Manuel fluttered a hand. "A very big man. And in case you're interested, the boat returned an hour ago." Plati wiped his thick lips with the back of his hand.

"From where?"

"Nobody knows. No one's talking—"

"Why?"

"Nobody wants trouble from Larado."

"Do you know him?"

Manuel glowered at the preposterousness of the question.

"What are you talking about? Of course I know who he is, and he knows who Manuel Plati is," he said proudly. "For another hundred dollars I'll arrange a meeting for you with him. Right now. You can hear everything you want to know from the horse's mouth."

"Why won't he tell you?"

"Me?" asked Plati, clucking his surprise at the naiveté of Jil's question. "You don't understand. Why should I suddenly ask about his business? But if you come to him as someone who wants to hire the boat, eh? When two important people talk, it's possible to ask all sorts of questions. The person who asks sometimes gets answered, too. Eh?"

What Manuel said seemed reasonable. Jil drew another hundred-dollar bill from his wallet and placed it on the windowsill.

"Arrange the meeting," he said.

Manual glanced covetously at the money, then turned and walked out of the apartment; there was a public telephone in the hall. Through the open door Jil heard Plati conversing fluently in Spanish. A minute later he returned, and smiling broadly, went over to the window and grabbed the hundred-dollar bill.

"It's mine," he said, stuffing the money into his pocket. "Antonio Larado is ready to discuss business. He's waiting for us at the shipyard."

On the way to the wharves Plati pattered on in praise of Antonio Larado. From this stream of chatter Jil culled one interesting bit of information: the entire shipyard belonged to this apparently important and influential figure. And he also decided that Manuel Plati was an extremely dangerous blabbermouth.

As they alighted from Manuel's car, Jil caught the first pungent whiff of the ocean: the distinctive, pervasive odor of oil and salt water wafting in on a gentle breeze from the murky waters of the bay. The clear phosphorescent glow of the moon and stars in a cloudless sky illuminated the far corners of the shipyard. At the edge of the dock, near the main building, a giant derrick used to hoist disabled ships ashore for removal to drydock loomed spectrally in the pearly light.

Manuel led Jil to a stone path that encircled the shipyard. At the back of the yard was a small entrance illuminated by a dim electric light. Plati pounded on the door with his fist and in a few seconds they heard a key turning in the lock. The door opened a crack and a man peered suspiciously at them through the thin slit, then swung the door wide. Manuel grabbed Jil by the shoulder and pulled him inside.

Jil caught the scent of death—like the fetid stench of streaming entrails after they have been torn open by a knife-thrust to the belly. Death had an unmistakable odor that could be neither swallowed nor spit out. From his long years as a KGB agent Jil had learned to sense where death lurked, even if he could not know its intended victim. His legs were heavy with fear, as if they had been cast in lead.

As the door creaked closed behind him, he knew he had been drawn into a trap. No one had locked the door; no one stood over him brandishing a weapon. No one, in fact, had even threatened him. The big man with the shoulders of a weight-lifter who opened the door didn't even give him a second glance, but nevertheless Jil sensed that trouble lay ahead. Plati, breathing heavily beside him, sniffled from time to time and wiped his nose with a filthy handkerchief.

At the end of the corridor another door opened onto a small staircase. The ominously rhythmic beat of their footsteps as they descended the stairs kept perfect cadence with the palpitations of fear that shook Jil's body. He felt the familiar queasiness in the pit of his stomach.

They entered a long, narrow room, no more than twelve

feet wide, but at least three times as long. It was a hermetically sealed trap: except for the door through which they had come, there was no other opening, not even a window. Running the length of the wall to Jil's left was the largest aquarium he had ever seen. It appeared to be about eight feet high and more than three feet deep. Lights inside the tank illuminated lush vegetation and thousands of beautiful tropical fish of myriad color and shape; they swam in schools, stopping from time to time, hanging suspended in water, then changing formation and gliding swiftly away to vanish behind the thick greenery.

The right-hand wall was covered with an impressive display of ancient fishing equipment and beautifully fashioned nautical instruments: large compasses embedded in dull copper plates, wooden steering bars, and wheels of various shapes and designs. In the middle of the wall a row of anchors, large and small, hung from a heavy wooden plank. And farther down was a display of fishing tackle—long, flexible angling rods used for casting from the shore and short, thick, deep-sea fishing poles.

This was Antonio Larado's private office. The dockyard boss sat at the far end of the room behind a massive wooden desk that looked as if it had been hewn from a large tree trunk. He didn't have to rise from the enormous upholstered chair for Jil to realize that he was in the presence of a man of gargantuan size. His weight was probably equal to that of two husky men. Jil had rarely seen such enormous shoulders. The short, thick neck supported a head that seemed altogether misplaced: it was gaunt and elongated, and the flat forehead—which seemed to have been compressed in a vise—was considerably narrower than the broad expanse of his thick jowls. The wide, flattened nose arched down to a thin, lipless sliver of a mouth. His large, round eyes held a look of perpetual surprise.

Except for an antique Chinese vase containing three long-stemmed red roses, the desk was bare. From time to time, Larado drew the vase toward him and inhaled the flowers' fragrance. He gazed in silence at Jil, who was standing with Manuel Plati at his left and Larado's brawny, intimidating henchman behind him.

No one spoke. Larado again sniffed the roses, his nostrils distended, his eyes closed; he seemed wholly absorbed in sensual gratification. Then he raised his head and nodded. Jil heard the man behind them stride to the door, and a key turned in the lock.

Manuel Plati seemed utterly petrified. "This is the man," he blurted in consternation, his voice shaking.

Antonio nodded again to indicate his comprehension. "What do you want?" Under other circumstances the youthful, high-pitched squeak that emanated from his huge body might have elicited laughter.

"To hire a boat," Jil replied.

"That's all?"

"Yes."

"So why does this little worm buzz in my ear that you are interested in knowing where my boat went yesterday?" Again he raised the small vase and buried his nose in the red roses.

So Manuel Plati had intended to profit from both sides.

"Just a rumor," said Jil.

The blood pounded in his temples. Although he wanted to avoid it at all costs, he knew he would have to kill. He felt the muscles of his throat constrict, and perspiration suddenly oozed from his palms.

"Rumors, you say." Larado chuckled. The wattles of flesh hanging in loose folds between his small chin and chest undulated as he laughed. "The worm knows I hate rumors. Isn't that right, worm?"

"*Sí*, Senor Larado, *sí* . . ."

From the corner of his eye Jil saw the terror mount in Plati's face. Plati knew what Jil could not: that the word "worm" meant death; a man who had been so designated knew that his final hours were approaching, that soon the worms would be eating his flesh. Jil glanced at the stain on Plati's trousers and then looked down at the pool of urine forming on the floor around his shoes.

Antonio Larado grinned at Plati's incontinence and turned back to Jil. "If I were to tell you that the boat sailed for Havana, would you believe it?"

"Perhaps." Jil was mildly surprised. He was certain the man was telling the truth; indeed, candor seemed to be part of the game Larado was playing with Plati and himself. He was like a great hulking cat toying with a family of mice that cowered helplessly before him.

"Perhaps, you say." Larado gave a thin little chuckle that

grated on Jil's ears. "I tell this charmer the truth and he says 'perhaps'!" He was obviously enjoying himself. He slammed down his hand and the desk shook under the powerful impact of the blow. "What do you think of your friend, worm?"

"He's not my friend!" Manuel Plati was pleading for his life. His expression, the tone of his voice, every gesture indicated an awareness of the deadly peril of his situation.

"He's not your friend!" mocked the big man slowly. "If not for your stupidity, he would not even know that Antonio Larado exists. But I know you, Manuel, and I'm tired of your scratching around for a few miserable dollars. That's why you are a worm—"

Jil heard the soft groan, saw Plati's eyeballs turn up as he slid to the ground. The man behind them had moved like lightning. He drew the long blade from between Manuel Plati's ribs and it came out almost clean. Plati lay on the ground; bright rivulets of blood began to pool on the floor. He shuddered convulsively for a few seconds, groaned again, and turned over on his side. His head was thrown back, a look of dumb amazement frozen on his face. Death had come swiftly.

"I apologize," said Antonio Larado, again burying his nose in the flowers. Larado closed his eyes and inhaled the fragrance of the roses. Jil watched him, at the same time alert to his henchman's every move.

"Well," said Larado, opening his eyes and looking up at Jil, "I am waiting." He smiled.

"For what?"

"Surely you intend to tell me why you—and perhaps not only you—are interested in the *Sierra Madre*'s trip to Havana yesterday. Certainly you are not interested in me—then again, maybe you are."

Jil knew Larado did not intend to let him out of his office alive. Again, he caught the cloying, pervasive odor of death. Larado's henchman did not even wait for instructions from his boss, whose face had turned crimson with anger. He leaped at Jil, aiming an outstretched fist at his face. Jil sidestepped and the man flew past, nearly impaling himself on the sharp prong of an anchor mounted on the wall.

"Kill him!" Antonio Larado screamed.

The man studied the distance between himself and Jil, who stood with his back to the aquarium. His hand flicked back and he seized an anchor from the wall. His expression was cold and calculating, almost devoid of emotion. With the anchor raised high in his right hand, he lunged forward. Jil held his ground until his opponent was almost on him. Then he leaped aside.

The man sailed past Jil and brought the heavy anchor down with tremendous force on the aquarium. An anguished, bloodcurdling scream broke from his throat as he fell through the jagged hole and a sharp glass spike severed his jugular vein. He lay impaled on the picket of glass, his head inside the aquarium, blood spurting from the wound in his neck. The water surging out of the tank carried the fish onto the floor, where they flapped about in wild panic.

A deluge of curses burst from Antonio Larado.

"Son of a bitch," he squealed. "You murdered my fish . . . you killed my fish . . ." He seemed indifferent to the fate of his henchman, whose lifeless body hung half in and half out of the tank.

Only when Larado stood up did Jil see for the first time the man's size. As he heaved himself up from behind the desk, he looked like Neptune rising from the depths of the ocean. He was as strong as he was huge. He lifted the heavy desk and tossed it like a match box in Jil's direction. It hit the floor and broke apart from the force of the impact. Jil retreated quickly and prepared to meet his advance. In pitting himself against this colossus, he knew that he could make no miscalculation.

He detached a large fish-knife from the wall, assessing its weight and feeling for its center of balance as he took it down. Larado, shrieking curses, lumbered toward him. In his rage, Larado did not see Jil raise his hand and hurl the knife, until he stopped suddenly, tottered, and gasped for air. The knife had found its mark, plunging through the layers of fat to pierce his throat. Antonio Larado grasped the handle of the knife and dislodged it from his neck with a sharp tug. The blood began to pour down his throat, choking off his breath.

Larado opened his mouth to bellow at his antagonist but the only sound that emerged was a faint squeal like a pig at slaughter. He continued to advance toward Jil, slogging through water and flapping fish, blood streaming from the open wound in his neck. Jil stepped aside hastily, afraid he would have to engage the man again, this time with his bare hands.

But the knife had severed nerves and Larado was fast succumbing to paralysis. Suddenly, he halted in his tracks and stood absolutely still for a few seconds. Then, like a heavy tree sawed off at its base, he toppled forward, crashing on his face into the water from the shattered aquarium.

Jil took in the scene of carnage—the three bodies, the fish flapping in their death struggle—before he plunged across the room to the door. As he opened it, the water that had accumulated in the closed chamber overflowed the staircase and flushed the gaily colored tropical fish down the stairs. They accompanied him all the way to the exit of the building, where they finally came to rest in a puddle of water, a few still moving their gills and flapping feebly.

Jil found Manuel Plati's old Chevrolet in the parking area, and, crossing the ignition wires, tripped the motor. He drove toward the downtown commercial area; he would be able to find a taxi there. He wanted to ditch the car as soon as possible, before the bodies were discovered and the Miami police began their search for the killer. By that time he would be on his way to Europe.

He should have guessed that Cuba had served as the springboard for Horst's illegal entry into the United States. The German was a wanted man who would not have risked entering the country in any other way. Jil remembered the last time he had seen Horst, when he took him out of Vienna and brought him to Miguel de Salit's villa near Toledo. Now he understood the significance of Da'ud el-Za'id's presence in Spain; the Palestinians were involved in this operation. Horst had been smuggled out of Europe and transported to one of their bases in the Middle East. But which of the Arab guerrilla organizations was involved? And where was their base? Although he was certain that the fox was on his way back to brief the hit team on the plan he had developed for the operation, without answers to these two questions, it was impossible to try to go after Horst.

He would have to find out exactly where the German was once he arrived in Europe. There were people there who could help him. Moreover, in Europe, he was likely to find other links in the chain of command. Horst Welsh wasn't giving orders; he was receiving them. And the Palestinians were no more than the darting tongue of a venomous snake; he had to expose the serpent's head. Jil recalled Sergei's parting instructions to him in Moscow: beyond his mission of protecting the Rebbe, he was to try to prove the Soviet Union's complicity in the terrorist operation. The Russians had no desire for a direct confrontation with the United States. A Soviet-inspired terrorist action, carried out on American soil, was tantamount to an act of war. If Ramizor believed that the KGB's involvement in the operation had been exposed, the reprisal plan would be abandoned immediately. So it was imperative that he uncover the individuals operating in Europe under the aegis of the KGB; this was the only way he could bring about the collapse of the entire scheme.

26

On his return from Riga, Pavel Ramizor ordered an investigation into Dr. Grisha Rostovitch's past. To Boris Borodov this was a clear indication that Ramizor had not been able to get the information he wanted. The old man had already alerted his contacts in Riga and he now set off for that city himself.

He stayed for three days and was met on his return by Sergei Padayev, who drove him to his apartment on Kalinin Boulevard.

Although the trip had been arduous, Boris's mood was exalted. He was no longer accustomed to shuttling about the country, but, at every place he stopped, his men had been waiting to ease the burdens of the journey and to offer whatever assistance he required.

"Riga was as beautiful as ever," the old man remarked as they ascended the stairs to the first floor. "Not even the war could extinguish its loveliness."

Zina opened the door and embraced first her brother and then Sergei. She helped them out of their coats and led them into Boris's room. She put a bottle of vodka on the table and began boiling water in the samovar, and as she bustled about, she asked him questions about Riga. She, too, remembered the city with nostalgia, for she had been there many times during her childhood.

After she left to prepare food, Boris opened the bottle of vodka and filled two glasses.

"And so, brother Sergei," said the old man, after taking a sip of vodka, "how is Pavel Ramizor?"

"He is closing in on Grisha Rostovitch."

"As I anticipated."

"The investigation has branched out. They've made inquiries at the Medical School, the Central Hospital, the Lenin Research Laboratories—every place where Grisha worked, Ramizor's men are to be found."

"A thorough job."

"Yes, indeed."

"And Grisha is prepared for what is to come?"

"I explained the situation to him. He is frightened. He is all too familiar with Pavel's character. He knows what awaits him if he has to take the hard way."

"That we still don't know."

Sergei Padayev knew exactly what the old man meant. What happened to Grisha would depend on circumstances outside the borders of the Soviet Union, wherever Yan happened to be. In due course, they would know which route Grisha was to follow: immediate confession, or the more difficult path of silence in order to gain time, for time could be of tremendous value to Yan.

"What are we to do now?"

Boris studied Padayev's anxious face. "As I've said, Sergei, I've done my part. I am ready. At the proper time, you will bring Ramizor to me. I am prepared to face him."

The words were uttered quietly, but the power that lay in back of them was intimidating. The old clown had his trap laid and now needed nothing but to wait for the opportune moment.

27

VOLODIA KANTOR WAS cleaning up after the lunch crowd when Evyatar Miller entered the restaurant in St. Germain des Près. The Israeli came down the stairs with his hand extended before him.

"Reb Kantor, it's good to see you," he said, grasping the old man's hand.

"Reb Miller." A smile flickered across Volodia's face as he straightened up. "I'm glad to see that you are still with us." It was unusual for Evyatar to disappear for such an extended period of time. The Israeli looked tense and tired, Volodia observed. "Sit," he said, removing an upturned chair from a table and setting it down on the floor.

"Do you remember the subject of our last meeting?" Evyatar asked as he sat down.

"I do indeed: the Soviet Circus."

"Were you able to get any more information?"

"I've told you everything I know."

"I was hoping . . ."

"I'm sorry, Evyatar. But I'm sure that you have made some discoveries."

"I've discovered that there is someone who knows at least

241

as much as you do about the Circus. He's used it as the basis of a terrorist group that's currently operating in Europe. The members of this unit, which has KGB links, use the same code names as the old group. We're looking for them, Volodia."

"The last time you were here you showed me a sketch of one of them."

"A composite sketch of the Clown."

"Do you have others?"

"We've managed to put together pretty accurate descriptions of two others: the Acrobat and the Miracle Worker."

Evyatar drew a small leather billfold from his breast pocket and pulled out the sketches. He first showed Volodia the picture of the Miracle Worker: a very ordinary face distinguished only by a moustache that drooped down below the corners of the mouth in a style popular during the '60s. Thick-rimmed glasses sat somewhat askew and the hair was carefully brushed back and parted in the middle. The Acrobat, wearing a cap in the sketch, had thick eyebrows, plump, rounded cheeks, and a remarkably self-satisfied expression.

"Here's the third one, the Clown," said Evyatar, placing the drawing on the table alongside the others. "You've already seen this one."

Something in the picture again caught Volodia's attention. Something about the eyes. Volodia's pulse quickened, and he felt as if his throat had been gripped by a cold, unseen hand. He had seen that piercing look—a mixture of irony and profound sorrow—in the face of the young Russian immigrant who had come to seek assistance on his way to Crown Heights.

"Do you recognize him?" asked Evyatar, his eyes fixed on the old man.

Volodia felt sick. The resemblance between the young immigrant and the man depicted in the sketch could be coincidental. But the Russians were capable of such a ploy: infiltrating one of their agents into the Rebbe's very court. And he had recommended the man to the Hasidic leadership in Crown Heights!

"Volodia!" The sharp note in Evyatar's voice wrenched the restaurateur from his meditation. "You know something, don't you?"

Volodia hesitated, annoyed with himself for having allowed his expression to betray him.

"Who says I know something? I don't know anything."

"Volodia." Evyatar placed his hand on the old man's shoulder. "It's important for us to know; it's a matter of life and death. Maybe one man's life is at stake, maybe the lives of many more. What do you know?"

"I need time," said Volodia feebly. "Time to check something out . . ."

"How much time?"

"Maybe a few hours. Perhaps a day."

Evyatar removed his hand from Volodia's shoulder. Experience over their years of collaboration had taught Evyatar to trust the old man implicitly.

"I'll wait," Evyatar agreed. "But, in the name of God, it's important!"

He reached out for the picture, but Volodia pulled it back. He wanted to study the face in privacy.

"I'll call you later tonight," he said and, locking the door behind Evyatar, he went to the telephone. He had to reach Yudke at once. He wasn't yet convinced that the young Russian immigrant was indeed the Clown. Only one man could confirm his true identity: the Rebbe.

Paul Mansfield was waiting for Evyatar at a small café around the corner from the American Embassy.

"Did you get anything?" Evyatar asked as he joined him at the small, round table.

Paul shook his head and took a long swig of wine. "Nope . . . What about you?"

"I may have something tangible," Evyatar answered cautiously. Their glances met. "I hope so," he added.

"So, you've had a fruitful day, you bastard!" The American folded his arms over his chest and assumed the pose of a pupil listening intently to the words of his teacher. "Go ahead and talk. I'm listening."

"There is someone who can identify the Clown."

"We've had a number of those," Paul mumbled.

"This time it's different. It's not just an identification. It's my impression that this person can do more . . . maybe even help us find him."

"When are we likely to know more?"

243

"Maybe in an hour. Maybe not till morning."

They studied one another in silence. Each seemed to have aged during the past weeks; their faces had a grayish cast. At this point they could only wait. Outside the café, they hailed a cab and returned to their hotel. Once in his room, Evyatar stretched out in an armchair and propped his long legs on the bed.

He awoke with a start to the jangle of the telephone.

"I have something." Volodia's voice was unmistakable.

"I'm listening."

"It isn't for the telephone."

"I'll be right over."

Evyatar found Volodia sitting at the same table, beside him a steaming coffeepot and two large cups. As the Israeli entered the room, the old man motioned him to the chair opposite.

"Sit down and have some coffee," he said. "We both need it."

In his agitation and impatience to hear Volodia's report, Evyatar sat down abruptly without bothering to remove his coat.

"Well?" he asked.

"The man you're looking for is not exactly what you think he is," said Volodia.

"What do you mean?" He stared at the old man dubiously.

"He's all right," Volodia declared with a smile. "He's one of us. A good Jew."

"Just a minute . . ." The Israeli was perplexed. "First of all, have you identified him? Is he the Clown?"

"Yes, he is the Clown. And you can stop looking for him. Your search is completely unnecessary. You must wait."

Evyatar gave a brief, incredulous look. "You are telling me to stop looking for him?"

"I am not the one who decided. It is the Rebbe who said you are to halt the search." Volodia's voice was firm and confident, his manner calm.

"We're looking for him all over the world, Volodia!" In his anger Evyatar felt the blood rush to his head. "Can't you understand that? If you know who is he, then I want to remind you that he is involved in a terrorist operation!"

"Calm down," Volodia said, smiling serenely. "The Rebbe

says that if the man you're looking for wishes to get in touch with you, then contact will be made, and only then."

The Israeli gazed at Volodia in disbelief. With the approval of the Rebbe, Volodia had cooperated with the Mossad for many years. He was a clever man who possessed the abilities and reflexes of a superb espionage agent, and he had worked tirelessly to expose Soviet agents. Now, at the Rebbe's bidding, he was instructing Evyatar to abandon his search.

"Volodia," said Evyatar, clearing his throat. His voice was hoarse with fatigue. "We're not on the same wave-length this time. What you are saying makes the situation even worse. That the man we suspect of being an agent of Department V is a Jew only complicates things."

Volodia did not reply.

"Look," said Evyatar, dropping his voice to a whisper, "they are preparing to murder Jews and Christians in the United States, important supporters of Israel: Kissinger, Church, Jackson ... We are up to our necks in trouble, Volodia. They are attacking Israel from all sides. Don't you understand?"

Still Volodia did not reply.

"Just tell me one thing," said Evyatar. His voice carried a note of desperate pleading. "Where is he now?"

"Nobody knows."

"What does that mean?"

"He's gone." Volodia shrugged. "He was in Crown Heights."

Evyatar was speechless. His prey had been within grasp, but now the elusive Clown had vanished into the shadows.

"At least let me meet him, ask him a few questions ..."

Volodia remained silent.

"Oh, God," sighed the Israeli. "What's so special about the damned Clown that even the Rebbe is trying to protect him?"

"I don't know," the old man replied. "There are things that only the Rebbe knows."

Evyatar rose to leave. He knew it was hopeless to argue further. As he stepped out into the narrow street he was assailed by a sense of helpless despair. He was stalemated, and time was running out.

28

BECAUSE THE DREAM kept recurring, Jil dreaded sleep and staved it off as long as possible. When he could no longer cope with fatigue, he would fall into a deep, uneasy slumber, and the scene in Antonio Larado's shipyard would be replayed. Slithering from every direction across the vast, eerie panorama of his dreams, in a kaleidoscopic array of color, the fish flapped and leaped in the water as it poured down over the wooden stairs. He would wake with a low, tortured groan, shaking with terror.

Perhaps it came from his dread of death. It could so easily have ended differently. It could have been him sprawled with his face in the water. Lately, the scene had even begun to come to him in shockingly vivid daydreams as he made his way in rented cars across the European continent.

In Rome, he tried to locate two West Germans who had found refuge with the help of members of the Red Brigades. He thought that perhaps they would know from whom Horst Welsh was receiving orders. But the Germans hiding in Rome did not know. He drew blanks in Brussels and Vienna as well. He could find no one who could help him solve the mystery.

Faced with this situation, Jil found he had no alternative. He would have to meet with François Ripoll: there was no other way. The French lawyer probably knew who had recruited Welsh. Although their last meeting had left Jil with the strong suspicion that Ripoll might be playing a double game, he had no other choice. He would have to take that risk.

He arrived in Paris at midnight on Wednesday, and that same night the artistic inspiration for which he had yearned, toward which he had groped for months, perhaps even years, came to him. As he wandered along the picturesque alleyways of Montmartre, in solitude and silence, he decided what he wanted to do when it was all over and he was free.

As long as he was involved in murder and espionage, he could not express what he felt within, could not draw out the characters who lived within him—as yet unidentified, but viable. There were occasional moments of lucidity during which he seemed to catch fleeting glimpses of some of them.

That night, walking in Montmartre, Jil found relief from his nightmares, a brief interlude of tranquility, after which he would resume his murderous course. He thought about the characters he would one day create onstage. He needed to identify them.

The moment of recognition came in a flash. While he stood on the hilltop, with Paris stretched out below under the first soft flush of morning light, Jil remembered where he had seen these characters and he understood why he sought them now. They were the figures that flowed from the enchanted brush of the Jewish painter Marc Chagall: the quaint villagers who inhabited the Jewish townlets of eastern Europe, the characters who populated Daidushka's stories. He could make out the musicians among them, who hovered over the roofs of the houses: the fiddlers, the cellist, the drummer, the trumpeter. The lovers—the young boys and girls—were present too. He saw them in flight, drifting gently toward one another, their hands outstretched. There was also the Wandering Jew, striding, staff in hand, sack slung over his shoulder, roving from city to town, from one tiny village to the next. And there were innumerable other characters; Jil himself was one—a winged creature transformed into a man.

He stood still for a long time, watching the endless procession of images. The diaphanous veils of mist melted before him and silver-gray tufts of clouds shifted silently across the sky, assuming and discarding shapes almost human in contour. He had found complete peace. The inspiration he had sought so long had burst suddenly upon him: he would recreate the world of Marc Chagall.

At eleven o'clock on Thursday morning Louis Etienne received a telephone call from François Ripoll.

"I know you are busy, Monsieur Etienne, but I have news for you. The Clown is back."

Not certain that he had heard the lawyer correctly, Etienne asked him to repeat his words.

"The Clown is here in Paris."

"Where?"

"I don't know."

"*Merde!*" the inspector swore in exasperation. "What *do* you know?"

"That he will be at my office tonight. Between eight and nine. Or so he has informed me."

"So!" The inspector heaved a sigh of relief. "Monsieur Ripoll, I appreciate this information very much. We will be at your place at seven." And Louis Etienne put through an immediate call to Evyatar Miller and Paul Mansfield.

François Ripoll received the three in his fifth-floor office. He was patently nervous, his tension mounting steadily since Jil's unexpected telephone call. The two tranquilizers he had taken with some cognac provided no relief.

Ripoll was finding it difficult to serve two masters, particularly since each one represented a very real danger to himself. He wanted to buttress his position with the establishment, yet he found himself no calmer after his conversation with Louis Etienne.

At twenty minutes to eight, his three guests left Ripoll and went to join their men, who were waiting in ambush outside. They were stationed in a cordon around the building, the plan being to apprehend the Clown outside, in order to avoid incriminating Ripoll. They had agreed to wait until after the meeting before seizing him. When he emerged from the building he would be shadowed and picked up at a distance from Avenue Victor Hugo.

As time passed, tempers began to fray. Sitting in the solitude of his office, François Ripoll's malaise increased steadily. The three men staked out in Etienne's car opposite the building's impressive façade began to show signs of strain, too; Paul Mansfield chain-smoked his cigars, Evyatar Miller's hands were sweat-covered, and Louis Etienne kept chewing on his lower lip. They did not exchange a word until a few minutes after nine.

"I suspect that the Clown will not come," said Etienne.

"Son of a bitch," Paul swore.

Evyatar said nothing. There seemed to be little point in complaining. There was still time; the Clown's delay might have been caused by any one of a number of reasons.

"I'm going to call Ripoll," Etienne declared several minutes after ten. He got out of the car and walked to the public telephone at the Metro station a few hundred yards away. He returned shortly thereafter, got back into the car, and started the motor.

"The lawyer is petrified," he said. "He can't explain why the Clown didn't show up; he's afraid he smelled a rat." Louis Etienne was limp from exhaustion. The evening with its endless waiting, its unfulfilled expectations, its relentless tension had exacted a heavy physical and emotional toll. "Shall I take you to the hotel?" he asked.

"Fine," Evyatar answered, his voice heavy with disappointment.

Alone in his office, an overwrought François Ripoll resolved to confront his dilemma. He would stop working on behalf of the terrorists, drop out, so to speak, for a while, until those with whom he had collaborated had forgotten him. He had already accumulated a great deal of money and could live comfortably for the remainder of his life. Perhaps he would retire to the villa in St. Tropez and reappear after a few years to devote himself exclusively to business activities. This might be his last opportunity to pull out.

He poured another drink and got into the private elevator to go to his living quarters on the floor above. As the elevator came to a stop on the sixth floor, he immediately noted the slender rim of light framing its heavy brass door. His pulse quickened. He stepped out of the elevator into the lounge and halted dead in his tracks.

The chandelier was ablaze with lights, and there in the deep armchair near the window sat Jil.

"Welcome, Monsieur Ripoll."

Ripoll's heart fluttered wildly. "We set a time," he said angrily. The pressure mounting in his temples induced sharp spasms of pain.

"I simply changed the place and waited for you here."

"You could have informed me."

Then François Ripoll suddenly fell silent, his eyes riveted on Jil. Understanding had come in a flash: Jil set a trap and he had fallen into it. Ripoll laughed bitterly.

"Now I understand," he exclaimed. "You never before set up a meeting with me by phone, Jil."

"True."

"So now you undoubtedly know what you wanted to find out."

"That also is true."

Ripoll's knees grew weak, and he felt his legs begin to tremble. He strode quickly to the bar and took down a bottle of cognac. His hand shook as he filled a glass; he reached into his pocket and withdrew some pills, which he washed down with cognac.

"Will you have something to drink?" he asked.

Jil shook his head, his gaze fixed on the lawyer. Ripoll knew now where he had slipped up. At their last meeting, Jil had realized there was a possibility, perhaps a very strong one, that he was cooperating with the law, that he might even have fingered Jil as an important operative in the world of terror. Jil had had to find out the extent of his duplicity. This time Ripoll had stumbled badly.

"Who were those men down there waiting for me?" Jil asked.

"One of them was from the DST."

"And the others?"

"They're working with the DST to uncover members of the Baader-Meinhof gang and their supporters."

"What do they know about me?" Jil seemed totally relaxed but his eyes never left the lawyer's perspiring face.

At this stage, evasion was pointless. "I'm sorry," Ripoll mumbled. His tongue was thick in his mouth—the combined effect of cognac and tranquilizers. His sentences were short and somewhat disjointed, and a note of plaintive desperation had crept into his voice. "You understand . . . they forced me . . . I knew you were leaving, would never come back . . . I had to open up one valve . . . to let off some pressure . . . otherwise they would never have left me alone."

Jil was silent.

"You weren't here," Ripoll went on. "I was the one stuck here with them . . . to take the rap."

"You've made a bad mistake, Ripoll."

"I know . . . What do you want from me?" The cry was torn from his heart. He gaped at Jil in round-eyed terror. His face was pallid; the pressure on his chest unbearable. "They would have found out that you're here . . . they'd have known that you spoke to me . . . and they would have hounded me. Don't you understand? You must understand!"

Still Jil said nothing.

"What do you want, Jil?" He sank heavily into the armchair opposite the man who was torturing him with his silence.

"You called me a few months ago to get Horst Welsh out of Vienna. Where is he now?"

"I don't know." Ripoll interlaced his fingers nervously. "I swear . . . the only thing they told me to do was to find you and have you smuggle Horst from Vienna to Spain."

"And then what?"

"I don't really know." Ripoll heard how hollow his voice sounded. A feeling of hopelessness enveloped him. "I think they were going on to the Middle East. The Palestinians needed him."

"Where in the Middle East?"

"That's what I'm trying to tell you . . ." He felt as if he were suffocating. He raised his hand to his chest and breathed deeply, expanding his lungs in an effort to ease the pain. "I don't know."

"You don't know where Horst might be," said Jil dryly, "but you know who manipulates him. Whoever told you to get him out of Vienna knows where he is. Who gave the order?"

The lawyer swallowed hard. "You know what will happen to me if they find out I've told you anything." His throat went dry. He passed a hand over his forehead. It was damp with perspiration. "Jil, you know the rules as well as I do . . . You don't ask questions, he doesn't ask, we don't ask . . . It's better that way."

Jil's expression did not change.

"It was you who forgot the rules, Monsieur Ripoll."

The threat was implicit. Ripoll ran his tongue over his parched lips.

"All right. I'll tell you. I'm sure you've heard the name
. . . the Twin."

"Klaus?"

"Klaus Schmidt," confirmed the lawyer.

Jil was well acquainted with the German nightclub owner.
His next stop would be Hamburg. But first he had to settle
his account with François Ripoll in such a way that the
Frenchman's death would appear to be the result of too
much alcohol and tranquilizers. He rose slowly and walked
toward Ripoll.

The lawyer's frightened eyes left no doubt that he was
aware of his final judgment. He wanted to say something, but
before the words had formed in his mouth he felt Jil's hand
cover his face, cutting off the supply of air to his lungs. He
turned his head aside in an attempt to shake Jil off, but there
was no force left in him. His body heaved with the sharp pul-
sations of pain that racked his temples and chest. Finally, an
odd sensation crept over him, and his heart gave in to the
silent, soothing darkness.

29

THAT NIGHT, JIL left Paris for Hamburg, arriving there in the early morning. He knew the city well, having visited it often in the past; on several occasions, Klaus Schmidt had enlisted his services. He had always treated Jil with the greatest respect, fully appreciating his expertise in smuggling human contraband.

In a small hotel, not far from the harbor's entertainment district, Jil rented a room with a private bath where he showered and shaved off his red beard. He would be meeting with men to whom he would have to be immediately recognizable. He examined the smooth contours of his face for some time; once again, he was the ageless youth. He stretched out on the bed and slept through the day. He was familiar with Klaus Schmidt's daily routine. The nightclub owner remained in his apartment until late in the evening, and then went straight to his office at the Cassandra.

Jil awakened at nine o'clock; it was time to leave for the nightclub. The Cassandra was famous for its superb food and liquor and for the city's most beautiful prostitutes who graced its bar, waiting till all hours of the night for the sailors whose ships had docked at the port.

As the owner of this successful and lucrative nightclub, Klaus Schmidt was very much in the public eye. But his image and the nightclub itself were elements of a cleverly devised and very effective cover which enabled the East German agent to operate in West Germany. His nickname, "the Twin," which he had received many years before, derived from his readiness to personally replace any suddenly disabled or indisposed terrorist.

One measure of his success was the fact that, over the years, he had avoided exposure by West German authorities and had also never been recalled by his government to East Germany. Once Schmidt had succeeded in creating a solid West German identity, he gradually insinuated himself into leftist circles, finally acquiring a firm foothold in the Baader-Meinhof gang. Thereafter, he played an important role in every terrorist operation carried out by the group. In recent years, in accordance with instructions received from his superiors in East Germany, he had maintained a low operational profile since direct participation in any terrorist ventures involved a risk of exposure that his government was unwilling to assume.

Instead, he recruited and manipulated other agents like Horst Welsh. If anyone was in a position to answer questions about the Fox, Jil reasoned, Klaus Schmidt was. The problem was just how to extract the answers from him. Time was at a premium and events were moving quickly, so Jil would have to take certain short-cuts, regardless of the dangers they posed. He thought briefly of Anna-Maria, Horst Welsh's girlfriend. It was doubtful whether she had any idea of where her lover might be, but if Klaus Schmidt refused to talk, Jil would turn to her.

When Jil entered the Cassandra, it was still almost empty. The bartender was polishing beer glasses with a soft cloth and lining them up in straight rows before him. Two prostitutes, neither more than eighteen years old, perched on high wooden stools at the bar. At the center of the room, a noisy group of four sailors, each with a girl, sat around a small table laden with empty beer mugs.

Jil sat down on a stool at the end of the long bar. He had to find out whether Klaus Schmidt had arrived at his office on the floor above. The second-story office could be reached from the yard by an iron staircase attached to the side of the building. Facing the office, from the other side of the court-yard, was the rear of the apartment building, in which Schmidt shared an apartment with two brothers, Heinrich and Rudolph. Thus, by merely crossing the yard, Klaus Schmidt could get from his home to his office unseen. Regardless of where his underground activities took him, he could always claim—and no witness could contradict him—that he had been either in his office or in his apartment.

The bartender placed a mug of beer before Jil, who waited until the froth had settled before taking his first sip. The beer was excellent. When he had drained the glass, the bartender offered another, but Jil refused.

"You can't just sit here," the man explained politely but firmly.

"I am waiting for Herr Schmidt," Jil answered calmly.

"Is Herr Schmidt waiting for you?"

"No." Jil smiled. "I don't think he knows I'm here."

The bartender picked up a mug and polished it assiduously. "Herr Schmidt will not come before ten-thirty," he said.

"I know," said Jil, glancing at his watch. It was ten minutes to ten. "I'll wait. Only please inform him that some-one is waiting to see him."

"Does that someone have a name?"

"Tell him Jil."

In the year that had passed since Jil's last visit to the Cassandra, there had been a complete turnover in staff. Klaus Schmidt was careful not to keep his employees too long. Only two people had remained with him since his initial appearance a few years before: the brothers Heinrich and Rudolph. Their origins were shrouded in mystery. They had appeared suddenly, soon after Schmidt's arrival in Hamburg, and seem-ingly never left their employer's side; at meetings and in the course of his travels, they clung to him like shadows. There had been some gossip about homosexual relations between Schmidt and the two brothers, but all this was of little consequence to Jil.

A few minutes after ten-thirty, Heinrich and Rudolph ap-peared at the club. Men of average height, both had tight, compact, athletic bodies. Their features were bland, their faces nondescript, and, except for Rudolph's flamboyant black-and-white striped jacket, their clothing was unremark-able. The bartender called them over to have a look at the young man waiting to see Schmidt. They identified Jil immediately and nodded to the bartender.

He leaned over toward Jil. "Herr Schmidt is here," he said. "Do you know where to find him?"

"Yes," said Jil, slipping down from the high stool.

He walked to the other end of the club and through a narrow hallway leading to a staircase which led to a small anteroom on the second floor.

Jil entered the small room preceded by the two brothers. Now, up close, Jil noted the strong resemblance between them. Both had straight hair the color of straw that sloped like thatch over their foreheads. Their eyes were so limpid they appeared utterly lifeless. Jil stopped at the door so Rudolph could frisk him for a concealed handgun.

Rudolph gestured to his brother.

"He's clean," he said. Heinrich nodded and pressed a switch on the wall. There was a buzz as the security lock sprang open, and Rudolph pushed back the door, letting Jil pass.

Klaus Schmidt was sitting behind a small wooden table, his close-set eyes fixed on the young man entering his office. He did not greet Jil, nor did the expression on his face alter. Knowing the man's eccentricities, Jil didn't wait to be asked but pulled a chair up to his desk and sat down.

The German continued to chew on a piece of sausage, his square jaw moving slowly, the muscles constricting and slackening. His gaze remained fixed on Jil, his expression inscrutable. Neither his thoughts nor his feelings ever found expression on Klaus's face.

"So, what do you want?" he asked.

Klaus seemed to be picking up the threads of an unfinished conversation. He abhorred unnecessary words, preferring to pass over superfluous amenities and go directly to the core of the matter. Jil had to deal cautiously with this man. Because one never knew what was going on behind Klaus's mask of imperturbability, the German had the capacity to surprise.

"I had a few things to take care of in Hamburg," Jil declared with complete composure. "I simply stopped by for a visit."

"Is that so."

Klaus lowered his eyes. A dozen fat sausages lay in a wooden bowl on the desk before him, several mugs of frothy beer beside it. Klaus played with a long, sharp, two-pronged fork. The light glinted from the polished steel as he raised the fork and speared one of the sausages. He bit off half and, as he chewed, pointed to the bowl, inviting Jil to share in the repast. Jil shook his head in refusal.

"At my age, I still don't get fat from this," said Klaus dryly. "I worry about my heart as I get older, but cholesterol is not yet one of my problems."

Klaus was a fanatic about his health. He never shook hands, having an obsessive fear of disease, which he believed could readily be transmitted by a contaminated hand. His apartment was spotless; Heinrich and Rudolph were responsible for maintaining its cleanliness.

"I hope that you have no problems with your health, Klaus."

"No." Again, Jil heard the sound of the square jaws chomping on a sausage. "I have no problems. I just keep away from unclean people."

He thrust another sausage into his mouth and bit a large chunk from it. He attacked the food as if it were a quarry, grinding it between his powerful jaws.

"Look," he said, extending an upturned palm. "They say you can read the future. Will I die of illness?"

Jil smiled. Klaus had not changed. Jil studied his palm, tracing the web of lines. Then he looked up. Klaus continued to wolf down the sausages.

"You will not die of illness," Jil said.

"That's good," said Klaus, compressing his lips in satisfaction. "I never wanted to die in bed. So, tell me, what do you want?" He raised one of the mugs and drank down a long draft of beer. Jil studied his lean, angular face: a blank, inscrutable mask that betrayed neither emotion nor age.

"I told you—business," said Jil diffidently. "I'm also looking for Horst Welsh."

Klaus's eyes, which were so close-set that each seemed to be pressing against the bridge of his nose, focused on Jil's face. He took his time answering. He speared another sausage, swallowed half, and washed it down with more beer, then replaced the mug on the table.

"This is most irregular, you know—your looking for Horst."

"True," Jil concurred. "But it is a fact."

"A fact that doesn't please me."

"I've taken that into account. But you will have to help me, Klaus. I've assisted you many times. I know that you are not one who forgets such things."

Klaus screwed up his face and sucked his teeth.

"I don't know what you need him for," declared Klaus finally, "but there is no chance of your seeing him before the middle of April. Come back then."

"That's no good," said Jill. "I need him now."

"What's so urgent?"

"A personal matter."

Klaus Schmidt shook his head. "As I said, he'll be busy for another three weeks. Sure you don't want one?" he asked, pointing to the bowl of sausages.

"No, thanks." Jil rose and turned to leave. When he reached the door, he stopped. "Three weeks, you say?"

"That's what I said," Klaus confirmed, taking up a small napkin and wiping his lips. "Remember something else. I don't want you to go looking for him. It's unhealthy. Don't get in touch with anyone."

"That sounds like a threat," said Jil. His tone was icy.

"That's exactly what I meant." Klaus drew a deep breath. "Don't go to Anna-Maria, Jil," he said, casting a sharp glance at his visitor. "I wouldn't like to think of you talking to a drug addict. She has a loose tongue."

They studied each other for several moments. Then Klaus speared another sausage. "Too bad you're not hungry tonight," he said, running his tongue the length of the sausage before snapping off a piece between his teeth.

Outside the nightclub, Jil was troubled. It was clear now, beyond a shadow of a doubt, that the actual date of the operation was much closer than he had thought: only three weeks away. He had to find Horst right away. Wherever he was, there, too, would be the men who were to carry out the attack in Crown Heights. Anna-Maria was now the only one in Hamburg from whom he might learn of Horst's whereabouts. He had to see her in spite of Klaus's warnings.

She lived at the wharves in the section where the houseboats were docked. Jil hadn't known she was a drug addict, but he accepted Klaus's statement at face value. Nevertheless, he doubted whether she had forgotten her debt to him. He had rescued her from the Argentinian government forces, and it was through him that she had met Horst.

Jil strode through the darkened area near the docks. Street lamps cast a dim glow over the narrow alleyways running between the large warehouses. He was careful to walk in the middle of the deserted street. In this way, if someone were lying in ambush, waiting to attack, he would be in a position to repel them.

His ears picked up the sound of rapid footsteps. He waited. The patter ceased. Someone was following him. He continued walking slowly. Nothing happened. No further sounds. Perhaps the footsteps had been the product of his overwrought imagination.

The wharves were about a quarter of an hour's walk from Klaus Schmidt's nightclub. Jil reached the yacht basin at eleven. The night was grim and overcast; heavy clouds moving ponderously across the sky eclipsed the stars. The narrow walkways leading to the wharves were dimly illuminated by light spilling from the houseboats.

Horst Welsh had named his boat the *Anna-Maria*. Jil searched for it among the array of craft at the pier and finally found the boat tied to the end of the last wharf. The *Anna-Maria* was almost twelve yards long and some three across. Light blazed from its portholes, and as Jil approached, he heard sounds of music and the murmur of voices coming from the hold. Anna-Maria was entertaining guests.

Jil peered through one of the portholes into the spacious cabin. Two young women and two men were lounging with drinks in their hands on the low wooden benches. He climbed the tall iron ladder to the deck, walked to the hatch, which opened into the cabin, and called down: "Anna-Maria!"

The voices died out; only the sound of the music lingered in the air. Jil heard the light scamper of footsteps mounting the narrow staircase and Anna-Maria emerged from the hold. Jil's back was to the lanterns that burned from the mast, and she could not immediately identify him. Then, drawing close, she caught a glimpse of his face.

"Jil!" she cried hoarsely, and she opened her arms wide. Jil came to her and gave her a gentle hug. She threw back her head and laughed blissfully.

"What a surprise!" she said, her eyes gleaming playfully. "But then you always surprise."

She spoke to him in French. In that language, her rich voice had a light, gay, musical lilt. She sounded precisely as Jil had remembered her.

"Come on down," she said. "I'm having fun with a few young comrades who love to hear stories about failed revolutions."

He caught the note of bitterness that suddenly crept into her voice. She took his arm and pulled him down the stairs after her. The cabin was larger than it appeared when viewed from the outside through the porthole. It seated six people comfortably. Anna-Maria introduced him to her guests, presenting him as a dear friend—"like a brother, really"—but refraining from mentioning his name. Such caution—the scrupulous avoidance of names—was an ingrained habit learned in the course of her years with the underground. She conversed with her friends in German, and her knowledge of the language, Jil noted, had greatly improved.

As the company chattered away merrily, if somewhat disjointedly, Jil watched their eyes and quickly detected the telltale signs: the frantic sparkle, the glassy look, the grossly dilated pupils. Now that he had joined them, they returned to sniffing cocaine. It was a cheap grade and their reaction was immediate, each recoiling as if he had received a stunning blow. A few minutes later, under the narcotic's influence, they became alert and vivacious.

Jil studied Anna-Maria and was shocked at how radically her appearance had altered. Her face had lost its vitality; deep lines furrowed her brow, and tiny wrinkles flared at the corners of her eyes and mouth. Her skin looked slack and dull. Anna-Maria's youth had been extinguished. Her hair, jet-black once, was dull and lank and uncared-for. Jil took in the delicate curve of her jaw, then his eyes moved downward to her neck, which looked withered and scrawny. She seemed so brittle and fragile that even a gentle caress might hurt her.

Anna-Maria lost the thread of her friends' conversation as she stole glances at Jil. She wanted to be alone with him; the next time the cocaine was passed she refused it, complaining of a headache. Her friends rose to leave shortly after, and Anna-Maria accompanied them to the upper deck to say good-bye. When she returned, she was quiet, almost introspective. She sat down opposite Jil.

"What's happened to you, Anna-Maria," he asked gently,

taking her hand. He noticed how cold it was, and how drained of vitality.

"It's a long story," she said, twisting her mouth into a wry smile. "Jil, I'm so glad to see you . . ."

He was silent.

"You're like a breath of fresh air . . . a special greeting from a past that will never return . . ."

His gaze did not waver as he studied Anna-Maria's face.

She smiled and closed her eyes for a moment. "You know, in my innocence I always believed that there was a world that could not be touched, that would somehow escape the violence and pain. The inner world. The spirit. Do you understand what I mean?"

"I understand, Anna-Maria."

"I thought you would." She took a cigarette and then struck a match, but her hands were trembling too much to light it. She saw Jil looking at her. "All right, so I'm hooked—so what? I have an out, Jil. Do you know what it is? I hallucinate. I escape. I fled from my country . . . and I continue to flee . . ."

"This is a different kind of escape," said Jil, placing a hand on her shoulder. He felt the sharp jut of her bones through her blouse. "Have you talked with Horst about your condition?"

She waved a hand futilely.

"We've talked many times, Jil. But, you know, I have dreams that will never be realized. And Horst is completely fettered; he's in a situation that he will never get out of." She spoke without bitterness; rather, her voice echoed a profound disappointment laced with resignation. She seemed no longer capable of confronting a situation that appeared difficult. "We belong to that corps of revolutionaries who will find liberation only in death. When you wake up one morning and find that you haven't even the strength to dream, then what is left but hallucinations?"

She told Jil how she had begged Horst to go away with her; she wanted him to find a tiny, remote island—one that did not even appear on the map—where they could live out their lives in isolation. She pleaded with Horst to escape now from a world that held out only one prospect for the future: the final, ultimate revolution, which would be followed swiftly, inevitably, by a conflagration that would wholly consume civilization.

"Horst understood up to a point and then suddenly became frightened. Klaus had warned him about me. He'd told Horst I was no good, a negative influence. He went to Klaus and repeated what I'd said, that I had begged him to leave with me. Then he cried. He said he was sorry he had told him, but it was too late. Klaus is not the sort of man to whom you tell such things."

Suddenly it all became clear to Jil.

"It was Klaus who hooked you on drugs?"

"Yes," she whispered.

"Horst knew?"

"Yes."

"Didn't he try to stop you?"

Anna-Maria gave a bitter little laugh. "Horst is addicted, too," she said. "Don't you know the system Klaus uses?"

"No," Jil admitted.

"Horst is strong; he can hide his problems. It didn't bother him when I became addicted. That's how it is when you're hooked. It isn't easy to live with a partner who isn't on drugs. Klaus supplies both of us. At first, though, I resisted his offer; he had to force me to take morphine. Horst would go to the North Pole if Klaus told him to. Klaus knows how to control people."

"Have you tried to stop?"

"Me?" She laughed again. It was a laugh resonant with pain. "Look, Jil," she said, pulling the sleeve of her sweater above her elbow and displaying the black and blue tracks of the hypodermic needle. "The brothers help me . . . Klaus's watchdogs. They see that I get my supply while Horst is away, so I don't go running around the streets like a bitch in heat. I am dangerous; have to be kept quiet, calm. Not for Klaus. For Horst."

She fell silent. There seemed to be nothing more to say. Jil too was silent. They sat gazing at one another.

"Jil . . ."

"Yes, Anna-Maria?"

"Do you remember how you used to impersonate the peasants we'd run across in the mountains? Do them for me again, Jil. Please!"

He smiled. That was how he had entertained Anna-Maria

when he spirited her through the Andes and out of Argentina. He portrayed the farmers who lived in the seclusion of the mountain ranges, cut off completely from society. First he mimicked the men, then the women. Anna-Maria would laugh until tears gleamed in the corners of her eyes.

"Only for you," he said. "They are coming back to see you, Anna-Maria." And he lured them back from the distant mountains, one comical figure after the other, capering along the mountain passes. He picked out their most comical traits and exaggerated them, delicately but meticulously laying bare their grotesqueness. For ten minutes he staged a performance especially for her, and she watched him intently, in silence at first; then the glimmer of a smile appeared on her face, and, finally, tears welled until she was laughing and crying simultaneously. He had brought her the breath of the mountains and provided a glimpse of the birthplace to which she would never again return.

"Thank you, Jil. Thank you." He smiled and sat down opposite her. "It's too bad Horst couldn't see you just now," she added.

"Where is Horst?"

She was completely taken aback at the question. "You don't know? Klaus said you got him out of Vienna. You should know where he is. Why are you asking me?" She reached for the bottle of gin and then picked up a bottle of tonic, only to find it was empty. She checked the refrigerator but found no tonic there either, and remembered leaving a few bottles on deck.

"I'm going up on deck," she said dully. "I'll be right back . . ."

"Anna-Maria."

She stopped.

"Who really operates Horst and Klaus?"

She smiled evasively. "Why don't you ask Klaus?" she asked.

Jil smiled ruefully. "You and I used to be friends," he said.

"We still are, Jil," she responded quietly. "I'll be right back . . . then we'll talk . . ."

She started up the stairs unsteadily, holding the bannister to maintain her balance. Jil leaned back, his eyes closed, and listened to the music drifting from the stereo.

When Anna-Maria didn't return, he went to the stairs.

"Anna-Maria?"

There was no answer.

He had reached the seventh step, his head and hands exposed at the level of the deck, when something heavy slammed into the back of his neck. Before he lost consciousness, Jil heard the clatter of rapidly departing footsteps. Before his eyes glazed over, he caught a glimpse of a black-and-white striped jacket, and, through the thickening haze, images of the wharf bobbed wildly, surrealistically about him. A scherzo of colors flashed before his eyes and was swallowed by a thick cloud of gray. Then blackness.

When he regained consciousness, Jil found himself stretched out at the foot of the staircase. He thought at first that hours had passed, but glancing at his watch, he discovered that it had been only a matter of minutes since his ascent to the deck. As his vision cleared, he became aware of a sharp pain at the nape of his neck. He touched the spot and his hand came away smeared with blood. Whoever administered the blow had meant to kill.

As he rose slowly, his knees buckled. He grasped the handrail to steady himself and then walked to the sink and splashed cold water on his face and on the wound. He felt immediate relief. The flow of blood from the wound stopped, but a large lump was forming at the point of impact. Jil wet a towel and applied more cold water to the area.

It was then that he remembered that Anna-Maria had gone up on deck.

He ran to the staircase and clambered up the steps, taking them two at a time. A few broad strides and he reached the center of the deck, and there he stopped dead. Anna-Maria lay face down, immobile, at his feet. He bent over her and felt for her pulse. She was alive, but her heartbeat was weak and fitful.

Grasping her by the shoulders, he turned her over and cradled her in his arms. He recoiled at the sight of her face. It was so swollen it was all but unrecognizable. Her mouth had been reduced to a pulpy mass of raw flesh, and blood streamed from her lips. Her tongue had been cut from her throat.

Lifting her, he carried her in his arms like an infant to the hatch. He descended the steps slowly, cautiously, easing her

264

body between the narrow walls of the staircase, and placed her on the bed. With a damp towel, he began to wipe away the blood. She blinked and opened her eyes, two black pools of deadly fear. He laid his hand on her forehead and concentrated his entire being in his fingertips, in the empathetic touch of his hand, as if by so doing he could draw away some of her pain. Anna-Maria breathed heavily. She felt an odd swelling in her mouth and the gentle, pleasant stroke of his hand. She implored him with her eyes to continue.

"You need medical help," he said quietly. "If you understand me, open and close your eyes. Do you have any painkiller? It will help until I can bring a doctor."

Her eyes twitched shut; then, reopening them, she glanced toward a nearby cupboard.

"I understand . . ."

As he removed his hand from her forehead, a long, low moan escaped from her throat. He found a small wooden box in the cupboard and took out a hypodermic needle and a tiny dish of morphine, which he quickly injected into her arm.

Her convulsive writhing gave way to an overpowering lassitude as she began to feel the effects of the narcotic. Jil took the damp towel and wiped the beads of perspiration from her brow.

"I am going Anna-Maria," he said. "I know who did this to you . . ."

Her face suddenly reflected intense fear and she clutched his arm, as if to caution him of the danger and to warn him off this pursuit of revenge.

"Don't worry, Anna-Maria," he whispered.

He felt her eyes boring into his back as he started up the stairs. The image of her face—mauled, contorted in terror, her eyes narrowed, her shredded lips puckered in supplication—remained fixed in his mind as he telephoned a nearby hospital and returned to the wharves to wait. In five minutes he heard the wail of the siren; when the ambulance pulled up to the wharf where the *Anna-Maria* was moored, he turned and went on his way.

Jil was assailed by guilt. He felt responsible for what had happened. He had committed an intolerable error, one which not even an inexperienced intelligence agent would make. Klaus Schmidt had not dared touch Anna-Maria previously for fear that he would lose control over Horst Welsh. But Jil had provided him with a reason to punish her. Under ordinary circumstances she could be trusted to keep silent about Horst and Klaus and their activities. But from Jil, to whom she owed her life and her happiness with Horst, she would hide nothing. Jil had provoked this assault on Anna-Maria, and his mind reeled under the weight of that terrible responsibility. He should have realized the deadly intent of Klaus Schmidt's threat.

Now he was really fighting against time. Pavel Ramizor would soon learn of his attempt to thwart the reprisal against the Rebbe. Then a manhunt for him would be mounted. The best liquidators in the KGB would be put on his trail. He now had to change his tactics, and Klaus Schmidt had simply and unwittingly given him a justification for the shortcut he was about to take.

It was one o'clock in the morning. At this hour Klaus would still be in his office, holding the last of his clandestine meetings, telephoning final instructions to the outer reaches of his far-flung terrorist network. This time Jil would get to him from the yard.

Klaus's apartment was on the first floor. Jil quickly pried open the two locks and then slowly, cautiously, swung open the door to the apartment. He slid in and closed the door behind him. Through a wall mirror he caught the reflection of the long hall, which ended at the bathroom door. Draped over a chair, adjacent to the door, was a black-and-white striped jacket. He heard the sound of water running in the bathtub.

Jil strode rapidly down the hall, pausing only to take in the bloodstained jacket. He pushed open the door slowly and entered the bathroom. The tub was abrim with soapsuds. Heinrich, the older brother, lay in the aromatic froth. Jil raised his hand, rigid as a sword, and brought it down between neck and clavicle. Heinrich recoiled from the blow, too stunned to comprehend what had occurred; Jill struck again, landing a powerful blow on his throat and smashing his windpipe. The German gave a low, savage sound and sank beneath the froth, his mouth agape in a vain effort to breathe. As he inhaled, a tiny gurgle came from his shattered windpipe, then he slid slowly back under the water, which enveloped him.

Jil heard the light, nimble footsteps even before Rudolph

entered the hall. He slid behind the door and waited silently
for the younger brother.

"Heinrich?"

Rudolph's voice reverberated through the apartment. He
approached the bathroom and, seeing Heinrich submerged in
the water, rushed toward him. He kneeled down and tried to
lift the motionless body. He did not have time to consider the
implications of the situation before Jil, standing behind him,
kicked him in the back with the tip of his heavy boot. The
blow had been accurately placed; it broke Rudolph's spine,
paralyzing him. He collapsed on the floor, his eyes widening
slowly in astonishment and terror.

"My legs," he murmured. "My legs . . ."

His eyes were riveted on Jil, but it was doubtful that he
saw him. Jil's second kick, which struck him in the temple,
was the coup de grace.

Klaus Schmidt heard the door leading to the yard creak
open behind him. Confident that it was the brothers who had
returned to the office, he did not bother to turn around. A
bowl of sausages lay on the table, and a smaller plate of
beans cooked in tomato sauce stood next to it. The beer mugs
lining his desk had been replenished and most were still full.
Klaus was enjoying his last meal of the evening. He had just
raised a spoonful of beans to his mouth and was about to
shovel them in when he saw Jil. He froze.

"Don't trouble yourself, Klaus," said Jil, pulling a chair up
and sitting down, uninvited, as he had done earlier in the evening. "I have come to the conclusion that those sausages fuel
your imagination, so please don't stop eating."

Something had gone wrong. Jil had come to the office from
the direction of the apartment.

Jil seemed to read the nightclub owner's thoughts. "That's
right, Klaus," he said quietly. "They won't disturb us while
we have our little talk."

The two-pronged steel fork dropped from Klaus's hand.
His face was transfixed with astonishment.

"What did you do to them?"

"That is completely inconsequential," answered Jil. He
lifted a mug and took a quick drink of beer. Then he went
on: "I killed them," he said flatly. "I killed them because I

had received proof that you are a man who follows through on your threats."

Klaus nodded in confirmation. "I always keep my word."

"So do I," Jil declared. "I promised you that you would not die of illness."

For the first time, Klaus's courage and resolution faltered. He hesitated before responding, wavering between consternation and sheer terror. His lips parted and his jaw dropped, marring his look of rugged, square-jawed aggressiveness.

"What do you want?" he asked.

Jil detected a trace of fear in the German's voice. As he gazed quietly into Klaus's gray eyes, he watched that fear grow. To Klaus Schmidt, Jil was not and had never been the droll clown, the talented pantomimist. To him, Jil was a dangerous man with an aptitude for murder and, when the need arose, a capacity for savagery.

Something had gone wrong. He had ordered his henchmen to kill Jil. When they returned from the wharves, they had reported that his instructions had been carried out, but they had been mistaken. They had acted like amateurs; obviously they had not made sure Jil was dead, and for this reason, they themselves were now dead.

"What do you want?" Klaus repeated.

"I want to know who you work for. Who gives you your orders." Jil pushed the beer mug aside, picked up the iron fork, and place it on its side next to him.

"I don't know what you are talking about . . . "

Jil's reaction was instantaneous. He picked up the fork and drove it hard into the nightclub owner's hand. The prongs passed through his flesh and lodged in the wooden desk top, pinning his hand to the table.

Jil kept an iron grip on the fork as the German groaned and struggled fruitlessly to free his hand from the prongs. But through his pain and fear, he said grimly, "You know you won't hear anything from me . . ."

Before he completed the sentence, Jil withdrew the fork and plunged it again into Klaus's hand, then pulled it out. As the German gazed in horror, Jil's arm rose and fell like a piston over the desktop, as he repeatedly, mercilessly, stabbed Klaus's hand. Blood oozed in rivulets from the holes the prongs had made and streamed over Klaus's skin and onto the table. His hand had been torn to shreds. He clenched his other hand into a fist and flailed at Jil, trying desperately to drive him back, but he dodged the blows and Klaus's fist jabbed impotently at the air. Before the German could begin to defend himself in earnest, Jil smashed a beer mug onto his skull. The glass splintered, and beer mixed with blood flowed over the German's face. He groaned and a wave of nausea and dizziness overtook him.

"You know now that you won't die of illness, right, Klaus?"

Jil lifted the fork once again, freeing the German's mangled hand. Most of the bones in the hand had been crushed and he could barely drag it across the desk.

The confusion and fear he had felt in the face of Jil's frantic attack had been replaced by the realization that he was now utterly powerless to defend himself.

"Look," Klaus mumbled, his body sagging behind the desk, "let's make a deal . . ."

"You sadden me, Klaus." Jil regarded him with loathing. "I'd expected more from you. I'm going to kill you."

"You're mad!"

"I asked a question. I want an answer. Otherwise I'll tear you apart piece by piece."

Klaus was on the verge of fainting.

"I get my orders from the STB," he croaked.

The Czech Secret service: the Czechs had been one of the possibilities Jil had considered.

"Which one of their men?" he asked, his eyes fixed on Klaus Schmidt's pallid, bloody face.

"Who?" he demanded again, when Schmidt remained silent.

Then, without warning, Jil gave the table a hard shove toward Klaus, delivering a stunning blow to the midriff and pinning him to the wall. At the sudden surge of pain, the German let out a low, tortured groan.

"Who?"

Jil grabbed the table and pulled it away from Klaus, permitting him a brief breathing spell, then once more drove it hard against him. The grunt Klaus emitted was accompanied by the sound of ribs cracking under the viselike pressure of the table. A faint tinge of yellow crept into his pallid face.

"Is it Kindler?"

Klaus did not respond.

"If not Kindler, then Kropte?"

269

Klaus bit his lips and remained silent, but his resolve had been broken; the strength and will to resist were rapidly draining from him. Jil pulled the table away and again slammed it against him.

"Maybe it's Anton Karlov?"

Klaus Schmidt reacted in a desperate last-ditch effort to save his life. He managed to heave the table away from himself and lunge at Jil. He bared his teeth and attempted to sink them into his antagonist's jugular vein.

Jil's reaction was immediate. He clamped the German's head between his palms and boxed both ears simultaneously. Klaus Schmidt's eardrums burst, and he released Jil with a groan and began to vomit. Jil pulled the German up from behind the table and banged a knee into his stomach. As he sagged forward, Jil brought his knee up again, against his chin, shattering his lower jaw.

Klaus Schmidt lay prostrate on the floor. It would take him several hours to die and it would not be a merciful death.

Jil bent over him. "So it *is* Anton Karlov," he said quietly.

Klaus opened his mouth to speak but could not. Jil straightened up and turned to leave. His business in Hamburg was at an end.

30

KNOWING THAT IT was Anton Karlov who was working for Pavel Ramizor clarified Jil's plan of action. He would go to Czechoslovakia in order to leave a blatant trail that pointed unmistakably to just one conclusion: that the plan had been uncovered by a Soviet deserter who was probably working as a double agent.

As Jil knew, Anton Karlov and Pavel Ramizor had one trait in common: a finely developed sense of caution. In order to stop them, Jil would have to play on their fear of exposure. They had to be made to realize that he was not just an ordinary deserter but someone who was actively assisting the other side. To this end, he had to get his hands on documents that would provide solid proof of the Soviet Union's involvement. Then Pavel Ramizor would be compelled to freeze the operation, perhaps even abandon it entirely.

Even as he came to this conclusion, his thoughts turned to Boris and Zina and Sergei. In his wrath, Ramizor was fully capable of crushing them. Jil remembered Daidushka's promise that they would be safe. The old man never made vows he did not keep. He would have to have faith in him, just as Boris had faith, unshakable faith, in God. Now more than ever, Jil wished he had that faith too. But in his experience God did not always respond to the prayers of men. God dreams, Jil thought, while men die.

Rousing himself to action, he put through a call to Regensburg in West Germany where a Rumanian associate of his, Karol Timmish, lived. Timmish had crossed the Czech border with Jil on numerous occasions, smuggling terrorists. He worked in collaboration with his cousin, Oscar, who lived in Czechoslovakia, in the city of Palzen. The two cousins would be able to help him. Karol could take him through the forests to a point just beyond the border, and from there, Oscar could bring Jil to the STB farm near Prague and wait until he had completed his business, then take him back to the forests to Karol.

Jil always arrived at Karol and Irma Timmish's house laden with presents for their three small children, and this time would be no exception. Jil purchased toys at the Hamburg airport and cakes and sweets at the Munich terminal right after his plane landed in the afternoon. From the airport he took a bus to Regensburg where Karol Timmish met him.

"I see that Santa Claus has arrived," said Timmish, pointing to Jil's bulging canvas suitcase.

"As always, Karol." Jil laughed. "It's good to see you again. Is everything in order?"

"Rest assured, everything has been arranged. We'll leave after dark. Oscar will be waiting for us on the other side. He'll take you to the farm. I'll wait for you in the area until you return. How long do you think you will be there?"

"I don't know. A day maybe."

"I'll wait for you tomorrow night at the same time and place. If you are delayed, wait at Oscar's house. I'll let him know when to bring you to the forest, to the regular meeting place."

It was typical of Karol to ask no idle questions. Jil's reasons for coming and going did not concern him. His only role was to insure that Jil reach and return from his destination safely.

Karol's wife and children received Jil with great excitement, and he busied himself distributing the gifts and sweets. In the past, during Jil's visits, the children would go to bed only after he had portrayed the animals of the circus: lions, bears, dancing elephants, monkeys, trained dogs and horses. On this occasion, too, when their mother ordered them to bed, they rebelled, demanding that Jil "make animals" for them.

"Please, Jil," Irma implored, "give them their zoo, and then we'll be able to get some rest."

As the three children sat breathless, their eyes following Jil's every movement, he presented the trained dogs who paced the arena on their hind legs, flipping over backward from time to time in spruce sommersaults. He punctuated their antics with short, sharp barking sounds. Using his hands and legs, Jil depicted a promenade of all the animals of the circus, imitating their sounds as well: the growl of the tiger, the whinny of the horse, and the frightening roar of the lion. He concluded his performance with an impersonation of a mammoth bear. As he lumbered over to the children and patted their heads, he was joined by Karol, who mimicked Jil's portrayal of the animal. Then the two great bears, with Irma's assistance, swept the children up in their arms and carried them off, squealing with joy, to their bedrooms.

After dinner, Jil excused himself and went to lie down. He was asleep at once, and in what seemed only minutes later Karol awakened him. It was time to leave. They traveled in Karol's car to a point midway up the mountain and from there began their penetration of the vast forest on foot. Walking was difficult because the melting snow had turned the ground to mud.

The course was not without its dangers, for during the winter months both the Czechs and the Germans increased their patrols: the Czechs in order to prevent citizens from fleeing to the West and the Germans so as to be on hand to lend assistance to any who succeeded in escaping. Fortunately Karol knew precisely when the Czechs and Germans changed watches, and when certain areas were left unpatrolled by the border guards.

At eleven o'clock they crossed the border. Now they had to climb to the summit of the mountain, then down the other side, to the foot; Oscar Timmish would be waiting for them there with a car.

Oscar Timmish proved no less proficient than his cousin

Karol, and he, too, did not ask questions. Jil was a confederate and, as such, was given assistance. The STB training farm was fifteen miles from Prague, near the town of Kaladnow. This was only one of a large network of such farms, all under the auspices of the KGB. Some were within the borders of the Soviet Union, and the remainder were located in Czechoslovakia, Bulgaria, and East Germany. The Czechoslovakian farm was under the direct supervision of Anton Karlov. Jil had stayed there many times over the past three years when terrorists from Germany, Ireland, Spain, and other noncommunist countries convened for advanced courses in sabotage and terror. The Czech instructors knew him and Jil hoped that his visit to the farm would help him locate Horst Welsh's base of operations.

Darkness overtook them a few miles from Kaladnow. When they reached the town, they parted, Oscar going to a friend's house to await Jil's return, and the latter continuing to the farm in Oscar's car.

Jil could see the glow of the floodlights that ringed the farm from afar. It wasn't a large area; approximately four and a half acres, with four buildings: two for the trainees, one for the instructors, and the last for the hive of administrative offices. There was, in addition, an old granary that served as a garage for the instructors' and administrators' automobiles. The training center could accommodate twenty trainees at a time—not a large number, but more than adequate, since sixteen sessions were held in the course of a single year.

Jil recognized the gate to the farm and the small shack next to it, where three guards were permanently stationed. Six others were generally assigned to the gatehouse behind it.

He stopped the car before the gate, turned toward the gatehouse, and shouted: "Yanek!"

The heavy door swung open and the tall, husky figure of the man responsible for security at the farm emerged from the gatehouse.

"Hello, Yanek."

The hulking figure suddenly halted in surprise. It was impossible to mistake that voice: it was the Clown.

"Jil!" he called exuberantly. "By God, Jil!" He hurried toward the car, a friendly smile spreading over his good-natured face. "Welcome!"

As Jil got out of the car and came toward him, Yanek stretched out his arms.

"It's good they've invited you too!" he said, beaming. "How about a drink?" He led the way to the gatehouse and as the two men passed a bottle of vodka back and forth, Jil began to ask deliberately casual questions. As he knew from the past, Yanek was a man with extensive knowledge of the workings of the farm.

From him, Jil learned that Anton Karlov was absent from the training center, summoned away that afternoon. Something had happened and he had left the farm in great haste.

"It's strange," admitted Yanek. "During the past few weeks he didn't leave the farm once. Right now a special course is being conducted to prepare candidates for a very important mission, and Karlov has personally supervised all the briefings. You should have seen the sour face on him when he left here. Something serious must have happened."

Thanks to Yanek's thirst for conversation, Jil left the gatehouse armed with very important information. He learned that Karlov's right-hand man, Vladimir Zoska, had been away for several months. He weighed this fact carefully. It meant that the group presently training at the farm was only the backup team. The unit that was to carry out the reprisals must be located elsewhere, probably at a base in another country—and with that group would be Horst Welsh and Zoska.

Jil crossed the dark courtyard lit by a single light from one of the windows of the administration building. He was going to check in with Thomas Kraptow, one of Karlov's personal aides, and someone who could be counted on to tell his boss of Jil's unexpected visit to the training farm. He wanted to put Karlov on notice; he had left a trail of blood in his wake. Jil knew how Karlov would react once he had weighed the tell-tale signs and fitted together all the loose pieces. Karlov subscribed wholeheartedly to the domino theory of international espionage, and Jil was the piece that had fallen: a KGB deserter striving, for reasons unknown to Karlov, to frustrate a terrorist operation. His motives were immaterial; given the situation, Karlov would look out for his own neck and that of his master, Pavel Ramizor.

Jil knocked on the door of the lighted office on the first

floor and opened it a crack. Kraptow was sitting behind his desk. He lifted his head and his eyes widened.

"Jil! I didn't expect to see you." Kraptow's surprise was genuine. "All the trainees are already here and this time there was no problem with borders. None at all."

He was visibly perplexed. Jil came to the farm only when he had to smuggle someone enrolled in a course either in or out of Czechoslovakia. Nevertheless, he clasped Jil's hand warmly and invited him to sit down.

"I know that nobody had a problem arriving this time," said Jil. "Still, it's possible that someone will have a problem getting out."

Kraptow chuckled. "Who has a problem like that?"

"I don't know," Jil responded. "That I'll hear from Karlov. I got a message that he was looking for me, so I came."

"I'm sorry, Jil. Karlov left for Hamburg. He'll be back in a day or two."

Jil's expression was placid but within him the tension was mounting. He gazed at Thomas. He was a stocky man with broad shoulders, a powerful build, and a sharp mind. Jil had to deal cautiously with him. Thomas was no Yanek.

"If Karlov isn't around," commented Jil diffidently, "I suppose nobody knows anything."

"Correct," said Thomas, smiling. "That's Karlov's system. He gets to know everything, but no one else does. The less we know, the better."

"Karlov will never change," Jil declared. He screwed his face into the sour expression of one who has suddenly, unexpectedly, swallowed something awful. At that moment he bore a striking resemblance to the Czech commander, and Thomas burst into peals of thunderous laughter. He pounded Jil's shoulder amicably.

"That was perfect!"

"And do you remember this character?" Jill knitted his eyebrows into an expression of deadly seriousness, a perfect likeness of Vladimir Zoska's gloomy countenance. Jil shrugged his shoulders slightly, as Zoska habitually did, then rose and began to pace the room, his head cocked to the side as if weighted down by the gravity of his ruminations.

"You don't have to look for anyone!" Thomas exclaimed. "You carry them all with you. You meet someone and steal

276

a little part of him. And you keep him with you until you need him. I could have sworn just then that you were Zoska."

Jil smiled and sat down. "I heard that he's with Horst right now." As he said it, Jil sucked in his cheeks and his face instantly assumed a hollow, austere, ascetic appearance—a superb evocation of Horst Welsh's eternally anguished, self-mortified countenance. Thomas burst into paroxysms of laughter. Jil drew a breath and waited for Thomas's response. The question was fraught with peril since it could easily arouse the Czech's well-developed sense of caution, but he had no choice but to pose difficult, hazardous questions, for tomorrow or the day after, when Karlov questioned Thomas about Jil's highly irregular visit to the farm, these questions would take on special importance. Jil knew that Thomas Kraptow would meticulously report every detail of their meeting, would repeat Jil's questions verbatim, and Karlov would understand immediately the significance of the message that Jil had left for him.

"I don't know," said Thomas, after he had stopped laughing. "He might be with Horst and then again, he might not. I heard that he's working with Palestinians."

Jil's face expressed utter indifference, but Thomas's statement bolstered his belief that Palestinian units would provide the spine of the entire operation. It was typical of Department V to strike at a target using that target's sworn enemy. He now lacked only one piece of information: the location of the base at which the Palestinians were presently stationed.

They talked until midnight, and then Kraptow, who was tired, suggested that Jil could use Zoska's room, a perfect arrangement from Jil's point of view. He waited in Zoska's room for a short while, then exited and headed through the darkened hallway for Anton Karlov's office on the second floor. Jil cautiously climbed up the old wooden staircase, every footfall producing an excruciating creak, and opened the lock to Karlov's office with a small strip of steel. The room was partially illuminated by the floodlights that ringed the headquarters.

Karlov's office was modestly furnished. A plain square desk was set beside the window, an office cabinet to the right, four simple wooden chairs placed in a row along the length of one wall, and a blackboard for use during briefings on the opposite wall; a screen on which slides could be projected hung next to it.

Jil opened the desk drawers, one after the other, and burrowed through the papers and documents. He leafed through instructors' evaluations of the terrorists who had been selected for the backup unit. He recognized several of the names. Under the pile of evaluations he found bogus English, French, and Dutch passports. He examined the faces of the young men who stared out at him from the counterfeit booklets, then placed the passports on the desk, next to an envelope in which he had gathered together all the documents that would shed light on the details of the terrorist action.

In the metal cabinet, whose lock he jimmied open, he discovered Anton Karlov's personal papers: letters from members of his family and friends; an old photograph album; government documents, diplomas that had yellowed with age, and two office diaries, one for the previous year and the other for the current year. He quickly checked the entries that had been made during the past few months. The letters "Z" and "R" appeared frequently in the journal: *"Monday: See Z." "Thursday: Meeting with R."* "Z" was unquestionably Vladimir Zoska, and "R" had to be Pavel Ramizor. But beyond these cursory words, there was nothing to indicate either the place or purpose of the meetings. Karlov had been cautious. On the pages for December of 1979, Jil found two sentences that were more explicit. The first was written one day after his arrival in Spain: *"The Clown took H. out of Vienna,"* and five days later, *"H. reached Z."* From the diaries Jil extracted pages containing entries that would enable him to reconstruct Karlov's movements over the past few months.

The Czech appeared to move in a geographic triangle: from Prague to Moscow, then on to a point as yet unknown, at which Zoska and Horst were located, and back again to Prague. Jil folded the pages and set them down next to the passports. He resumed his search but discovered nothing more of interest. Only when he started to close the doors of the cabinet did he notice the slide projector on the top shelf. There was one slide in the magazine; perhaps this is what aroused his curiosity. He removed it from the metal sleeve and held it up to the window, utilizing the light of the floodlamps.

At first glance, there appeared to be nothing unusual about

the slide, except for a number of dots which had seemingly been drawn in at random. He decided to check it out, but to do this he needed better light. After closing the wooden shutters, he stood the projector on top of the desk and, directing its lens at the screen, he turned the machine on. Projected on the screen before him, the tiny dots appeared as black circles of equal diameter, each one about the size of a coin. One circle, to the right, was set in a yellow ring and had what appeared to be a date—4/5—inscribed above it.

Jil sat on the edge of the desk and studied the screen. The question was, what was needed to complete the information contained in the slide; as it was, it appeared to be completely meaningless. He again headed toward the metal cabinet; in its bottom drawer lay a roll of maps. He took them out and spread them on the floor. The fourth one was a map of the United States. Jil withdrew it from the roll and hung it over the screen. Then he went back to the projector and turned it on again. His conjecture had been absolutely right. The six dots were superimposed over the locations of six American cities. He exhaled slowly. The yellow ring encircled the city of New York. Before him was conclusive proof that the first assassination would be carried out in that city on the fifth of April.

The door burst open and Jil spun around to see Thomas Kraptow standing in the threshold.

"I thought that Karlov had returned." There was a clear note of surprise in Kraptow's voice as his glance wandered from Jil to the projector on the desk top and then to the map of the United States. In a flash, he understood the reason for the Clown's surprise visit to the training base and he leaped at Jil.

"Filthy bastard."

Kraptow missed Jil, as the master of movement stepped to one side and brought his fist down like a hammer on the Czech's head. Kraptow grunted; his eyes misted over as he wobbled clumsily to and fro. Then his knees gave way, and he crashed to the floor. Jil quickly removed Kraptow's belt and tied his wrists behind his back, binding his ankles together with his shoelaces. Sensing that the Czech was regaining consciousness, Jil stuffed a handkerchief into his mouth.

Kraptow tried to twist free of his bonds, but ultimately he abandoned the effort as fruitless and lay still, his eyes on Jil, who now approached the blackboard. He had a personal message for Anton Karlov—one that would let him know that the cover on the operation had been blown. Taking up a piece of chalk, he proceeded to list the fifteen names.

Even if he hurried, Jil realized he would still need several hours to reach the border. He could not leave the Czech to spread the alarm. He approached him and, crouching over his body, thrust his thumbs behind Kraptow's ears and pressed down hard on the acoustic nerve centers. The sharp pain gave way to a loud clap, as if an explosive charge had gone off in the center of his skull, and Kraptow sank into unconsciousness.

Jil gathered up the passports, the pages he had taken from Karlov's diaries, and the slide, and placed them in an envelope, which he stuffed into the breast pocket of his coat.

The moment had arrived to turn to Volodia Kantor. Through him, he would make contact with the Mossad and the CIA. But first he wanted to try to pinpoint Welsh's base of operations. One other avenue of investigation remained open: Margaret.

Margaret was sitting on the veranda that ran along the eastern side of Miguel's house. The rays of the morning sun were already strong enough to warm the porch, and she felt relaxed and comfortable working there.

On the table lay the notebooks containing her translation of the book on Miguel and his work; only a few more pages remained. She was alone in the house. Miguel had gone to Córdoba two days earlier to help with the preparations for a surprise party in honor of the matador Pepe Manuelete's fiftieth birthday, and the servants had been given a day's holiday.

Winter had passed and the weather had turned warm and balmy. A few early flowers were in bloom, and a thin blanket of vegetation covered the cliffs and foothills with shimmering tints of delicate green. Margaret felt a subtle correspondence between the change in weather and the changes that she herself had undergone. She was totally at peace with her decision to abandon all political activism. Being here, safe from the storms that swept over and battered the outside world, had made it easier for her to arrive at this decision. And so, of course, had Miguel—he had treated her with discretion, delicacy, and great understanding. He had never interrogated her, never asked any questions at all, but whenever she had needed an attentive ear, he had been available.

Over the past few weeks, her desire to write had become overpowering, but first she wanted to complete the translation. After that, she would be free to write something of her own, something totally different from her previous writings.

Perhaps she could begin even today, with the approach of evening. Or tomorrow, the dawn of a new day.

Inspired by the profound silence, Margaret was concentrating on the remaining pages of the translation when something came between her and the sun, casting a shadow over the table. She looked up in surprise and her eyes widened.

"Jil!" she cried out exuberantly.

"Hello, Maggie."

"Hello, clown," she responded, smiling. Jil contorted his face ludicrously and Margaret burst into laughter.

"You haven't changed," she said, taking up his hands and examining the long, expressive fingers. Then, looking up, she scanned his face: the large dark eyes flecked with gold, eternally searching, questioning, the mouth, curled in a shy smile as enchanting as ever.

Jil sat on the edge of the table, his arms folded over his chest. He studied her face and saw the sadness in her lovely gray eyes.

"It's good to see you, Margaret—though you have changed."

She smiled and said nothing. If only she had the courage, she would rush to him, embrace him, lay her head on his shoulder and say the words lodged deep in the hidden recesses of her heart. If only she had the boldness to tell him how many times she had thought of him . . . every day. But, instead, she merely smiled and said conversationally, "I'm glad you're here, you surprised me."

He gestured at the notebooks. "A new story?"

"No." She told him what she had been doing for the past few months in Spain—her occupational therapy, as she called the work for Miguel. And then she described the events that had eventually led her to break with the terrorist organizations.

"And you," she concluded in a whisper, "what have you been doing?"

"Envisioning a new world, populated by Chagall's people."

"Tell me about it, Jil."

"It's a world you don't know very much about, Maggie," he said, turning serious. "It's a world that's connected with my past."

"I don't really know anything about your past."

"I know," he said, turning to look at the walls of Toledo. "What would you say if I told you that my ancestors were born in Toledo? That their predecessors came from a distant country, a very different culture . . . It's a long story, one that spans thousands of years . . ."

"Was it the search for your past that prompted you to come here so suddenly?" she asked.

His reply was brief. "Not really. I checked your apartment in London and was told you were here. I had to see you. Something extremely urgent came up and I needed your help."

"How so?"

"I'm looking for Horst Welsh."

Jil was quick to notice the almost imperceptible cloud that passed over Margaret's face.

"Is anything wrong?" he asked gently.

"No," she answered abruptly.

He gazed at her for a moment. "Margaret, where did you take him?"

She hesitated briefly and then answered. "To Larnaca."

"Larnaca," Jil repeated, drawing a deep breath.

"Why do you want to know?"

Jil regarded her, weighing the advisability of giving a direct response to her question. He felt a sudden sense of relief. The circle had been closed. He had located the last link of the chain.

"To prevent murder," he answered forthrightly. "Horst, as you know, is involved in a terrorist action that will result in the liquidation of a number of innocent people. I want to head off that operation, Margaret."

She looked at him in consternation. "I thought that you . . ." She was unable to complete the sentence.

"I know what you thought. As you said, you really don't know anything about me."

"What else do you want to know?" she asked.

"Everything that you know."

She told him about delivering Horst to Cyprus, about Mussa el-Dalil, about everything she had observed while in Larnaca.

Now he had the last piece of the puzzle: the reprisals would be carried out by a unit of Palestinians briefed by Horst Welsh. He had to work swiftly to stop them. He must leave at once. Every hour was important. He had to reach Paris as quickly as possible; he needed Volodia's assistance to make immediate contact with the Israelis and Americans.

"Thank you, Maggie," he said quietly. "I'm on my way again."

"You are always appearing and vanishing. Do you know that, Jil? I'm beginning to think of you as someone who doesn't really exist at all. It's as if you're some figure my imagination conjured up. Or maybe you are someone that I once wrote into existence in a story. Perhaps you are made of words, Jil." Involuntarily, she reached out to caress him but curbed her impulse.

"Then I'll return, Maggie, and let you write more of my story," he said, smiling. Flecks of gold sparkled in the inky depths of his eyes.

"I'll be here," she replied.

The sun's rays glinted in Margaret's golden hair and her gray eyes glistened. Jil stood an arm's length away, longing to reach out but afraid to touch her. He feared that if he did, he would be unable to ever let her go. And he still had another stop: a final destination which he was compelled to reach. Afterward, perhaps he would learn to express what was in his mind and heart, the desire of a man for a woman.

31

PAVEL RAMIZOR FINALLY took the step that Boris Borodov had long anticipated he would. Having spent the afternoon going over the reports on Grisha Rostovitch, he asked his secretary to call Dr. Rostovitch to his office for his weekly medical examination to monitor his blood pressure.

Within a few minutes, Grisha Rostovitch entered the office, his black bag in hand. He took out the blood pressure apparatus while Ramizor removed his jacket and rolled up the sleeve of his shirt.

"Your blood pressure is fine," the physician said as he concluded his examination. "Exactly what it was last week."

"So I should be satisfied." Ramizor chuckled. He regarded the doctor's youthful face. Only the gray hairs that peppered the ludicrous little beard that sprouted wildly from his chin gave a hint of his actual age.

"Sit down, brother Grisha. Let's have a drink together."

The doctor was not surprised by the department head's display of sociability. Occasionally, when Ramizor was in high spirits he would invite Rostovitch to join him in a drink. He placed a bottle of vodka and glasses on the desk, removed the cork from the bottle, and poured out two drinks.

"*Nazdrovya!*" He toasted the doctor and emptied his glass.

"And so, we are satisfied, eh?"

"Satisfied with what, brother Pavel?"

"With the clinic, of course."

"Yes indeed. A modern facility with excellent equipment. I am quite satisfied."

"You aren't bored there?"

"No . . ." Rostovitch hesitated. He put the glass down on the desk with great deliberateness and began to clean his eyeglasses with a handkerchief. "I find the work at the clinic interesting and challenging. Don't forget, I am responsible medically for all the hundreds of people who work in this building."

"I haven't forgotten. Incidentally," Ramizor paused and poured another glass of vodka, "you know, of course, that from time to time I review the personal files of employees of the department. Oh, don't worry!" He held his hand up at the doctor's startled glance. "It's just a matter of habit—a disgraceful habit. Curiosity, I suppose."

"I see."

"And, needless to say, I've seen your file."

"Needless to say."

Pavel chose to ignore the ironic tone. "It's very interesting. I wasn't aware that you've known our Sergei for so many years."

The doctor gave a thin, hesitant smile but said nothing.

"Yes, indeed. He appears as one of your references."

"Ah, yes. I'd forgotten. The truth is, he's an old acquaintance of mine. In fact, I met him when I treated him at the Central Hospital. That was many years ago, brother Pavel."

"How would you describe his condition now?"

"Static. No change."

"Is that the diagnosis of a general practitioner or a heart specialist?"

"In this instance, I'm speaking as a specialist . . ."

For a moment Grisha Rostovitch thought he had perhaps erred. The corners of Pavel Ramizor's mouth turned up slightly and the faintest glimmer of a smile appeared on his face. He refilled the glasses.

"A specialist," said the department head. "A heart specialist. Yes. That's what I've heard."

The doctor raised the glass to his mouth and tossed down his drink before speaking. He had anticipated this exchange. Sergei Padayev had prepared him for the confrontation and warned him that he would probably be detained. He had told him, moreover, that in the course of the interrogation he might be subjected to physical abuse. But despite the advance notice and the preparation, he now felt a strange quaking in his stomach.

"In any case, Sergei is definitely not well," remarked the doctor casually, hoping to conclude the discussion with this comment.

"A specialist," repeated the department head aggressively. He glanced up at the doctor. "Yes, my dear Grisha, I know you are a heart specialist. I heard that a brilliant future had been predicted for you, if only you had chosen to remain in that field."

"But I didn't choose to do so."

"Quite true. You didn't. Here you are the director of a medium-sized clinic whose primary function is to provide medical consultations and first aid. That's a poor substitute for a brilliant medical career. How do you explain it?"

"I guess it's just how life works out," the doctor ventured cautiously.

"How life works out? I wonder what you could possibly mean by that."

"You wake up one morning and discover that you don't really want to practice medicine in a hospital day after day, year after year. The atmosphere is depressing. You know, there are certain individuals who aren't able to be among the sick and dying. I am one of them."

Pavel Ramizor made no attempt to respond. Since he controlled the situation, he could take his time. He glanced again at the reports lying on his desk and slowly leafed through them. Grisha Rostovitch felt his mouth go dry.

"There are a number of well-known physicians, friends of yours, who are today eminent professors," Ramizor went on. "And in the practical day-to-day work at the hospital, you were among the best of them."

"I was."

"Doesn't that contradict what you said about your not finding hospital work satisfying?"

"No. There's no contradiction. I'm a workhorse, brother

Pavel. I didn't enjoy the work at the hospital, but I didn't shirk it. I continued doing my job until I found more suitable employment."

"And how *did* you find your present position?"

"I heard they were looking for a physician here . . ."

"You heard . . . from whom did you hear?"

"I don't recall at the moment . . . I heard . . ."

"You don't remember?"

"No . . . let me think . . ."

"I'm not preventing you from thinking. Surely you can recall who it was, Grisha."

"Let me take just a minute to think . . ."

"Take as much time as you want. Do you remember yet, Grisha?"

"No! . . . What is it you want of me, Comrade Ramizor?"

It was no longer "brother Pavel." The man sitting opposite Grisha Rostovitch had suddenly reassumed his official role as head of Department V. The mask had been torn aside and he was again the shrewd, forceful inquisitor, impatient to receive answers. And Grisha Rostovitch was merely a doctor, a man of science, inexpert in the ways of official interrogation. He drew out a handkerchief; his hand trembled as he raised it to wipe the perspiration from his face.

"Aren't you feeling well, brother Grisha?"

"I'm a bit warm," the doctor admitted. "You are questioning me as if I had done something wrong . . . What do you hope to get out of me?"

"Nothing at all. I've been asking just one question all along: from whom did you hear that we had an opening here for a doctor? And, yet," he added with a smile, "I keep hearing that you don't remember. Tell me, is that possible? A man takes such an important step in his life and he doesn't recall who assisted him?"

"I don't remember," Rostovitch repeated feebly.

"Perhaps I can help you."

The doctor was silent.

"I'm just guessing, of course, Grisha. It doesn't appear in your file. But my conjectures are usually correct. You tell me if I'm right. The man who recommended the job to you was Sergei Padayev."

"I don't remember."

"You still don't remember, Grisha?"

"No."

Pavel Ramizor pursed his lips and sucked in his cheeks. He exhaled through his mouth and the dry whisper of air passing through his lips suggested a shortness of breath. So the doctor chose to be obstinate. Very well. Very well. He would play his game.

"Grisha," said Pavel Ramizor slowly, modulating his voice. "I like you. I know you are a fine doctor and nobody would want to lose you. Please don't allow that to happen."

"I wouldn't want it to happen. I am happy here."

"Then tell me who told you about the job. Your memory must certainly be functioning by now. Who, Grisha? Perhaps someone called the Grand Emissary?"

"I've never heard of anyone who goes by that name." The doctor's face was white.

"Very well." Pavel Ramizor returned the bottle of vodka to his desk drawer. "Go back to your clinic."

Utterly disconcerted, the doctor picked up his bag. He felt ill and pallid but he was determined to follow Sergei Padayev's directions. At this stage, he still had to play down his long association with Sergei, even though Pavel Ramizor was now well aware of it. He was at the door when the department head halted him.

"Grisha."

He stopped.

"I want you to telephone your family and tell them you won't be coming home."

"I understand," said the doctor. His voice had dropped almost to a whisper.

"At least not until you hear from me."

"Am I under detention?"

"There is no label for it, Grisha. But you are not to leave the clinic unless I instruct you to."

The doctor's hand tightened on the doorknob.

"One other thing, Grisha. Did anyone speak to you about the possibility of my detaining you?"

Grisha Rostovitch's heart beat wildly. His grip on the doorknob increased until he felt pain shoot through his hand.

"No."

Ramizor made a note of the terse reply but said nothing, his eyes never leaving the doctor until he had left the office. His conjecture had been right on target; someone had indeed prepared Grisha Rostovitch for this interrogation. It could be only one man: the head of the Hasidic network, the Grand Emissary.

"Damn it," Pavel Ramizor muttered, "who is he?"

He analyzed the events of the past few months. Somewhere along the line he had made a mistake, and by dint of this mistake his adversary had been able to anticipate his moves. The Grand Emissary had foreseen the detention of Grisha Rostovitch and had prepared the frightened physician for it.

For some time Ramizor had had the feeling that this Jew had anticipated his every action, as if he knew precisely what went on in his office. The head of the network had to be someone who was very close to him, perhaps someone of Sergei Padayev's caliber and position. Sergei probably was not the Grand Emissary, but if he wasn't, he was certainly in contact with him. It will be interesting to see what develops, Ramizor thought, when Sergei finds out that Grisha Rostovitch has been placed in detention. Undoubtedly when he learns of it, he will hasten to report to the Grand Emissary, whoever and wherever he might be.

Ramizor lifted the receiver of the house phone and spoke to the head of the Surveillance Unit.

"Place Sergei Padayev under surveillance immediately."

32

Over the past few weeks, the intelligence reports that had been flowing into Earl Dickson's task force headquarters in Washington were sketchy at best, based more on rumor than fact. Agents operating in Europe reported that known terrorists were being trained on a farm near Prague, confirming Czech involvement in the operation, and the Israelis had forwarded information which indicated that the Palestinians would constitute the main strike force. However, their base of operations was as yet unknown.

Earl Dickson spent a day in Tel-Aviv in consultation with General Negbi. After sifting through the mass of information obtained from various sources, they concluded that their efforts should now be focused in two areas: protecting the targeted individuals and locating the Palestinians' training base. If the base were found, they would eventually strike at it, but in order to do this, they would first have to bring additional men to the Middle East.

Then Dickson flew on to Europe. He had already decided to transfer most of the agents operating on the continent to the Middle East. There were several agents with whom Earl

Dickson wanted to confer personally, among them Paul Mansfield.

Mansfield arrived at the Embassy Building on Boulevard Gabriel at two o'clock in the afternoon. The meeting was to take place in the office of the CIA representative in France. Mansfield was well aware that the pressures on Dickson were enormous since Washington was becoming increasingly nervous about the reprisals, but he was unprepared for Dickson's statement that the hunt for the Clown was an exercise in futility, or for his request that Mansfield transfer to the Middle East where agents were trying to locate the Palestinians' base.

"Just give me a few more days," Mansfield pleaded. He rose abruptly and walked to the window. Outside a misty rain descended, streaking the windows of the building. "Just a few more days," he repeated. "The Israeli is going to wait it out, and I want to wait with him. We've been in on this together from the beginning."

He took out a cigar and lit it. He knew that part of his anger was directed at himself, for, in truth, he and Evyater Miller were very close to admitting defeat.

Earl Dickson moved next to him and put his arm around Paul's broad shoulders. "Believe me, I know what you're going through. But do you remember what you always said to me—all those times we worked together over the years and we'd find ourselves up against a brick wall? You'd say that even if we failed in our mission we had to have the strength to look the facts straight in the eye, to see things as they really were."

"That's a nice way of telling me I don't even have enough strength left to admit failure!"

"Paul . . ."

"Aw—to hell with it!"

Mansfield turned away from the window and Dickson's hand fell from his shoulder.

"Maybe I'm wrong, Paul. How much more time do you want here?"

"Give me a few days."

"Okay. They're yours."

"Thanks, Earl."

"Don't thank me, Paul. I only hope you're right. Because if

you aren't, you'll be cursing yourself out—and you have a special talent for that. I don't want to be around to hear it."

The conversation was interrupted by the jangle of the telephone. The CIA man answered and passed the receiver to Paul.

"For you. The Israeli Embassy."

Mansfield took the phone and listened intently, a slow smile lighting up his face.

"Thanks, pal," he said. "Thanks again. I haven't felt this good in weeks." He replaced the receiver and turned to Earl Dickson.

"Okay," Dickson exclaimed, "I know you're holding all the cards. What happened?"

"That was Miller," said Paul. "The Clown's here in Paris. We've got him."

"Not to dampen your enthusiasm," Dickson said, "but this isn't the first time you were sure you had the Clown."

"This time it's a different story."

"How?"

"The Clown has caught us!" Paul couldn't hide the note of excitement in his voice. "We have a meeting with him tonight at the Israeli Embassy. That's the difference this time, Earl. How do the French say it? *Vive la petite différence!*"

Volodia Kantor closed the doors of his restaurant after the last dinner guest had departed and returned to Jil, who was sitting at the back of the room sipping a cup of coffee. In a few minutes they were to leave for the Israeli Embassy. He regarded the young man's faraway expression; he seemed to be in another world.

"Are you worried?"

"A little nervous maybe," said Jil, rubbing his hands together.

"That can also be a kind of fear."

"Perhaps."

"I understand how you feel," said Volodia, tugging gently at his beard. "I know what fear is."

They fell silent. The young man was a strange individual, thought Volodia. No wonder he had failed to recognize him the first time Evyatar showed him the composite sketch. He looked so odd in his new suit, completely different from the young Jew with the scraggly red beard who had come to him directly from Moscow. At present he didn't even look like a Jew. But his eyes—yes, his eyes were filled with Jewish melancholy.

"What happens after all this is over? You go back to Crown Heights?" Volodia asked.

"I don't know."

"You are performing a mission for the Rebbe," said Volodia, dropping his voice. "A sacred mission. You must return to the Rebbe. He would want you to come back to him."

"I don't know if I'll want to."

Volodia heaved a sigh. These were words of heresy. "You are a Hasid," he declared. "You cannot cease being a Hasid."

Jil was silent. There was no point in arguing the question with Volodia—whether or not it was possible to cease being a Hasid. He gazed at the old man. Although he looked somewhat like Yudke, he was different from his brother. Yudke's personality was characterized by a rare simplicity, a guilelessness. What distinguished Volodia was his extraordinary acuity and wit.

He wondered how he could explain to Volodia that he wished to begin his life over, from a different point, without mortgaging his future to the past. He wanted the right to be himself.

"You are a Hasid," Volodia repeated stubbornly.

"Volodia, I am here because my father and his ancestors were Hasidim. But I am the product of different times, of different conditions . . ."

"You have an obligation to them. To the generations that came before you!"

"I don't owe them anything. I paid my debt when I pledged myself to two men. That's the only obligation I have. And after I discharge that, I'm a free man. You understand, Volodia? A free man . . ."

"You'll return."

"Maybe."

Volodia placed a hand on his shoulder.

"They are waiting for us."

He stepped outside onto the narrow street and walked a few paces and then, looking back, saw that Jil had remained standing by the door. He halted. The younger man was looking about uncertainly, as if he were struggling to take in the unknown that lay beyond his range of vision. Then he turned up the collar of his coat and began to trudge slowly toward Volodia. As he approached him, his pace increased as if his doubts and hesitations had been obliterated.

Volodia Kantor and Jil sat on one side of the conference room in the Israeli Embassy, and opposite them, in twin armchairs, were Paul Mansfield and Evyatar Miller.

The two agents studied the man they had been pursuing for months. His expression shifted continually; each movement completely altered his look, though the contours of his face remained unchanged. They had tried every conceivable means to capture him, and at least once had nearly succeeded in apprehending him in Paris, only to have him slip through their fingers.

"I didn't think you'd come," Evyatar admitted, looking at Jil.

"This is the man you've been looking for," Volodia said with a smile. "Yacov-Moshe Levinson . . . One of ours. A Hasid."

Evyatar glanced over at Paul Mansfield, but he did not appear to have caught the significance of the remark.

"You see, Evyatar," Volodia went on, "it was as the Rebbe said: When he was ready, he would find you."

Did he ever find us! thought the Israeli. They had chased him across Europe for weeks, had, in effect, breathed the Clown day and night. They would rise in the morning, puzzling over his whereabouts, sifting through the information from people claiming to have seen him, planning where to pick up the trail the following day. And now he was here. And he was a Jew. A Jew named Yacov-Moshe Levinson.

"I understand you want help from the Israeli Security Services and the CIA," said Evyatar.

Jil nodded.

"Paul Mansfield is a senior representative of the CIA," explained Evyatar. "And, to put it mildly, he has been interested in meeting you personally for a long time, as have I. You've eluded us all along the way. I wasn't prepared for anyone named Yacov-Moshe Levinson. What name have you been using with the KGB?"

"I grew up with the name Yan Borodov; that's the only name that appears in my KGB records. But I've used a number of aliases. One of them you know: the Clown."

"Well, if you are the one known as the Clown, maybe you're familiar with the other members of the so-called Soviet Circus?"

"There aren't any others."

"Meaning?"

"I am the Clown, and I am also the Miracle Worker, the Fortune Teller, all the others. I used a variety of code names and disguises to cover my activities. I distributed the burden, so to speak, among a large number of individuals. The system proved effective. You, perhaps better than anyone else, know just how effective it was."

Paul Mansfield and Evyatar Miller exchanged rueful glances. This man with the naive, youthful expression was hard to reconcile with the image they had conjured of the wily agent who had dodged across Europe, evading them. For months, the cream of the western European intelligence community had tried unsuccessfully to snare at least one of the members of the Soviet Circus.

"Perhaps you'll let me ask a few questions," Jil went on. "After all, I am the one who initiated this little get-together." He glanced at Paul Mansfield, then turned back to the Israeli. "Why have you been looking for me?"

"We knew that you were in some way involved in the planning of a terrorist operation," responded Evyatar. "We were convinced that catching you would help us expose the Soviet Union's involvement in the operation. And if we succeeded in doing that, then we would be able to abort the action while it was still in the planning stages."

"You are mistaken," Jil said with a faint smile. "I am not involved in it at all."

"That can't be!" Paul Mansfield exclaimed heatedly. "We know you've been in close contact with that German bastard in the Baader-Meinhof gang."

"Horst Welsh," Jil interjected.

"Right! That's his name." Paul moved up to Jil and confronted him face to face. "Do you mean to tell me that you have no connection with Horst Welsh's operation?"

"Not the kind of connection you're suggesting. I know about the action Welsh is currently involved in. I, too, am looking for him."

"What do you know about it?" Evyatar cut in.

"A great deal. I defected from the KGB to thwart it at all costs . . ."

"I don't get it." Evyatar was obviously confused.

"It's a very long story," said Jil. "I had better give you all the information I have so that you can begin to act." He took out the envelope containing the forged passports, the pages torn from Anton Karlov's diaries, and the slide depicting the targets.

33

ON THE THIRTEENTH of March, Anton Karlov received word that Antonio Larado had been killed by persons unknown. The murder itself was not so unexpected but its occurrence exactly one day after Larado had smuggled Horst Welsh out of the United States alarmed Karlov. It might well have been a coincidence, but nevertheless, the Czech instructed his men in Miami to follow the local police investigation to try to extract information that would shed light on the killer or his motives.

And, then, six days later, an informer in Hamburg transmitted the startling and, for Karlov, extremely distressing news that Klaus Schmidt and his two bodyguards had been murdered. This was a heavy blow; Schmidt was the most effective operator that the East German espionage services had placed at Karlov's disposal.

The Czech left for Hamburg to personally investigate the triple murder. Interrogation of the Cassandra staff revealed that on the night of the murders Klaus Schmidt had met a young man in his office whom he apparently knew well. After uncovering most of the details connected with the killings, including an account of Anna-Maria's savage mutilation, he concluded that Klaus Schmidt and the brothers Rudolph and Heinrich had been liquidated by a professional killer and evidently—since he had been able to overcome all three of them—one of exceptional ability. Here, too, there was a connection with Horst Welsh.

In this instance, Karlov was certain that the connection with Welsh was not coincidental. Someone had apparently found the end of a thread and was trying to pull it in an attempt to unravel the entire operation in which the Fox was a key man.

The Czech returned to the STB farm to prepare a detailed report for Pavel Ramizor on both the Hamburg and Miami murders. However, on his arrival, he was obliged to alter his plans. Thomas Kraptow was waiting for him in the second-floor corridor. He was unable to conceal his nervousness; his face was pallid and his look downcast as Karlov approached him. Kraptow described the events of the previous evening when the Clown had shown up at the training farm, how he had gone up to Karlov's office thinking that his boss had returned, how when he had arrived there, he found the Clown rifling the desk drawers.

Karlov did not wait for him to finish his story. With a panic-stricken look, he brushed past Kraptow and flung open the door to his office. He froze in his tracks, thunderstruck as he took in the overturned desk drawers, the open cabinet, and then the blackboard where the names of the fifteen men targeted for death were written. The implications were not lost on Anton Karlov. The individual who knew those names must already know other details of the operation.

Suddenly, everything made sense. Karlov now knew the identity of the young man who had visited Klaus Schmidt on the evening of the nightclub owner's murder. And he knew also that Jil's appearance at the farm was meant as a signal to him and to the others involved in the operation. The Clown had exposed himself intentionally.

Yan Borodov was clearly a double agent, a KGB deserter who, for reasons as yet unknown, was working to thwart the terrorist action. Karlov decided to fly to Moscow at once. He wanted to call a halt to the operation, but to do this, he had to get Pavel Ramizor's approval.

Ramizor received Karlov with a great show of ebullience,

but his exuberance faded as he observed the severe expression on the Czech's face.

"The operation has been exposed," Karlov stated matter-of-factly, in an effort to conceal his distress.

"What do you mean?" Ramizor's tiny eyes scrutinized the Czech's broad face. "Don't tell me one of your sons of bitches has deserted. Which one is it?"

"It's not someone connected with *my* organization." Karlov shifted restlessly in his chair.

Pavel Ramizor banged his heavy fist on the desk. "What are you driving at?"

"I'm afraid that it's one of your men . . ."

The explosion erupted the moment Karlov mentioned Yan Borodov's name. He had witnessed Pavel Ramizor's wrath before, but today's reaction exceeded anything he had ever seen. Ramizor's face turned scarlet; the veins pulsating in his temples swelled till they seemed on the verge of bursting.

"Yan Borodov," he growled between clenched teeth. "And it's been going on under my nose—is that what you are telling me?"

"Yes," Anton Karlov confirmed, "this is not something that developed overnight, Comrade Ramizor."

Pavel Ramizor regained his composure. "What do you suggest?"

"We have to halt the operation," the Czech responded.

"Yes, precisely the approach I would consider," agreed Ramizor, "until we can determine Borodov's motives and uncover proof of his treason."

Karlov remained in Moscow for three more days. During his stay, KGB agents stationed in New York confirmed that Yan Borodov had vanished without a trace.

The defection of Yan Borodov caused great concern among the leadership of the KGB, which was apprehensive about criticism from the Politburo. Pavel Ramizor was asked to make sure that the KGB's involvement had been well concealed, and if it had not, then to what extent representatives of the Soviet Union would be able to deny a connection with the terrorist operation. Aided by Anton Karlov, Ramizor conducted an inquiry, and delivered his conclusions to Chairman Yuri Andropov. Only then did Ramizor find time to weigh the significance of Borodov's defection from the point of view of his own secret investigation of the Jewish network.

The more Ramizor thought about it, the more Sergei Padayev stood out as a key figure. Yan's desertion pointed more and more to a link between the section head, Dr. Rostovitch, and the defector.

It occurred to Ramizor that all three were Jews who had managed, most effectively, to conceal their religious identity. And if this were indeed the case, then it would explain their collaboration with the Hasidic network. He knew he had to proceed very cautiously so as not to stumble and fall a second time. The memory of his previous unsuccessful attempt to prove the existence of the Hasidic network to Yuri Andropov was fresh in the minds of his colleagues and he still smarted from his failure.

One thing was clear: to obtain the proof he needed, he would first have to break the doctor who, until now, had maintained a stubborn silence. Once he accomplished this, he would then approach Sergei Padayev armed with irrefutable evidence. Through Sergei, he might very well reach the Grand Emissary.

For the first few days, the defection remained a closely guarded secret, confined to the agency's ruling cadre. Only on the afternoon of the third day did Ramizor summon Sergei Padayev to his office to discuss the measures and the personnel they would have to employ to apprehend Yan Borodov. Ramizor had hoped in the course of the meeting to learn something from the section head's reactions, but being familiar with Sergei's ability to mask his emotions, he was not overly optimistic.

Sergei's response was very much in keeping with what the department head had anticipated; his face remained utterly expressionless as he listened to the news of Yan Borodov's sudden defection.

"Up to now there has never been a defection from your section," said Ramizor softly, "and of all your men, it had to be Yan Borodov . . . I know the significance this desertion must have for you."

"It is painful, Pavel. Very painful." Sergei's bloodless lips trembled slightly.

"We've been ordered to find him. I'm sorry, Sergei," Ramizor added, quietly drawing in his breath as if fearful of upsetting the warm and convivial atmosphere he had been striving to create. "I can imagine how you must feel, having to hunt down a man who you were so very fond of." As he spoke, he kept his glance on the section head's emaciated countenance. He tried to capture any change, no matter how slight, in his expression. But the mask remained intact. "We shall have to begin preparations immediately."

"First of all, we'll have to prepare a 'defector's file.' I'll take care of that at once," offered Sergei dryly.

"Make a number of copies, Sergei. We'll put as many agents as we can on this. Our men should have every detail that might assist them in identifying Borodov, even if he should appear in disguise. You must emphasize that he is an expert actor, capable of completely altering his identity."

Padayev nodded.

"You will have to ignore your personal feelings, Sergei. I liked the young man too."

"I know."

"The Borodovs were like family to you."

"I consider them among my closest friends."

"I was always envious of your friendship with the old clown . . ." Ramizor detected the slightest crack in the frozen mask of Sergei's face. A tiny muscle seemed, momentarily, to constrict in the corner of his left eye, causing it to narrow ever so slightly. Ramizor wondered if he hadn't hit upon something of significance when he mentioned the elder Borodov. It was possible that he—like his grandson—was connected with the same network. And if Sergei was indeed a member of the Hasidic network, then the clown, despite his advanced age, might very well serve as a connecting link between Sergei and the Grand Emissary.

"My friendship with Boris Borodov was formed during the war."

"A friendship like that will withstand any test," Ramizor pointed out gently. "I feel very sorry for the old clown. I don't understand how his grandson could have let him down so badly . . ."

"We will have to wait, brother Pavel. Time will provide us with the answer to that question."

"I find it very difficult to stop turning the affair over in my mind," conceded the department head. "I ask myself again and again if this was really something sudden, done on impulse, or if he had perhaps been operating as a double agent for a long time."

"I don't know."

"Maybe a probe of the Borodov family's past would yield some background on the defection."

"What do you mean?"

"The period before the war. What do we know about the Borodov family's roots?"

"Not a great deal," conceded Sergei. "They are a very old family, descendants of one of the Cossack tribes that wandered up and down the Don River. Still, I don't think it will be very easy to make an investigation into the Borodovs' roots."

"It might not be easy, but it is certainly within the realm of possibility. The history of the Cossack tribes is far from being as ancient as, say, that of the Jews, for example . . ."

"I couldn't say. I'm not very familiar with the subject."

A disquieting silence fell between them. Sergei chose to interpret it as an indication that Ramizor wanted to terminate their meeting. He rose from his chair and walked slowly toward the door, then halted and turned to Ramizor.

"Yan Borodov's file will be ready within a few hours," he said, gripping the doorknob. "When I deliver it to you, I'll also bring along a list of the men I'd recommend we use in the search for him." He brushed a frail, bony hand across his high forehead. "I'm still at a loss as to how to break the news of Yan's defection to Boris Borodov."

"I wouldn't want him to know about it, at least not now. Don't meet with him for the time being, Sergei."

"As you wish, Pavel."

Outside, in the wide corridor, Sergei found himself bathed in perspiration. Ramizor had sunk his fangs in him. He had actually ordered him to break off contact with Borodov, which meant that Ramizor attributed an importance that transcended mere friendship to his long-standing relationship with the old clown. Pavel would begin to move very soon.

On the fourth day of Karlov's stay in Moscow, Pavel Ramizor was summoned several times to the office of Yuri Andropov to discuss various aspects of the mysterious disappearance of the KGB agent and to decide what to do about the terrorist operation. After weighing various opinions and considering the options, Yuri Andropov and Pavel Ramizor decided that Anton Karlov should leave immediately for Larnaca to postpone the implementation of the plan. Whether or not they would cancel it entirely or merely delay it was something they would decide later, when they had a clearer picture of what was going on and why Yan Borodov had defected.

When Pavel Ramizor was not occupied with whether to postpone or cancel the terrorist action, he was concentrating on his inquisition of the frightened physician, Dr. Grisha Rostovitch.

At the beginning, Pavel Ramizor conducted the examination with a degree of restraint. Though he devoted many hours to the inquiry, he avoided using physical force. Shortly after the decision to postpone the reprisal plan, however, Ramizor shifted his method to one he found more congenial. He was a master at the most appalling brutal methods of interrogation, and for several hours that afternoon he dealt personally with the doctor. At six o'clock he summoned Sergei Padayev to the Bureau of Investigations.

As yet, no one in the agency's hierarchy, Yuri Andropov included, had held Sergei Padayev responsible for the plan's miscarriage as a result of the unexplained desertion of Yan Borodov. Such things had happened before. Nonetheless, Pavel Ramizor burned with determination to expose the roots of this latest departmental failure. Grisha Rostovitch was in some way connected with Sergei Padayev, and they were both linked to Yan Borodov. He recalled Padayev's curiously stubborn insistence that only Borodov be considered for the extended mission in the United States. It was as if Padayev had carefully planned all his steps in advance. Perhaps he received instructions from an individual whose identity was as yet shrouded in mystery—the same individual who headed the Hasidic network.

Ramizor kept his hypothesis, and the few shreds of evidence upon which it was based, strictly to himself. He wanted to verify the theory on his own. Only when he had, would he present the proof to Yuri Andropov. And he was close to attaining that proof.

Every man has a dream. Pavel Ramizor's had been to expose and crush the Jewish network, and after the thwarting of "Operation Red Immigrants" this vision was transformed into an obsession. Yuri Andropov told him months before that only someone willing to devote himself to the matter in earnest would succeed in uncovering the representatives of the network operating within the KGB. Behind his back, senior KGB officials referred to Ramizor sneeringly as the "Jew Hunter." That sobriquet had stuck, and its use was fanned by his outspoken hatred of Jews.

From his point of view, exposure of the Hasidic network would be an accomplishment that would clear the slate of all his recent failures and ensure that his prospects of being appointed head of the First Chief Directorate would be far better than those of any other candidate. For some years he had considered the possibility of advancement to the number two position in the agency. The grade the job carried would significantly affect his pension, but, more importantly, he wanted the promotion because he believed that he merited it.

During the session that afternoon, he had employed every means conceivable to crack the doctor's resistance. The department head was in a state of great excitement, convinced that he was nearing his ultimate goal—the revelation of the Grand Emissary's identity.

A few minutes after calling Sergei Padayev, he heard a light tap on the door, and the head of the Liquidation Section entered his office. Ramizor pointed to the armchair before his desk and Sergei sat down. They faced one another in silence with only the desk between them, but the distance separating them was greater than it seemed. Between the two men, whose intimate association spanned dozens of years, who had together celebrated victories and lamented defeats, there yawned an impassable chasm. Ramizor regarded Sergei's pallid, ascetic countenance and wondered if he had ever really known the man sitting opposite him; perhaps he had merely deluded himself into thinking he had.

"And so, Sergei," he said quietly, "do you want to speak, or shall I?"

"I am listening."

"You knew I would get to you; it was just a question of time."

"And also of luck."

"No. You are wrong. I planned my steps carefully."

Sergei Padayev made no response.

"I set a trap for you and your friends. And it worked, Sergei. I think that tonight I'll finally be able to complete what has been a very long and difficult job, work that required months of planning. I checked every step, every point meticulously. I had to smoke you out of your holes in order to expose the network. And I succeeded, Sergei."

Padayev said nothing.

"Do you understand?" Ramizor asked.

"Not yet."

Which was not true. Sergei had assumed that the meeting would mark the end of the long, tortuous road he had traveled in the KGB. He had known of Grisha Rostovitch's grueling interrogation, and he was now prepared to act in accordance with Boris Borodov's orders.

"Then I'll explain." Ramizor settled back, relaxed and in a tranquil mood. His voice was low and restrained. "For years you've been creeping treacherously around the agency—like serpents. The hierarchy knew of your presence, but no one could prove that you existed or find out how you operated against the KGB. You showed extraordinary power and resolve, careful and thorough analysis, and superb planning. The Grand Emissary!" he exclaimed, pounding his fist. "You understand, Sergei, it wasn't you who I had to contend with. It was him, all along, only with him. Tonight I will close the trap."

"I don't know anything about a trap."

"You haven't discovered it?"

"No," admitted Sergei.

"Then you deserve to have it disclosed, Sergei. For you helped me solve the problem of the Hasidic network."

"How?"

"Patience, brother Sergei. The whole story begins with one simple fact: the fact that the network is run by Hasidim. You know as well as I the kind of allegiance Hasidim have to their Rebbe. Why, you yourself, Sergei, are a Hasid. I don't have to describe the Rebbe's significance to you. And so, Sergei," he continued, watching with pleasure as the color slowly drained from the section head's gaunt face, "was this not an important step to have reached in my thinking?"

"Yes," Sergei said dryly.

"I believe you would have proceeded precisely as I did. You understand, Sergei, I acted as if I had first consulted with you. I asked myself, how would Sergei react? What would he propose in a situation like this? And then I reached a simple conclusion: to strike at your most vulnerable point; to strike in such a manner as to compel you to expose yourselves. And that is precisely what happened."

"The trap."

"That's right, Sergei, the trap." He drew a deep breath and continued. "Yuri Andropov knows that there is an underground network operating against us. But, up until now, he had no idea that it was a network comprised of Hasidim. That finding I'll keep for him until after I've reached the Grand Emissary. But, let us return to the trap. Yes. I decided to devise a strategy that would force you to act, regardless of the risk of exposure."

"I understand that we exposed ourselves . . ."

"Without a doubt, Sergei. The trap succeeded. You see, when I conceived of a plan of reprisals against fifteen Jews and non-Jews connected with the Jewish lobby, I had an ulterior motive. I persuaded all those who had a say in the matter to approve it, despite its inherent dangers. From a policy point of view, it met current needs. From a personal point of view, it served my purpose superbly."

"I understand."

"I thought you would."

"You placed the Rebbe's name on this list, knowing how we would react."

"Yes, Sergei." Pavel Ramizor dropped his voice almost to a whisper. "The Rebbe was my bait. I knew what effect the discovery of his name on the list would have on you. Therefore, I opened a narrow crack for you, to reveal just a little, but no more."

"A narrow crack," agreed Sergei. He recalled how he had uncovered the names of those on the reprisal list by checking the card index and noting which files Ramizor's secretary had taken from the archives.

"Then I proceeded from two directions. You made two mistakes I would never have expected you to make Sergei, not a man of your caliber, with your experience. First, you falsified medical reports, but it is impossible to distort medical records without the cooperation of a compliant doctor. True?"

Sergei Padayev nodded his head.

"Grisha Rostovich was an excellent physician, a doctor who relinquished a brilliant career to come to us. Why?"

Sergei kept silent.

"I'll tell you why, Sergei. You needed a cover—a drop—within our headquarters, a central point from which orders could be transmitted to the men in your network operating within the KGB. Could there be a better place, or one less likely to arouse suspicion than the Central Clinic? Who would dream that a simple friendly doctor like Grisha was in fact serving as a walking drop for an underground network? Who would believe such a thing, Sergei?"

"A commendable discovery," affirmed Padayev quietly.

"Oh, yes," agreed Pavel Ramizor, "but it's you who deserve the praise for coming up with an idea like that. For years you succeeded in supervising your men, individuals planted right here in the KGB, without coming into direct contact with any of them. You had the doctor. Who would suspect a man who enters the clinic for an examination or to receive treatment?" He laughed. "As I said, the falsification of the reports aroused my suspicions and eventually put me on the right track. I knew then and I know now what your condition really is, Sergei. You are a very sick man. Your life expectancy is very short indeed." He spoke these last words with cold malevolence.

"You mentioned two mistakes . . ."

"Your thirst for the details increases by the minute." Ramizor settled himself comfortably in his chair. "I found the other error only after I uncovered your indiscretion with regard to the medical reports. It concerned Yan Borodov. I recalled our discussions about the liquidation mission in the United States—how you fought for his appointment, trying, it seemed, to elbow aside all other candidates. It was not characteristic of you. So, after I learned of Borodov's desertion, I made a simple deduction. Was I right?"

"You were right."

"You are a strange adversary," admitted Ramizor. "I'm sorry the contest is about to end. To tell you the truth, Sergei, I haven't any real friends; I've avoided making friends. But I always felt close to you. And I never underestimated your very rare abilities. Despite what I've discovered, I can still find words of praise for you."

"And I, likewise, for you, Pavel," remarked Sergei.

"Despite your plan to strike at the Jewish lobby. For that you will receive the prize: the Grand Emissary."

"A proper characterization, Sergei. He is indeed the prize."

"I must admit that you succeeded in duping us. Not one of us dreamed that this operation was also meant to serve you personally as a means of getting to us. You succeeded, Pavel. I assume you have shared your findings."

"I wouldn't share a success like this with anyone, Sergei."

"You haven't even passed your information on to Yuri Andropov?"

"Not yet. I want to present him with the entire picture."

"What do you want of me now?"

"You know."

"I suppose I do." Events had gone precisely as the old man had said they would. He wondered how Boris Borodov would fare in his face-to-face confrontation with Ramizor.

Pavel Ramizor had been surprised at first by Sergei Padayev's immediate accession to his demand for a meeting with the Grand Emissary. Then he realized that Sergei must have felt so incapable, in his debilitated condition, of withstanding any pressure—whether physical or psychological—that he had capitulated at once.

During the drive from KGB headquarters, Ramizor had been filled with a delicious sense of anticipation, a feeling of intoxication. At long last, he was to meet the Grand Emissary, the man whom he had longed to unmask and whom he would have paid any price to expose.

Now, however, he stood rooted to the floor in the apartment on Kalinin Boulevard. Opposite him, at ease in a comfortable armchair, sat the thin old man with the sweeping Cossack moustache.

"Boris Borodov," Ramizor exclaimed in a hoarse whisper. Somehow he could not conceive of Boris Borodov in any role other than that of the famous circus clown.

"Sit down," Borodov said in a quiet but decisive voice.

"I didn't come to sit, Comrade Borodov," said Ramizor, his voice laced with sarcasm. "Who would have thought that the legendary clown was in fact the most serious of men!" He laughed wryly. "I'll never forget your appearances with the circus, Borodov, but I must tell you that you gave your greatest performance behind the scenes."

"Do sit," repeated the old man. "We have several matters to discuss."

"Is there very much more for me to learn here?"

"I believe so."

"I hadn't thought to carry on an extended conversation. In any case, my office would be more suitable for our purposes."

"We'll get to that later, Comrade Ramizor. In the meantime, we are here."

Pavel Ramizor hesitated. He glanced at Sergei, who was sitting to his left, then looked back at Borodov. The old man's eyes were cold and penetrating, and his look imperious. His manner gave Ramizor a feeling of profound discomfort. He grumbled and sat down.

It was an odd situation. Ramizor's sharp senses were instantly alert. He had begun to suspect that he had misunderstood Sergei Padayev's immediate acquiescence to his request that he be brought to the Grand Emissary. He had interpreted his willingness as an indication of weakness, yet, at the moment, Sergei seemed completely at ease, as did the old clown. Indeed, Boris Borodov's tranquility was so profound that it seemed hard to believe he was a traitor who had been unmasked and whose entire underground network was about to be exposed.

"For years I have wanted to know who you were," Ramizor said. He was surprised to find that his voice was hoarse. "You have engaged me in a brilliant battle of wits. And you were always ahead of me, sometimes by only one step, at times by two but always ahead. This time I have gained the ascendancy."

"So it seems."

"I am a step ahead of you, Comrade Borodov. Only one. But, from your point of view, I have a deadly advantage."

The old man nodded. "I would never disparage your ability, Pavel Ramizor. You are unquestionably an extremely astute and competent man. There was always the possibility of your forestalling me. I must admit that the battle of wits in which we engaged provided me with an intellectual challenge. And that is a very important thing for a man of my age. We tend to become unimaginative and set in our ways."

"Who would have thought it possible?" Pavel Ramizor regarded Borodov for a moment and then his glance wandered to Sergei Padayev. "Sergei served you faithfully. To trick and deceive me for so many years was no simple matter. But the moment of truth has arrived, Borodov. From the instant I began to suspect that a key member of your network had infiltrated my department, I was spurred to action. I started to think in a different way, to react in a different manner, to look for mistakes. Sergei blundered. And you are a partner to his error."

"True. I am a partner to his mistake."

Borodov's voice held the tiniest trace of mockery, and a vague feeling of discomfort again welled up in Ramizor, but he squelched it.

"Everyone makes mistakes, and every mistake has its price. You will pay a price as will Sergei."

"And you will pay a price for your glory."

The old clown's response seemed almost mocking. Ramizor again had the odd feeling that perhaps something was amiss. A man like Borodov could surprise him even now. He was well aware of the man's endowments: the capacity of his intellect; the power of his will.

"Very caustic remarks, Borodov," said the department head dryly. "And very inappropriate considering your situation. You have many hours of interrogation before you. I will want to know everything about you, every detail that can shed light on your methods of operation. I will want to receive a complete list of your people. Who they are. Where they are. I want, once and for all, to lay your network to eternal rest—to bury it and place a headstone over its grave."

"I have no doubt that those are your intentions."

"You know that you have no alternative. A man like you knows when to throw in his cards."

"I do indeed."

"So, Borodov, let's go." Ramizor rose from the chair, but to his amazement, the old man did not stir, nor did Sergei.

"I suggest you sit," said Borodov. "We haven't finished yet."

"What remains to be discussed will be dealt with in a different arena. Under different spotlights. The audience, too, will be a far cry from the audience of your circus days."

"You are still in *my* arena, however," responded the old clown, quietly. "And I haven't yet completed my part. Your sense of fairness, brother Pavel, should permit me to finish this little performance."

Ramizor hesitated.

"You must have noticed that I anticipated your arrival," said Borodov, smiling.

"Since you mention it—yes, I did notice."

"You will also admit that at times I have anticipated your moves and checked them, particularly when it was a matter of saving human lives, physically or spiritually. And it's possible that this time, too, I am ahead of you, brother Pavel, perhaps by just one step, not a very large step, but a very important one."

Ramizor found himself sitting down involuntarily. His sense of caution was alerted. Although it wasn't clear what was happening, it appeared the old man still held a few cards.

"What are you talking about?"

"Sergei and I are not the only ones who made mistakes. You made them as well."

"I have, quite true. But I don't know which mistake you're referring to at the moment."

"I won't keep it from you, brother Pavel. You deserve to know what it is."

"Enlighten me."

"You found the mistake that Sergei Padayev made," said the old man, "when you read Grisha Rostovitch's file."

"True."

"The moment you located the error, you went to work with commendable caution. You first checked the ground very thoroughly before you stepped down on it. But the more you progressed, the less cautious you became. Ultimately you reached a stage where you galloped ahead blindly; you began to check things on your own."

"I don't understand what you're getting at."

"I'm referring to Riga."

"Riga?"

"Yes. Grisha Rostovitch's birthplace. Riga particularly aroused your curiosity. In his personal file, Grisha Rostovitch appears as a bona fide pure-blooded Russian. You had to find some motive for him that would point to a connection with Sergei Padayev—and such a motive, if you truly believed that Padayev was one of my men, had to focus on Judaism. You had a hunch that Sergei Padayev was a Jew but in order to prove it, you had to find the weak link in the chain. That link was Grisha Rostovitch. If you could prove that the doctor was a Jew, then you would have your answer. Isn't that so?"

"But he isn't!" exclaimed Pavel Ramizor.

"*Now* you know this to be a fact," the old man agreed, "but you didn't then. And because you didn't, you made an error. Only someone familiar with Riga would have taken it upon himself to go there to conduct this inquiry. And you had two good reasons for personally undertaking the investigation. First, because you yourself were born in Riga." Boris Borodov paused. "But there was a much better reason."

"A better reason," murmured Pavel Ramizor. He suddenly felt very tired, as if he had aged years in the course of this brief meeting.

The old man went on relentlessly. "And that error, Pavel, assumed increasingly greater significance. You returned from Riga empty-handed, having failed to find proof that Grisha was a Jew. Perhaps you were not aware that there are Christians who believe in the validity of Judaism and work on its behalf, even performing actions that may endanger themselves and those they love. Grisha Rostovitch is one of that group we call 'the Righteous Among the Nations,' the most exalted title that we Jews can bestow on a Gentile.

"You had to look for another motive or for some inconsistency in his background that might point to a connection with the network and with Sergei Padayev. You uncovered it when you began to investigate Grisha's past—his attendance at medical college and his employment at the Central Hospital—and discovered that he had cut short a brilliant future in the profession. Having located an inconsistency which you believed might lead you to a motive, you detained him. When Yan's desertion followed, you succeeded in putting the pieces together. But I have put some pieces together myself. Just before you arrived, it dawned on me, finally, what a brilliant trap you had laid for us. You set the Rebbe up as the first target of a savage terrorist operation. Even if I had uncovered the trap earlier, I doubt whether I'd have acted any differently. I was obliged to take chances, even if it meant risking the exposure of the whole network. Curiously enough, you understood the significance of the Rebbe to his Hasidim."

"Yes," Ramizor whispered.

"And this knowledge wasn't recent. You always knew."

Pavel Ramizor was silent.

"You see, brother Pavel," continued Boris Borodov, "everyone has something in his past he wishes to hide. A blemish . . . a secret of some kind. For years I was unable to uncover your secret. And, believe me, I looked for it. I like to prepare myself for every eventuality. I am obliged to know the vulnerabilities of people who have a connection with my world. Do you know when I began to close in on your Achilles' heel?"

"When I went to Riga?"

"Correct."

"How did you uncover it?"

"Your hatred of Jews, Pavel. Your rabid anti-Semitism. You traveled to Riga because you knew what you might find. As one who was born in Riga, who knew the city well from his youth, you were convinced that you'd find there proof of Grisha Rostovitch's Jewishness. And you went by yourself because none of your investigators had the kind of connections with the Riga Jewish community that you once had. When you came back empty-handed, I went to Riga to conduct my own investigation. I also had good contacts in the Jewish community there, as you know. I found that I hadn't been mistaken. I discovered what I was looking for."

Sweat beaded Pavel Ramizor's forehead. His body was clammy with perspiration and there was a strange taste of fear in his mouth.

"You simply went overboard with your anti-Semitism, Pavel. That was a serious mistake. A Jew must remember his roots. Even if he denies them."

"I had no alternative," said Ramizor, his voice so low as to be nearly inaudible.

"You chose your way of life. But what did you think? That you'd be able to bury your past?" Boris Borodov shook his head. "That is impossible to do. Now you are in a difficult position. You see, I uncovered your origins in Riga, Pavel."

The old man fixed his penetrating gaze on the department head's sallow, perspiring face. Ramizor sat limply in his chair, his face slack and bloodless. He found himself totally impotent before this old man. For dozens of years he had worked meticulously, cautiously, with resolution and cunning, to build a new image for himself. To create a new world. A different life.

"Why, Pavel?"

"I had the right . . ."

"The right to do what?"

"To live like all the others. To be Russian—pure, untainted." He wanted to scream; he tried but failed to raise his voice. "You know as well as I do there's no hope for us here." His tone was almost supplicating.

"True."

"I didn't want to live like you, or like Sergei, hunched over with the weight of two thousand years of suffering on my back. Not me."

"You lived a monstrous lie. That is worse than the weight we carry with us."

Pavel Ramizor gave a bitter chuckle. "You and Sergei, you don't live with lies?"

"We didn't choose to do so."

"What's the difference? Ultimately, everyone chooses his way of life. And each has his own reasons for the choice he makes. I saw what happened to millions of Jews during the war. And nobody cared. Nobody went out into the streets shaking a fist and railing at the slaughter, screaming at death to halt in its tracks. No one tried to block even one of the thousands of chimneys that poured smoke from the gas chambers . . . that spewed out my parents, my brothers and sisters. Why?" The words choked in his throat; he drew a deep breath and continued. "I wasn't willing to remain part of a minority. Not in the world we live in."

Boris Borodov regarded him sadly. "Nobody forced you to live like a Jew. But you lost all semblance of humanity, Pavel. You became a Jew-hater in order to justify to yourself your estrangement from your past. You sank to the lowest level possible: you became the persecutor of your brothers."

Sergei Padayev studied Boris Borodov's handsome, tranquil face with undisguised admiration. He knew the old man had been preparing himself for this encounter with Ramizor but he had had no idea what turn it would take. Like a clever circus magician, Boris had put into his hat a dubious Christian and pulled out a turncoat Jew.

"Surely, Comrade," Borodov concluded, "it's clear to you what will happen when it becomes known that all through the years you concealed the fact that you were a Jew." The old man's voice was dry and flat. "If your origins had been known, you would never have attained your present position. Unfortunately for you, your need to distinguish yourself as a

Jew-hater undermined your logic. In order to expose us, you initiated an important KGB operation without any of your superiors knowing your highly personal reasons for doing so. You might have brought the Soviet Union, by dint of this mission, to a dangerous confrontation with the United States. The ugly, self-hating Jew in you wanted to totally crush us."

Ramizor was unable to meet the old man's withering glance. He lowered his eyes and, drawing a handkerchief from his pocket, began to dab at his sweaty face.

"Without doubt, Pavel, you succeeded in tripping us up. You completely deluded us with the trap you laid. Placing the Rebbe—may he live a long and blessed life—at the head of the list of targets was a brilliant ploy to get us to expose ourselves. But look at what else you accomplished. Because of you, the Americans have in their hands at this moment concrete proof of the KGB's involvement in a terrorist plot. You have contributed to the failure of an important mission. And one always pays a price for a failure. If this information—which at present is known only to Sergei, to me, and to you—were brought to the attention of your colleagues, all the privileges you enjoyed in the past would immediately vanish as if they had never existed."

Borodov paused to let Ramizor digest his remarks, to consider the hopelessness of his situation. The turnabout in their positions in the last hour could not have been more dramatic.

"There is only one way you can escape this threat to your future," said the old man, as if he were a teacher explaining a difficult lesson to his pupil. "You will in any event have to pay a price, but the price that I'll exact will be infinitely smaller than the one demanded by Chairman Andropov. If you do as I say, you'll have a real prospect of continuing to live your life as you've ordered it. You understand, Pavel, that if an investigation is opened now into the causes underlying Yan's desertion, unless you exert an influence on its conduct, the investigators will get to me. And, from me, I promise you, they will reach you. Thus, the trap you laid so expertly will be closed. But not only on Sergei and myself."

Pavel Ramizor knew he had no alternative but to follow the course of action Boris Borodov had proposed. Still, it was difficult to admit defeat, especially when it had been administered in the very room that was to be the scene of his most glorious triumph. The disappointment was crushing, but there could be no other solution. His fate lay completely in Boris Borodov's hands.

"What do you want of me?" he asked, his voice quavering.

"An accord of silence. You will remain silent and so shall we. Nothing will change. You have to oversee the investigation of Yan's desertion. Look after it properly, Pavel. As of now, your well-being is dependent on his. Don't send your bloodhounds after him. Despite this failure, your standing has not been impaired."

Ramizor had no alternative. A feeling of self-contempt welled up in him as he slowly rose from the chair and walked wearily to the door. He realized that the old clown had been temperate, perhaps even generous. But for Pavel Ramizor this had not been just a failure, it had been a shattering, humiliating defeat.

34

ANTON KARLOV ARRIVED in Larnana on Monday, the fourth of March, and immediately telephoned the villa where Vladimir Zoska was staying. There had been some concern about Zoska's welfare, for employees in Karlov's office had tried unsuccessfully to reach him to inform him of the section head's arrival in Larnaca.

Karlov was therefore very relieved when he heard Zoska's voice on the other end of the line.

"We tried to reach you earlier," he said.

"I've just returned from Beirut."

Karlov paused for a moment. Zoska would not have gone to Beirut unless it was absolutely necessary. "I hope it was a good trip," he said finally.

"From a business point of view—bad."

There was no use discussing the matter over the telephone; they arranged to meet later at Karlov's room in the harbor-front hotel.

Karlov greeted Zoska warmly when he arrived. He was genuinely fond of his assistant. The section head drew a bottle of plum brandy—the Yugoslavian slivovitz they both enjoyed—from his suitcase and filled two glasses, and as they

317

took their first sips of the liqueur, Karlov explained why he had flown to Larnaca. He brought Zoska up to date on the previous week's developments, beginning with the first report from Miami and concluding with Chairman Yuri Andropov's decision on the fate of the mission.

"As you no doubt understand, I have been given full authority to decide," said Karlov. "But we must be careful that no matter what happens, you and I are not crushed in the process, eh?"

"I can provide you with arguments for a very radical decision," Zoska commented, refilling his glass.

Karlov gazed meditatively at Zoska's pale countenance. His assistant was not given to flip comments. His statement had to have been prompted by some very compelling considerations.

"Horst Welsh called me," said Zoska calmly, though a look of deep concern was etched on his face. "That's why I went to Beirut."

"I understand something went wrong there," said Karlov, choosing his words carefully.

"Precisely. And in my opinion you have to recommend not just postponing the operation but cancelling it entirely."

"That's a very drastic conclusion."

"There's a good reason for it."

"I'm listening."

Vladimir Zoska related the information he had acquired in Beirut from his protégé, Da'ud el Za'id, and from Horst Welsh. The time he had spent cultivating the Palestinian had proven to be a worthwhile investment. Against the background of their special relationship, Da'ud had decided to share the information he'd obtained from el-Dalil, information that was highly explosive.

"They plan to use us to perpetrate mass slaughter," explained Zoska. "Mussa el-Dalil has no intention at all of stopping with the assassination of the old Jew. He intends to use us and the mission simply as the means for carrying out his own deranged plan."

Anton Karlov's mouth dropped open in astonishment. "What are you talking about?" he asked in disbelief.

"About the fact that we have chosen dangerous and unreliable partners."

"I want to hear everything you know," Karlov demanded.

Vladimir Zoska proceeded to describe Mussa el-Dalil's covert plan: the Palestinian commander intended to train a special unit patterned on the one Horst Welsh had trained in Larnaca. This second group would reach New York on its own and, once there, would join Horst's unit, but from then on, the action would proceed in accordance with el-Dalil's plan. They would mount an attack on the synagogue after the Rebbe had entered the building. Mussa el-Dalil's intention was to set fire to the structure from all sides, so that no one inside the synagogue would come out alive.

"Vladimir, we're folding up here as fast as possible."

"That won't stop el-Dalil now."

"We'll worry about that later," declared the section head. "Right now, I'm thinking of you and me. For my part, el-Dalil can carry out his pact with the Devil. We're getting out. Later on, we'll figure out how to cover our tracks."

"When are we taking off?"

"Tonight. We'll take the first plane out of here."

"What will we do about Horst Welsh? He's arriving in Larnaca on Thursday with el-Dalil."

"What is el-Dalil coming here for?"

"In Limmasol there is a neighborhood similar to Crown Heights," explained Vladimir Zoska. "They want to study the area and then bring the men there for a final briefing. We can't leave without Horst."

Anton Karlov hesitated. "Listen, Vladimir," he began. He wavered briefly and then came to a decision: "You wait for Horst, I have to get back to Moscow at once and report on the new developments."

Soon after their boat docked at the anchorage south of Larnaca's commercial harbor, Horst and el-Dalil stopped at the villa on their way to Limmasol to pick up Zoska. To their surprise, they found him in the midst of packing.

"I must fly to Prague," Zoska explained flatly. "We are forced to postpone the operation." Mussa el-Dalil stared incredulously at the Czech for several moments; then he gave a short, bitter laugh.

"That's a very bad joke," he said. "We're not accustomed to that kind of humor here in the Middle East."

His black eyes glittered ominously. Despite the moderation of his tone, the Palestinian's anger was manifestly mounting.

"It's no joke," stated the Czech dryly. "I am simply acting on orders. I waited especially to inform you."

Mussa el-Dalil lost his self-control; he grabbed the lapels of Zoska's jacket. "Is this the way you people plan to wind up the affair? I demand to know what's behind this decision."

Although the Czech knew him to be extremely dangerous, he did not flinch from the Palestinian. He encircled el-Dalil's wrists with his hands and wrenched his arms away from the lapels, shoving him backward at the same time.

"Don't use force with me," he said quietly. "I have told you what I was instructed to tell you. The reasons?" He shrugged. "I don't know. But the intention is to put it off a few days, perhaps a week or two, maximum."

The Palestinian's eyes moved from Zoska to Horst Welsh. He made an obvious effort to regain his composure and finally succeeded, convinced that restraint might serve him more effectively as a means of getting at the truth.

Finally, el-Dalil asked: "Will you please tell me what caused the postponement?"

"I don't know."

"But you are certain it's only a postponement?"

"That's what I was told."

"I would like you to remain in Larnaca," said el-Dalil slowly, "until I receive a reliable explanation of the exact situation."

"They're waiting for me," the Czech responded calmly, though he felt his pulse quicken. He did not dismiss the possibility that el-Dalil might hold him in Larnaca by force.

Mussa el-Dalil was bitterly disappointed. He needed the Czechs as a springboard from which to launch his own operation. Yet, the apparent lost opportunity only made him more determined to carry out the operation according to his original timetable. To do so, however, one man was indispensable. He glanced at Horst Welsh. The German had said nothing so far.

"Are you taking Welsh, too?"

Zoska immediately grasped the Palestinian's intent. He took a deep breath. Drawing the rope too tight was unnecessarily perilous. Mussa el-Dalil had offered him an opportunity to leave Larnaca safely.

"No, not now," said Zoska abruptly. "I hadn't thought of

taking him. One of us must remain here until a new date is set. Welsh will be the contact."

Horst opened his mouth to protest, but the Czech flashed him a withering look and he remained silent. He was trapped.

"That's good," declared el-Dalil. "Welsh will be the contact man . . . that's very good."

They rose as one. The three were experienced professionals; as such, each knew that his colleagues had been less than candid, that each, in reaching the apparent present accord, had dissembled and distorted facts and concealed personal motives. Yet they continued the game. Mussa el-Dalil, in particular, was obliged to proceed with circumspection, for if the Czechs had any reason to suspect that he might proceed without them, they would undoubtedly try to stop him.

"I'm sorry about the delay," said the Czech, taking leave of el-Dalil at the entrance to the villa, "but this is not the end of the story, you know."

"You're right," agreed the Palestinian as he trotted down the stone steps and got into the Mercedes idling in front of the villa. "This is by no means the end of the line." He closed the door and the blue car sped away.

When Zoska returned to the villa, Welsh was waiting for him. The German's expression was dour.

"I understand that el-Za'id's information caused a minor earthquake," said Welsh quietly.

"It's more than that, Horst. Someone in Europe uncovered some compromising information on the operation. A KGB defector," Zoska explained. "But I can't go into it now. I must get to the airport."

"What about me?"

Although he had little doubt as to what it would be, Welsh's eyes were filled with supplication as he awaited the Czech's response.

"You can't come with me, Horst," explained Zoska calmly. "I'm sure you don't want to cause unnecessary problems, do you?"

"But—"

"Everything will be arranged," Zoska interrupted. "I didn't want to aggravate the situation while the Arab was here. But there's something you should know: we're getting out of the whole affair. There will be no new date."

"But what about me?" Horst ran his tongue over parched

lips. "Don't leave me stuck here. You can get me out the same way you brought me here. I won't try to prevent you from going, Vladimir, but don't forget about me."

His eyes were again on the Czech's face, imploring.

"You have no need to worry." Zoska was genuinely distressed that he had to abandon the German. "In a few days one of our men will come to Larnaca to get you out."

Zoska caught the four o'clock flight to Athens; Horst Welsh, who had accompanied him to the airport, watched the plane take off, feeling very alone and extremely jittery.

"So he's gone has he?"

Horst whirled around at the sound of el-Dalil's voice. "Yes," he said, "he's gone."

El-Dalil had four burly men with him. Welsh was certain that their elegant sports jackets concealed revolvers, and it suddenly dawned on him that he had been followed.

"I'm glad you didn't try to get on the plane," said Mussa el-Dalil with a smile.

"Why?"

"Because then I would have had to kill you." The smile faded from his thick lips. "Come, let's go."

He grabbed the German roughly by the arm and pulled him toward the exit. The blue Mercedes was waiting in front of the terminal. Horst was certain that he was not merely being held hostage by el-Dalil: a plan was brewing in the Palestinian's fevered mind and he was meant to assist in its execution.

They drove in silence up the palm-lined boulevard and as they approached the hotel, Mussa el-Dalil turned to the German: "There is no point in trying to get away from Larnaca. You will join us. Isn't that so, Horst?"

Welsh's heart skipped a beat in terror. "Of course I'll join you." His voice was so hoarse he thought he might not have been understood. "I'll join, but what are you planning?"

"We intend to carry out the operation. Now do you understand? I need you with us. You will guide the men step by step through the operation."

"I'm with you," Horst said, barely able to keep his teeth from chattering. This madman was about to lead all of them to certain death.

"You and your bodyguards are to stay here—we have reserved rooms for you," el-Dalil directed. "In another four days I'll bring the men over in the boat. Wait for me at the port."

"On Monday?"

"Yes."

"I'll be waiting."

As Welsh opened the door and stepped out of the car, the two husky, grim-faced men got out with him.

"You might just as well get to know them," el-Dalil called from the window. "The tall one is Murad and the other is Abed. They'll accompany you like two shadows. At a distance, of course." He laughed expansively and closed the window.

Horst Welsh turned slowly and walked toward the yacht basin. He would spend his free time here in the wharves, watching the boats, remembering the dreamy, carefree days he had spent with Anna-Maria.

35

Much as Jil longed to be done with it all, to hurdle this final obstacle on the road to independence and freedom, he found he wanted to be there when the curtain descended on the final act of the operation.

The briefing sessions with Earl Dickson, General Negbi, and the CIA and Mossad agents went on for three days, leaving Jil drained and weary. When it was over, they were all in agreement: they wanted him to fly to Larnaca to help locate and question Horst Welsh. They intended to liquidate the unit that was to serve as the operational spearhead.

He had described Welsh to them many times; the Fox, in point of fact, resembled nothing so much as a fox. They would identify him easily, but until they had, Jil was to remain in his hotel room in Larnaca. Once Welsh had been located, Jil was to establish contact with him.

On Thursday, March twenty-seventh, he flew to Larnaca with Evyatar Miller and Paul Mansfield. Rooms had been reserved for them in the hotel near the harbor. For the first time in several days, Jil found himself completely alone, a situation he was enjoying as he sat by the window and watched the play of light and shade on the still, gloomy waters of the harbor. A storm was brewing in the west.

A few minutes before midnight he heard a light tap on his door, and he rose to admit Evyatar and Paul.

"We've located Welsh," said Paul, with satisfaction. "In a hotel next to ours."

"Then we mustn't lose him. A tail has to be put on him immediately."

"That's been done," Evyatar said with a smile. "Our men and Paul's have already surrounded the place. You should try to make contact with him in the morning."

As Jil locked the door behind them, he found himself thinking of Margaret. She had led them here.

"Many thanks, Maggie," he murmured with a nod and a smile, as if her spirit were hovering in the room.

The next morning Jil was notified that Horst Welsh, followed by his two bodyguards, had left the hotel and was walking in the direction of the harbor.

Jil went outside and crossed the palm-lined boulevard. A few minutes later he caught sight of Horst, deep in conversation with an elderly fisherman. He waited until Horst was alone. Jil was not concerned about the two Arabs lingering near the breakwater since Paul and Evyatar were bringing up the rear.

"Jil!" It was the exuberant cry of a drowning man at long last catching hold of a life belt. Horst gazed in happy disbelief as Jil sat down next to him.

"So they didn't throw me to the wolves," he mumbled. "They promised—and damnit, they kept their promise. You know, I'd almost stopped believing, but you're actually here. Listen," he said, his eyes suddenly clouding over. "Be careful of those two back there, at the edge of the breakwater . . ."

Jil turned slowly to catch a glimpse of the Arabs, realizing now that they were not Horst's bodyguards at all, but had been attached to him for reasons wholly unrelated to personal security. Horst was their captive.

"Who did you think had abandoned you?"

"Vladimir Zoska and the rest of them." Horst's breathing was labored. He brought a hand up to his head and ran his fingers through his damp, matted hair. "They left . . . they went away . . . and left me here alone, until they could get me out . . . that's what they said. You understand, Jil?"

"I understand," said Jil slowly. "They left suddenly, is that it?"

"Exactly." Horst lit a cigarette, inhaled too much smoke and began to cough. "Sorry," he said. "So you see how it is now? I'm stuck here alone. They all left . . . I understand that they didn't have time to bring you up to date, did they?"

"Time was in short supply," Jil murmured, "but I was given to understand that someone in Europe got wind of the plan . . ."

"That's not all," said Horst. He felt uncomfortable, for the two Arabs were standing a short distance away.

"What else?"

"These madmen want to start a barnfire over there . . . burn thousands of people alive." He clutched at Jil's arm. "They're planning to force me to go with them. You probably can't understand what I'm talking about, but it's terrible . . . Jil, I need you . . . you have to get me out of here. But first we have to get rid of those two dogs. They're armed . . ."

"Who are they?"

"Mussa el-Dalil's men." Horst seemed on the verge of losing his grip. Observing him, Jil thought he probably needed a fix, but there was no time for that. The German had to be made to talk, and quickly too. It was essential they get rid of the two guards. He cast a quick glance at them. They seemed restless as they stood catching some of the spray from the sea splashing up from the breakwater. The storm was about to break, and tall waves rolling in to the harbor pounded the jetty.

"Get up," he ordered.

"Where are we going?"

"Back to the shore," explained Jil. "Do you know the area?"

"Yes."

"Do you know of any isolated spot where we can draw those two into a trap?"

"Do you mean . . ."

"Exactly," was Jil's curt reply. "Where?"

"There are groves not far from here. On the way to Limmasol."

"That sounds right. As long as there are other people around, they won't do anything that's likely to endanger you."

Jil jumped to his feet. At first, the German hesitated, but a moment later, braced by Jil's determination, he too got up.

From a distance they looked like two friends engaged in a casual conversation. Murad and Abed watched them closely, as they had watched Horst and the fisherman earlier. Jil explained to Horst precisely what he was to do. He told him there was an American car, a gray Chevrolet, parked near the boulevard. He would go directly to the automobile, and Horst was to follow a few minutes later. He would find the car waiting, with the door open and the engine running. He was to jump in, close the door, and drive toward the grove. Jil left it at that, making no mention of the plan of action once they reached their destination. He turned and walked toward the shore.

Horst waited five minutes, then he strode shoreward back along the jetty. He walked slowly so as not to arouse any suspicion on the part of the Arabs. Reaching the boulevard, he found the gray car and sprang into the driver's seat. Jil was sitting beside him. The engine was idling and Horst had only to release the handbrake and step down on the accelerator. He picked up speed quickly. Murad and Abed ran to their Mercedes and, within seconds, were barreling after the Chevrolet.

The two Arabs were completely engrossed in the chase. Craning their necks, straining to keep track of the gray car, they were oblivious of the orange BMW following them. Evyatar Miller was behind the wheel of this third automobile, Paul Mansfield beside him.

A flash of lightning, like a thin, blue tongue of fire, zigzagged across the darkened sky. Thunder rolled in the distance, drawing nearer as the fury of the storm increased. Rain fell in torrents.

Though he was tense, Horst drove well. The Mercedes stayed close behind them. The third car kept a fixed distance behind the Mercedes. Paul unbuttoned his jacket. His old Smith & Wesson revolver hung from a shoulder holster under his armpit.

Another flash of lightning snaked across the sky and was followed by a deafening peal of thunder. Suddenly the Chevrolet took a sharp right turn down a narrow dirt road toward the groves. Skidding and bouncing along the wet, bumpy path, the car neared a high locked gate. Horst, as ordered, accelerated, and the heavy car lunged forward, breaking the chain strung across the gate and plunging headlong down the muddy path, its front smashed. They drove for another thirty yards and then stopped.

"Jump out and run toward the trees," called Jil, looking back at the Mercedes, which was just then approaching the iron gate. "I'll be right behind you."

They leaped from the car and Jil dashed around to the driver's side, following Horst into the trees. The low-slung citrus boughs were at face level, so they had to run almost completely doubled over. They heard the door of the Mercedes slam shut and knew that the Palestinians had started after them.

In their haste, the Arabs did not think to look behind them. They did not, therefore, notice the orange car that pulled up after their own and disgorged two men. They did, however, hear an abrupt sharp whistle somewhere to their rear.

At the sound, the Palestinians stopped in their tracks, as Paul Mansfield had assured Evyatar Miller they would, and looked back. Steadying his right forearm with his left hand, Paul raised the revolver, took aim, and pumped one round after the other into the Palestinians. The two men, their mouths agape in shock and wonder, slumped forward into the mud.

The rain, driven by fierce winds, formed muddy rivulets that swept torrentially across the ground. Horst and Jil emerged from the trees and paused for an instant over the dead men. Then Jil moved toward Paul and Evyatar, a completely baffled Horst in his wake.

The downpour increased, and by the time the four men reached their cars, they were thoroughly drenched. The branches of the trees moaned and crackled under each savage blast of the storm. Horst shivered uncontrollably—a reaction due as much to fear as to the cold and dampness.

"I can't drive now," he said, his lower lip trembling.

Jil slid behind the wheel; Horst went around to the other side and got in next to him. A few minutes later, they were heading back to the hotel on the Limmasol-Larnaca highway.

The windshield wipers were useless against the deluge. Jil, barely able to see through the rain-streaked windows, had to drive slowly and cautiously just to stay on the road, but there was no need to hurry now.

"Who are those men?" Horst asked suspiciously. He drew a pack of cigarettes from his pocket and placed one between his lips, then fumbled with his lighter, but could not get it to work.

Jil paused; he would have to explain certain things to the German.

Horst's eyes were riveted on Jil. "You don't want to tell me?"

"You'll be introduced to them, Horst. They came to Larnaca with me to look for you."

"Jil . . ."

He glanced at the German. His hair was matted down on his head like the fur of a drenched animal, and his face was pale. Fear was evident in his eyes.

"Nobody is going to hurt you, Horst," said Jil icily. "But the game is up. For me. For you. Even for Anna-Maria . . ."

"What about Anna-Maria? Why did you mention her?"

"You knew about the drugs; Klaus supplied both of you."

"Yes," Horst whispered. "That's right. But what do drugs have to do with it?"

"Anna-Maria is not the same young woman," said Jil.

"I know . . ."

"No, you don't know."

Jil described in explicit detail what Heinrich and Rudolph, acting on instructions from Klaus Schmidt, had done to Anna-Maria. As he spoke, Horst's eyes widened and his jaw slowly dropped open. His body, reacting to the sudden onslaught of pain, anger, and hatred, shook uncontrollably from head to foot. He wanted to weep but the tears would not come. His chest rose and fell rapidly as he fought back a sensation of suffocation.

"I'll kill Klaus," he whispered. "I'll murder the brothers . . ."

"There's nothing you can do to hurt them," said Jil. "They're dead, Horst. I killed them. First the brothers, then Klaus . . ."

Horst placed his hand on Jil's shoulder. "I'll never forget that," he murmured. "I won't forget."

As the car approached the boulevard, the towering palms were swaying to and fro in the wind. Immense breakers were visible on their right. The huge waves rolled helter-skelter toward shore, clashing against one another and scattering a shower of foam and seaweed across the bay and onto the beach.

"Are those two from the German police?"

"No," said Jil, slowing down. "One is an American; the other is an Israeli. But they'll turn you over to the West Germans. You realize that, don't you?"

"I understand," Horst said with resignation.

Jil glanced into the rear-view mirror as he pulled up in front of the hotel. The BMW was a short distance behind. Horst remained frozen in place as Jil got out and walked around the front of the car. He opened the door for the German, and without speaking, took him by the arm.

Once in the hotel, they went straight to Jil's room where they removed their jackets and muddy shoes.

"Your things will be brought here," said Jil. "You'll be able to change your clothes soon."

In a few minutes, a man the German had never seen before apppeared with his suitcase, which had been brought over from his hotel. By the time they had changed into dry clothes, Paul Mansfield and Evyatar Miller arrived. Fully aware of the hopelessness of his present situation, Horst decided nonetheless that it was still preferable to falling once again into Mussa el-Dalil's clutches.

He sat down on the edge of the bed and began to talk. For a full hour he discussed his role in the operation, and what he told them corroborated Jil's information and the hypothesis he had formulated. Only now did the three men learn that the operation had been called off, insofar as the KGB and STB were concerned, but that Mussa el-Dalil's terrorist unit was nevertheless planning to go ahead with the action on its original date, the fifth of April.

They were appalled by Horst's description of el-Dalil's projected bloodbath. He recounted in great detail how the Palestinian intended to subvert the original plan and use it as a springboard for mass murder.

"On Monday, el-Dalil will come to Larnaca with his unit. I was supposed to brief the men here for two days," explained

Horst. "And on Thursday, the third of April, we were all to leave for New York."

"Tell us everything you know about how el-Dalil intends to bring his men from Beirut to Larnaca," said Evyatar. "What port are they sailing from?"

"From Junia. Six miles north of Beirut."

"I need a description of the boat. And everything relevant to the trip—the time of departure, makeup of the crew, any layovers, and so on."

Horst Welsh was able to describe el-Dalil's boat very explicitly since he had traveled in it several times from Cyprus to Lebanon and back. By late afternoon, they had all the information they needed to prepare an assault on el-Dalil and his unit, and at four o'clock, two American Embassy officials, who had been summoned by Paul Mansfield, arrived to take Horst Welsh to the Larnaca airport, where they would board a flight to West Germany.

Before he left, Horst approached Jil.

"Will they let me visit Anna-Maria at the hospital?"

Jil looked at his anxious face. "I think so," he replied.

"I love her, you know," Horst said with almost childlike simplicity.

After everyone had gone, Jil went to the window. The rain had continued all day without let-up, as if winter were hurling a final defiant challenge at spring. The dark windowpane mirrored his figure, and he stood examining the reflection with detached curiosity. He thought it strange that for so long he had given no thought whatsoever to his external appearance; his thoughts had been turned inward. He gazed at the image formed on the wet glass. This hazy likeness was part of him. Or perhaps it was all of him—a combination of sharply defined and completely blurred fragments.

At nine o'clock Sunday evening a thick sheet of clouds moved across the moon and the sky was instantly engulfed in total darkness. A light breeze wafted over the still waters of the harbor. Following the violent storm two days before, the sea had calmed and its surface now was as smooth as a finely polished mirror.

Two missile boats—part of the Israeli Navy fleet—had sailed from Haifa and were on their way to the Lebanese coast, where they would take positions opposite the Junia harbor. They were to take part in the final stage of an operation to liquidate Mussa el-Dalil's terrorist unit, an operation that had been put together during the previous twenty-four hours by the intelligence and defense branches of both the Mossad and the Israeli Defense Forces.

A short time before their departure from Haifa, the weather had begun to change dramatically. Now the transformation was becoming steadily more pronounced. The wind radiated a strange heat, and its direction had reversed; it now wafted from the land seaward. It was the same warm blast that burst forth periodically from the desert and blew out to sea. It skimmed over the waters with a soft whistle, flattening waves, smoothing and buffing the face of the sea, which now seemed as rigid and lustrous as a slab of polished granite.

An hour after the moon's eclipse by clouds, the darkness was partially lightened by the glow of the stars as the two missile boats, the *Ra'am* and the *Soufa*, plowed the still waters at a speed of twenty knots, leaving in their wake a wide, roiling swath of foam shaped like a giant fan that flared out behind the ships as they moved northward.

The intelligence officials had worked quickly. By Sunday morning, confirmation of Horst Welsh's information had been checked and found accurate. The small ship to be used by Mussa el-Dalil was presently anchored at the port of Junia. The Palestinian's timetable had also been corroborated: the small boat was to sail from Junia at precisely two o'clock in the morning.

Six members of an elite unit of the Israeli Navy had been ordered to penetrate the port, which served as a maritime base for terrorist organizations, and attach mines to the stern of the ship. The charge was set to go off at three o'clock in the morning, so that the devastating explosion would not occur until the ship had reached open sea.

Paul, Evyatar, and Jil were huddled together on the deck of one of the Israeli missile boats. The wind buffeted their faces as they watched the ship's prow cleave a sharp furrow in front of them. Evyatar studied Jil and wondered what passed through his mind—this man was a Jew like himself, yet totally unlike him—light-years away from him. Even if he were to reach out and touch him, he could in no way bridge the gap that separated them.

Jil was aware of the Israeli's prolonged stare and, on his

other side, the riveting gaze of the American; each darting glance possessed its own vital force, as if both men sought to find an opening through which to approach Jil, man to man. But the barriers stood.

The whistle of the wind, the whisper of the engine, the sound of the sea as the prow of the ship cut a path mingled hypnotically in Jil's ears. The wind continued to lash his face, as it had the day before at the Larnaca airport when he boarded the small plane that brought him to Tel-Aviv. As the missile boat engine began to decelerate, Jil looked at his watch, his body vibrating to the pulse of time, and his heart throbbing in tempo.

The gale gradually subsided, and within minutes a soft breeze caressed his face. The powerful engines fell silent. The boats were now five miles from the Palestinians' sea base.

Only a few hours remained, and then the Clown would be resurrected. Wings outstretched, he would soar aloft, free, unencumbered, knowing his vow had been fulfilled to the letter.

About a mile away, in the bay directly opposite the missile boats, a throng of Lebanese fishing craft had cast anchor for the night. Aglow with the light of numerous fishing lanterns, this broad sweep of water seemed a mirror image of the star-flecked sky above. Farther on, facing the inlet, lay Port Junia.

Jil leaned against the railing of the boat, his eyes penetrating the thick gloom of the moonless night, his gaze fixed on the harbor. He remembered the layout of the port perfectly. The slides they had been shown at the Israeli naval base were so vivid that, even while viewing them, he had felt as if he were actually standing in the midst of the port.

Several officers, led by the major in charge of the operation, joined the commander of the vessel on deck. Jil overheard their conversation: a series of pointed questions, immediately followed by terse replies. The atmosphere on the ship was heavy with tension; the strain seemed almost palpable. Nature, it appeared, had chosen to cast her lot with the enemy. The attackers had counted on choppy seas, for the waves would have provided the launches with a cover, enabling them to reach the entrance to the port without fear of discovery. But rather than allying herself with them, the sea had instead assumed the role of antagonist. The eerie calm induced a feeling of apprehension. All the fishing boats carried weapons, and any one of their crew members might notice the incoming boats and fire a warning shot. Once the enemy was alerted to their presence, it would compel them to change their plan of mining el-Dalil's boat and engage in an open battle with the Palestinians upon reaching the port. The commander of the Israeli missile boat turned to Evyatar and muttered something under his breath in Hebrew. Evyatar nodded and then repeated what the officer had said.

"He says there's an ancient seaman's superstition that the wind blowing from the land toward sea—which is unnatural—means bad luck." Evyatar drew a deep breath of the warm, damp air and continued: "They're evaluating the situation, trying to decide whether it'll be necessary to make any changes in the plan." Evyatar turned back to the group of officers.

"Shitty business," remarked Paul. "I know what it's like when a soldier goes into battle with the feeling that everything's working against him. I was in the Marines once. I fought in the goddamned Korean War."

He directed his comments to Jil, as if impelled by the need to share something of his own background with the man about whom he already knew so much. He paused, pulled a handkerchief from his pocket, and wiped away the mixture of sweat and brine that covered his face. "I remember what it was like just before going into action. You thought your brain wasn't functioning, that you were completely empty. But it wasn't really like that. During those last few minutes you thought about what might happen to you. Sometimes you didn't even understand what the hell you were doing there . . . Your own thoughts would start to drive you crazy. You'd feel a big spring in your chest—where your heart is—winding tighter and tighter . . ."

Paul fell silent. His eyes were on the young men who had begun to lower the three Zodiac launches into the water. Then, turning back to Jil, he continued: "Afterward," he said, "the tension breaks. The big spring coiled up in your chest snaps and empties you out completely. And then, while you're in action, you forget everything. With a little bit of luck and damn good timing, you come out alive. But even then, you come back a different man . . ."

"You feel you've lost a part of yourself," Jil remarked quietly.

"Yeah, I guess that pretty well explains it." Paul straightened up and turned around, his back to the shore. Then he drew a half-smoked cigar from his pocket and stuck it into his mouth. "Something is lost, that's for sure. It could be part of your body. Part of your soul—if you come back without your buddy . . ."

Suddenly the commotion around them escalated. Orders were issued in rapid succession, and the soldiers began descending to the flat rubber craft which bobbed in the water alongside the boat.

Evyatar turned to Jil. "The three of us will be in the major's Zodiac. You'll be able to follow the whole operation from beginning to end."

"No change in plans?"

"No," replied Evyatar, glancing toward the fishing boats anchored in the bay. "The only change is in the amount of time we have at our disposal. We'll have to go in very slowly because of this lousy weather."

Six frogmen lowered themselves from the missile boat into the first launch; another six men climbed into the second Zodiac. It was the duty of the latter group to protect the divers in the event of a mishap. Jil, Paul, and Evyatar boarded the third Zodiac with the major and two sergeants. A large assortment of firearms and medical equipment was piled at their feet in the middle of the craft.

The motor of the commander's boat rumbled into life; then the engines of the two other launches turned over, and the convoy of three Zodiacs plowed through the water toward the second missile boat. When the convoy had almost reached it, they were joined by a fourth Zodiac with six soldiers who were to serve as part of the backup unit. The motors revved up and, with a thunderous roar, the four boats surged forward, the still waters parting before them as if cleaved by a broadsword. It was a few minutes after midnight.

The wind blowing in from the shore actually muffled the roar of the engines so that the launches could advance to a point some two hundred yards from the area in which the fishing boats were anchored. From here they would proceed without the benefit of outboard motors. The navigators in each boat cut the engines, and oars were distributed. The boats slid noiselessly across the water. The men had been ordered to maintain complete silence and to hunch as low as possible in the rubber boats as they rowed.

They could now make out the outlines of the fishing boats, which were anchored directly in front of them at intervals of a hundred to a hundred and fifty yards. The commander of the Israeli force veered right in order to pass midway between the two furthermost trawlers, the most feasible route; the three other launches followed. The sea stretched out before them like a great lake. The air was filled with strains of Arab music—wailing, plaintive cries of singers accompanied by Oriental string and percussion instruments—that blared from the fishermen's radio sets.

The wan starlight reflecting on the sea lent a slick, oily sheen to the deep waters. A keen eye would be able to pick out any object protruding above its surface. No one could accurately judge the risk of exposure, and the tension in the launches steadily mounted. In accordance with the major's instructions, the distance between the rubber boats was significantly increased. Their chances of proceeding undetected were far better if they were spread out.

The seconds passed like minutes, and the minutes crept like hours. The command launch drifted slowly between two fishing boats, and after pulling away, waited for the other three boats to complete the crossing. They now confronted another cordon of trawlers, this one thicker than the last.

Jil was certain that the others shared his sense of dread. He felt like an animal caught in a net; the harder he struggled to free himself, the more entangled he became, the tighter the net pulled around him. Although the young major had made a decided effort to conceal his concern, Jil was aware of the man's dilemma. The sea with its flat unrippled surface was like a huge surrealistic bathtub. Had there been even shallow waves they could easily have piloted their launches through the thicket of fishing boats without being noticed.

The four Zodiacs listed for some time beyond the cluster of trawlers while the major tried to reach a decision. It was clear that further progress would most certainly lead to premature discovery, and any exchange at sea would provide ample warning to Mussa el-Dalil and his men. It was imperative that the silence not be broken as they made their way to the harbor area.

"We're playing with fire," whispered the major. They had thus far crossed only a small portion of the bay. If they did not step up their pace, the mission might very well be aborted.

He surveyed the area before them, studying the broad sterns of the vessels anchored to their left and right, then turned to the commander of the diving squad and exchanged a few words with him. The two men scrutinized the large trawler to their right. There was no evidence of any activity on board. Only the sound of music blaring from a portable radio testified to the presence of a crew, which was apparently asleep.

The lieutenant turned from his commanding officer and relayed the instructions to his men. The six divers slid into the water. They carried no diving equipment and were armed only with pistols and knives. In their black wetsuits they merged almost totally with the dark waters of the sea. They broke immediately into a rapid breaststroke and in a few moments had disappeared from sight.

The divers reached the deck of the vessel by climbing up a sturdy fishing net that was slung over the craft's port side. The lieutenant was the first to scramble up the net. He released it only after he reached the rim of the deck, along which a row of old rubber tires had been hung to protect the ship's hull from the impact of the wharf while mooring. The lieutenant grabbed the nearest tire and freed the net for the next man. He then swung from tire to tire along the side of the boat. Two minutes later, all six men hung from tires just below the railing, their heads low like cats about to pounce.

Three members of the crew lay sprawled on mattresses, sound asleep. Two others sat crosslegged on the deck, engrossed in a game of backgammon. One of the men chanted in a low wail, accompanying the soulful lament that poured from the radio at his side. Neither of the men saw the dark figures slip furtively onto the deck, thread their way between the crates of fish, and advance rapidly toward them.

The major's plan worked well. By the time he and his men had reached the boat and climbed aboard, the crew members had been taken captive. All five lay side by side, face down on the deck, their arms raised above their heads. Two divers, their pistols still drawn, stood over them. The other four soldiers were busy binding the crew members' hands and feet with a length of rope they had found on deck. The fishermen had already been gagged with strips of cloth torn from one of their shirts.

The launches were secured to the hull of the vessel, two on each side. The entire force boarded the boat and, in accordance with the major's instructions, lay flat on its deck. Only the two sergeants and the major himself, who was well acquainted with that type of craft and intended to steer her into port, remained erect and moved freely about the vessel. The major turned his attention to the old engine and soon had it operating. Meanwhile, the sergeants released the fishing net, which had been hung from a winch fixed to the stern of the boat, and the vessel began to move in the direction of the harbor.

Fish had been scarce all night, and many fishermen who tired of waiting had already returned to port with their hatches and crates empty. Therefore, the captured trawler received hardly a passing glance as it slowly made its way to the harbor.

The major's confidence had been restored; he was certain now that they would meet their tight schedule. A short time later, as they sailed clear of the fishing area, the port and town of Junia loomed up to their left, less than a mile away.

The boat's engine was cut and the major gathered his men for a final briefing. He went over every phase of the plan in detail, up to and including the final rendezvous. After the briefing was completed, the major announced that he would enter the port in the captured fishing boat and dock it in the harbor. The vessel, he explained, would serve as an excellent forward observation point. The men assigned to his launch—the two sergeants and three security agents—would remain on board with him.

The divers' launch was to follow a separate course to the entrance of the port. Once within the harbor, the frogmen would make their way underwater to el-Dalil's boat. The backup units would move shoreward from a point about half a mile south of the port. The intelligence officers, in presenting their recommendations, had selected this spot for a final rendezvous following the completion of the mission.

By one-thirty all the men were to be in their assigned positions. The backup units were, by then, to have fanned out to various locations in the port, carrying with them explosive charges. At the first indication of danger to the divers, these would be detonated as a means of distracting the enemy. Having entered the harbor, the diving squad would have fifteen minutes in which to attach the mines to the hull of el-Dalil's boat and leave the port area.

The major now moved to the railing of the boat to watch his men descend to their launches. The divers were the first to pull away, and they were followed immediately by the three other craft. The Zodiacs were quickly swallowed up by the darkness. There were no visible obstacles between the fishing boat and the shore. The major found some old fishermen's garb in a foot locker and asked each of his men to put on one article of clothing so that they would appear to be the boat's legitimate crew, who, after a night's fishing, were making their way back to shore with their catch.

The divers' launch sped quickly toward the harbor. The lieutenant who commanded the frogman unit was familiar with the port. In the past two years he had participated in several actions in the area. The Zodiac's motor purred softly as the lieutenant piloted the craft effortlessly over the still waters. He cut the engine a short distance from the port; from here on in, they would use oars. His men were silent. As a group, they were all very young; the lieutenant, the eldest of the lot, was only twenty-one.

Mussa el-Dalil had worked quickly to adapt his plan to the new situation created by the cancellation of the operation and the departure of the Czechs. His unit consisted of eleven combatants who had been forced into hardened, disciplined troops. They knew what lay before them. They realized that perhaps not even one of their group would return safely from the mission, yet they were prepared to carry it out for the glory they and their families would reap. This was to be the culmination of many years of training—a fiery climax in blood, tears, and exaltation.

They boarded the small ship at one-fifteen in the morning and each man took his assigned position on the deck. Mussa el-Dalil had closeted himself with Da-ud el-Za'id in the small cabin adjacent to the engine room.

Da'ud hadn't an inkling of what el-Dalil wished to discuss with him before their departure to Cyprus, but his heart was heavy. The commander's attitude toward him was strange. He had sensed the change even yesterday although el-Dalil hadn't actually said anything that indicated a shift in his approach to him. He had simply been moody and had all but ignored him. But now he was speaking.

"I've never kept anything from you," el-Dalil said dryly.

"No, never," agreed el-Za'id.

"I told you that the Czechs have fled. That we're left alone."

"And that we would proceed alone."

"Yes. We shall continue, true. But without you."

Mussa el-Dalil's expression was pained. El-Za'id's look reflected profound fear.

"One thing I didn't tell you," continued el-Dalil in a whisper. "I suspect that the Czechs and the others left because they had learned what they were prohibited from knowing."

"That's impossible!"

"Is that all you have to say? Only two men knew about my plan: I spoke to only one person about it—you, Da'ud."

"I didn't discuss the plan with anyone."

"That lie is a mark of your disgrace. I know the truth," said el-Dalil, his words coming with difficulty. "I conducted a brief investigation. The answers I received to my inquiries were incomplete and vague. But yesterday I was informed of a meeting you had in Beirut with Horst Welsh and the Czech, Zoska."

Da'ud el-Za'id was unable to meet his commander's gaze. He lowered his eyes and felt a slight twitch in his cheek.

"I treated you like a son," whispered el-Dalil. His glance was riveted on the youth's handsome face. "I don't have any sons of my own. For that reason, I treated you with leniency on the one hand, but at the same time with firmness. I wanted you to be a man."

Da'ud raised his head and held it stiffly upright. The young Palestinian wished to retain a soldierly posture at least. He owed that to himself.

"Yes," he admitted. "I told them."

"Why?"

"You don't know? You can't guess?"

"You hate me?"

"Perhaps," Da'ud said, and felt himself suddenly adrift in time and space, remote from el-Dalil. "You degraded me. I thought I hated you . . . now I don't know . . . I simply don't know . . ."

"You pain me, Da'ud. I have no further use for you. Go!"

"I . . ."

Mussa el-Dalil would never know what the young freedom fighter had meant to say, for he turned his head away, and el-Za'id fell silent.

There was no need for further words between them. El-Dalil heard the youth place his gun on the table. Da'ud knew the punishment that awaited him.

"Will you shoot me in the back?" el-Za'id asked.

Mussa el-Dalil remained silent, head lowered. He looked up only when he heard el-Za'id's footsteps on the wooden stairs.

The heavy fishing boat entered the harbor area at one-ten at night. The major lazily guided the vessel into her berth like one, who after long years of practice, was capable of mooring his craft with his eyes closed. The crew members lay on the deck, covered by a sheet of tarpaulin and surrounded by empty fishing crates. Their captors—who within a few moments would have to act under the major's instructions like an experienced crew—crouched nearby.

At that late hour there was little activity in the harbor area. The port would come to life a few hours later when, after their lengthy stays at sea, throngs of fishermen would return home, and merchant ships bound for the shores of Turkey and Greece to the north, Cyprus to the west and Egypt to the south would set off for their destinations. The port itself seemed sorely neglected, and its loading docks were conspicuously lacking in modern equipment.

The major scanned the quays and the stone buildings behind them. Some of the structures obviously served as warehouses, while others appeared to be government offices. He identified the green ship moored at the western tip of the jetty as Mussa el-Dalil's. Another smaller vessel was docked behind her, and beyond this craft were several additional berths. The entire area was dimly lit. Beginning from the point at which el-Dalil's ship was docked, a row of searchlights extended along the jetty toward the port.

The fishing boat rolled slowly toward the tip of the

shadow-shrouded quay and stopped. The commanding officer glanced at his watch: at that moment the two backup units would be planting explosives at the foundations of several of the nearby stone buildings. He was convinced, however, that the mission would proceed smoothly and that these diversionary measures would not be needed. By a quarter to two he would be guiding the fishing boat out of the harbor and heading toward the rendezvous point.

Jil and Paul jumped down from the deck onto the jetty, where they stood, arms extended, waiting to catch the ropes that Evyatar hurled down at them. They were winding the thick ropes around the mooring pegs when Jil suddenly froze. He had caught sight of the young man who had just emerged from the belly of the green ship and was now standing on the vessel's upper deck. He seemed to vacillate for a moment before ambling to the stepladder that descended to the wharf. Something about him was vaguely familiar to Jil. As Jil studied him, he realized how closely the man resembled Da'ud el-Za'id. As the young man vaulted the bannister and started down the narrow stairway, his face was momentarily illuminated by the pale glow of the searchlight positioned on the jetty beside the boat. There was no longer any question: it was el-Za'id. Jil was astounded at the change in his appearance. What could have caused his hair to turn white in so short a time?

In that instant of recognition, whatever doubts that Jil may have had completely evaporated: the ship was indeed their target, the vipers' nest they had set out to destroy.

"What is it?" asked Paul, drawing close to Jil.

"It's el-Za'id."

As they watched, four figures leaped from the shadows of the nearby buildings. In the dim light of the wharf, the watchers saw the upraised arms and the flash of knives as the quartet fell like a pack of wolves upon el-Za'id. They watched the daggers rise and fall, plunging repeatedly into Da'ud's writhing body until he lay lifeless in a pool of blood.

Mussa el-Dalil ascended the narrow staircase to the deck of the ship to check on the final arrangements prior to sailing. He had to efface all recollection of Da'ud, to blot out his memory as if the youth had never existed. He would concentrate exclusively on the eleven men who would be working with him in Crown Heights. He was pleased he had left Horst Welsh in Larnaca in the custody of two of his best men. The German fox would brief his troops well. From now on, everything would go precisely according to plan.

Because of Da'ud's treachery, he had had to change the method of infiltrating his men into the United States. His contact in Europe informed him that the Libyans were prepared to provide any assistance he needed. They would supply the diplomatic passports with which his men were to travel from Paris to the United States. Each man would be on a different flight. The weapons and explosives were already at the destination. Diplomats representing countries that supported his Palestinian faction had been running guns and ammunition into the United States on a regular basis. The stock of weapons brought in in diplomatic pouches, with the assistance of envoys and official couriers, was formidable—enough to implement large-scale terrorist operations.

Impulsively, el-Dalil strode to the stern of the ship and surveyed the spot where his men had executed el-Za'id. When he saw Da'ud's corpse on the ground and his men crouched over it, his throat went dry. As he started back toward the stairs, he felt the hand of one of the sailors on his shoulder. The man pointed down at the water.

"Frogmen!" he shouted.

Mussa el-Dalil gave a start. The meaning of the divers' presence was clear: the frogmen represented the first fruits of el-Za'id's treason. The irony of fate, thought el-Dalil: the man lying dead on the wharf was already wreaking his vengeance. The divers had to be Israeli commandoes; only the Israelis were capable of penetrating the port of Junia in so daring a manner. Nor did he doubt for a moment that his boat was the frogmen's target.

One of the divers had remained in the launch, which was concealed among a cluster of rocks at the entrance to the port. The lieutenant and four other commandoes, with oxygen tanks strapped to their backs and limpet mines fastened to their utility belts, had gone under. Led by the lieutenant, the group progressed in a loose-wedge formation. They had to hurry. Mussa el-Dalil's ship was due to sail shortly. The divers made a strenuous effort to increase their pace.

At the entrance to the port, blue seawater mixed with the

turbid waters of the harbor. The light cast by searchlights on the wharves was diffused through the water into a myriad of colors, but as they advanced, visibility decreased. The port itself was a murky sewer; its waters, churning with refuse, fuel waste, and oily substances, formed a dark, opaque curtain before the divers' eyes. They crossed the harbor as if blindfolded, guided solely by the lieutenant's instinct. Although he was well acquainted with the area, he would soon have to surface, for he needed to determine their exact location in order to lead them to the green vessel's keel.

The four divers remained beneath the surface of the dark, polluted waters as the lieutenant split off from them and quickly ascended. At the surface of the water, he removed his diving mask, and the harbor came vividly into view. He found himself floating near a familiar quay that had been built many years before atop a huge rock formation. The stones and boulders of which it was composed had, in the course of time, come naturally together in great scattered heaps. His glance traveled the length of the jetty. He immediately spotted the two boats: the fishing trawler they had commandeered at sea, and their target—the green ship belonging to Mussa el-Dalil. The vessels, separated at the jetty by only a small merchant craft, were moored very close to one another. A few men moved about the upper deck of the green ship. He noticed someone approaching the railing and tossing something into the water. Suddenly the man froze; he wheeled around and caught the attention of a man nearby. With lightning speed, the second man charged to the railing, then raised and lowered his arm in one rapid movement.

The lieutenant knew he had been spotted. Before he could dive underwater, a grenade exploded at his side. He felt immediately that he had been hit. The blast shattered his eardrums.

Then the entire port erupted in a cacophony of gunfire. Besides the men on the green boat, there were others in the harbor area who were armed, and he became the target of all of them.

The lieutenant's mouth filled with blood. He spit it out and coughed; a strange but pleasant sensation filtered through his body. His eyes grew dim. The lights about him faded, and he was presently enveloped in a black void. He could not remember where he was, but he knew there was something else that had to be done . . . something important . . . He had a vague recollection that it had to do with his men. Where were they? Somewhere in the sea waiting for him . . . He had to warn them that the plan had miscarried . . . that things had gone terribly amiss. It was his duty. But the lieutenant had lost consciousness before he could feel the arms of two of his men encircling his body and dragging him beneath the water.

Jil and Paul stood on the quay unarmed. Evyatar quickly leaned over the railing of the trawler and handed each of them a submachine gun and a combat belt equipped with grenades. He then dropped to the deck and sprawled beside the major and his two sergeants. There wasn't time to discuss what had happened. It was evident that they would have to engage the enemy. Their success would depend upon the backup units. If those men set off the diversionary charges as planned, it might be possible to exterminate Mussa el-Dalil and his men within a matter of minutes.

Clutching the guns close to their bodies at waist level, Jil and Paul took aim at el-Dalil's assassins, who were now barreling toward the green ship. At that moment, a powerful explosion erupted at the eastern corner of the harbor about eighty yards away. The backup unit had detonated the first charge. A building crumbled to its foundations: pieces of stone and wood, flung high in the air by the impact of the blast, rained down over the harbor. In the wake of the explosion, intense shock waves passed through the air. Jil was hurled against the side of the fishing boat. Paul too was badly shaken, as were the four assassins. They staggered around in a daze, as Paul and Jil fired at them. Shortly, all four lay motionless on the quay, at the foot of the narrow stepladder leading to el-Dalil's ship.

A second explosion, this one louder than the first, shook the harbor. Rock fragments sailed through the air, many landing close to the ships. The diversionary explosions proved effective. The Palestinian troops guarding the port, convinced that the main body of the strike force was behind them, hurriedly abandoned their posts and directed their fire at the gray stone buildings. Then, as the gunfire began to close in around them, they were seized with panic: it seemed that they were surrounded by massive enemy forces. Every niche and cranny, every shadow and darkened corner of the port might harbor hostile troops.

Mussa el-Dalil, however, saw through the Israelis' plan. The danger to him lay not in the dark recesses of the port; it lurked a few feet away, perhaps in the water, perhaps overhead. He knew exactly how the Israelis operated. But this knowledge would be of little help, he suddenly realized, since only seven of his men were with him on deck. The other four had apparently been cut down by enemy fire. Common sense dictated that he sail out of the port immediately, while he was still able to do so. But when he tried to locate the captain, he found the man was missing, along with his crew members. At first, Mussa el-Dalil thought that they had gone below and were hiding in the belly of the ship. He instructed his men to continue firing into the water in the immediate vicinity of the ship to prevent any frogmen from approaching the vessel. Then he ran to the staircase and scrambled quickly below deck. There was no one anywhere in the ship's belly. The sailors had apparently jumped overboard and fled for their lives. El-Dalil trembled with rage. He and his men were trapped.

The third building exploded while Jil and Paul were making a dash for the deck of the fishing boat to pick up more ammunition. In a few minutes their backup force, in accordance with the emergency plan, would begin making its way to the rendezvous. They had very little time to finish their job and clear out of the harbor.

With guns trained on the deck of the green ship, the major and his two sergeants stepped up their fire. Most of el-Dalil's men were congregated behind the ship's wheelhouse, where they continued shooting into the water. Only when one of the men had been hit did the group comprehend the nature of the Israeli trap. The wounded man screamed out that the bullet had come from the direction of the last boat on the wharf, the fishing trawler, and Mussa el-Dalil immediately sized up the situation. He ordered his men to drop to the deck at once and to fire at the searchlights. He and his few remaining troops would escape under cover of darkness. He was familiar with the physical layout of the harbor and was certain to find a way out.

Paul, Evyatar, the major and the sergeants continued

shooting at the deck of the green ship, intensifying their fire. Wanting to take advantage of the cover provided by the hail of bullets to storm the terrorists' ship, Jil tapped the Israeli on the shoulder and pointed to the low deck of the boat docked between theirs and el-Dalil's. Evyatar nodded his approval and turned back to the target.

Mussa el-Dalil's men were now shooting at the searchlights. Only a few bullets were on target, but the number of hits was sufficient to plunge the port into darkness. As the lights began to go out one by one, Jil moved rapidly through the thickening gloom. He cleared the wide gap separating the fishing boat from the small merchant vessel in one leap. Landing gracefully on the craft's low deck, he immediately flattened himself against its surface. Evyatar dropped down next to him and hurried to the other side of the deck, which faced the enemy vessel. The terrorists, meanwhile, continued to fire frantically at the searchlights, spreading darkness in the wake of their bullets.

Paul and the major jumped onto the quay, leaving only the sergeants aboard the fishing boat, firing their submachine guns. The plan was clear. Jil and Evyatar would bombard the ship with grenades, forcing the terrorists on board to flee in the direction of the quay. Once they were in flight, Paul and the commander would cut them down with their submachine guns.

Jil threw the first hand grenade, Evyatar the next. The consecutive blasts were followed by soul-rending screams of agony. Jil pointed to the deck of el-Dalil's boat, which loomed out of the darkness overhead. Evyatar nodded. They crouched and jumped; each grabbed a tire hanging from the side of the hull, hauled himself over the railing, and rolled onto the deck. None of the figures lying on deck stirred. Jil ran to the staircase and descended to the cabin, while Evyatar stayed on deck.

"Dog!"

The word, hissed venomously over the clatter of gunfire, sizzled in the air like the spitting of water on dying embers. Evyatar wheeled around and started in the direction of the voice, but he reacted a fraction of a second too late. The Palestinian who had uttered the insult emerged from behind the wheelhouse, his machine gun upraised, and discharged a volley of bullets which struck Evyatar in the chest. In the instant before he slumped to the ground, the thought flickered through Evyatar's brain that he had finally come face to face with Mussa el-Dalil.

Even as the Israeli lay dead at his feet, Mussa el-Dalil continued to pump bullets into his body until he had emptied the contents of his magazine into Evyatar Miller's corpse.

Jil heard the shots and bounded up from the cabin of the ship. He saw the man from behind and, leveling his Uzi, he squeezed the trigger. The gun made a hollow click. Empty. Grabbing the gun by the stock, he hurled it at Mussa el-Dalil, striking him in the back. The Palestinian turned slowly like a wounded animal. Jil had never encountered a face like his. It was distorted by fathomless fury and hatred; the dark eyes protruded from their sockets, as if they would burst from his head, the lips curled back, baring a row of sharp, uneven teeth.

Uncoiling like a tightly wound steel spring, the Palestinian pounced upon his antagonist. Jil was astonished by the older man's speed and agility. He attempted to draw back but banged into the wheelhouse door. As he felt the Palestinian's powerful fingers closing around his throat, Jil's reaction was swift. He rammed his knees into el-Dalil's groin and, with clenched fists, hammered at his temples.

A sharp pain exploded in the Arab's head; then a feeling of numbness spread through his body. But his grip only tightened. His fingers sank deeper and deeper into Jil's neck. In a practiced movement, Jil swung his hands between el-Dalil's arms and wrenched his own head backward. The impact of his arms against his opponent's elbows broke the stranglehold. But el-Dalil would not give up. He lunged forward and sank his teeth into Jil's arm. Jil brought the hard edge of his hand down on the Palestinian's neck. Mussa el-Dalil reeled back, moaning in pain, and Jil broke away from him once again.

The Arab recouped his strength. He drew himself erect and, growling like a frenzied beast, he seized Jil's legs and hoisted them aloft, pitching his body backward, over the railing and into the dark waters below.

Jil hit the water, still stunned by the abruptness and violence of the Palestinian's assault. El-Dalil dived in after him and, before Jil could resurface, clasped him around the neck and attempted to hold him under water. Jil's lungs were bursting for want of oxygen. Finally, he struggled to the surface of the water and drew in a deep breath of air.

Mussa el-Dalil tightened his grip around Jil's midriff and, steadily increasing the pressure, began to bite his neck, chest, and shoulders. Jil placed his hand on el-Dalil's forehead and pushed his head back, breaking the Palestinian's hold on him. Then, thrashing behind el-Dalil, Jil wrapped an arm around his neck. Interlocking the fingers of his hands, he clamped the Arab's throat in a viselike grip and then gradually increased the pressure of his forearm. Mussa el-Dalil flailed with his arms and legs in vain; he still remained in the stranglehold. His entire body began to jerk convulsively. Within a few moments, his heart gave out and his body went limp. Jil released him and watched el-Dalil's corpse bob momentarily on the surface of the sea before vanishing beneath the water.

The last charges left behind by the backup force exploded as the four launches sped away from the rendezvous and headed out to sea. Two claps of thunder shattered the air, and then a single ball of fire rose slowly like a giant fist, flames thrusting skyward and gradually uncurling over Junia. The echo of the explosion swelled in the ears of the men as they approached the area where the fishing boats had been anchored. Now there was nothing to prevent their escape. The trawlers had scattered to the four winds at the first reports of gunfire and explosives from the port. No one wanted to be caught in the path of the Israelis.

Jil gazed out into the darkness. Beyond, he could make out the elongated silhouettes of the missile boats waiting to take them back to Haifa, to the Israelis' home port.

From the moment the first hand grenade had been tossed from the deck of the terrorists' boat to Jil's slaying of Mussa el-Dalil, only a few minutes had elapsed, but in that time the strike force had suffered casualties—three men killed and five wounded. The dead included the commanding officer of the frogmen, a sergeant from the backup unit, and Evyatar Miller, Mossad agent and ex-combat officer.

No one spoke in the Zodiac that carried the dead men. This boat was piloted by the major. Paul sat next to Evyatar's body, his eyes fixed on the lifeless form stretched out before him. Evyatar's head lay at an awkward angle, as if his neck had been bent to one side and broken. Paul leaned over and with his large hands gently righted the head so that it appeared the Israeli was asleep. Before Paul took his hands from Evyatar's head, he stroked the dead man's forehead, as if wishing him a peaceful rest. The touch was ever so slight, and then Paul again sat upright and motionless over his friend's body.

36

O N SUNDAY, THE thirteen of April, the CIA's interrogation of Jil, conducted in Washington, was completed. Earl Dickson advised him to go into hiding for a few months until he had decided what he wanted to do; the agency would select a place and provide for his security. But Jil refused; he had a place to go. He asked Paul Mansfield to take him to New York. From there, he said, he would assume responsibility for himself.

On Monday morning Paul drove him to New York. Jil asked first to be taken around Crown Heights. He explained to Paul that he wished to return for one more look at the community to which his father, grandfather, and all his ancestors on both sides of his family had belonged. He particularly wanted to see Yudke; perhaps during the past few days some news had arrived from Moscow.

As usual, the door of the shop was slightly ajar. As Jil pushed it open, the creak of the hinges drew Yudke's attention and he turned and stared suspiciously at the young man standing on the threshold.

"Yes?" he asked curtly, obviously annoyed at the disturbance.

Jil smiled.

"Reb Yudke, don't you remember me?"

The voice was unmistakable. Yet the man facing him was not the young Hasid from Moscow; this man with the smooth-shaven face hardly resembled that Jew. Yudke stared incredulously.

"It's me," said the young man; the smile didn't leave his face.

"Reb Levinson?" asked Yudke hesitantly. "You came back to us?"

"Just for a moment, Reb Yudke."

Yudke considered the situation carefully before speaking, his expression grave. It was unquestionably the same man, despite the drastic change in his external appearance.

"You'll be back to stay," he declared finally. "You must come back. You are one of the Rebbe's emissaries. Do not forget that."

"I will not forget."

"I knew you would return. I've been expecting you."

"You knew?" asked Jil in surprise.

"Your Zaide knew."

"You have news from Moscow?" Jil's pulse quickened. The intense longing to know that the old man, Zina, and Sergei were well blazed up in his heart. Perhaps it was naive of him to believe they would all pass through this ordeal unscathed; the chances were so terribly slight.

"You have news from Zaide?" he repeated, this time with trepidation.

"I do," replied Yudke, his smile exuberant, his cheeks glowing with elation. "The news reached my brother in Paris and he passed it on to me. Zaide wants you to know that he realizes you fulfilled your vow to the letter. And he also wants you to know that he, too, carried out his vow. Completely."

It suddenly seemed to Jil that Yudke stood in Daidushka's stead; he stifled the urge to rush to the old carpenter and gather him in his arms, perhaps even lay his head on the powerful shoulder and weep in joy and relief, to ease the tensions that had accumulated for so long.

"God bless you, Reb Yudke."

"May He bless us all," replied Yudke, moving closer to Jil. "Your Zaide wants you to know that you have his blessing—

in whatever you do, wherever you go—but you must always remember your origins. Always, Reb Levinson."

Jil's lips parted to respond, but the words would not come.

"Before you go," Yudke said in a whisper, turning toward the partition at the back of the shop, "I want to show you something. Something that is now whole because of you."

He drew the partition aside. On a small wooden platform stood the chair of the Tzadikim. Without a blemish. Totally restored. Jil's eyes filled and he saw through the thin veil of tears a procession of his loved ones; they wound majestically through the shop, their faces aglow, and formed a semicircle behind the holy chair. He could not speak. He went to Yudke, pressed the carpenter's calloused hand, and turned to leave. When he reached the door, he stopped and looked back at the old man.

"Yudke . . ."

Again, although he wanted to speak, although there was so much to say, so much that lay on his heart, the words choked in his throat.

Once outside, he drew a deep breath, and then another, in an effort to erase his feelings and confusion. He opened the car door and sat down next to Paul. The American observed him in silence, then asked:

"Where to, Jil?"

"Manhattan," Jil responded softly. "Let me off near Times Square. That will be our last stop."

"Are you sure you have a place to stay?"

Jil nodded. In recent days he had thought a great deal about Margaret. He had told her he would return to the house facing Toledo, his ancestral home. There he would begin to frame the Chagall figures; one by one, he would fashion an entire gallery of these bewitchingly lively characters, pursuing their quiet workaday lives, feet rooted to the muddy village roads, while with arms upraised, their hands caressed the heavens.

Manhattan basked in the soft, golden glow of a spring sun. The skies overhead were bright and cloudless. The heady fragrance of grass and flowers drifted through the window of the car.

"Spring," Jil murmured wistfully. "For the ancients, springtime symbolized rebirth—they began the new year in spring."

"Like a new life," Paul said.

Jil turned his head toward the American. His eyes sparkled.
"Yes, Paul. Like a new life."

He thrust his hand out the window. The long, graceful fingers fluttered and closed around the stem of an imaginary blossom. He went through the slow, deliberate motions of a man picking a flower. His portrayal was so realistic that it left Paul in wonderment. Jil went through the gestures again and again, and then drew his arm back into the car. Gently clutching the bouquet in his hands, he raised it to his nose and slowly inhaled the aroma of the imaginary flowers. He smiled and extended them to Paul.

"Look after them, Paul, and they'll last forever."

To Paul it almost seemed that the car had become filled with the intoxicating scent of spring, that the seat between them, where Jil had placed the imaginary bouquet, was ablaze with color. He suddenly felt elated.

"Thank you, Jil."

They were approaching Times Square. Crowds of people thronged the streets, drinking in the sunshine and luxuriating in the warmth of the fine, clear day. Paul pulled over to the curb.

Jil started to open the door, then suddenly wavered. Paul saw the sad look on his youthful face. He wondered then if they would ever meet again, and he wanted to tell Jil he was sorry to say good-bye, that he would miss him, but he said nothing. Paul felt suddenly awkward and confused. Perhaps the flowers had inspired these feelings, or the scent of spring in the air. Whatever it was, it had aroused in him a yearning for something that had been lost.

"Do you need anything, Jil?"

"No, Paul. Thanks."

Jil opened the door and seemed to hesitate briefly again before he stepped out onto the crowded sidewalk. He turned, closed the door, and walked slowly to the corner. He halted at the curb and waited for the traffic light to change. Standing in place, he lifted first one leg, then the other, and swung his arms at his sides in slow alternation, as if walking. Paul, observing him through the car window, was entranced. The crowd at the street corner jostled closer to Jil, necks craned, laughing aloud at the sight of a man cheerfully walking along and going nowhere.

The light changed and Jil moved forward with the crowd. He stopped in the middle of the street, turned around, and waved good-bye. Paul Mansfield sat immobile at the steering wheel while behind him horns began to sound impatiently. For some reason he found it difficult to press down on the accelerator. When the car at last lurched from the curb, he peered through the crowd to catch another glimpse of Jil. But the Clown had vanished.

ABOUT THE AUTHOR

Amos Aricha was born and educated in Tel-Aviv where he has been actively involved in the theater, art, and literature. He served for twelve years with the Israeli police force, rising to the rank of chief superintendent. In the course of his work, he became familiar with worldwide terrorist and anti-terrorist activities.

Following his retirement from the police, Aricha devoted himself to writing novels of political intrigue, one of which was the recent bestseller PHOENIX, available in both NAL hardcover and Signet editions.

Bestsellers from SIGNET

- ☐ **TWO LUCKY PEOPLE** by Tony Kenrick. (#E9725—$2.50)
- ☐ **THE 81st SITE** by Tony Kenrick. (#E9600—$2.75)
- ☐ **THE NIGHTTIME GUY** by Tony Kenrick. (#E9111—$2.75)*
- ☐ **FOOLS DIE** by Mario Puzo. (#E8881—$3.50)
- ☐ **THE REBELLION OF YALE MARRATT** by Robert H. Rimmer.
  (#E8851—$2.50)*
- ☐ **COME LIVE MY LIFE** by Robert H. Rimmer. (#E7421—$2.25)
- ☐ **LOVE ME TOMORROW** by Robert H. Rimmer.
  (#E8385—$2.50)*
- ☐ **PROPOSITION 31** by Robert H. Rimmer. (#J7514—$1.95)
- ☐ **THURSDAY, MY LOVE** by Robert H. Rimmer. (#E7109—$1.75)
- ☐ **A GARDEN OF SAND** by Earl Thompson. (#E9374—$2.95)
- ☐ **TATTOO** by Earl Thompson. (#E8989—$2.95)
- ☐ **CALDO LARGO** by Earl Thompson. (#E7737—$2.25)
- ☐ **DANIEL MARTIN** by John Fowles. (#E8249—$2.95)†
- ☐ **THE EBONY TOWER** by John Fowles. (#E9658—$2.95)
- ☐ **THE FRENCH LIEUTENANT'S WOMAN** by John Fowles.
  (#E9003—$2.95)
- ☐ **THE DHARMA BUMS** by Jack Kerouac. (#J9138—$1.95)
- ☐ **ONE FLEW OVER THE CUCKOO'S NEST** by Ken Kesey.
  (#E8867—$2.25)
- ☐ **THE GRADUATE** by Charles Webb. (#W8633—$1.50)
- ☐ **YOUR CHEATIN' HEART** by Elizabeth Gilchrist.
  (#E9061—$2.25)

* Price slightly higher in Canada
† Not available in Canada

Buy them at your local

bookstore or use coupon

on next page for ordering.